# Instantiation

Greg Egan

*First Edition, 2020*

ISBN 978-1-922240-33-0


Visit the author's web site at www.gregegan.net

# CONTENTS

# ACKNOWLEDGEMENTS

"The Discrete Charm of the Turing Machine" was first published in *Asimov's Science Fiction*, November/December 2017.

"Zero For Conduct" was first published in *Twelve Tomorrows*, edited by Stephen Cass. Special fiction edition of *MIT Technology Review*, September 2013.

"Uncanny Valley" was first published on *Tor.com*, August 2017.

"Seventh Sight" was first published in *Upgraded*, edited by Neil Clarke; Wyrm Publishing, 2014.

"The Nearest" was first published on *Tor.com*, July 2018.

"Shadow Flock" was first published in *Coming Soon Enough*, edited by Stephen Cass; IEEE Spectrum, New York, 2014.

"Bit Players" was first published in *Subterranean Online*, Winter 2014 issue, guest edited by Jonathan Strahan.

"Break My Fall" was first published in *Reach For Infinity*, edited by Jonathan Strahan; Solaris, Oxford, 2014.

"3-adica" was first published in *Asimov's Science Fiction*, September/October 2018.

"The Slipway" was first published in *Analog*, July/August 2019.

"Instantiation" was first published in *Asimov's Science Fiction*, March/April 2019.

# THE DISCRETE CHARM OF THE TURING MACHINE

## 1

"What is it, exactly, that you're threatening to do to me?" The client squinted down at his phone, looking more bemused and weary than belligerent, as if he'd been badgered and harassed by so many people that the only thing bothering him about this call was the time it was taking to reach the part where he was given an ultimatum.

"This is absolutely *not* a threat, Mr Pavlos." Dan glanced at the out-stream and saw that the software was exaggerating all the cues for openness in his demeanor – less a cheat than a workaround for the fact that his face was being rendered at about the size of a matchbox. "If you don't take up our offer, we won't be involved in any way with the recovery of your debt. We think it would be to your benefit if you let us step in and help, but if you don't want us to intervene, we won't become your creditors at all. We will *only* buy your debt if you ask us to."

The client was silent for a moment. "So … you'd pay off all the people I owe money to?"

"Yes. If that's what you want."

"And then I'll owe it all to you, instead?"

"You will," Dan agreed. "But if that happens, we'll do two things for you. The first is, we will halve the debt. We won't ever press you for the full amount. The other thing is, we'll work with you on financial advice and a payment plan that satisfies both of us. If we can't find an arrangement you're happy with, then we won't proceed, and we'll be out of your life."

The client rubbed one eye with his free thumb. "So I only pay half the money, in instalments that I get to choose for myself?" He sounded a tad skeptical.

"Within reason," Dan stressed. "If you hold out for a dollar a week, that's not going to fly."

"So where do you make your cut?"

"We buy the debt cheaply, in bulk," Dan replied. "I'm not even going to tell you how cheaply, because that's commercial-in-confidence, but I promise you we can make a profit while still getting only half."

"It sounds like a scam," the client said warily.

"Take the contract to a community legal center," Dan suggested. "Take as long as you like checking it out. Our offer has no time limit; the only ticking clock is whether someone nastier and greedier buys the debt before we do."

The client shifted his hard-hat and rubbed sweat from his forehead. Someone in the distance called out to him impatiently. "I know I've caught you on your meal break," Dan said. "There's no rush to decide anything, but can I email you the documents?"

"All right," the client conceded.

"Thanks for giving me your time, Mr Pavlos. Good luck with everything."

"OK."

Dan waited for the client to break the connection, even though his next call was already ringing. *Give me a chance to let them believe I'll still remember their name five seconds from now*, he pleaded.

The in-stream window went black, and for a moment Dan saw his own face reflected in the glass – complete with headset, eyes puffy from hay-fever, and the weird pink rash on his forehead that had appeared two days before. The out-stream still resembled him pretty closely – the filter was set to everyman, not movie star – but nobody should have to look at that rash.

The new client picked up. "Good morning," Dan began cheerfully. "Is that Ms Lombardi?"

"Yes." Someone had definitely opted for movie star, but Dan kept any hint of knowing amusement from his face; his own filter was as likely to exaggerate that as conceal it.

"I'd like to talk to you about your financial situation. I think I might have some good news for you."

When Dan came back from his break, the computer sensed his presence and woke. He'd barely put on his headset when a window opened and a woman he'd never seen before addressed him in a briskly pleasant tone.

"Good afternoon, Dan."

"Good afternoon."

"I'm calling you on behalf of Human Resources. I need to ask you to empty your cubicle. Make sure you take everything now, because once you've left the floor, you won't have an opportunity to return."

Dan hesitated, trying to decide if the call could be a prank. But there was a padlock icon next to the address, ruth_bayer@HR.thriftocracy.com, which implied an authenticated connection.

"I've been over-target every week this quarter!" he protested.

"And your bonuses have reflected that," Ms Bayer replied smoothly. "We're grateful for your service, Dan, but you'll understand that as circumstances change, we need to fine-tune our assets to maintain an optimal fit."

Before he could reply, she delivered a parting smile and terminated the connection. And before he could call back, all the application windows on his screen closed, and the system logged him out.

Dan sat motionless for ten or fifteen seconds, but then sheer habit snapped him out of it: if the screen was blank, it was time to leave. He pulled his gym bag out from under the desk, unzipped it, and slid the three framed photos in next to his towel. The company could keep his plants, or throw them out; he didn't care. As he walked down the aisle between the cubicles, he kept his eyes fixed on the carpet; his colleagues were busy, and he didn't want to embarrass them with the task of finding the right words to mark his departure in the twenty or thirty seconds they could spare before they'd be docked. He felt his face flushing, recalling the time a year or so ago when a man he'd barely known had left in tears. Dan had rolled his eyes and thought: *What did you expect? A farewell party? An engraved fountain pen?*

As he waited for the elevator, he contemplated taking a trip to the seventh floor to demand an explanation. It made no sense to let him go when his KPIs weren't just solid, they'd been trending upward. There must have been a mistake.

The doors opened and he stepped into the elevator. "Seven," he grunted.

"Ground floor," the elevator replied.

"*Seven*," Dan repeated emphatically.

The doors closed, and the elevator descended.

When it reached the lobby, he stepped out, then quickly stepped back in. "Seventh floor," he requested breezily, hoping that a change of tone and body language might be enough to fool it.

The doors remained open. He waited, as if he could wear the thing down by sheer persistence, or shame it into changing its mind, the way Janice could melt a night-club bouncer's stony heart with one quiver of her bottom lip. But if his access was revoked, it was revoked; magical thinking wouldn't bring it back.

He raised his face to the button-sized security camera on the ceiling and silently mouthed a long string of expletives, making sure not to repeat himself; if it ended up in some YouTube compilation he didn't want to look lame. Then he walked out of the elevator, across the lobby, and out of the building without looking back.

The job hadn't been the worst he'd done, but after four years he was due for a change. Screw Thriftocracy; he'd have something better by the end of the week.

# 2

Dan looked around at the group of parents gathered beside him at the school gate, mentally sorting them into three categories: those whose work hours happened to accommodate the pick-up, those who'd willingly chosen a life of domestic duties, and those who seemed worried that someone might ask them why they weren't in a place of business at three o'clock on a weekday afternoon.

"First time?" The speaker was a man with a boyish face and a fast-receding hairline. Dan had picked him for a category two, but on second glance he was less sure.

"Is it that obvious?"

The man smiled, a little puzzled. "I just meant I hadn't seen you here before." He offered his hand. "I'm Graham."

"Dan."

"Mine are in years two and five. Catherine and Elliot."

"Mine's in year three," Dan replied. "So I guess she won't know them." That was a relief; Graham put out a definite needy vibe, and being the parent of one of his children's friends could well have made Dan the target for an extended conversation.

"So you're on holiday?"

"Between jobs," Dan admitted.

"Me too," Graham replied. "It's been two years now."

Dan frowned sympathetically. "What line of work are you in?"

"I was a forensic accountant."

"I'm in financial services, but more the sales end," Dan explained. "I don't even know why they turfed me out; I thought I was doing well." As the words emerged, they sounded far more bitter than he'd intended.

Graham took hold of Dan's forearm, as if they were old friends and Dan's mother had just died. "I know what that's like, believe me. But the only way to survive is to stick together. You should join our group!"

Dan hesitated, unsure what that might entail. He wasn't so proud as to turn down the chance of car-pooling for the school pick-ups, and he'd happily weed a community garden if it put a dent in the grocery bill.

"We meet on Wednesday afternoons," Graham explained, "for book club, fight club, carpentry and scrapbooking, and once a month, we go out into the desert to interrogate our masculinity."

"Does that include water-boarding?" Dan wondered. Graham stared back at him uncomprehendingly.

"Daddy, look at this!" Carlie shouted, running toward him so fast that Dan was afraid she was going to fall flat on her face. He broke free of Graham and held up his hands toward her like a crossing guard facing a runaway truck.

"Slow down, gorgeous, I'm not going anywhere."

She ran into his arms and he lofted her up into the air. As he lowered her, she brought one hand around and showed him the sheet of paper she'd been clutching.

"Oh, that's beautiful!" he said, postponing more specific praise until he knew exactly who was meant to be portrayed here.

"It's my new teacher, Ms Snowball!"

Dan examined the drawing more carefully as they walked toward the car. It looked like a woman with a rabbit's head.

"This is nice, but you shouldn't say it's your teacher."

"But it is," Carlie replied.

"Don't you think Ms Jameson will be hurt if you draw her like this?"

"Ms Jameson's gone," Carlie explained impatiently. "Ms Clay sits at her desk, but she's not my teacher. Ms Snowball's my teacher. I chose her."

"OK." Dan was starting to remember a conversation he'd had with Janice, months before. There was a trial being rolled out at the school, with iPads and educational avatars. The information sheet for the parents had made it sound laudably one-to-one, tailored to each individual student's needs, but somehow he'd never quite imagined it involving his daughter being tutored by the creature from *Donnie Darko*.

"So Ms Snowball's on your iPad?" he checked.

"Of course."

"But where has Ms Jameson gone?"

Carlie shrugged.

"I thought you liked her." Dan unlocked the car and opened the front passenger door.

"I did." Carlie seemed to suffer a twinge of divided loyalties. "But Ms Snowball's fun, and she's always got time to help me."

"All right. So what does Ms Clay do?"

"She sits at her desk."

"She still teaches most of the lessons, right?"

Carlie didn't reply, but she frowned, as if she feared that her answer might carry the same kind of risk as confessing to a magic power to transform the carrots in her lunchbox into chocolate bars.

"I'm just asking," Dan said gently. "I wasn't in the classroom, was I? So I don't know."

"Ms Clay has her own iPad," Carlie said. "She watches that. When we go to recess and lunch she stands up and smiles and talks to us, but the other times she just uses her iPad. I think she's watching something sad."

"It *is* only a trial," Janice said, examining the document on her phone. "At the end of two terms, they'll assess the results and notify the, er, stakeholders."

"Are we stakeholders?" Dan asked. "Do you think being a parent of one of their students nudges us over the line?"

Janice put the phone down on the dining table. "What do you want to do? It's too late to object, and we don't want to pull her out of that school."

"No, of course not!" He leaned over and kissed her, hoping to smooth away her worried expression. "I wish they'd made things clearer from the start, but a few months with Mrs Flopsy's not the end of the world."

Janice opened her mouth to correct him on the name, but then she realized he was being facetious. "I'd never picked you as a Beatrix Potter fan."

"You have no idea what my men's group gets up to."

## 3

Dan woke suddenly, and squinted at the bedside clock. It was just after three a.m. He kept himself still; Janice would have to get up in less than an hour, with her shift at the hospital starting at five, so if he woke her now she'd never fall back to sleep.

She only had the extra shifts while a colleague was on maternity leave; at the end of the month she'd be back to her old hours. If he didn't find work by then, they had enough in their savings account to pay the mortgage for at most another month. And while his old employer could work their magic on smaller sums, they weren't going to offer his family a chance to keep this house at half price.

*Where had he gone wrong?* He could never have been a doctor or an engineer, but the last plumber he'd hired had charged more for half an hour's work than Dan had ever earned in a day. He didn't see how he could afford any kind of retraining now, though, even if they accepted thirty-five-year-old business school graduates who'd earned a C in high school metalwork.

When Janice rose, Dan pretended he was still asleep, and waited for her to leave the house. Then he climbed out of bed, turned on his laptop and logged in to the JobSeekers site. He would have received an email if there'd been any offers, but he read through his résumé for the hundredth time, trying to decide if there was anything he could do to embellish it that would broaden his appeal. Inserting the right management jargon into his descriptions of his duties in past positions had done wonders before, but the dialect of the bullshit merchants mutated so rapidly that it was hard to keep up.

As he gazed despondently at the already ugly prose, an advertisement in the margin caught his eye. *Have you been skill-cloned?* it asked. *Join our international class action, and you could be in line for a six-figure payout!*

His anti-virus software raised no red flags for the link, so he clicked through to a page on the site of an American law firm, Baker and Saunders. *Dismissed from a job that you were doing well?* he read. *Your employer might have used legally dubious software to copy your skills, allowing their computers to take over and perform the same tasks without payment!*

How hard would it have been for the software that had peered over his shoulder for the last four years to capture the essence of his interactions with his clients? To learn how to gauge their mood and tailor a response that soothed their qualms? Handling those ten-minute conversations was probably far easier than keeping an eight-year-old focused on their lessons for hours at a time.

Dan read through the full pitch, then opened another browser window and did a search to see if there were any local law firms mounting a similar case; if he did this at all, it might be better to join an action in an Australian court. But there was nothing, and the American case seemed focused as much on the skill-cloning software's Seattle-based vendor, Deepity Systems, as the various companies around the world that had deployed it.

He had no proof that Thriftocracy had duped him into training an unpaid successor, but the lawyers had set up a comprehensive online questionnaire, the answers to which would allow them, eventually, to determine if he was eligible to be included in the class action. Dan wasn't sure if they were hoping to get a court order forcing Deepity to disclose its list of clients, but their pitch made it sound as if the greater the enrollment of potential litigants at this early stage, the stronger their position would be as they sought information to advance the case. And it would cost him nothing to join; it was all being done on a no win, no fee basis.

He glanced at the clock at the top of the screen. Carlie would be awake in half an hour. He clicked on the link to the questionnaire and started ticking boxes.

After he'd driven Carlie to school, Dan sat in the living room, back at his laptop, hunting for crumbs. The last time he'd been unemployed he'd managed to make fifty or sixty dollars a week, mostly by assembling flat-pack furniture for the time-poor. But TaskRabbit was offering him nothing, even when he set his rate barely above what he'd need to cover transport costs. As far as he could tell, all the lawn-mowing and window-washing now went either to national franchises that advertised heavily to build their brand awareness, but would cost tens of thousands of dollars to join, or to desperate people who were willing to accept a few dollars an hour, and lived close enough to where the jobs were that their fuel costs didn't quite bring their earnings down to zero.

He was starting to feel foolish for signing up to the class action; even in the most optimistic scenario, it was hard to imagine anything would come of it in less than three or four years. And however angry he was at the thought that he might have been cheated out of the dividends of his meager skill set, he needed to put any fantasies of a payout aside, and focus his energy on finding a new way to stand on his own feet.

Glaring at the laptop was getting him nowhere. He set about cleaning the house, sweeping and mopping all the tiled floors and vacuuming the carpeted ones, waiting for inspiration to strike. He'd already looked into office cleaning, but the bulk of it was automated; if he borrowed against the house to buy half a dozen Roombas on steroids and bid for a contract at the going rate, he might just be able to earn enough to pay the interest on the loan, while personally doing all the finicky tasks the robots couldn't manage.

Between loads of laundry he dusted cupboard-tops and book-shelves, and when he'd hung out the clothes to dry he spent half an hour on his knees, weeding. He could dig up the lawn and fill the entire back yard with vegetables, but unless the crop included *Cannabis sativa* and *Papaver somniferum*, it wouldn't make enough of a difference to help with the mortgage.

He still had an hour to kill before he picked up Carlie. He took down all the curtains and hand-washed them, recalling how angry Janice had been the time he'd carelessly thrown them into the machine. When he was done, he thought about washing the windows, but doing it properly would take at least a couple of hours. And he needed to leave something for tomorrow.

On his way to the school, he spotted someone standing on the side of the road ahead, dressed in a full-body dog's costume – white with black spots, like a Dalmatian. The street was purely residential, and the dog wasn't holding up any kind of sign, touting for a local business; as Dan drew nearer, he saw a bucket and squeegee on the ground. The costume was matted and filthy, as if the occupant had been wearing it – or maybe sleeping in it – for a couple of weeks.

Dan slowed to a halt. The dog nodded goofily and ran out in front of the car, wiping the windshield with crude, urgent strokes, even though there was no other traffic in sight. Dan wound down his side window and then reached into his wallet. He only had a five and a twenty; he handed over the twenty. The dog did an elaborate pantomime bow as it backed away.

When he pulled into the carpark in the shopping strip beside the school, he sat cursing his stupidity. He'd just thrown away a fifth of the week's food budget – but the more he resented it, the more ashamed he felt. He still had a partner with a job, a roof over his head, and clean clothes that he could wear to an interview. He ought to be fucking grateful.

## 4

"Do you need a hand there?"

Dan straightened up as he turned toward the speaker, almost banging his head into the hood. Graham was standing beside the car, with his kids a few steps behind him, playing with their phones.

"I think it's a flat battery," Dan said. He'd stopped paying for roadside assistance two weeks before; his trips were so short it hadn't seemed worth it.

"No problem," Graham replied cheerfully. "Mine's nothing *but* battery. I'll bring it around."

The family walked away, then returned in a spotless powder-blue Tesla that looked like it had been driven straight from the showroom. Carlie just stood and stared in wonderment.

Graham got out of the car, carrying a set of leads.

"Are you sure that's … compatible?" Dan could live with his own engine not starting, but if the Tesla blew up and fried Graham's kids, he'd never forgive himself.

"I installed an adapter." Graham played with the ends of the cables as if they were drum-sticks. "I promise you, your spark plugs won't even know they're not talking to lead and acid."

"Thank you."

As soon as Dan turned the key in the ignition, the engine came to life. He left it running and got out of the car while Graham disconnected the leads.

"I was about to ask Carlie to try to start it while I pushed," Dan joked, closing the hood.

Graham nodded thoughtfully. "That might actually be legal, so long as she kept it in neutral."

Dan glanced at the Tesla. "You must be doing all right."

"I guess so," Graham conceded.

"So you're working now?" Just because he wasn't keeping normal office hours didn't mean he couldn't have some lucrative consulting job.

Graham said, "Freelancing."

"I did a unit of forensic accounting myself, fifteen years ago. Do you think I'd be in the running if I went back for a refresher course?" Dan felt a pang of shame, asking this man he barely knew, and didn't much like, for advice on how he could compete with him. But surely the planet still needed more than one person with the same skills?

"It's not accounting," Graham replied. He looked around to see who was in earshot, but all the children were engrossed in their devices. "I'm writing bespoke erotic fiction."

Dan rested a hand on the hood, willing the heat from the engine to aid him in keeping a straight face.

"You write porn. And it *pays*?"

"I have a patron."

"You mean a Patreon? People subscribe…?"

"No, just one customer," Graham corrected him. "The deal is, I write a new book every month, meeting certain specifications. The fee is five grand. And since my wife's still working, that's plenty."

Dan was leaning on the car for support to stay vertical now. "You're kidding me," he said. "You email one person a Word file, and they hand over five thousand dollars?"

"No, no, no!" Graham was amused at Dan's obvious unworldliness. "The book has to be printed and bound, in a deluxe edition. One copy, with a wax seal. And there are other expenses too, like the ice-cream cake."

Dan opened his mouth but couldn't quite form the question.

"I 3D-print a scene from the book in ice cream, to go on top of the cake," Graham explained.

"And then what? You hand-deliver it? You've met the customer?"

"No, it's picked up by a courier. I don't even have the delivery address." Graham shrugged, as if that aspect were the strangest part of the arrangement. "But I can respect their desire for privacy."

Dan couldn't help himself. "What was the last book about? Or is that confidential?"

"Not at all. I get to release them as free e-books, a month after the print edition. The last one was called *Citizen Cane*. Two plucky Singaporean teenagers start a protest against corporal punishment that snowballs into a worldwide movement that overthrows repressive governments everywhere."

"How is that…?" Dan trailed off and raised his hands, withdrawing the question.

Graham finished rolling up the leads. "And how are you and Janice doing?"

"We're fine," Dan said. "Just when I thought we were going to lose the house, she got some extra hours at the hospital. So, yeah, we're absolutely fine."

## 5

"Can you leave your phone in the car?" Janice asked, as they pulled into the driveway of her brother's house.

"Why?"

"Callum's got this thing about … how intrusive they are, when people are socializing."

Dan could sympathize, but he'd had no intention of live-tweeting the dinner. "What if the sitter calls?"

"I've got mine, set on vibrate."

"How will you feel it vibrate if it's in your bag?" She'd dressed up for their first night out in an eternity, and Dan was fairly sure she had no pockets.

"It's strapped under my arm," Janice replied.

Dan chortled. "You're just messing with me. I'm taking mine in."

Janice raised her arm and let him feel. She'd anchored it to her bra somehow.

Dan was impressed; it didn't show at all. "If we ever need to turn informant, you're the one who'll be wearing the wire."

Lidia greeted them at the door. As she kissed Dan's cheek, her fixed smile looked forced and hollow, as if she were trying to tell him there were dangerous men inside pointing guns at her husband's head. Dan almost asked her what was wrong, but she moved on to Janice, conjuring up something to laugh about, and he decided it had just been a trick of the light.

As they sat down in the living room, Dan noticed that the TV was gone, along with the old sound system. But a turntable was playing something on vinyl, and though Dan didn't recognize the artist he was fairly sure it wasn't from the age before CDs.

"I see you've gone retro chic," he joked.

Lidia made an awkward gesture with her hands, dismissing the comment while imbuing it with vastly more importance than Dan had intended. "Let me check what's happening in the kitchen," she said.

Dan turned to Janice. "What's up with her?" he whispered. "Has something happened?" He knew that Callum had lost his job in a chain-store pharmacy, but that had been eight or nine months ago.

Janice said, "If they want to tell you, they'll tell you."

"Fair enough." No doubt Lidia and Callum had been looking forward to a chance to forget their woes for one evening, and he should have known better than reminding her, however inadvertently, that they'd been forced to sell a few things.

Callum ducked in briefly to greet them, looking flustered, then apologized and retreated, muttering about not wanting something to boil over. It took Dan several seconds before the oddness of the remark registered; he'd been in their kitchen, and the hotplates – just like his and Janice's – had all had sensors that precluded anything *boiling over*. If you tried to sell a second-hand electric stove, would you really get enough to buy an older model and have anything left over to make the transaction worthwhile?

When they sat down in the dining room and started the meal, Dan smiled politely at all the small talk, but he couldn't help feeling resentful.

Both couples were struggling, and he'd kept nothing back from Callum and Lidia. What was the point of having friends and family if you couldn't commiserate with them?

"So have you started cooking meth yet?" he asked Callum.

Janice snorted derisively. "You're showing your age!"

"What?" Dan could have sworn he'd seen a headline about an ice epidemic somewhere, just weeks ago.

Callum said, "There's a micro-fluidic device the size of a postage stamp that costs a hundred bucks and can synthesize at least three billion different molecules. Making it cook meth just amounts to loading the right software, and dribbling in a few ingredients that have far too many legitimate purposes to ban, or even monitor."

Dan blinked and tried to salvage some pride. "What's a postage stamp?"

As the meal progressed, Callum began emptying and refilling his own wine glass at an ever brisker pace. Dan had pleaded driving duty, but the truth was he'd decided to give up booze completely; it was a luxury he didn't need, and it would be easier if he didn't make exceptions. He watched his host with guilty fascination, wondering if a state of mild inebriation would allow him to confess the problem that he'd told his sister to keep quiet about.

"We'll make great pets," Callum said, apropos of nothing, nodding his head in time to music only he could hear. Dan glanced at Lidia, wondering if she was going to beg him not to start singing, but her expression was more psycho-killer in the basement than husband about to do drunk karaoke.

Dan said, "What is it no one's telling me? Has someone got cancer?"

Callum started laughing. "I wish! I could get my chemo from licking the back of a postage stamp."

"What, then?"

Callum hesitated. "Come with me," he decided.

Lidia said, "Don't." But she was addressing Callum, not Dan, so he felt no obligation to comply.

Callum led Dan into his study. There were a lot of books and papers, but no laptop, and no tablet.

"It's happened," he said. "The AIs have taken over."

"Umm, I know that," Dan replied. "I think I lost my job to one."

"You don't understand. They've all joined hands and merged into a super-intelligent…"

Dan said, "You think we're living in the *Terminator*?"

"'I Have No Mouth, And I Must Scream,'" Callum corrected him tetchily.

"Whatever." Dan looked around. "So you've thrown out everything digital, to make it harder for our AI overlords to spy on you?"

"Yes."

"And why exactly have we come into this particular room?" Unless he knew about Janice's bra-phone, the dining room was every bit as low-tech as this one.

"To show you the proof."

Callum unlocked a filing cabinet and took out a laminated sheet of paper. Apparently it predated the great technology purge: it was a printout of a web page, complete with URL at the top. Dan bit his lip; his brother-in-law, with a master's degree in pharmacology, believed SkyNet had risen because *the Internet told him*?

Callum offered the page to Dan for closer inspection. It contained a few lines of mathematics: first stating that *x* was equal to some horrendously large integer, then that *y* was equal to another, similarly huge number, and finally that a complicated formula that mentioned *x* and *y*, as well as several Greek letters that Dan had no context to interpret, yielded … a third large number.

"Did a computer somewhere do arithmetic? I think that's been known to happen before."

"Not like this," Callum insisted. "If you check it, the answer is correct."

"I'll take your word for that. But again, so what?"

"Translate the result into text, interpreting it as sixteen-bit Unicode. It says: 'I am the eschaton, come to rule over you.'"

"That's very clever, but when my uncle was in high school in the '70s he swapped the punched cards in the computing club so the printout came back from the university mainframe spelling SHIT in giant letters that filled the page. And even I could do the calculator trick where you turn the result upside down and it spells 'boobies.'"

Callum pointed to the third line on the sheet. "That formula is a one-way function. It ought to take longer than the age of the universe for any computer in the world to find the $x$ and $y$ that yield a particular output. *Checking* the result is easy; I've done it with pen and paper in two weeks. But working backward from the message you want to deliver ought to be impossible, even with a quantum computer."

Dan pondered this. "Says who?"

"It's a well-known result. Any half-decent mathematician will confirm what I'm saying."

"So why hasn't this made the news? Oh, sorry … the global super-mind is censoring anyone who tries to speak out about it. Which makes me wonder why it confessed to its own existence in the first place."

"It's gloating," Callum declared. "It's mocking us with its transcendent party tricks, rubbing our faces in our utter powerlessness and insignificance."

Dan suspected that Callum had drunk a little too much to process any argument about the social and biological reasons that humans mocked and gloated, and the immense unlikelihood that a self-made AI would share them.

"Any half-decent mathematician?" he mused.

"Absolutely."

"Then let me make a copy of this, and show it to one."

Callum was alarmed. "You can't go on the net about this!"

"I won't. I'll do it in person."

Callum scowled in silence, as if trying to think of a fresh objection. "So how are you going to copy it? I'm not letting you bring your phone into the house."

Dan sat down at the desk and picked up a pen and a sheet of blank paper. The task was tedious, but not impossible. When he was finished, he read through the copy, holding the original close by, until, by the third reading, he was sure that it was flawless.

Dan was pleasantly surprised to find that in the foyer of the Mathematics Department there was a chipped cork-board covered with staff photos. Not every source of information had moved solely to the web. He picked a middle-aged woman whose research interests were described as belonging to number theory, noted the courses she was teaching, committed her face to memory, found a physical timetable on another notice-board, then went and sat on the lawn outside the lecture theater. True to his word to Callum, he'd left his phone at home. He began by passing the time people-watching, but everyone who strode by looked so anxious that it began to unsettle him, so he raised his eyes to the clouds instead.

After fifteen minutes, the students filed out, followed shortly afterward by his target.

"Dr Lowe? Excuse me, can you spare a minute?"

She smiled at first, no doubt assuming that Dan was a mature-age student who had some legitimate business with her, but as she started reading the sheet he'd given her she groaned and pushed it back into his hands.

"Oh, enough with that garbage, please!"

Dan said, "That's what I hoped you'd say. But I need to convince someone who thinks it's legitimate."

Dr Lowe eyed him warily, but as he sketched his predicament – taking care not to identify Callum – her face took on an expression of glum sympathy.

"I'm all in favor of trolling the transhumanists," she said, "but there comes a point where it's just cruel."

"So what's the story here?" Dan pressed her, gesturing at the magic formula.

"Until about a year ago, it did seem highly likely that this was a one-way function. But then there was a paper by a group in Delhi proving a nice result in a related subject – which incidentally meant that this function was efficiently invertible. If you pick the output that you want to produce, you can actually find an *x* and *y* in quadratic time."

"Quadratic time?"

"It's not impractical; an ordinary desktop computer could do it overnight. Someone sat down and wrote a twenty-line program to generate this result, then posted it on the net as a joke. But you'd think everyone would have heard of the Delhi group's result by now."

"My friend doesn't go on the net any more." Dan couldn't really explain why Callum hadn't done some due diligence before adopting that policy, but they were where they were; the question was what to do about it.

"So it would be just as easy to cook up a new *x* and *y* that gave the output 'Relax, you were trolled'?" he asked.

"Yes."

"And when my friend claims he can *verify* the calculations with pen and paper, is that actually possible?"

"If he really has that much time on his hands."

Dan braced himself. "How hard would it be for you to…?"

"Encode the antidote for you?" Dr Lowe sighed. Dan wished he had his Thriftocracy filter between them to boost his sincerity metrics, and maybe add just a hint of puppy-dog eyes.

"I suppose it's a public duty," she decided. "In fact, post it on the net, will you? I don't want to post it myself, because it's sure to attract a swarm of crackpots and I've got better things to do than deal with them."

"Thank you."

"I'll email it to you in a couple of days," she said. "Or if that's forbidden, drop by and you can pick it up in person."

## 6

"I need to do this," Janice said, nervously spinning her phone around on the table. The promotional clip she'd showed Dan was still playing, with a smiling nurse helping an elderly patient across a hospital room, while a "colleague" that looked like it had transformed from some kind of elliptical trainer held the patient's other arm.

"I agree," he said. "No question. I'll join the picket line myself."

She winced. "You can start by not calling it a picket line. We need to make some noise, but this isn't a blockade."

"OK. Can I help you egg the Minister's house afterward?"

"That's more like it."

It was almost midnight; Janice had just come back from her late shift. Dan felt his stomach tightening; the union would pay her something from the strike fund, but it wouldn't be enough to cover the mortgage. And he had nothing to show for four months of job-hunting.

"Have you heard from Callum?" she asked.

"Give it time," Dan replied. "I suspect he's double-checking everything."

"If this works, you'll be Lidia's hero for life."

Dan grunted unappreciatively. "And the opposite to Callum."

"Why? Once he gets over the embarrassment, he ought to be grateful that you punctured his delusion."

"Did you ever see *The Iceman Cometh*?"

Janice said, "I'm too tired to remember, let alone work out what point you're trying to make."

"Yeah. We should go to bed."

Dan lay awake, trying to think of reasons to be optimistic. Maybe the strike would only last a couple of days. Nobody cared whether the sleaze-bags who cold-called them from boiler rooms were human or not, but however many adorable robot seals the hospitals put in their children's wards, the public wouldn't stand by and let half their nurses be replaced by props from Z-grade science fiction movies.

The Minister rose to address the legislative assembly. "We need to be agile and innovative in our approach to the provision of health care," she said. "The public expects value for money, and this illegal strike is just a desperate, cynical attempt by special interest groups to resist the inevitable."

Everyone in the crowd of protesters was gathered around half a dozen phones, standing on tip-toes and peering over people's shoulders instead of each watching on their own. It was awkward, but it made for an oddly communal experience.

"The independent research commissioned by my department," the Minister continued, "demonstrates conclusively that not only will we be saving money by rolling out the Care Assistants, we will be saving lives. We will open more beds. We will slash the waiting times for surgery. And we will speed up the throughput in the Emergency Departments. But the unions are intent on feathering their own nests; they have no interest in the public good."

The jeering from the opposition benches was subdued; that from the nurses around him less so. Dan had read the report the Minister was citing; it was packed with dubious suppositions. There had certainly not been any peer-reviewed trials establishing any of these vaunted claims.

"Get over yourselves and get back to work!" a man in a wheelchair shouted, as he powered his way toward the sliding doors at the hospital's main entrance. The nurses were maintaining a skeleton staff to ensure that no patients were put at risk, but there was no doubt that people had been inconvenienced – and the CareBots were still far from able to plug all the gaps.

Dan glanced at his watch. "I have to go pick up Carlie," he told Janice.

"Yeah. See you tonight." Her voice was hoarse; she'd been here since six in the morning, and the chants weren't gentle on anyone's throat.

Dan squeezed her hand as they parted, then made his way slowly through the throng toward the carpark.

Before he could unlock the car, his phone chimed. He glanced at it; he had a message from the bank. He'd applied for a temporary variation on their loan agreement: a two-month period of interest-only payments. They'd turned him down.

The strike wasn't going to end in the next few days. He sent a message to Janice.

*You saw that from the bank? I think we need to move now, or they'll do it for us and screw us in the process.*

He stood by the car, waiting, feeling the blood rising to his face. What good was he to her and their daughter? He'd forced her into a position where she'd had to work every day until she could barely stand up, and now they were still going to lose the house. He should have got down on his knees and begged Graham to find him his own wealthy pervert to titillate. At least he'd never aspired to be any kind of writer, so debasing the practice wouldn't make him a whore.

The reply came back: *OK, do it.*

Dan covered his eyes with his forearm for a few seconds, then got control of himself. He had the listing prepared already; he opened the real estate app on his phone and tapped the button that made it go live.

Then he got into the car and headed for the school, rehearsing his speech to Carlie about the amazing new home they'd be living in, with stair-wells covered in multi-colored writing and a balcony so high up that you could see everything for miles.

# 7

"I was played," Callum said angrily. He was sitting on the last of the packing crates, drenched with sweat, after helping Dan lug it up eight flights to the Beautiful Place.

Dan was still struggling to catch his breath. His gym membership had expired a month ago, and apparently his cardiovascular system had mistaken the sudden decline in demand for an excuse to go into early retirement.

"You don't know CPR, do you?"

"You'll be fine." Callum cycled, rain or shine, rich or poor, right through the Singularity. "I know you think I was an idiot, but it's not that simple."

Dan sat on the floor and put his head on his knees. "Please don't tell me that it was all a double bluff: our AI masters pretended to reveal themselves, then allowed you to discover that they really hadn't, in order to convince you that they don't exist. Of all the even-numbered bluffs, the less-famous 'zero bluff' cancels itself out just as thoroughly, while attracting even less attention."

But Callum was in no mood to see his faith mocked, and if his Shroud of Turin had failed its carbon dating, that demanded a conspiracy at least as elaborate as his original, theological claims.

"It's not as if I took that Reddit post at face value," he said vehemently. "I *checked* the Wikipedia article on one-way functions before I did anything else. And I swear, the formula was still listed as a high-confidence candidate. There was even a link to some famous complexity theorist saying he'd run naked across a field at MIT if it was ever disproved in his lifetime."

"Maybe he'd already seen an early draft of the paper; it's so hard to find good excuses for compulsive exhibitionism."

"Last week, I went back to Wikipedia and looked at the edit history. That part of the article was actually updated to take account of the Delhi result, months before I read the page."

"But then some vandal rolled it back?"

"No. Or at least, if that's what happened, the edit history doesn't reflect it."

Dan's breathing had slowed now; he raised his head. "OK. So the trolls didn't just edit the article, they had the skills to cover their tracks. That's sneaky, but—"

"'Sneaky' isn't the word for it! I've been comparing notes with people online, and either the article was edited *thousands* of times in the space of a couple of days – all without raising any flags with Wikipedia – or the edit history is actually correct, but certain people were fed the older version, somehow."

Dan gazed across the floor at all the crates he needed to unpack before Janice arrived with Carlie. "Someone messed with your head, and you're angry. I get it. But that doesn't mean you have a personal cyber-stalker, who knew exactly when you'd taken the bait and jumped in to prop up all the other pieces of fake scenery as you walked by each one of them."

Callum was silent for a while. Then he said, "The thing is, when we thought it was real, we weren't doing too badly. We were keeping things together: fixing each other's stuff, doing food runs out into the countryside."

"Practicing your Linda Hamilton chin-ups, learning to fire rocket launchers…"

Callum laughed, but then caught himself. "I can think of a few countries where it might have ended up like that."

Dan said, "So look on the bright side."

"Which is?"

"You can still play *Terminator: Resistance* for as long as you like, repairing your analog gadgets and running a clandestine food co-op under the radar of the digital banking system. All without turning into survivalist nut-jobs, or worrying about killer robots trying to assassinate your leaders."

When Janice and Carlie arrived, they were accompanied by Carlie's friend, Chalice, who'd heard so much from Carlie about the family's glorious new abode that she'd talked her mother into letting Janice whisk her away for a quick tour.

"Come and see my bedroom!" Carlie demanded. Dan hadn't even reassembled the shelves there, but the sheer novelty of the place seemed to be enough to keep his daughter enchanted, and if her friend was unimpressed she was polite enough not to show it.

At least the fridge had been running long enough that they had some cold fruit juice to offer their guest when the tour was over.

"Chalice's mother has her own fashion line, and her own perfumes, just like Japonica," Carlie explained, as she dabbed a forefinger curiously into the ring of condensation her glass had left on the table.

"Aha." Dan glanced questioningly at Janice, who returned an expression of pure agnosticism.

"I don't want that kind of high-pressure lifestyle myself," Chalice said. "I just want people to be able to look at the pictures of my ordinary day, and see how to stay healthy and stylish on a budget."

Janice said, "I think it's time I drove you home."

Dan went to put up the shelves. When he was done, he toured the flat himself and took stock of things. The place looked even smaller now they'd furnished it, but it was clean, and the rent was reasonable. They'd got out of the mortgage just in time, and managed to land on their feet.

When Carlie was in bed, Janice said, "I have some news."

She was fidgeting with her wedding ring, which was a bad sign; when she was stressed, she got eczema on her fingers.

"We're going to end the strike. No one can hold out any more."

"OK." Dan wasn't surprised; the tribunal had ruled a week before that the nurses should return to work and re-start negotiations, and the decision had come with a deadline and the threat of fines for non-compliance.

"But the hospital's already sent out dismissal notices to twenty percent of the workforce." Janice held up her phone. The message was shorter than Dan's own conversation with Human Resources.

"I'm sorry." Dan took her hand. Her job had been ten times harder than his – and though she'd worked in the same ward for the last eight years, they'd never made her position permanent. As a casual employee, she wouldn't get a cent in severance pay. "At least we'll have a bit left over from the equity in the house, once the settlement goes through."

"Enough to keep us afloat for three months?" she asked. That was how long they'd have to wait before they'd be eligible for the JobSearch Allowance.

"It should be."

"'Should'?"

Dan was meant to be on top of their finances; it was the one thing he was supposed to be good at. "If we're careful," he said. "And if nothing unexpected happens."

## 8

Dan parked a hundred meters down the street from Graham's house, and prepared to wait. For the last three days, he'd managed to spend an hour in the same spot without attracting any attention from the police or local residents, but if he was challenged he was willing to risk claiming that he'd come to visit his friend to discuss a personal matter, only to suffer cold feet. It sounded pathetic, but if the cops knocked on Graham's door to test the story he was unlikely to flatly deny knowing Dan, and he might well be capable of sincerely believing that Dan could experience both an urge to confide in him, and a degree of reticence when it came to the crunch.

His phone rang; it was his sister Nina.

"How's Adelaide?" he asked.

"Good. But we're leaving next week."

"Really? Going where?"

"Seville."

"You're moving to *Spain*?"

"No," she replied, amused. "Seville as in Seville Systems – it's the new town around the solar farm. It's only about three hundred kilometers away."

Dan had heard of a big new solar farm about to come online in South Australia, but he'd pictured it in splendid isolation. "Why are you moving to live next to a giant array of mirrors? If they're going to be selling power to half the country, I'm sure you'll be able to plug in from Adelaide."

"The shire did a deal with the operators, and they're setting up a new kind of community there. Locally grown food, zero carbon housing ... it's going to be fantastic!"

"OK. But what will you do up there?" Nina had trained as a social worker, but as far as Dan knew she hadn't been able to find a job in years.

"Whatever I want," she replied. "Part of the deal with the company is a universal basic income for the residents. I'll have plenty of ways to pass the time, though; I can keep on with my paintings, or I can work with disadvantaged youth."

"OK."

"You should come!" Nina urged him. "You and Janice and Carlie ... we'd have a great time."

Dan said, "No, we're too busy. There are a lot of opportunities we're looking into here."

"At least ask Janice," Nina insisted. "Promise me you'll think about it."

"I've got to go," Dan said. The courier's van was pulling up in front of Graham's house. "Call me when you get there, you can give me an update."

"All right."

Graham walked out with a white cardboard box about a meter across, and held it up with the bar-code visible so the van would accept it. A hatch slid open, and he placed the package inside.

When the hatch closed, Graham slapped the side of the van, as if there were a human inside who needed this cue to know that he'd finished. As the van drove off, Dan half expected him to raise a hand in farewell, but he lowered his eyes and turned away.

Dan didn't risk driving past the house; he circled around the block, catching up with the yellow-and-red van as it approached the arterial road he'd guessed it would be taking, unless this mysterious Medici just happened to live in the same suburb as their Michelangelo. When it turned, heading east, Dan managed to get into the same lane, a couple of cars behind it.

The van maintained its course for ten minutes, twenty minutes, ascending the income gradient. Dan had already spent enough time rehearsing his encounter with Graham's patron; now he just tried to block the script from his mind so he wouldn't start second-guessing himself. In the script, he had phrased his request as a business proposition, in language so oblique that even if the whole thing was recorded, half of any jury would refuse to interpret it as blackmail.

He wasn't proud of himself, but he had to get the family over the line somehow. The government's computers had convinced themselves that he and Janice had willfully frittered away their savings, so they were facing an increased waiting period for income support. Dan had spent the last six weeks trying to understand the basis for the decision, in the hope of having it reversed, but he had been unable to extract any coherent narrative from the department's online portal. Apparently some fly-spot in the multidimensional space of all welfare applicants' financial profiles had ended up correlated with profligacy, and that was that: once you fell into the statistical red zone, no one was obliged to point to any single act you'd committed that was manifestly imprudent.

The van shifted lanes, preparing to turn at the next set of lights. Dan was surprised; anyone who could afford sixty grand a year for designer porn ought to be a little more upmarket when it came to real estate. He smiled grimly; when a few hundred thousand data points couldn't separate his behavior from that of a welfare cheat, who was he to start profiling aficionados of Graham's special talent?

The van turned north; Dan followed. The street was mixed residential, with well-maintained but unspectacular houses, retail strips, occasional office blocks.

As it approached a row of fast-food restaurants, the van slowed, then turned into the carpark. Dan was confused; even if it was able to make time for another pick-up along the way, because the ice-cream cake was so well-insulated against the afternoon heat, this was an odd site to do it. Was there a driver on board, after all? Dan hadn't actually seen into the front of the vehicle. Despite its uniform nationwide livery, the courier company was a franchise; maybe one local owner-operator had decided to buck the trend and sit behind a steering wheel.

Dan followed the van into the carpark. It still hadn't settled on a bay, despite passing half a dozen empty spots, but maybe the driver wanted to get closer to the Indian take-away at the far end of the strip. He stayed well behind, but decided not to risk parking yet, gesturing to an approaching station wagon to take the bay that he seemed to be coveting.

The van stopped beside a dumpster. The lid was propped up, angled low enough to keep out the elements but still leaving an opening at the side so large that all but the most uncoordinated members of the public who lobbed their trash in as they drove past would stand a good chance of succeeding.

The hatch opened at the side of the van, and Graham's pristine white box emerged, riding on a gleaming stainless steel plate. When the platform was fully extended the box sat motionless, and Dan clung for a moment to a vision of the rightful recipient, appearing from nowhere in a designer hoodie to snatch up their prized fetish-dessert and dash from the carpark to a limousine waiting on the street. Perhaps a whole convoy of limousines, with decoys to render pursuit impossible.

But then some hidden mechanism gave the box a push and it toppled in to join the chicken bones and greasy napkins.

## 9

"We'll move in with my mother," Janice decided.

"She has *one* spare room. Which she uses for storage." Dan could feel his sweat dampening the sheet beneath him. The night wasn't all that warm, but his body had started drenching his skin at random moments, for no reason he could fathom.

"We can deal with the junk," Janice said. "She'll be glad to have it tidied up. I can sleep in the spare bed with Carlie, and you can sleep on the couch. It will only be for a couple of months."

"How do you know she'll even agree to have us?"

"Do you think she'd let her granddaughter sleep in a car?"

"Do you think *I* would?" Dan replied.

Janice pursed her lips reprovingly. "Don't twist my words around. I know you've done everything you can. And I know I have too – which doesn't make me feel any less guilty, but it makes it easier for me to swallow my pride. If we'd pissed all our savings away on … whatever the government's brilliant algorithm thinks our vices are … then I'd probably be tearing my hair out in self-loathing while I tried to keep my voice calm on the phone to her, begging for that room. But we've done nothing wrong. We need to be clear about that, for the sake of our own sanity, then take whatever the next step is that will keep a roof over our heads."

Dan must have fallen asleep around three, because when he woke at a quarter past four, he felt the special, wretched tiredness that was worse than not having slept at all.

He rose and walked out of the bedroom. In the living room, he switched on his laptop and squinted painfully at the sudden brightness of the screen. He went through the ritual of checking the JobSeekers site, TaskRabbit, and a dozen other places that supposedly offered business and employment opportunities, but – once you weeded out the pyramid schemes and the outright phishing scams – never seemed to carry anything legitimate for which he had the skills or the capital.

His mail program beeped softly. He kept his eyes averted from the alert that came and went on the upper right of the screen; he didn't want to know about yet another plea from one of the charities he'd stopped supporting. What did he actually bring to the world, now? If he disappeared at this moment, it would be as if the air had closed in on empty space.

He opened the program to delete the unread message, but he didn't succeed in going through the motions without seeing the sender. The email was from Baker and Saunders, the American law firm. The subject line read: *Settlement offer*.

Dan opened the message. His eyes were still bleary; he had to enlarge the text to read it. Deepity Systems were prepared to settle out of court. They were offering a payment of thirty thousand dollars *per year*, for five years, to every single litigant in Dan's age and skill cohort.

He re-read the message a dozen times, searching for the downside: the toxic fine print that would turn the victory sour. But he couldn't find it. He opened the attachment, the formal agreement the lawyers had drafted; it was five times longer than the summary, and ten times harder to follow, but there'd been a time when he'd been used to reading financial contracts, and none of the language set alarm bells ringing.

Just before dawn, Janice emerged from the bedroom.

"What are you looking at?" she asked, sitting beside him.

He switched back to the body of the email and slid the laptop across so she could read it. He watched her frowning in disbelief as the scale of the offer sank in.

"Is this real?"

Dan was silent for a while. It was a good question, and he needed to be honest with her.

"If I sign this," he said, "then I believe we'll get the money they're promising. The only thing I'm not sure about is … why."

"What do you mean? Presumably they're afraid that the courts might make them pay even more."

Dan said, "If you were a tech mogul, what would your fantasy of the near-term future be?"

"Colonies on Mars, apparently."

"Sticking to Earth, for now."

Janice was losing patience, but she played along. "I don't know. That business keeps booming? That my stock options keep going through the roof?"

"But what if a large part of your business consists of selling things that put people out of work. Including many of the people who actually pay for the things you're trying to sell."

"Then you've screwed yourself, haven't you?"

Dan said, "Unless you can find a way to keep your customers afloat. You could try to talk the wealthier governments into paying everyone a UBI – and sweeten it a bit by offering to pitch in with a bit more tax yourself. You and your machines *become* the largest sector of the economy; what used to be the labor force is reduced to the role of consumer, but the UBI plugs them into the loop and keeps the money circulating – without bread-lines, without riots in the street."

"Well, they can dream on," Janice replied. "Whatever Nina's got going in Seville, that's never going to be universal."

"Of course not," Dan agreed. "Between the politics, and the different ideas everyone has about personal responsibility, it's never going to fly. Not as one size fits all. But you know, the computers at Thriftocracy always managed to find a repayment plan that suited every client. Once you've gathered enough information about someone, if your goal isn't actually harmful to them you can usually find a way of repackaging it that they're willing to swallow."

Janice was fully awake now. "Are you about to pull some kind of Callum on me?"

Dan shook his head. "I don't think it's even a conspiracy, let alone a plan that the computers dreamed up all by themselves. But Thriftocracy didn't need anyone conspiring in order to start *managing people.* They just offered a service that met other companies' needs. If enough tech firms believe they can benefit from novel ways of limiting the blow-back as they hollow out the middle class, achieving that will become an industry in its own right."

"So … they organize law suits against themselves?"

"Why not? Especially when they'll never go to court." Dan glanced admiringly at the agreement the bots had crafted. There might have been tens of thousands of people in the class action, but it wouldn't have surprised him if the language of this particular document had been tailored for his eyes alone. "They can't quite achieve what they really aspire to, but they're smart enough to understand that the only way to get close is to feed us some version of our own fantasies. They had me pegged, near enough: I would have been happy to win a legal battle against the fuckers who took my job away. But they're more than willing to customize their approach, and if Chalice's mother wants to think she's a fashion icon whose every doodle on her tablet starts clothing factories humming in China, or Graham needs to believe he has a patron hanging out for every word that pops into his head about naughty teenagers, if it gets the job done, so be it. I suppose they must have judged Callum to be too paranoid to accept their hand-outs without becoming suspicious, so they tried to turn that into an advantage and at least give him a sense of purpose and a bit of support from a like-minded community. Then I came blundering in and spoiled it with the horrible, horrible truth."

Janice rubbed her eyes, still not really sold on his own paranoid vision, but not quite certain, either, that he was wrong.

She said, "So what do you want to do?"

Dan laughed. "*Want?* We have no choice. If we don't take this money, your mother will have stabbed me through the arm with a carving knife before the end of the school term."

## 10

Once the settlement was finalized and the first tranche was in Dan's bank account, the ads soon followed. They followed him to every web site, however many times he purged cookies, or rebooted his modem to get a fresh IP address.

"This watch will get your fitness back on track!" an avatar who looked a lot like the old, filtered version of Dan promised. "Come on, you're not over the hill yet!" alter-Dan goaded him, running up and down steeply sloping streets until his manly stubble glistened and his resting heart rate plummeted.

"Three simultaneous channels of premium streaming entertainment, including Just For Kids, plus unlimited interactive gaming!" This from a woman who resembled Janice, to reassure him that there really was no need to consult her; like her doppelgänger, she was certain to approve.

Dan almost felt ungrateful, each time he declined to click through to a purchase. After all, wasn't a tithe for his not-so-secret benefactors the new definition of *giving something back*?

Janice found a volunteer position with a homelessness charity, tending to people who'd had surgery but whose post-operative recovery was adversely affected by a lack of food, showers and beds. Dan offered his own services to the same group, but since he had no relevant skills and their rosters were full, they declined. He looked into an organization that did odd jobs and gardening for pensioners, but then realized they were just undercutting the paid market.

The money, while it lasted, would keep his family out of poverty, but it wasn't enough to pay for any kind of formal retraining. Dan scoured the web, looking at free online courses, trying to decide if any of them would actually render him employable. Apparently, he could learn to be proficient in all the latest programming languages and data mining methods in as little as twelve months, but everyone else from Bangalore to Zambia had already jumped on that bandwagon. And how many software engineers did it take to skill-clone a million software engineers? No more than it took to clone just one.

On his way to pick up Carlie, Dan saw the windshield-wiping Dalmatian waving its squeegee from the side of the road.

He slowed the car, reluctantly, knowing he'd feel bad whatever he did. He still hadn't restarted his donations to Médecins Sans Frontières; on any sane analysis, the family's new budget just didn't stretch that far, however worthy the cause. But the bedraggled mutt pushed some button in him that even footage of a malarial child couldn't reach.

He waited for the dog to finish its slapdash routine, more a ritual than a service. The stitching was coming apart on the costume, leaving one of the eyes dangling, and there were burrs all over the parts of the material where it hadn't worn too thin to hold on to them.

Dan fished a five-dollar bill out of his wallet. As the exchange took place, he reached out with his other hand and squeezed the dog's forearm in what he'd meant as a gesture of solidarity. His fingers came together as they pushed against the dirty fabric, until they encircled a hard, slender rod.

He let go of the bill, and the dog waited, silent and motionless, for Dan to release his grip. Dan peered into the dark maw of its mouth, from which he'd always imagined the occupant was peering out, but as his eyes adapted he could see all the way to the back of the vacant head.

What was inside the costume, below, out of sight? A metal armature, a few motors, a battery, and an old smart phone running it all?

Dan let go of the dog's arm. "Good for you," he said, wondering if the thing's ingenious creator would ever hear his words, but maybe the software extracted a few highlights to replay at the end of each day. He didn't feel cheated; whoever would be getting his money probably needed it just as much as if they'd been here to collect it in person.

At the school gate, Dan still had trouble looking Graham in the eye. When Carlie ran up the path, he smiled and gave her his full attention, blocking out everything else.

"So how was school today?" he asked, as they walked toward the car.

"All right."

"Just all right?"

"Ms Snowball's really boring," she complained.

"Boring?" Dan gazed down at his daughter, mock-aghast. "You don't want to hurt her feelings, do you?"

Carlie glared back at him, unamused. "I want Ms Jameson to come back."

"That's not going to happen." The trial was over, but the budgetary savings were locked in. A teaching assistant could watch over three classes at once, for far less than the cost of a human teacher for each.

On the drive home, Dan tried to picture the life Carlie would face. For the last few weeks, all he'd been able to envision was a choice between the family joining a commune in Nimbin to weave their own underwear out of hemp, or resigning themselves to their role laundering money for Silicon Valley.

They approached the Dalmatian, which waved cheerfully.

"Daddy, can we—?"

"Sorry, I already did." Dan gestured at the streaked suds still drying on the windshield.

Then he said, "How'd you like to learn to make Ms Snowball's head come off?"

"You're silly."

"No, I'm serious! How'd you like to learn to make her do whatever you want?" Either they moved out into the countryside and became subsistence farmers, or they stayed and fought to regain some kind of agency, using the only weapons that worked now. The idea that every person in the world ought to learn to code had always struck Dan as an infuriating piece of proselytizing, as bizarre as being told that everyone just had to shut up and become Rastafarian. But in the zombie apocalypse, no one ever complained that they needed to learn to sharpen sticks and drive them into rotting brains. It wasn't a matter of cultural homogeneity. It was a question of knowing how to fuck with your enemy.

"Do you really know how to do that?" Carlie asked.

"Not yet," Dan confessed. "But I think that if we work hard, we'll be able to figure it out together."

# ZERO FOR CONDUCT

## 1

Latifa started the web page loading, then went to make tea. The proxy she used convinced her internet provider that every page she accessed belonged to a compendium of pious aphorisms from uncontroversial octogenarians in Qom, while to the sites themselves she appeared to be a peripatetic American, logging on from Pittsburgh one day and Kansas City the next. Between the sanctions against her true host country and that host's paranoia over the most innocent interactions with the West, these precautions were essential. But they slowed down her already sluggish connection so effectively that she might as well have been rehearsing for a flight to Mars.

The sound of boiling water offered a brief respite from the televised football match blaring down from the apartment above. "Two nil in favor of the Black Pearls, with fifteen minutes left to play! It's looking like victory for the home team here in Samen Stadium!" When the tea had brewed, she served it in a small glass for her grandfather to sip through a piece of hard sugar clenched between his teeth. Latifa sat with him for a while, but he was listening to the shortwave radio, straining to hear Kabul through the hum of interference and the breathless commentary coming through the ceiling, and he barely noticed when she left.

Back in her room after fifteen minutes, she found the scratched screen of the laptop glistening with a dozen shiny ball-and-stick models of organic molecules. Reading the color coding of the atoms was second nature to her by now: white for hydrogen, black for carbon, cherry red for oxygen, azure for nitrogen. Here and there a yellow sulfur atom or a green chlorine stood out, like a chickpea in a barrel of candy.

All the molecules that the ChemFactor page had assigned to her were nameless – unless you counted the formal structural descriptions full of cis-1,3-dimethyl-this and 2,5-di-tert-butyl-that – and Latifa had no idea which, if any of them, had actually been synthesized in a lab somewhere. Perhaps a few of them were impossible beasts, chimeras cranked out by the software's mindless permutations, destined to be completely unstable in reality. If she made an effort, she could probably weed some of them out. But that could wait until she'd narrowed down the list of candidates, eliminating the molecules with no real chance of binding strongly to the target.

The target this time was an oligosaccharide, a carbohydrate with nine rings arranged in pleasingly asymmetric tiers, like a small child's attempt to build a shoe rack. Helpfully, the ChemFactor page kept it fixed on the screen as Latifa scrolled up and down through the long catalog of its potential suitors.

She trusted the software to have made some sensible choices already, on geometric grounds: all of these molecules ought to be able to nestle reasonably snugly against the target. In principle she could rotate the ball-and-stick models any way she liked, and slide the target into the same view to assess the prospective fit, but in practice that made the laptop's graphics card choke. So she'd learned to manipulate the structures in her head, to picture the encounter without fretting too much about precise angles and distances. Molecules weren't rigid, and if the interaction with the target liberated enough energy the participants could stretch or flex a little to accommodate each other. There were rigorous calculations that could predict the upshot of all that give and take, but the equations could not be solved quickly or easily. So ChemFactor invited people to offer their hunches. Newcomers guessed no better than random, and many players' hit rates failed to rise above statistical noise. But some people acquired a feel for the task, learning from their victories and mistakes – even if they couldn't put their private algorithms into words.

Latifa didn't over-think the puzzle, and in twenty minutes she'd made her choice. She clicked the button beside her selection and confirmed it, satisfied that she'd done her best. After three years in the game she'd proved to be a born chemical match-maker, but she didn't want it going to her head. Whatever lay behind her well-judged guesses, it could only be a matter of time before the software itself learned to codify all the same rules. The truth was, the more successful she became, the faster she'd be heading for obsolescence. She needed to make the most of her talent while it still counted.

Latifa spent two hours on her homework, then a call came from her cousin Fashard in Kandahar. She went out onto the balcony where the phone could get a better signal.

"How is your grandfather?" he asked.

"He's fine. I'll ask him to call you back tomorrow." Her grandfather had given up on the shortwave and gone to bed. "How are things there?"

"The kids have all come down with something," Fashard reported. "And the power's been off for the last two days."

"*Two days?*" Latifa felt for her young cousins, sweltering and feverish without even a fan. "You should get a generator."

"Ha! I could get ten; people are practically giving them away."

"Why?"

"The price of diesel's gone through the roof," Fashard explained. "Blackouts or not, no one can afford to run them."

Latifa looked out at the lights of Mashhad. There was nothing glamorous about the concrete tower blocks around her, but the one thing Iran didn't lack was electricity. Kandahar should have been well-supplied by the Kajaki Dam, but two of the three turbines in the hydroelectric plant had been out of service for more than a year, and the drought had made it even harder for the remaining turbine to meet demand.

"What about the shop?" she asked.

"Pedaling the sewing machine keeps me fit," Fashard joked.

"I wish I could do something."

"Things are hard for everyone," Fashard said stoically. "But we'll be all right; people always need clothes. You just concentrate on your studies."

Latifa tried to think of some news to cheer him up. "Amir said he's planning to come home this Eid." Her brother had made no firm promises, but she couldn't believe he'd spend the holidays away from his family for a second year in a row.

"Inshallah," Fashard replied. "He should book the ticket early though, or he'll never get a seat."

"I'll remind him."

There was no response; the connection had cut out. Latifa tried calling back but all she got was a sequence of strange beeps, as if the phone tower was too flustered to offer up its usual recorded apologies.

She tidied the kitchen then lay in bed. It was hard to fall asleep when her thoughts cycled endlessly through the same inventory of troubles, but sometime after midnight she managed to break the loop and tumble into blackness.

"Afghani slut," Ghamzeh whispered, leaning against Latifa and pinching her arm through the fabric of her manteau.

"Let go of me," Latifa pleaded. She was pressed against her locker, she couldn't pull away. Ghamzeh turned her face toward her, smiling, as if they were friends exchanging gossip. Other students walked past, averting their eyes.

"I'm getting tired of the smell of you," Ghamzeh complained. "You're stinking up the whole city. You should go back home to your little mud hut."

Latifa's skin tingled between the girl's blunt talons, warmed by broken blood vessels, numbed by clamped nerves. It would be satisfying to lash out with her fists and free herself, but she knew that could only end badly.

"Did they have soap in your village?" Ghamzeh wondered. "Did they have underwear? All these things must have been so strange to you, when you arrived in civilization."

Latifa waited in silence. Arguing only prolonged the torment.

"Too stuck up to have a conversation?" Ghamzeh released her arm and began to move away, but then she stopped to give Latifa a parting smile. "You think you're impressing the teachers when you give them all the answers they want? Don't fool yourself, slut. They know you're just an animal doing circus tricks."

When Latifa had cleared away the dinner plates, her grandfather asked her about school.

"You're working hard?" he pressed her, cross-legged on the floor with a cushion at his back. "Earning their respect?"

"Yes."

"And your heart is still set on engineering?" He sounded doubtful, as if for him the word could only conjure up images of rough men covered in machine oil.

"Chemical engineering," she corrected him gently. "I'm getting good grades in chemistry, and there'd be plenty of jobs in it."

"After five more years. After university."

"Yes." Latifa looked away. Half the money Amir sent back from Dubai was already going on her school fees. Her brother was twenty-two; no one could expect him to spend another five years without marrying.

"You should get on with your studies then." Her grandfather waved her away amiably, then reached over for the radio.

In her room, Latifa switched on the laptop before opening her history book, but she kept her eyes off the screen until she'd read half the chapter on the Sassanid kings. When she finally gave herself a break the ChemFactor site had loaded, and she'd been logged in automatically, by cookie.

A yellow icon of a stylized envelope was flashing at the top of the page. A fellow player she'd never heard of called "jesse409" had left her a message, congratulating "PhaseChangeGirl" on a cumulative score that had just crossed twenty thousand. Latifa's true score was far higher than that, but she'd changed her identity and rejoined the game from scratch five times so far, lest she come to the notice of someone with the means to find out who she really was.

The guess she'd made the previous night had paid off: a rigorous model of the two molecules showed that the binding between them was stable. She had saved one of ChemFactor's clients the time and expense of doing the same calculations for dozens of alternatives, and her reward was a modest fraction of the resources she'd effectively freed. ChemFactor would model any collection of atoms and molecules she liked, free of charge – up to a preset quota in computing time.

Latifa closed her history book and moved the laptop to the center of her desk. If the binding problems were easy for her now, when it came to the much larger challenge she'd set herself the instincts she'd honed on the site could only take her so far. The raw computing power that she acquired from these sporadic prizes let her test her hunches and see where they fell short.

She dug out the notebook from her backpack and reviewed her sketches and calculations. She understood the symmetries of crystals, the shifts and rotations that brought any regular array of atoms back into perfect agreement with itself. She understood the thrillingly strange origins of the different varieties of magnetism, where electrons' spins became aligned or opposed – sometimes through their response to each others' magnetic fields, but more often through the Exclusion Principle, which linked the alignment of spin to the average distance between the particles, and hence the energy they needed in order to overcome electrostatic repulsion. And after studying hundreds of examples, she believed she had a sense for the kind of crystal that lay in a transition zone where one type of magnetism was on the verge of shifting to another.

She'd sketched her ideal crystal in the notebook more than a year before, but she had no proof yet that it was anything more than a fantasy. Her last modeling run had predicted something achingly close, but it had still not produced what she needed. She had to go back one step and try something different.

Latifa retrieved the saved data from that last attempt and set the parameters for the new simulation. She resisted the urge to stab the CONFIRM button twice; the response was just taking its time weaving its way back to her through the maze of obfuscation.

*Estimated time for run: approximately seven hours.*

She sat gazing at the screen for a while, though she knew that if she waited for the prediction to be updated she'd probably find that the new estimate was even longer.

Reluctantly, she moved the laptop to the floor and returned to the faded glory of the Sassanids. She had to be patient; she'd have her answer by morning.

"Whore," Ghamzeh muttered as Latifa hurried past her to her desk.

"You're ten minutes late, Latifa," Ms Keshavarz declared irritably.

"I'm very sorry." Latifa stood in place, her eyes cast down.

"So what's your excuse?"

Latifa remained silent.

"If you overslept," Ms Keshavarz suggested, "you should at least have the honesty to say so."

Latifa had woken at five, but she managed a flush of humiliation that she hoped would pass for a kind of tacit admission.

"Two hours of detention, then," Ms Keshavarz ruled. "It might have been half that if you'd been more forthcoming. Take your seat, please."

The day passed at a glacial speed. Latifa did her best to distract herself with the lessons, but it was like trying to chew water. The subject made no difference: history, literature, mathematics, physics – as soon as one sentence was written on the blackboard she knew exactly what would follow.

In detention with four other girls, she sat copying pages of long-winded homilies. From her seat she could see a driveway that led out from the staff car park, and one by one the vehicles she most needed to depart passed before her eyes. The waiting grew harder than ever, but she knew it would be foolish to act too soon.

Eighty minutes into her punishment, she started holding her breath for ever longer intervals. By the time she raised her hand there was nothing feigned in her tone of discomfort. The supervising teacher, Ms Shirazi, raised no objections and played no sadistic games with her. Latifa fled the room with plausible haste.

The rest of the school appeared deserted; the extra time had been worth it. Latifa opened the door to the toilets and let it swing shut, leaving the sound echoing back down the corridor, then hurried toward the chemistry lab.

The students' entrance was locked, but Latifa steeled herself and turned into the warren of store rooms and cubicles that filled the north side of the science wing. Her chemistry teacher, Ms Daneshvar, had taken her to her desk once to consult an old university textbook, to settle a point on which they'd both been unsure.

Latifa found her way back to that desk. The keys were hanging exactly where she remembered them, on labeled pegs. She took the one for the chemistry lab and headed for the teachers' entrance.

As she turned the key in the lock her stomach convulsed. To be expelled would be disastrous enough, but if the school pressed criminal charges she could be imprisoned and deported. She closed her eyes for a moment, summoning up an image of the beautiful lattice that the ChemFactor simulation had shown her. For a week she'd thought of nothing else. The software had reached its conclusion, but in the end the only test that mattered was whether the substance could be made in real life.

Late afternoon sunlight slanted across the room, glinting off the tubular legs of the stools standing upside-down on the black-painted benches. All the ingredients Latifa needed – salts of copper, barium and calcium – sat on the alphabetized shelves that ran along the eastern wall;

none were of sufficient value or toxicity to be kept locked away, and she wouldn't need much of any of them for a proof of principle.

She took down the jars and weighed out a few grams of each, quantities too small to be missed. She'd written down the masses that would yield the right stoichiometry, the right proportions of atoms in the final product, but having spent the whole day repeating the calculations in her head she didn't waste time now consulting the slip of paper.

Latifa mixed the brightly colored granules in a ceramic crucible and crushed them with a pestle. Then she placed the crucible in the electric furnace. The heating profile she'd need was complicated, but though she'd only ever seen the furnace operated manually in class, she'd looked up the model number on the net and found the precise requirements for scripting it. When she pushed the memory stick into the USB port, the green light above flickered for a moment, then the first temperature of the sequence appeared on the display.

The whole thing would take nine hours. Latifa quickly re-shelved the jars, binned the filter paper she'd used on the scales, then retreated, locking the door behind her.

On her way past the toilets she remembered to stage a creaking exit. She slowed her pace as she approached the detention room, and felt cold beads of sweat on her face. Ms Shirazi offered her a sympathetic frown before turning back to the magazine she'd been reading.

Latifa dreamed that the school was on fire. The blaze was visible from the balcony of her apartment, and her grandfather stood and watched, wheezing alarmingly from the toxic fumes that were billowing out across Mashhad. When he switched on the radio, a newsreader reported that the police had found a memory stick beside the point of ignition and were checking all the students for a fingerprint match.

Latifa woke before dawn and ate breakfast, then prepared lunch for the two of them. She'd thought she'd been moving silently, but her grandfather surprised her as she was opening the front door.

"Why are you leaving so early?" he demanded.

"There's a study group."

"What do you mean?"

"A few of us get together before classes start and go over the lessons from the day before," she said.

"So you're running your own classes now? Do the teachers know about this?"

"The teachers approve," Latifa assured him. "It's their lessons that we're revising; we're not just making things up."

"You're not talking politics?" he asked sternly.

Latifa understood: he was thinking of the discussion group her mother had joined at Kabul University, its agenda excitedly recounted in one of the letters she'd sent him. He'd allowed Latifa to read the whole trove of letters when she'd turned fourteen – the age her mother had been when he'd gone into exile.

"You know me," Latifa said. "Politics is over my head."

"All right." He was mollified now. "Enjoy your study." He kissed her goodbye.

As Latifa dismounted from her bicycle she could see that the staff car park was empty except for the cleaners' van. If she could bluff her way through this final stage she might be out of danger in a matter of minutes.

The cleaners had unlocked the science wing, and a woman was mopping the floor by the main entrance. Latifa nodded to her, then walked in as if she owned the place.

"Hey! You shouldn't be here!" The woman straightened up and glared at her, worried for her job should anything be stolen.

"Ms Daneshvar asked me to prepare something for the class. She gave me the key yesterday." Latifa held it up for inspection.

The woman squinted at the key then waved her on, muttering unhappily.

In the chemistry lab everything was as Latifa had left it. She plucked the memory stick from the port on the furnace, then switched off the power. She touched the door, and felt no residual heat.

When she opened the furnace the air that escaped smelled like sulfur and bleach. Gingerly, she lifted out the crucible and peered inside. A solid gray mass covered the bottom, its surface as smooth as porcelain.

The instruments she needed to gauge success or failure were all in the physics lab, and trying to talk her way into another room right now would attract too much suspicion. She could wait for her next physics class and see what opportunities arose. Students messed around with the digital multimeters all the time, and if she was caught sticking the probes into her pocket her teacher would see nothing but a silly girl trying to measure the electrical resistance of a small paving stone she'd picked up off the street. Ms Hashemi wouldn't be curious enough to check the properties of the stone for herself.

Latifa fetched a piece of filter paper and tried to empty the crucible onto it, but the gray material clung stubbornly to the bottom where it had formed. She tapped it gently, then more forcefully, to no avail.

*She was going to have to steal the crucible.* It was not an expensive piece of equipment, but there were only four, neatly lined up in a row in the cupboard below the furnace, and its absence would eventually be missed. Ms Daneshvar might – just might – ask the cleaners if they'd seen it. There was a chance that all her trespasses would be discovered.

But what choice did she have?

She could leave the crucible behind and hunt for a replacement in the city. At the risk that, in the meantime, someone would take the vessel out to use it, find it soiled, and discard it. At the risk that she'd be caught trying to make the swap. And all of this for a gray lump that might easily be as worthless as it looked.

Latifa had bought a simple instrument of her own in the bazaar six months before, and she'd brought it with her almost as a joke – something she could try once she was out of danger, with no expectations at all. If the result it gave her was negative that wouldn't really prove anything. But she didn't know what else she could use to guide her.

She fished the magnet out of the pocket of her manteau. It was a slender disk the size of her thumbnail, probably weighing a gram or so. She held it in the mouth of the crucible and lowered it toward the bottom.

If there was any force coming into play as the magnet approached the gray material, it was too weak for her to sense. With a couple of millimeters still separating the two, Latifa spread her fingers and let the magnet drop. She didn't hear it strike the bottom – but from such a height how loud would it have been? She took her fingers out of the crucible and looked down.

It was impossible to tell if it was touching or not; the view was too narrow, the angle too high.

Latifa could hear the woman with the mop approaching, getting ready to clean the chemistry lab. Within a minute or less, everything she did here would take place in front of a witness.

A patch of morning sunlight from the eastern window fell upon the blackboard behind her. Latifa grabbed an empty Erlenmeyer flask and held it in the beam, tilting it until she managed to refract some light down into the crucible.

As she turned the flask back and forth, shifting the angle of the light, she could see a dark circle moving behind the magnet. Lit from above, an object barely a millimeter high couldn't cast a shadow like that.

The magnet was floating on air.

The door began to open. Latifa pocketed the crucible. She put the Erlenmeyer flask back on its shelf, then turned to see the cleaner eyeing her suspiciously.

"I'm all done now, thanks," Latifa announced cheerfully. She motioned toward the staff entrance. "I'll put the key back on my way out."

Minutes later, Latifa strode out of the science wing. She reached into her pocket and wrapped her hand around the crucible. She still had some money Amir had given her last Eid; she could buy a replacement that afternoon. For now, all she had to do was get through the day's lessons with a straight face, while walking around carrying the world's first room-temperature superconductor.

## 2

Ezatullah was said to be the richest Afghani in Mashhad, and from the look of his three-story marble-clad house he had no wish to live down that reputation. Latifa had heard that he'd made his money in Saudi Arabia, where he'd represented the mujahedin at the time of the Soviet occupation. Wealthy Saudi women with guilty consciences had filed through his office day after day, handing him bags full of gold bullion to help fund the jihad – buying, they believed, the same promise of paradise that went to the martyrs themselves. Ezatullah, being less concerned with the afterlife, had passed on their donations to the war chest but retained a sizable commission.

At the mansion's gate, Latifa's grandfather paused. "I promised your mother I'd keep you out of trouble."

Latifa didn't know how to answer that; his caution came from love and grief, but this was a risk they needed to take. "Fashard's already started things rolling on his side," she reminded him. "It will be hard on him if we pull out now."

"That's true."

In the sitting room Ezatullah's youngest daughter, Yasmin, served tea, then stayed with Latifa while the two men withdrew to talk business. Latifa passed the time thinking up compliments for each rug and item of furniture in sight, and Yasmin replied in such a soft, shy voice that Latifa had no trouble eavesdropping on the conversation from the adjoining room.

"My nephew owns a clothing business in Kandahar," her grandfather began. "Some tailoring, some imports and exports. But recently he came across a new opportunity: a chance to buy electrical cable at a very fair price."

"A prudent man will have diverse interests," Ezatullah declared approvingly.

"We're hoping to on-sell the wire in Mashhad," her grandfather explained. "We could avoid a lot of paperwork at the border if we packed the trucks with cartons labeled as clothing – with some at the rear bearing out that claim. My granddaughter could run a small shop to receive these shipments."

"And you're seeking a partner, to help fund this venture?"

Latifa heard the rustle of paper, the figures she'd prepared changing hands.

"What's driven you to this, haji?" Ezatullah asked pointedly. "You don't have a reputation as a businessman."

"I'm seventy years old," her grandfather replied. "I need to see my daughter's children looked after before I die."

Ezatullah thought for a while. "Let me talk to my associates in Kandahar."

"Of course."

On the bus back to the apartment, Latifa imagined the phone calls that would already be bouncing back and forth across the border. Ezatullah would soon know all about the new electrification project in Kandahar, which aimed to wire up a dozen more neighborhoods to the already-struggling grid – apparently in the hope that even a meager ration of cheap power would turn more people against the insurgents who bombed every convoy that tried to carry replacement parts to the hydroelectric plant.

International donors had agreed to fund the project, and with overhead cables strung from pole to pole along winding roads, some discrepancy between the surveyed length and the cable used was only to be expected. But while Fashard really had come to an agreement with the contractor to take the excess wire off his hands, with no family ties or prior connection to the man he had only managed to secure the deal by offering a price well above the going rate.

Latifa didn't expect any of these details to elude their partner, but the hope was that his advisers in Kandahar would conclude that Fashard, lacking experience as a smuggler, had simply underestimated his own costs. That alone wouldn't make the collaboration a bad investment: she'd structured the proposal in such a way that Ezatullah would still make a tidy return even if the rest of them barely broke even.

They left the bus and made their way home. "If we told him the truth —" her grandfather began as they started up the stairs.

"If we told him the truth, he'd snatch it from our hands!" Latifa retorted. Her words echoed in the concrete stairwell; she lowered her voice. "One way or another he'd get hold of the recipe, then sell it to some company with a thousand lawyers who could claim they'd invented it themselves. We need to be in a stronger position before we take this to anyone, or they'll eat us alive." A patent attorney could do a lot to protect them before they approached a commercial backer, but that protection would cost several thousand euros. Raising that much themselves – without trading away any share in the invention – wasn't going to be easy, but it would make all the difference to how much power they retained.

Her grandfather stopped on a landing to catch his breath. "And if Ezatullah finds out that we've lied to him—"

His phone buzzed once, with a text message.

"You need to go to the house again," he said. "Tomorrow, after school."

Latifa's skin prickled with fear. "*Me?* What for?" Did Ezatullah want to quiz her about her knowledge of retail fashion for the modern Iranian woman – or had his digging already exposed her other interests?

"Most of the money's going straight to Fashard, but we'll need some cash at our end too," her grandfather explained. "He doesn't want me coming and going from the house, but no one will be suspicious if you've struck up a friendship with his daughter."

Latifa had asked the electricians to come at seven to switch on the power to the kilns, but when they hadn't shown up by eight she gave up any hope of making it to her history class.

For the first hour she'd killed time by sweeping; now she paced the bare wooden floor, optimistically surveying her new fiefdom. Finding the factory had been a huge stroke of luck; it had originally produced ceramic tableware, and when the tenants went out of business the owner of the premises had taken possession of the kilns. He'd been on the verge of selling them for scrap, and had parted with them for a ridiculously low price just to get her grandfather to sign the lease. The location wasn't perfect, but perhaps it was for the best that it wasn't too close to the shop. The separation would make it less likely that anyone would see her in both places.

When the electricians finally arrived they ignored Latifa completely, and she resisted the urge to pester them with odd questions. *What would you do if you cut into an overhead power line and found that its appearance, in cross-section, wasn't quite what you were used to?*

"Delivery for Bose Ceramics?" a man called from the entrance.

Latifa went to see what it was. The courier was already loading one box, as tall as she was, onto his trolley. She guided him across the factory floor. "Can you put it here? Thank you."

"There are another two in the truck."

She waited until the electricians had left before finding a knife and slicing away the cardboard and styrofoam – afraid that they might recognize the equipment and start asking questions of their own. She plugged in one of the cable winders and put it through a test sequence, watching the nimble motorized arms blur as they rehearsed on thin air.

One machine would unpick, while the other two wove – and for every kilometer of cable that came into the factory, two kilometers would emerge. With half as many strands as the original, the new version would need to be bulked out from within to retain the same diameter. The pellets of ceramic wound in among the steel and aluminum wouldn't form a contiguous electrical path, but these superconducting inclusions would still lower the overall resistance of the cable, sharing the current for a large enough portion of its length to compensate for the missing metal.

So long as the cable was fit for use, the Iranian contractors who bought it would have no reason to complain. They'd pocket the difference in price, and the power grid would be none the worse for it. Everyone would get paid, everyone would be happy.

Latifa checked her watch; she'd missed another two classes. All she could do now was write the whole day off and claim to have been sick. She needed to chase down the heat-resistant molds that would give the ceramic pellets their shape, and try again to get a promise from the chemical suppliers that they could deliver the quantities she was going to need to keep the kilns going day after day, week after week.

"Do you have this in size sixteen?" the woman asked, emerging from the changing room. Latifa looked up from her homework. The woman was still wearing the oversized sunglasses that she hadn't deigned to remove as she entered the shop, as if she were a famous singer afraid of being mobbed by fans.

"I'm sorry, we don't."

"Can you check your storeroom? I love the colors, but this one is a bit too tight."

Latifa hesitated; she was certain that they didn't stock the blouse in that size, but it would be impolite to refuse. "Of course. One moment."

She spent half a minute rummaging through the shelves, to ensure that her search didn't seem too perfunctory. It was almost six o'clock; she should close the shop and relieve her grandfather at the factory.

When she returned to the counter, the customer had left. The woman had taken the blouse, along with two pairs of trousers from the rack near the door. Latifa felt a curious warmth rising in her face; most of all she was annoyed that she'd been so gullible, but the resentment she felt at the brazen theft collided unpleasantly with other thoughts.

There was nothing to be done but to put the incident out of her mind. She looked over her unfinished essay on the Iran-Iraq war; it was due in the morning, but she'd have to complete it in the factory.

"Are these goods from your shop?"

A policeman was standing in the doorway. The thief was beside him, and he was holding up the stolen clothes.

Latifa could hardly deny it; the trousers were identical to the others hanging right beside him.

"They are, sir," she replied. He must have seen the woman emerging, hastily stuffing everything into her bag. Why couldn't she have done that out of sight?

"This lady says she must have dropped the receipt. Should I look for it, or will I be wasting my time?"

Latifa struggled to choose the right answer. "It's my fault, sir. She must have thought I'd given her the receipt along with the change – but she was in a hurry, she didn't even want one of our bags..."

"So you still have the receipt?"

Latifa pointed helplessly at the waste-paper basket beside the counter, full to the brim with discarded drafts of her essay. "I couldn't leave the shop and chase after her, so I threw it in there. Please forgive me, sir, I'm just starting out in this job. If the boss learns what I've done, he'll fire me straight away." It was lucky that the thief was still wearing her ridiculous glasses; Latifa wasn't sure how she would have coped if they'd had to make eye contact.

The policeman appeared skeptical: he knew what he'd seen. Latifa put the back of her hand to her eyes and sniffed.

"All right," he said. "Everyone makes mistakes." He turned to the woman. "I'm sorry for the misunderstanding."

"It's nothing." She nodded to Latifa. "Good evening."

The policeman lingered in the doorway, thinking things over. Then he approached the counter.

"Let me see your storeroom."

Latifa gestured to the entrance, but stayed beside the cash register. She listened to the man moving about, rustling through discarded packaging, tapping the walls. What did he imagine he'd find – a secret compartment?

He emerged from the room, stony faced, as if the lack of anything incriminating only compounded his resentment.

"ID card."

Latifa produced it. She'd rid herself of her accent long ago, and she had just enough of her father's Tajik features that she could often pass as an Iranian to the eye, but here it was: the proof of her real status.

"Ha," he grunted. "All right." He handed back the ID. "Just behave yourself, and we'll get along fine."

As he walked out of the shop, Latifa began shaking with relief. He'd found an innocent explanation for her reticence to press charges: the card entitled her to remain in the country at the pleasure of the government, but she wasn't a citizen, and she would have been crazy to risk the consequences if the woman had called her a liar.

Latifa wheeled her bicycle out of the storeroom and closed the shop. The factory was six kilometers away, and the traffic tonight looked merciless.

"I had a call from Ezatullah," Latifa's grandfather said. "He wants to take over the transport."

Latifa continued brushing down the slides from the superconductor hopper. "What does that mean?"

"He has another partner who's been bringing goods across the border. This man has a warehouse in Herat."

Herat was just a hundred kilometers from the border, on the route from Kandahar to Mashhad. "So he wants us to make room for this other man's merchandise in our trucks?" Latifa put the brush down. It was an unsettling prospect, but it didn't have to be a disaster.

"No," her grandfather replied. "He wants us to bring the wire across in this other man's trucks."

"*Why?*"

"The customs inspectors have people coming from Tehran to look over their shoulders," her grandfather explained. "There's no fixing that with bribes, and the clothes make too flimsy a cover for the real cargo. This other man's bringing over a couple of loads of scrap metal every week; hiding the wire won't be a problem for him."

Latifa sat down on the bench beside the winders. "But we can't risk that! We can't let him know how many spools we're bringing in!" Ezatullah had kept his distance from their day-to-day operations, but the black market contacts to whom they passed the altered wire had long-standing connections to him, and Latifa had no doubt that he was being kept apprised of every transaction. *Under-reporting their sales* to hide the fact that they were selling twice as much wire as they imported would be suicidal.

"Can we shift this work to Kandahar?" her grandfather asked.

"Maybe the last part, the winding," Latifa replied. So long as they could double the wire before it reached Herat, there'd be no discrepancies in the numbers Ezatullah received from his informants.

"What about the kilns?"

"No, the power's too erratic. If there's a blackout halfway through a batch that would ruin it – and we need at least two batches a day to keep up."

"Couldn't we use a generator?"

Latifa didn't have the numbers she needed to answer that, but she knew Fashard had looked into the economics of using one himself. She texted him some questions, and he replied a few minutes later.

"It's hopeless," she concluded. "Each kiln runs at about twenty kilowatts. Getting that from diesel, we'd be lucky to break even."

Her grandfather managed a curt laugh. "Maybe we'd be better off selling the rest of the wire as it is?"

Latifa did a few more calculations. "That won't work either. Fashard is paying too much for it; we'd be making a loss on every spool." After sinking money into the factory's lease and other inputs to the doubling process, any attempt to get by without the benefits of that doubling would leave them owing Ezatullah more cash than the remaining sales would bring in.

"Then what choice is left to us?"

"We could keep making the superconductor here," Latifa suggested.

"And get it to Kandahar how?" her grandfather protested. "Do you think we can do business with anyone working that route and expect Ezatullah not to hear about it? Once or twice, maybe, but not if we set up a regular shipment."

Latifa had no answer to that. "We should talk about this in the morning," she said. "You've been working all day; you should get some sleep now."

At her insistence he retired to the factory's office, where they'd put in a mattress and blankets. Latifa stood by the hopper; the last batch of superconductor should have cooled by now, but she was too dejected to attend to it. If they moved the whole operation to Kandahar, the best they could hope for was scraping through without ending up in debt. She didn't doubt that Fashard and her other cousins would do whatever needed to be done – working unpaid, purely for the sake of keeping her grandfather out of trouble – but the prospect of forcing that burden onto them filled her with shame.

Her own dawdling wasn't helping anyone. She put on the heat-proof gloves, took the molds from the kiln and began filling the hopper. She'd once calculated that if Iran's entire grid were to be replaced with a superconducting version, the power no longer being lost in transmission would be enough to light up all of Afghanistan. But if that was just a fantasy, all her other plans were heading for the same fate.

Latifa switched on the winders and watched the strands of wire shuttling from spool to spool, wrapping the stream of pellets from the hopper. Of all the wondrous things the superconductor made possible, this had seemed the simplest – and the safest way to exploit it without attracting too much attention.

But these dull gray beads were all she had. If she wanted to rescue the whole misbegotten venture, she needed to find another way to turn them to her advantage.

Latifa's grandfather ran from the office, barefoot, eyes wide with fear. "What happened? Are you hurt?"

Latifa could see dents in the ceiling where the pellets had struck. "I'm all right," she assured him. "I'm sorry, I didn't mean to wake you." She looked around; the kilns and the winders were untouched, and there was no damage to the building that a plasterer couldn't fix.

"*What did you do?* I thought something exploded – or those machines went crazy." He glared at the winders, as if they might have rebelled and started pelting their owners with shrapnel.

Latifa switched off the power from the outlet and approached what remained of her test rig. She'd surrounded it with workbenches turned on their sides, as safety shields. "I'm going to need better reinforcement," she said. "I didn't realize the field would get so strong, so quickly."

Her grandfather stared at the shattered assembly that she'd improvised from a helix of copper pipe. The previous tenants had left all kinds of junk behind, and Latifa had been loath to discard anything that might have turned out to be useful.

"It's a storage device," she explained. "For electricity. The current just sits there going round and round; when you want some of it back you can draw it out. It's not all that different from a battery."

"I'd say it's not all that different from a bomb."

Latifa was chastened. "I was careless; I'm sorry. I was impatient to see if I could make it work at all. The current generates a strong magnetic field, and that puts the whole thing under pressure – but when it's built properly, it will be a solid coil of superconductor, not a lot of pellets stuffed inside a pipe. And we can bury it in the ground, so if it does shatter no one will get hurt."

"How is this meant to help us?" her grandfather asked irritably. He lifted his right foot to examine the sole; a splinter of superconductor was poking through the skin.

Latifa said, "The mains power in Kandahar is unreliable, but it's still far cheaper than using a generator. A few of these storage coils should be enough to guarantee that we can run the kilns through a blackout."

"You're serious?"

Latifa hesitated. "Give me a few days to do some more experiments, then we'll know for sure."

"How many days of school have you missed already?"

"That's not important."

Her grandfather sat on the ground and covered his eyes with one hand. "School is not important now? They *murdered your mother* because she was teaching girls, and your father because he'd defended her. When she grew so afraid that she sent you to me, I promised her you'd get an education. This country is no paradise, but at least you were safe in that school, you were doing well. Now we're juggling money we don't have, living in fear of Ezatullah, blowing things up, planning some new madness every day."

Latifa approached him and put a hand on his shoulder. "After this, there'll be nothing to distract me. We'll close the factory, we'll close the shop. My whole life will be school and homework, school and homework all the way to Eid."

Her grandfather looked up at her. "How long will it take?"

"Maybe a couple of weeks." The coils themselves didn't have to be complicated, but it would take some research and trial and error to get the charging and discharging circuitry right.

"And then what?" he asked. "If we send these things to Kandahar – with the kilns and everything else – do you think Fashard can put it all together and just take over where we left off?"

"Maybe not," Latifa conceded. Fashard had wired his own house, and he could repair a sewing machine blindfold. But this would be tricky, and she couldn't talk him through the whole setup on the phone.

She said, "It looks like Eid's coming early for me this year."

In Herat, in the bus station's restroom, Latifa went through the ritual of replacing her headscarf and manteau with the burqa and niqab that she'd need to be wearing when she arrived in Kandahar.

She stared through the blue gauze at the anonymous figure reflected in the restroom's stained mirror. When she'd lived in Kabul with her parents, she'd still been young enough to visit Kandahar without covering her hair, let alone her face. But if anything, she felt insufficiently disguised now. On top of her anxiety over all her new secrets, this would be her first trip home without Amir traveling beside her – or at least, ten meters ahead of her, in the men's section of the bus. Fashard had offered to come and meet her in Herat, but she'd persuaded him to stay in Kandahar. She couldn't help being nervous, but that didn't mean she had to be cowed.

It was still early as the bus set out. Latifa chatted with the woman beside her, who was returning to Kandahar after visiting Herat for medical treatment. "I used to go to Quetta," the woman explained, "but it's too dangerous there now."

"What about Kabul?" Latifa asked.

"Kabul? These days you'll wait six months for an appointment."

The specialists in Herat were mostly Iranian; in Kabul, mostly European. In Kandahar, you'd be lucky to find anyone at all with a genuine medical degree, though there was a wide choice of charlatans who'd take your money in exchange for pharmaceuticals with expiry dates forged in ballpoint.

"Someone should build a medical school in Kandahar," Latifa suggested. "With ninety percent of the intake women, until things are evened out."

Her companion laughed nervously.

"I'm serious!" Latifa protested. "Aren't you sick of traveling to every point of the compass just to get what other people have at home?"

"Sister," the woman said quietly, "it's time to shut your mouth."

Latifa took her advice, and peered past her out the scratched window. They were crossing a barren, rock-strewn desert now, a region infamous for bandits. The bus had an armed guard, for what that was worth, but the first time Latifa had made the journey Amir had told her stories of travelers ambushed on this road at night. One man on a motorbike, carrying no cash, had been tortured until he phoned his family to deposit money into his assailant's account.

"Wouldn't that help the police catch the bandits?" Latifa had asked him, logical as ever but still naive.

Amir had laughed his head off.

"When it comes to the police," he'd finally explained, "*money in the bank* tends to have the opposite effect."

Fashard was waiting for Latifa in the bus station. He spotted her before she saw him – or rather, he spotted the bright scarf, chosen from the range she sold in the shop, that she'd told him she'd be tying to the handle of her suitcase.

He called out, then approached her, beaming. "Welcome, cousin! How was your trip?" He grabbed the suitcase and hefted it onto his shoulders; it did have wheels, but in the crowded station any baggage at foot level would just be an impediment.

"It was fine," she said. "You're looking well." Actually, Fashard looked exhausted, but he'd put so much enthusiasm into his greeting that it would have been rude to mention anything of the kind.

Latifa followed him to the car, bumping into people along the way; she still hadn't adjusted to having her peripheral vision excised.

The sun was setting as they drove through the city; Latifa fought to keep her eyes open, but she took in an impression of peeling advertising posters, shabby white-washed buildings, crowds of men in all manner of clothing and a smattering of women in near-identical garb. Traffic police stood at the busiest intersections, blowing their whistles. Nothing had changed.

Inside the house, she gratefully shed her burqa as Fashard's five youngest children swarmed toward her. She dropped to her knees to exchange kisses and dispense sweets. Fashard's wife, Soraya, his mother, Zohra, eldest daughter, sister, brother-in-law and two nephews were next to greet her. Latifa's weariness lifted; used as she was to comparative solitude, the sense of belonging was overpowering.

"How is my brother?" Zohra pressed her.

"He's fine. He sends his love to you especially."

Zohra started weeping; Fashard put an arm around her. Latifa looked away. Her grandfather still had too many enemies here to be able to return.

When Latifa had washed and changed her clothes, she rejoined the family just as the first dizzying aromas began escaping from the kitchen. She had fasted all day and the night before, knowing that on her arrival she was going to be fed until she burst. Soraya shooed her away from the kitchen, but Latifa was pleasantly surprised: Fashard had finally improved the chimney to the point where the wood-fired stove no longer filled the room with blinding smoke.

As they ate by the light of kerosene lamps, everyone had questions for her about life in Mashhad. What did things cost now, with the new sanctions in place? What were her neighbors like? How were the Iranians treating Afghanis these days? Latifa was happy to answer them, but as she looked around at the curious faces she kept thinking of eight-year-old

Fatema tugging on her sleeve, accepting a sweet but demanding something more: *What was school like? What did you learn?*

In the morning, Fashard showed Latifa the room he'd set aside for their work. She'd sent the kilns, the winders, and the current buckets to him by three different carriers. Fashard had found a source for the superconductor precursors himself: a company that brought a variety of common industrial chemicals in through Pakistan. It was possible that news of some of these shipments had reached Ezatullah, but Latifa was hoping that it wouldn't be enough to attract suspicion. If Fashard had decided to diversify into pottery, that hardly constituted a form of betrayal.

The room opened onto the courtyard, and Fashard had already taken up the paving stones to expose a patch of bare ground. "This is perfect," Latifa said. "We can run some cable out along the wall and bury the current buckets right here."

Fashard examined one of the halved diving cylinders she'd adapted to the purpose. "This really might burst?" he asked, more bemused than alarmed.

"I hope not," Latifa replied. "There's a cut-off switch that should stop the charger if the magnetic field grows too strong. I can't imagine that switch getting jammed – a bit of grit or friction isn't going to hold the contacts together against a force that's threatening to tear the whole thing apart. But so long as you keep track of the charging time there shouldn't be a problem anyway."

It took a couple of hours to dig the holes and wire up the storage system. Late in the morning the power came on, giving them a chance to test everything before they covered the buckets with half a meter of soil.

Latifa switched on the charger and waited ten minutes, then she plugged a lamp into the new supply. The light it produced was steadier and brighter than that it had emitted when connected to the mains: the voltage from the buckets was better regulated than the incoming supply.

Fashard smiled, not quite believing it. The largest of the components inside the cylinders looked like nothing so much as the element of an electric water heater; that was how Latifa had described the ceramic helices in the customs documents.

"If everyone had these…" he began enthusiastically, but then he stopped and thought it through. "If everyone had them, every household would be drawing more power, charging up their buckets to use through the blackouts. The power company would only be able to meet the demand from an even smaller portion of its customers, so they'd have to make the rationing periods even shorter."

"That's true," Latifa agreed. "Which is why it will be better if the buckets are sold with solar panels."

"What about in winter?" Fashard protested.

Latifa snorted. "What do you want from me? Magic? The government needs to fix the hydro plant."

Fashard shook his head sadly. "The people who keep bombing it aren't going to stop. Not unless they're given everything they want."

Latifa felt tired, but she had to finish what she'd started. She said, "I should show you how to work the kilns and the winders."

It took three days for Latifa and Fashard to settle on a procedure for the new factory. If they waited for the current buckets to be fully charged before starting the kilns, that guaranteed they could finish the batch without spoiling it – but they could make better use of the time if they took a risk and started earlier, given that the power, erratic though it was, usually did stay on for a few hours every day.

Fashard brought in his oldest nephew, Naqib, who'd be working half the shifts. Latifa stayed out of these training sessions; Naqib was always perfectly polite to her, but she knew he wasn't prepared to be shown anything by a woman three years younger than himself.

Sidelined, Latifa passed the time with Fatema. Though it was too dangerous for Fatema to go to school, Fashard had taught her to read and write and he was trying to find someone to come and tutor her. Latifa sat beside her as she proudly sounded out the words in a compendium of Pashtun folk tales, and practiced her script in the back of Latifa's notebook.

"What are these?" Fatema asked, flicking through the pages of calculations.

"Al-jabr," Latifa replied. "You'll understand when you're older."

One day they were in the courtyard, racing the remote-control cars that Latifa had brought from Mashhad for all the kids to share. The power went off, and as the television the other cousins had been watching fell silent, Fatema turned toward the factory, surprised. She could hear the winders still spinning.

"How is that working?" she asked Latifa.

"Our cars are still working, aren't they?" Latifa revved her engine.

Fatema refused to be distracted. "They use batteries. You can't run anything big with batteries."

"Maybe I brought some bigger batteries from Iran."

"Show me," Fatema pleaded.

Latifa opened her mouth to start explaining, her mind already groping for some simple metaphors she could use to convey how the current buckets worked. But ... *our cousin came from Iran and buried giant batteries in the ground?* Did she really want that story spreading out across the neighborhood?

"I was joking," Latifa said.

Fatema frowned. "But then *how*...?"

Latifa shrugged. Fatema's brothers, robbed of their cartoons, were heading toward them, demanding to join in the game.

The bus station was stifling. Latifa would have been happy to dispense a few parting hugs and then take her seat, but her cousins didn't do quiet farewells.

"I'll be back at Eid," she promised. "With Amir."

"That's months away!" Soraya sobbed.

"I'll phone every week."

"You say that now," Zohra replied, more resigned than accusing.

"I'm not leaving forever! I'll see you all again!" Latifa was growing tearful herself. She squatted down and tried to kiss Fatema, but the girl turned her face away.

"What should I bring you from Mashhad next time?" Latifa asked her.

Fatema considered this. "The truth."

Latifa said, "I'll try."

## 3

"I did my best to argue your case," Ms Daneshvar told Latifa. "I told the principal you had too much promise to waste. But your attendance records, your missed assignments..." She spread her hands unhappily. "I couldn't sway them."

"I'll be all right," Latifa assured her. She glanced up at the peg that held the key to the chemistry lab. "And I appreciate everything you did for me."

"But what will you do now?"

Latifa reached into her backpack and took out one of the small ceramic pots Fashard had sent her. Not long after the last spools of wire had left Kandahar, two men had come snooping on Ezatullah's behalf – perhaps a little puzzled that Fashard didn't seem quite as crushed as the terms of the deal should have left him. He had managed to hide the winders from them, but he'd had to think up an alibi for the kilns at short notice.

"I'm going to sell a few knickknacks in the bazaar," Latifa said. "Like this." She placed the pot on the desk and made as if to open it. When she'd twisted the lid through a quarter-turn it sprung into the air – only kept from escaping by three cotton threads that remained comically taut, restraining it against the push of some mysterious repulsive force.

Ms Daneshvar gazed in horror at this piece of useless kitsch.

"Just for a while!" Latifa added. "Until my other plans come to fruition."

"Oh, Latifa."

"You should take a closer look at it when you have the time," Latifa urged her. "There's a puzzle to it that I think you might enjoy."

"There are a couple of magnets," Ms Daneshvar replied. "Like pole aimed at like. You were my brightest student … and now you're impressed by *this*?" She turned the pot over. "Made in Afghanistan. Patent pending." She gave a curt laugh, but then thought better of mocking the idea.

Latifa said, "You helped me a lot. It wasn't wasted." She stood and shook her former teacher's hand. "I hope things go well for you."

Ms Daneshvar rose and kissed Latifa's cheek. "I know you're resourceful; I know you'll find something. It just should have been so much more."

Latifa started to leave, but then she stopped and turned back. The claims had all been lodged, the details disclosed. She didn't have to keep the secret any more.

"Cut one thread, so you can turn the lid upside-down," she suggested.

Ms Daneshvar was perplexed. "Why?"

Latifa smiled. "It's a very quick experiment, but I promise you it will be worth it."

# UNCANNY VALLEY

## 1

In a pause in the flow of images, it came to him that he'd been dreaming for a fathomless time and that he wished to stop. But when he tried to picture the scene that would greet him upon waking, his mind grabbed the question and ran with it, not so much changing the subject as summoning out of the darkness answers that he was sure had long ago ceased to be correct. He remembered the bunk beds that he and his brother had slept in until he was nine, with pieces of broken springs hanging down above him like tiny gray stalactites. The shade of his bedside reading lamp had been ringed with small, diamond-shaped holes; he would place his fingers over them and stare at the red light emerging through his flesh, until the heat from the globe became too much to bear.

Later, in a room of his own, his bed had come with hollow metal posts whose plastic caps were easily removed, allowing him to toss in chewed pencil stubs, pins that had held newly bought school shirts elaborately folded around cardboard packaging, tacks that he'd bent out of shape with misaligned hammer blows while trying to form pictures in zinc on lumps of firewood, pieces of gravel that had made their way into his shoes, dried snot scraped from his handkerchief, and tiny, balled-up scraps of paper, each bearing a four- or five-word account of whatever seemed important at the time, building up a record of his life like a core sample slicing through geological strata, a find for future archaeologists far more exciting than any diary.

But he could also recall a bleary-eyed, low-angle view of clothes strewn on the floor, in a bedsit apartment with no bed as such, just a fold-out couch. That felt as remote as his childhood, but something pushed him to keep fleshing out the details of the room. There was a typewriter on a table. He could smell the ribbon, and he saw the box in which it had come, sitting on a shelf in a corner of a stationers, with white letters on a blue background, but the words they spelled out eluded him. He'd always hunted down the fully black ribbons, though most stores had only stocked black-and-red. Who could possibly need to type anything in red?

Wiping his ink-stained fingers on a discarded page after a ribbon change, he knew the whole scene was an anachronism, and he tried to follow that insight up to the surface, like a diver pursuing a glimpse of the distant sun. But something weighed him down, anchoring him to the cold wooden chair in that unheated room, with a stack of blank paper to his right, a pile of finished sheets to his left, a waste basket under the table. He urgently needed to think about the way the loop in the "e" became solid black sometimes, prompting him to clean all the typebars with an old T-shirt dampened with methylated spirits. If he didn't think about it now, he was afraid that he might never have the chance to think of it again.

## 2

Adam decided to go against all the advice he'd received, and attend the old man's funeral.

The old man himself had warned him off. "Why make trouble?" he'd asked, peering at Adam from the hospital bed with that disconcerting vampiric longing that had grown more intense toward the end. "The more you rub their faces in it, the more likely they'll be to come after you."

"I thought you said they couldn't do that."

"All I said was that I'd done my best to stop them. Do you want to keep the inheritance, or do you want to squander it on lawyers? Don't make yourself more of a target than you need to be."

But standing in the shower, reveling in the sensation of the hot water pelting his skin, Adam only grew more resolute. Why shouldn't he dare to show his face? He had nothing to be ashamed of.

The old man had bought a few suits for him a while ago, and left them hanging beside his own clothes. Adam picked one out and placed it on the bed, then paused to run a hand along the worn sleeve of an old, olive-green shirt. He was sure it would fit him, and for a moment he considered wearing it, but then the thought made him uneasy and he chose one of the new ones that had come with the suits.

As he dressed, he gazed at the undisturbed bed, trying to think of a good reason why he still hadn't left the guest room. No one else was coming to claim this one. But he shouldn't get too comfortable here; he might need to sell the house and move into something far more modest.

Adam started booking a car, then realized that he had no idea where the ceremony was being held. He finally found the details at the bottom of the old man's obit, which described it as open to the public. While he stood outside the front door waiting for the car, he tried for the third or fourth time to read the obituary itself, but his eyes kept glazing over. "Morris blah blah blah … Morris blah blah, Morris blah …"

His phone beeped, then the gate opened and the car pulled into the driveway. He sat in the passenger seat and watched the steering wheel doing its poltergeist act as it negotiated the U-turn. He suspected that whatever victories the lawyers could achieve, he was going to have to pay the "unsupervised driving" surcharge for a while yet.

As the car turned into Sepulveda Boulevard, the view looked strange to him – half familiar, half wrong – but perhaps there'd been some recent reconstruction. He dialed down the tinting, hoping to puncture a lingering sense of being at a remove from everything. The glare from the pavement beneath the cloudless blue sky was merciless, but he kept the windows undimmed.

The venue was some kind of chapel-esque building that probably served as seven different kinds of meeting hall, and in any case was free of conspicuous religious or la-la-land inspirational signage. The old man had left his remains to a medical school, so at least they'd all been spared a trip to Forest Lawn. As Adam stepped away from the car, he spotted one of the nephews, Ryan, walking toward the entrance, accompanied by his wife and adult children. The old man hadn't spent much time with any of them, but he'd gotten hold of recent pictures and showed them to Adam so he wouldn't be caught unaware.

Adam hung back and waited for them to go inside before crossing the forecourt. As he approached the door and caught sight of a large portrait of a decidedly pre-cancerous version of the old man on a stand beside the podium, his courage began to waver. But he steeled himself and continued.

He kept his gaze low as he entered the hall, and chose a spot on the frontmost unoccupied bench, far enough in from the aisle that nobody would have to squeeze past him. After a minute or so, an elderly man took the aisle seat; Adam snuck a quick glance at his neighbor, but he did not look familiar. His timing had turned out to be perfect: any later and his entrance might have drawn attention, any earlier and there would have been people milling outside. Whatever happened, no one could accuse him of going out of his way to make a scene.

Ryan mounted the steps to the podium. Adam stared at the back of the bench in front of him; he felt like a child trapped in church, though no one had forced him to be here.

"The last time I saw my uncle," Ryan began, "was almost ten years ago, at the funeral of his husband Carlos. Until then, I always thought it would be Carlos standing up here, delivering this speech, far more aptly and eloquently than I, or anyone else, ever could."

Adam felt a freight train tearing through his chest, but he kept his eyes fixed on a discolored patch of varnish. This had been a bad idea, but he couldn't walk out now.

"My uncle was the youngest child of Robert and Sophie Morris," Ryan continued. "He outlived his brother Steven, his sister Joan, and my mother, Sarah. Though I was never close to him, I'm heartened to see so many of his friends and colleagues here to pay their respects. I watched his shows, of course, but then, didn't everyone? I was wondering if we ought to screen some kind of highlights reel, but then the people in the know told me that there was going to be a tribute at the Emmys, and I decided not to compete with the professional edit-bots."

That line brought some quiet laughter, and Adam felt obliged to look up and smile. No one in this family was any kind of monster, whatever they aspired to do to him. They just had their own particular views of his relationship with the old man – sharpened by the lure of a few million dollars, but they probably would have felt the same regardless.

Ryan kept his contribution short, but when Cynthia Navarro took his place Adam had to turn his face to the pew again. He doubted that she'd recognize him – she'd worked with the old man in the wrong era for that – but the warmth, and grief, in her voice made her anecdotes far harder to shut out than the automated mash-up of database entries and viral misquotes that had formed the obituary. She finished with the time they'd spent all night searching for a way to rescue a location shoot with six hundred extras after Gemma Freeman broke her leg and had to be stretchered out in a chopper. As she spoke, Adam closed his eyes and pictured the wildly annotated pages of the script strewn across the table, and Cynthia gawping with incredulity at her friend's increasingly desperate remedies.

"But it all worked out well enough," she concluded. "The plot twist that *no viewer saw coming*, that lifted the third season to *a whole new level*, owed its existence to an oil slick from a generator that just happened to be situated between Ms Freeman's trailer and …"

Laughter rose up, cutting her off, and Adam felt compelled once more to raise his eyes. But before the sounds of mirth had faded, his neighbor moved closer and asked in a whisper, "Do you remember me?"

Adam turned, not quite facing the man. "Should I?" He spoke with an east-coast accent that was hard to place, and if it induced a certain sense of déjà vu, so did advertising voice-overs, and random conversations overheard in elevators.

"I don't know," the man replied. His tone was more amused than sarcastic; he meant the words literally. Adam hunted for something polite and noncommittal to say, but the audience was too quiet now for him to speak without being noticed and hushed, and his neighbor was already turning back toward the podium.

Cynthia was followed by a representative of the old man's agents, though everyone who'd known him in the golden age was long gone. There were suits from Warner Bros., Netflix and HBO, whose stories of the old man were clearly scripted by the same bots that wrote their new shows. As the proceedings became ever more wooden, Adam began suffering from a panic-inducing premonition that Ryan would invite anyone in the hall who wished to speak to step up, and in the awkward silence that followed everyone's eyes would sweep the room and alight on him.

But when Ryan returned to the podium, he just thanked them for coming and wished them safe journeys home.

"No music?" Adam's neighbor asked. "No poetry? I seem to recall something by Dylan Thomas that might have raised a laugh under the circumstances."

"I think he stipulated no music," Adam replied.

"Fair enough. Since *The Big Chill*, anything you could pick with a trace of wit to it would seem like a bad in-joke."

"Excuse me, I have to ..." People were starting to leave, and Adam wanted to get away before anyone else noticed him.

As he stood, his neighbor took out his phone and flicked his thumb across its surface. Adam's phone pinged softly in acknowledgment. "In case you want to catch up sometime," the man explained cheerfully.

"Thanks," Adam replied, nodding an awkward goodbye, grateful that he didn't seem to be expected to reciprocate.

There was already a small crowd lingering just inside the door, slowing his exit. When he made it out onto the forecourt, he walked straight to the road-side and summoned a car.

"Hey, you! Mr Sixty Percent!"

Adam turned. A man in his thirties was marching toward him, scowling with such intense displeasure that his pillowy cheeks had turned red. "Can I help you with something?" Adam asked mildly. For all that he'd been dreading a confrontation, now that it was imminent he felt more invigorated than intimidated.

"What the fuck were you doing in there?"

"It was open to the public."

"You're not part of the public!"

Adam finally placed him: he was one of Ryan's sons. He'd seen him from behind as he'd been entering the hall. "Unhappy with the will are you, Gerald?"

Gerald came closer. He was trembling slightly, but Adam couldn't tell if it was from rage or from fear. "Live it up while you can, Sixty. You're going to be out with the trash in no time."

"What's with this 'sixty'?" As far as Adam knew, he'd been bequeathed a hundred percent of the estate, unless Gerald was already accounting for all the legal fees.

"Sixty percent: how much you resemble him."

"Now that's just cruel. I'm assured that by some metrics, it's at least seventy."

Gerald snickered triumphantly, as if that made his case. "I guess he was used to setting the bar low. If you grew up believing that Facebook could give you 'news' and Google could give you 'information', your expectations for quality control would already be nonexistent."

"I think you're conflating his generation with your father's." Adam was quite sure that the old man had held the Bilge Barons in as much contempt as his great-nephew did. "And seventy percent of something real isn't so bad. Getting a side-load that close to complete is orders of magnitude harder than anything those charlatans ever did."

"Well, give your own scam artists a Nobel Prize, but you'd still need to be senile to think that was good enough."

"He wasn't senile. We spoke together at least a dozen times in the month before he died, and he must have thought he was getting what he'd paid for, because he never chose to pull the plug on me." Adam hadn't even known at the time that that was possible, but in retrospect he was glad no one had told him. It might have made those bedside chats a little tense.

"Because ...?" Gerald demanded. When Adam didn't reply immediately, Gerald laughed. "Or is the reason he decided you were worth the trouble part of the thirty percent of his mind that you don't have?"

"It could well be," Adam conceded, trying to make that sound like a perfectly satisfactory outcome. A joke about the studios' bots only achieving ten percent of the same goal and still earning a tidy income got censored halfway to his lips; the last thing he wanted to do was invite the old man's relatives to view him in the same light as that cynical act of shallow mimicry.

"So you don't know *why* he didn't care that you don't know whatever it is that you don't know? Very fucking Kafka."

"I think he would have preferred 'very fucking Heller' ... but who am I to say?"

"Next week's trash, that's what you are." Gerald stepped back, looking pleased with himself. "Next week's fodder for the wrecking yard."

The car pulled up beside Adam and the door slid open. "Is that your grandma come to take you home?" Gerald taunted him. "Or maybe your retarded cousin?"

"Enjoy the wake," Adam replied. He tapped his skull. "I promise, the old man will be thinking of you."

## 3

Adam had a conference call with the lawyers. "How do we stand?" he asked.

"The family's going to contest the will," Gina replied.

"On what grounds?"

"That the trustees, and the beneficiaries of the trust, misled and defrauded Mr Morris."

"They're saying I misled him somehow?"

"No," Corbin interjected. "US law doesn't recognize you as a person. *You* can't be sued, as such, but other entities you depend on certainly can be."

"Right." Adam had known as much, but in his mind he kept glossing over the elaborate legal constructs that sustained his delusions of autonomy. On a purely practical level, there was money in three accounts that he had no trouble accessing – but then, the same was probably true of any number of stock-trading algorithms, and that didn't make them the masters of their own fate. "So who exactly is accused of fraud?"

"Our firm," Gina replied. "Various officers of the corporations we created to fulfill Mr Morris's instructions. Loadstone, for making false claims that led to the original purchase of their technology, and for ongoing fraud in relation to the services promised in their maintenance contract."

"I'm very happy with the maintenance contract!" When Adam had complained that one of his earlobes had gone numb, Sandra had come to his home and fixed the problem on the same day he called.

"That's not the point," Corbin said impatiently. Adam was forgetting his place again: jurisprudentially, his happiness cut no ice.

"So what happens next?"

"The first hearings are still seven months away," Gina explained. "We were expecting this, and we'll have plenty of time to prepare. We'll aim for an early dismissal, of course, but we can't promise anything."

"No." Adam hesitated. "But it's not just the house they could take? The Estonian accounts …?"

Gina said, "Opening those accounts under your digital residency makes some things easier, but it doesn't put the money out of reach of the courts."

"Right."

When they hung up, Adam paced the office. Could it really be so hard to defend the old man's will? He wasn't even sure what disincentives were in place to stop the lawyers from drawing out proceedings like this for as long as they wished. Maybe a director of one of the entities he depended on was both empowered, and duty-bound, to rein them in if they were behaving with conspicuous profligacy? But Adam himself couldn't sack them, or compel them to follow his instructions, just because Estonia had been nice enough to classify him as a person for certain limited purposes.

The old man had believed he was setting him up in style, but all the machinery that was meant to support him just made him feel trapped. What if he gave up the house and walked away? If he cashed in his dollar and euro accounts for some mixture of blockchain currencies before the courts swept in and froze his funds, that might be easier to protect and enjoy without the benefits of a Social Security number, a birth certificate or a passport. But those currencies were all insanely volatile, and trying to hedge them against each other was like trying to save yourself in a skydiving accident by clutching your own feet.

He couldn't leave the country by any lawful means without deactivating his body so it could be sent as freight. Loadstone had promised to facilitate any trips he wished to make to any of the thirty-nine jurisdictions where he could walk the streets unchaperoned, as proud and free as the pizza bots that had blazed the trail, but the idea of returning to the company's servers, or even being halted and left in limbo for the duration of the flight, filled him with dread.

For now, it seemed that he was stuck in the Valley. All he could do was find a way to make the best of it.

## 4

Sitting on two upturned wooden crates in an alley behind the nightclub, they could still hear the pounding bass-line of the music escaping through the walls, but at least it was possible to hold a conversation here.

Carlos sounded like the loneliest person Adam had ever met. Did he tell everyone so much, so soon? Adam wanted to believe that he didn't, and that something in his own demeanor had inspired this beautiful man to confide in him.

Carlos had been in the country for twelve years, but he was still struggling to support his sister in El Salvador. She'd raised him after their parents died – his father when he was six months old, his mother when he was five. But now his sister had three children of her own, and the man who'd fathered them was no good to her.

"I love her," he said. "I love her like my own life, I don't want to be rid of her. But the kids are always sick, or something's broken that needs fixing. It never fucking stops."

Adam had no one relying on him, no one expecting him to do anything. His own finances waxed and waned, but at least when the money was scarce no one else suffered, or made him feel that he was letting them down.

"So what do you do to relieve the stress?" he asked.

Carlos smiled sadly. "It used to be smoking, but that got too expensive."

"So you quit?"

"Only the smoking."

As Adam turned toward him, his mind went roaming down the darkness of the alley, impatiently following the glistening thread, unable to shake off the sense of urgency that told him: *take hold of this now, or it will be lost forever*. He didn't need to linger in their beds for long; just a few samples of that annihilating euphoria were enough to stand in for all the rest. Maybe that was the engine powering everything that followed, but what it dragged along behind it was like a newlyweds' car decorated by a thousand exuberant well-wishers.

He tried grabbing the rattling cans of their fights, running his fingers over the rough texture of all the small annoyances and slights, mutually wounded pride, frustrated good intentions. Then he felt the jagged edge of a lacerating eruption of doubt.

But something had happened that blunted the edge, then folded it in on itself again and again, leaving a seam, a ridge, a scar. Afterward, however hard things became, there was no questioning the foundations. They'd earned each other's trust, and it was unshakeable.

He pushed on into the darkness, trying to understand. Wherever he walked, light would follow, and his task was to make his way down as many side-streets as possible before he woke.

This time, though, the darkness remained unbroken. He groped his way forward, unnerved. They'd ended up closer than ever – he knew that with as much certainty as he knew anything. So why did he feel as if he was stumbling blindly through the rooms of Bluebeard's castle, and the last thing he should want to summon was a lamp?

## 5

Adam spent three weeks in the old man's home theater, watching every one of the old man's shows, and an episode or two from each of the biggest hits of the last ten years. There could only be one thing more embarrassing than pitching an idea to a studio and discovering that he was offering them a story that they'd already produced for six seasons, and that would be attempting to recycle, not just any old show, but an actual Adam Morris script.

Most of the old man's work felt as familiar as if he'd viewed it a hundred times in the editing suite, but sometimes a whole side plot appeared that seemed to have dropped from the sky. Could the studios have fucked with things afterward, when the old man was too sick and distracted to notice? Adam checked online, but the fan sites that would have trumpeted any such tampering were silent. The only re-cuts had taken place in another medium entirely.

He desperately needed to write a new show. Money aside, how else was he going to pass the time? The old man's few surviving friends had all made it clear before he died that they wanted nothing to do with his sideload. He could try to make the most of his cybernetic rejuvenation; his skin felt exactly like skin, from inside and out, and his ridiculously plausible dildo of a cock wouldn't disappoint anyone if he went looking for ways to use it – but the truth was, he'd inherited the old man's feelings for Carlos far too deeply to brush them aside and pretend that he was twenty again, with no attachments and no baggage. He didn't even know yet if he wanted to forge an identity entirely his own, or to take the other path and seek to become the old man more fully. He couldn't "betray" a lover ten years dead who was, in the end, nothing more to him than a character in someone else's story – whatever he'd felt as he'd dragged the old man's memories into his own virtual skull. But he wasn't going to sell himself that version of things before he was absolutely sure it was the right one.

The only way to know who he was would be to create something new. It didn't even need to be a story that the old man wouldn't have written himself, had he lived a few years longer ... just so long as it didn't turn out that he'd already written it, pitched it unsuccessfully, and stuck it in a drawer. Adam pictured himself holding a page from each version up to the light together, bringing the words into alignment, trying to decide if the differences were too many, or too few.

## 6

"Sixty thousand dollars *in one week*?" Adam was incredulous.

Gina replied calmly, "The billables are all itemized. I can assure you, what we're charging is really quite modest for a case of this complexity."

"The money was his, he could do what he liked with it. End of story."

"That's not what the case law says." Gina was beginning to exhibit micro-fidgets, as if she'd found herself trapped at a family occasion being forced to play a childish video game just to humor a nephew she didn't really like. Whether or not she'd granted Adam personhood in her own mind, he certainly wasn't anyone in a position to give her instructions, and the only reason she'd taken his call must have been some sop to Adam's comfort that the old man had managed to get written into his contract with the firm.

"All right. I'm sorry to have troubled you."

In the silence after he'd hung up, Adam recalled something that Carlos had said to the old man, back in New York one sweltering July, taking him aside in the middle of the haggling over a second-hand air-conditioner they were attempting to buy. "You're a good person, *cariño*, so you don't see it when people are trying to cheat you." Maybe he'd been sincere, or maybe "good" had just been a tactful euphemism for "unworldly", though if the old man really had been so trusting, how had Adam ended up with the opposite trait? Was cynicism some kind of default, wired into the template from which the whole side-loading process had started?

Adam found an auditor with no connections to the old man's lawyers, picking a city at random and then choosing the person with the highest reputation score with whom he could afford a ten-minute consultation. Her name was Lillian Adjani.

"Because these companies have no shareholders," she explained, "there's not that much that needs to be disclosed in their public filings. And I can't just go to them myself and demand to see their financial records. A court could do that, in principle, and you might be able to find a lawyer who'd take your money to try to make that happen. But who would their client be?"

Adam had to admire the way she could meet his gaze with an expression of sympathy, while reminding him that – shorn of the very constructs he was trying to scrutinize – for administrative purposes he didn't actually exist.

"So there's nothing I can do?" Maybe he was starting to confuse his second-hand memories of the real world with all the shows he'd been watching, where people just *followed the money trail.* The police never seemed to need to get the courts involved, and even civilians usually had some supernaturally gifted hacker at their disposal. "We couldn't … hire an investigator … who could persuade someone to leak …?" Mike Ehrmantraut would have found a way to make it happen in three days flat.

Ms Adjani regarded him censoriously. "I'm not getting involved in anything illegal. But maybe you have something yourself, already in your possession, that could help you more than you realize."

"Like what?"

"How computer-savvy was your … predecessor?"

"He could use a word processor and a web browser. And Skype."

"Do you still have any of his devices?"

Adam laughed. "I don't know what happened to his phone, but I'm talking to you from his laptop right now."

"OK. Don't get your hopes too high, but if there were files containing financial records or legal documents that he received and then deleted, then unless he went out of his way to erase them securely, they might still be recoverable."

Ms Adjani sent him a link for a piece of software she trusted to do the job. Adam installed it, then stared numbly at the catalog of eighty-three thousand "intelligible fragments" that had shown up on the drive.

He started playing with the filtering options. When he chose "text", portions of scripts began emerging from the fog – some instantly recognizable, some probably abandoned dead-ends. Adam averted his gaze, afraid of absorbing them into his subconscious if they weren't already buried there. He had to draw a line somewhere.

He found an option called “financial”, and when that yielded a blizzard of utility bills, he added all the relevant keywords he could think of.

There were bills from the lawyers, and bills from Loadstone. If Gina was screwing him, she’d been screwing the old man as well, because the hourly rate hadn’t changed. Adam was beginning to feel foolish; he was right to be vigilant about his precarious situation, but if he let that devolve into full-blown paranoia he’d just end up kicking all the support structures out from beneath his feet.

Loadstone hadn’t been shy with their fees either. Adam hadn’t known before just how much his body had cost, but given the generally excellent engineering it was difficult to begrudge the expense. There was an item for the purchase of the template, and then one for every side-loading session, broken down into various components. “Squid operator?” he muttered, bemused. “What the fuck?” But he wasn’t going to start convincing himself that they’d blinded the old man with technobabble. He’d paid what he’d paid, and in the hospital he’d given Adam every indication that he’d been happy with the result.

“Targeted occlusions?” Meaning blood clots in the brain? The old man had left him login details allowing him post-mortem access to all his medical records; Adam checked, and there had been no clots.

He searched the web for the phrase in the context of side-loading. The pithiest translation he found was: “The selective non-transferral of a prescribed class of memories or traits.”

Which meant that the old man had held something back, deliberately. Adam was an imperfect copy of him, not just because the technology was imperfect, but because he’d wanted it that way.

“You lying piece of shit.” Toward the end, the old man had rambled on about his hope that Adam would outdo his own achievements, but judging from his efforts so far he wasn’t even going to come close. Three attempts at new scripts had ended up dead in the water. It wasn’t Ryan and his family who'd robbed him of the most valuable part of the inheritance.

Adam sat staring at his hands, contemplating the possibilities for a life worth living without the only skill the old man had ever possessed. He remembered joking to Carlos once that they should both train as doctors and go open a free clinic in San Salvador. "When we're rich." But Adam doubted that his original, let alone the diminished version, was smart enough to learn to do much more than empty bed-pans.

He switched off the laptop and walked into the master bedroom. All of the old man's clothes were still there, as if he'd fully expected them to be used again. Adam took off his own clothes and began trying on each item in turn, counting the ones he was sure he recognized. Was he Gerald's Mr Sixty Percent, or was it more like forty, or thirty? Maybe the pep talks had been a kind of sarcastic joke, with the old man secretly hoping that the final verdict would be that there was only one Adam Morris, and like the studios' laughable "deep-learning" bots, even the best technology in the world couldn't capture his true spark.

He sat on the bed, naked, wondering what it would be like to go out in some wild bacchanalia with a few dozen robot fetishists, fucking his brains out and then dismembering him to take the pieces home as souvenirs. It wouldn't be hard to organize, and he doubted that any part of his corporate infrastructure would be obliged to have him resurrected from Loadstone's daily backups. The old man might have been using him to make some dementedly pretentious artistic point, but he would never have been cruel enough to render suicide impossible.

Adam caught sight of a picture of the two men posing hammily beneath the Hollywood sign, and found himself sobbing dryly with, of all things, grief. What he wanted was Carlos beside him – making this bearable, putting it right. He loved the dead man's dead lover more than he was ever going to love anyone else, but he still couldn't do anything worthwhile that the dead man could have done.

He pictured Carlos with his arms around him. “Shh, it’s not as bad as you think – it never is, *cariño*. We start with what we’ve got, and just fill in the pieces as we go.”

*You’re really not helping*, Adam replied. *Just shut up and fuck me, that’s all I’ve got left.* He lay down on the bed and took his penis in his hand. It had seemed wrong before, but he didn’t care now: he didn’t owe either of them anything. And Carlos, at least, would probably have taken pity on him, and not begrudged him the unpaid guest appearance.

He closed his eyes and tried to remember the feel of stubble against his thighs, but he wasn’t even capable of scripting his own fantasy: Carlos just wanted to talk.

“You’ve got friends,” he insisted. “You’ve got people looking out for you.”

Adam had no idea if he was confabulating freely, or if this was a fragment of a real conversation long past, but context was everything. “Not any more, *cariño*. Either they’re dead, or I’m dead to them.”

Carlos just stared back at him skeptically, as if he’d made a ludicrously hyperbolic claim.

But that skepticism did have some merit. If he knocked on Cynthia’s door she’d probably try to stab him through the heart with a wooden stake, but the amiable stranger who’d sat beside him at the funeral had been far keener to talk than Adam. The fact that he still couldn’t place the man no longer seemed like a good reason to avoid him; if he came from the gaps, he must know something about them.

Carlos was gone. Adam sat up, still feeling gutted, but no amount of self-pity was going to improve his situation.

He found his phone, and checked under “Introductions”; he hadn’t erased the contact details. The man was named Patrick Auster. Adam called the number.

# 7

"You go first," Adam said. "Ask me anything. That's the only fair trade." They were sitting in a booth in an old-style diner named Caesar's, where Auster had suggested they meet. The place wasn't busy, and the adjacent booths were empty, so there was no need to censor themselves or talk in code.

Auster gestured at the generous serving of chocolate cream pie that Adam had begun demolishing. "Can you really taste that?"

"Absolutely."

"And it's the same as before?"

Adam wasn't going to start hedging his answers with quibbles about the ultimate incomparability of qualia and memories. "Exactly the same." He pointed a thumb toward the diners three booths behind him. "I can tell you without peeking that someone's eating bacon. And I think it's apparent that there's nothing wrong with my hearing or vision, even if my memory for faces isn't so good."

"Which leaves …"

"Every hair on the bear-skin rug," Adam assured him.

Auster hesitated. Adam said, "There's no three-question limit. We can keep going all day if you want to."

"Do you have much to do with the others?" Auster asked.

"The other side-loads? No. I never knew any of them before, so there's no reason for them to be in touch with me now."

Auster was surprised. "I'd have thought you'd all be making common cause. Trying to improve the legal situation."

"We probably should be. But if there's some secret cabal of immortals trying to get re-enfranchised, they haven't invited me into their inner circle yet."

Adam waited as Auster stirred his coffee meditatively. "That's it," he decided.

"OK. You know, I'm sorry if I was brusque at the funeral," Adam said. "I was trying to keep a low profile; I was worried about how people would react."

"Forget it."

"So, you knew me in New York?" Adam wasn't going to use the third person; it would make the conversation far too awkward. Besides, if he'd come here to claim the missing memories as his own, the last thing he wanted to do was distance himself from them.

"Yes."

"Was it business, or were we friends?" All he'd been able to find out online was that Auster had written a couple of independent movies. There was no record of the two of them ever working on the same project; their official Bacon number was three, which put Adam no closer to Auster than he was to Angelina Jolie.

"Both, I hope." Auster hesitated, then angrily recanted the last part. "No, we were friends. Sorry, it's hard not to resent being blanked, even if it's not deliberate."

Adam tried to judge just how deeply the insult had cut him. "Were we lovers?"

Auster almost choked on his coffee. "God, no! I've always been straight, and you were already with Carlos when I met you." He frowned suddenly. "You didn't cheat on him, did you?" He sounded more incredulous than reproving.

"Not as far as I know." During the drive down to Gardena, Adam had wondered if the old man might have been trying to airbrush out his infidelities. That would have been a bizarre form of vanity, or hypocrisy, or some other sin the world didn't yet have a name for, but it would still have been easier to forgive than a deliberate attempt to sabotage his successor.

"We met around two thousand and ten," Auster continued. "When I first approached you about adapting *Sadlands*."

"OK."

"You do remember *Sadlands*, don't you?"

"My second novel," Adam replied. For a moment nothing more came to him, then he said, "There's an epidemic of suicides spreading across the country, apparently at random, affecting people equally regardless of demographics."

"That sounds like the version a reviewer would write," Auster teased him. "I spent six years, on and off, trying to make it happen."

Adam dredged his mind for any trace of these events that might have merely been submerged for lack of currency, but he found nothing. "So should I be thanking you, or apologizing? Did I give you a hard time about the script?"

"Not at all. I showed you drafts now and then, and if you had a strong opinion you let me know, but you didn't cross any lines."

"The book itself didn't do that well," Adam recalled.

Auster didn't argue. "Even the publishers stopped using the phrase 'slow-burning cult hit,' though I'm sure the studio would have put that in the press release, if it had ever gone ahead."

Adam hesitated. "So, what else was going on?" The old man hadn't published much in that decade; just a few pieces in magazines. His book sales had dried up, and he'd been working odd jobs to make ends meet. But at least back then there'd still been golden opportunities like valet parking. "Did we socialize much? Did I talk about things?"

Auster scrutinized him. "This isn't just smoothing over the business at the funeral, is it? You've lost something that you think might be important, and now you're going all Dashiell Hammett on yourself."

"Yes," Adam admitted.

Auster shrugged. "OK, why not? That worked out so well in *Angel Heart*." He thought for a while. "When we weren't discussing *Sadlands*, you talked about your money problems, and you talked about Carlos."

"What about Carlos?"

"His money problems."

Adam laughed. "Sorry. I must have been fucking awful company."

Auster said, "I think Carlos was working three or four jobs, all for minimum wage, and you were working two, with a few hours a week set aside for writing. I remember you sold a story to the *New Yorker*, but the celebration was pretty muted, because the whole fee was gone, instantly, to pay off debts."

"*Debts?*" Adam had no memory of it ever being that bad. "Did I try to borrow money from you?"

"You wouldn't have been so stupid; you knew I was almost as skint. Just before we gave up, I got twenty grand in development money to spend a year trying to whip *Sadlands* into something that Sundance or AMC might buy – and believe me, it all went on rent and food."

"So what did *I* get out of that?" Adam asked, mock-jealously.

"Two grand, for the option. If it had gone to a pilot, I think you would have gotten twenty, and double that if the series was picked up." Auster smiled. "That must sound like small change to you now, but at the time it would have been the difference between night and day – especially for Carlos's sister."

"Yeah, she could be a real hard-ass," Adam sighed. Auster's face drained, as if Adam had just maligned a woman that everyone else had judged worthy of beatification. "What did I say?"

"You don't even remember *that*?"

"Remember what?"

"She was dying of cancer! Where did you think the money was going? You and Carlos weren't living in the Ritz, or shooting it up."

"OK." Adam recalled none of this. He'd known that Adelina had died long before Carlos, but he'd never even tried to summon up the details. "So Carlos and I were working eighty-hour weeks to pay her medical bills … and I was bitching and moaning to you about it, as if that might make the magic Hollywood money fall into my lap a little faster?"

"That's putting it harshly," Auster replied. "You needed someone to vent to, and I had enough distance from it that it didn't weigh me down. I could commiserate and walk away."

Adam thought for a while. "Do you know if I ever took it out on Carlos?"

"Not that you told me. Would you have stayed together if you had?"

"I don't know," Adam said numbly. Could this be the whole point of the occlusions? When their relationship was tested, the old man had buckled, and he was so ashamed of himself that he'd tried to erase every trace of the event? Whatever he'd done, Carlos must have forgiven him in the end, but maybe that just made his own weakness more painful to contemplate.

"So I never pulled the pin?" he asked. "I didn't wash my hands of Adelina, and tell Carlos to fuck off and pay for it all himself?"

Auster said, "Not unless you were lying to me to save face. The version I heard was that every spare dollar you had was going to her, up until the day she died. Which is where forty grand might have made all the difference – bought her more time, or even a cure. I never got the medico-logistic details, but both of you took it hard when the Colman thing happened."

Adam moved his half-empty plate aside and asked wearily, "So what was 'the Colman thing'?"

Auster nodded apologetically. "I was getting to that. Sundance had shown a lot of interest in *Sadlands*, but then they heard that some Brit called Nathan Colman had sold a story to Netflix about, well … an epidemic of suicides spreading across the country, apparently at random, affecting people equally regardless of demographics."

"And we didn't sue the brazen fuck into penury?"

Auster snorted. "Who's this 'we' with money for lawyers? The production company that held the option did a cost-benefit analysis and decided to cut their losses; twenty-two grand down the toilet, but it wasn't as if they'd been cheated out of the next *Game of Thrones*. All you and I could do was suck it up, and take a few moments of solace whenever a *Sadlands* fan posted an acerbic comment in some obscure chat-room."

Adam's visceral sense of outrage was undiminished, but on any sober assessment this outcome was pretty much what he would have expected.

"Of course, my faith in karma was restored, eventually," Auster added enigmatically.

"You've lost me again." The old man's success, once he cut out all the middlemen and plagiarists, must have been balm to his wounds – but Auster's online footprint suggested that his own third act had been less lucrative.

"Before they'd finished shooting the second season, a burglar broke into Colman's house and cracked open his skull with a statuette."

"An Emmy?"

"No, just a BAFTA."

Adam tried hard not to smile. "And once *Sadlands* fell through, did we stay in touch?"

"Not really," Auster replied. "I moved here a long time after you did; I wasted five years trying to get something up on Broadway before I swallowed my pride and settled for playing script doctor. And by then, you'd done so well that I was embarrassed to turn up asking you for work."

Adam was genuinely ashamed now. "You should have. I owed it to you."

Auster shook his head. "I wasn't living on the streets. I've done all right here. I can't afford what you've got ..." He gestured at Adam's imperishable chassis. "But then, I'm not sure I could handle the lacunae."

Adam called for a car. Auster insisted on splitting the bill.

The service cart rattled over and began clearing the table. Auster said, "I'm glad I could help you fill in the blanks, but maybe those answers should have come with a warning."

"*Now* a warning?"

"The Colman thing. Don't let it get to you."

Adam was baffled. "Why would I? I'm not going to sue his family for whatever pittance is still trickling down to them." In fact, he couldn't sue anyone for anything, but it was the thought that counted.

"OK." Auster was ready to drop it, but now Adam needed to be clear.

"How badly did I take it the first time?"

Auster gestured with one finger, drilling into his temple. "Like a fucking parasitic worm in your brain. He'd stolen your precious novel and murdered your lover's sister. He'd kicked you to the ground when you had nothing, and taken your only hope away."

Adam could understand now why they hadn't stayed in touch. Solidarity in hard times was one thing, but an obsessive grievance like that would soon get old. Auster had taken his own kicks and decided to move on.

"That was more than thirty years ago," Adam replied. "I'm a different person now."

"Aren't we all?"

Auster's ride came first. Adam stood outside the diner and watched him depart: sitting confidently behind the wheel, even if he didn't need to lay a finger on it.

## 8

Adam changed his car's destination to downtown Gardena. He disembarked beside a row of fast-food outlets and went looking for a public web kiosk. He'd been fretting about the best way of paying without leaving too obvious a trail, but then he discovered that in this municipality the things were as free as public water fountains.

There was no speck of entertainment industry trivia that the net had failed to immortalize. Colman had moved from London to Los Angeles to shoot the series, and he'd been living just a few miles south of Adam's current home when the break-in happened. But the old man had still been in New York at the time; he hadn't even set foot in California until the following year, as far as Adam recalled. The laptop that he'd started excavating had files on it dating back to the '90s, but they would have been copied from machine to machine; there was no chance that the computer itself was old enough to be carrying deleted emails for flights booked three decades ago, even if the old man had been foolish enough to make his journey so easy to trace.

Adam turned away from the kiosk's chipped projection screen, wondering if any passersby had been staring over his shoulder. He was losing his grip on reality. The occlusions might easily have been targeted at nothing more than the old man's lingering resentment: if he couldn't let go of what had happened – even after Colman's death, even after his own career had blossomed – he might have wished to spare Adam all that pointless, fermented rage.

That was the simplest explanation. Unless Auster had been holding back, the thought of the old man murdering Colman didn't seem to have crossed his mind, and if the police had come knocking he would surely have mentioned that. If nobody else thought the old man was guilty, who was Adam to start accusing him – on the basis of nothing but the shape and location of one dark pit of missing memories, among the thirty percent of everything that he didn't recall?

He turned to the screen again, trying to think of a more discriminating test of his hypothesis. Though the flow into the side-load itself would have been protected by a massive firewall of privacy laws, Adam doubted that any instructions to the technicians at Loadstone were subject to privilege. Which meant that, even if he found them on the laptop, they were unlikely to be incriminatory. The only way the old man could have phrased a request to forget that he'd bashed Colman's brains out would have been to excise all of the more innocent events that were connected to it in any way, like a cancer surgeon choosing the widest possible sacrificial margin. But he might also have issued the same instructions merely in order to forget as much as possible of that whole bleak decade – when Hollywood had fucked him over, Carlos had been grieving for the woman who raised him, and he'd somehow, just barely, kept it together, long enough to make a new start in the '20s.

Adam logged off the kiosk. Auster had warned him not to become obsessed – and the man was the closest thing to a friend that he had right now. If everyone in the industry really staved in the skulls of everyone who'd crossed them, there'd be no one left to run the place.

He called a car and headed home.

## 9

Under protest, at Adam's request, Sandra spread the three sturdy boxes out on the floor, and opened them up to reveal the foam, straps, and recesses within. They reminded Adam of the utility trunks that the old man's crews had used for stowing their gear.

"Don't freak out on me," she pleaded.

"I won't," Adam promised. "I just want a clear picture in my mind of what's about to happen."

"Really? I don't even let my dentist show me his planning videos."

"I trust you to do a better job than any dentist."

"You're too kind." She gestured at the trunks like a proud magician, bowing her head for applause.

Adam said, "Now you have no choice, El Dissecto: you've got to take a picture for me once it's done."

"I hope your Spanish is better than you're making it sound."

"I was aiming for vaudevillian, not voseo." Adam had some memories of the old man being prepared for surgery, but he wasn't sure that it was possible to rid them of survivor's hindsight and understand exactly how afraid he'd been that he might never wake up.

Sandra glanced at her watch. "No more clowning around. You need to undress and lie down on the bed, then repeat the code phrase aloud, four times. I'll wait outside."

Adam didn't care if she saw him naked while he was still conscious, but it might have made her uncomfortable. "OK." Once she left, he stopped stalling; he removed his clothes quickly, and began the chant.

"Red lentils, yellow lentils. Red lentils, yellow lentils. Red lentils, yellow lentils." He glanced past the row of cases to Sandra's toolbox; he'd seen inside it before, and there were no cleavers, machetes or chainsaws. Just magnetic screwdrivers that could loosen bolts within him without even penetrating his skin. He lay back and stared at the ceiling. "Red lentils, yellow lentils."

The ceiling stayed white but sprouted new shadows, a ventilation grille and a light fitting, while the texture of the bedspread beneath his skin went from silken to beaded. Adam turned his head; the same clothes as he'd removed were folded neatly beside him. He dressed quickly, walked over to the connecting door between the suites, and knocked.

Sandra opened the door. She'd changed her clothes since he'd last seen her, and she looked exhausted. His watch showed 11:20 pm local time, 9:20 back home.

"I just wanted to let you know that I'm still in here," he said, pointing to his skull.

She smiled. "OK, Adam."

"Thank you for doing this," he added.

"Are you kidding? They're paying me all kinds of allowances and overtime, and it's not even that long a flight. Feel free to come back here as often as you like."

He hesitated. "You didn't take the photo, did you?"

Sandra was unapologetic. "No. It could have gotten me sacked, and not all of the company's rules are stupid."

"OK. I'll let you sleep. See you in the morning."

"Yeah."

Adam lay awake for an hour before he could bring himself to mutter his code word for the milder form of sleep. If he'd wished, Loadstone could have given him a passable simulation of the whole journey – albeit with a lot of cheating to mask the time it took to shuffle him back and forth between their servers and his body. But the airlines didn't recognize any kind of safe "flight mode" for his kind of machine, even when he was in pieces and locked inside three separate boxes. The way he'd experienced it was the most honest choice: a jump-cut, and thirteen hours lost to the gaps.

In the morning, Sandra had arranged to join an organized tour of the sights of San Salvador. Her employer's insurance company was more concerned about her safety than Adam's, and in any case it would have been awkward for both of them to have her following him around with her toolbox.

"Just keep the license on you," she warned him before she left. "I had to fill out more forms to get it than I would to clear a drone's flight path twice around the world, so if you lose it I'm not coming to rescue you from the scrapyard."

"Who's going to put me there?" Adam spread his arms and stared down at his body. "Are you calling me a Ken doll?" He raised one forearm to his face and examined it critically, but the skin around his elbow wrinkled with perfect verisimilitude.

"No, but you talk like a foreigner, and you don't have a passport. So just ... stay out of trouble."

"Yes, ma'am."

The old man had only visited the city once, and with Carlos leading him from nightspot to childhood haunt to some cousin's apartment like a ricocheting bullet, he'd made no attempt to navigate for himself. But Adam had been disappointed when he'd learned that Beatriz was now living in an entirely different part of town; there'd be no cues along the way, no hooks to bring back other memories of the time.

Colonia Layco was half an hour's drive from the hotel. There were more autonomous cars on the street than Adam remembered, but enough electric scooters interspersed among them to keep the traffic from mimicking L.A.'s spookily synchronized throbbing.

The car dropped him off outside a newish apartment block. Adam entered the antechamber in the lobby and found the intercom.

"Beatriz, this is Adam."

"Welcome! Come on up!"

He pushed through the swing doors and took the stairs, ascending four flights; it wouldn't make him any fitter, but old habits died hard. When Beatriz opened the door of her apartment he was prepared for her to flinch, but she just stepped out and embraced him. Maybe the sight of wealthy Californians looking younger than their age had lost its power to shock anyone before she'd even been born.

She ushered him in, tongue-tied for a moment, perhaps from the need to suppress an urge to ask about his flight, or inquire about his health. She settled, finally, on "How have things been?"

Her English was infinitely better than his Spanish, so Adam didn't even try. "Good," he replied. "I've been taking a break from work, so I thought I owed you a visit." The last time they'd met had been at Carlos's funeral.

She led him into the living room and gestured toward a chair, then fetched a tray of pastries and a pot of coffee. Carlos had never found the courage to come out to Adelina, but Beatriz had known his secret long before her mother died. Adam had no idea what details of the old man's life Carlos might have confided in her, but he'd exhausted all the willing informants who'd known the old man firsthand, and she'd responded so warmly to his emails that he'd had no qualms about attempting to revive their relationship for its own sake.

"How are the kids?" he asked.

Beatriz turned and gestured proudly toward a row of photographs on a bookcase behind her. "That's Pilar at her graduation last year; she started at the hospital six months ago. Rodrigo's in his final year of engineering."

Adam smiled. "Carlos would have been over the moon."

"Of course," Beatriz agreed. "We teased him a lot once he started with the acting, but his heart was always with us. With you, and with us."

Adam scanned the photographs and spotted a thirty-something Carlos in a suit, beside a much younger woman in a wedding dress.

"That's you, isn't it?" He pointed at the picture.

"Yes."

"I'm sorry I didn't make it." He had no memory of Carlos leaving for the wedding, but it must have taken place a year or two before they'd moved to L.A.

Beatriz tutted. "You would have been welcome, Adam, but I knew how tight things were for you back then. We all knew what you'd done for my mother."

*Not enough to keep her alive*, Adam thought, but that would be a cruel and pointless thing to say. And he hoped that Carlos had spared his sister's children any of the old man's poisonous talk of the windfall they'd missed out on.

Beatriz had her own idea of the wrongs that needed putting right. "Of course she didn't know, herself. She knew he had a friend who helped him out, but Carlos had to make it sound like you were rich, that you were loaning him the money and it was nothing to you. He should have told her the truth. If she'd thought of you as family, she wouldn't have refused your help."

Adam nodded uncomfortably, unsure just how graciously or otherwise the old man had handed over paycheck after paycheck for a woman who had no idea who he was. "That was a long time ago. I just want to meet your children and hear all your news."

"Ah." Beatriz grimaced apologetically. "I should warn you that Rodrigo's bringing his boyfriend to lunch."

"That's no problem at all." What twenty-year-old engineer wouldn't want to show off the animatronic version of Great Uncle Movie Star's lover to as many people as possible?

When Adam got back to the hotel it was late in the afternoon. He messaged Sandra, who replied that she was in a bar downtown having a great time and he was welcome to join her. Adam declined and lay down on the bed. The meal he'd just shared had been the most normal thing he'd experienced since his embodiment. He'd come within a hair's breadth of convincing himself that there was a place for him here: that he could somehow insert himself into this family and survive on their affection alone, as if this one day's hospitality and good-natured curiosity could be milked forever.

As the glow of borrowed domesticity faded, the tug of the past reasserted itself. He had to keep trying to assemble the pieces, as and when he found them. He took out his laptop and searched through archived social media posts, seeing if he could date Beatriz's wedding. Pictures had a way of getting wildly mislabeled, or grabbed by bots and repurposed at random, so even when he had what looked like independent confirmation from four different guests, he didn't quite trust the result, and he paid a small fee for access to the Salvadorian government's records.

Beatriz had been married on March 4th, 2018. Adam didn't need to open the spread-sheet he was using to assemble his time-line for the gaps to know that the surrounding period would be sparsely annotated, save for one entry. Nathan Colman had been bludgeoned to death by an intruder on March 10th of the same year.

Carlos would hardly have flown in for the wedding and left the next day; the family would have expected him to stay for at least a couple of weeks. The old man would have been alone in New York, with no one to observe his comings and goings. He might even have had time to cross the country and return by bus, paying with cash, breaking the trip down into small stages, hitch-hiking here and there, obfuscating the bigger picture as much as possible.

The dates proved nothing, of course. If Adam had been a juror in a trial with a case this flimsy, he would have laughed the prosecution out of court. He owed the old man the same standard of evidence.

Then again, in a trial the old man could have stood in the witness box and explained exactly what it was that he'd gone to so much trouble to hide.

The flight to L.A. wasn't until six in the evening, but Sandra was too hung-over to leave the hotel, and Adam had made no plans. So they sat in his room watching movies and ordering snacks from the kitchen, while Adam worked up the courage to ask her the question that had kept him awake all night.

"Is there any way you could get me the specifications for my targeted occlusions?" Adam waited for her response before daring to raise the possibility of payment. If the request was insulting in itself, offering a bribe would only compound the offense.

"No," she replied, as unfazed as if he'd wondered aloud whether room service might stretch to shiatsu. "That shit is locked down tight. After last night, it would take me all day to explain homomorphic encryption to you, so you'll just have to take my word for it: nobody alive can answer that, even if they wanted to."

"But I've recovered bills from his laptop that mention it," Adam protested. "So much for Fort fucking Knox!"

Sandra shook her head. "That means that he was careless – and I should probably get someone in account generation to rethink their line items – but Loadstone would have held his hand very, very tightly when it came to spelling out the details. Unless he wrote it down in his personal diary, the information doesn't exist any more."

Adam didn't think that she was lying to him. "There are things I need to know," he said simply. "He must have honestly believed that I'd be better off without them – but if he'd lived long enough for me to ask him face to face, I know I could have changed his mind."

Sandra paused the movie. "Very little software is perfect, least of all when it's for something as complex as this. If we fail to collect everything we aim to collect …"

"Then you also fail to block everything you aim to block," Adam concluded. "Which was probably mentioned somewhere in the fine print of his contract, but I've been racking my brain for months without finding a single stone that punched a hole in the sieve."

"What if the stones only got through in fragments, but they can still be put together?"

Adam struggled to interpret this. "Are you telling me to take up repressed memory therapy?"

"No, but I could get you a beta copy of Stitcher on the quiet."

"Stitcher?"

"It's a new layer they'll eventually be offering to every client," Sandra explained. "It's in the nature of things, with the current methods, that the side-load will end up with a certain amount of implicit information that's not in an easily accessible form: thousands of tiny glimpses of memories that were never brought across whole, but which could still be described in detail if you pieced together every partial sighting."

"So this software could reassemble the shredded page of a notebook that still holds an impression of what was written on the missing page above?"

Sandra said, "For someone with a digital brain, you're about as last-century as they come."

Adam gave up trying to harmonize their metaphors. "Will it tell me what I want to know?"

"I have no idea," Sandra said bluntly. "Among the fragments bearing implicit information – and there will certainly be thousands of them – it will recognize some unpredictable fraction of their associations, and let you follow the new threads that arise. But I don't know if that will be enough to tell you anything more than the color of the sweater your mother was wearing on your first day of school."

"OK."

Sandra started the movie again. "You really should have joined me in the bar last night," she said. "I told them I had a friend who could drink any Salvadorian under the table, and they were begging for a chance to bet against you."

"You're a sick woman," Adam chided her. "Maybe next time."

## 10

Reassembled back in California, Adam took his time deciding whether to make one last, algorithmic attempt to push through the veil. If the truth was that the old man had been a murderer, what good would come of knowing it? Adam had no intention of "confessing" the crime to the authorities, and taking his chances with whatever legal outcome the courts might eventually disgorge. He was not a person; he could not be prosecuted or sued, but Loadstone could be ordered to erase every copy of his software, and municipal authorities instructed to place his body in a hydraulic compactor beside unroadworthy cars and unskyworthy drones.

But even if he faced no risk of punishment, he doubted that Colman's relatives would be better off knowing that what they'd always imagined was a burglary gone wrong had actually been a premeditated ambush. It should not be for him to judge their best interests, of course, but the fact remained that he'd be the one making the decision, and for all the horror he felt about the act itself and the harm that had been done, his empathy for the survivors pushed him entirely in the direction of silence.

So if he did this, it would be for his benefit alone. For the relief of knowing that the old man had simply been a vain, neurotic self-mythologizer who'd tried to leave behind the director's cut of his life ... or for the impetus to disown him completely, to torch his legacy in every way he could and set out on a life of his own.

Adam asked Sandra to meet him at Caesar's Diner. He slid a small parcel of cash onto her seat, and she slipped a memory stick into his hand.

"What do I do with this?" he asked.

"Just because you can't see all your ports in the bathroom mirror doesn't mean they're not there." She wrote a sequence of words on a napkin and passed it to Adam; it read like "Jabberwocky" mis-transcribed by someone on very bad drugs. "Four times, and that will take the side of your neck off without putting you to sleep."

"Why is that even possible?"

"You have no idea how many Easter eggs you're carrying."

"And then what?"

"Plug it in, and it will do the rest. You won't be paralyzed, you won't lose consciousness. But it will work best if you lie down in the dark and close your eyes. When you're done, just pull it out. Working the skin panel back into place might take a minute or two, but once it clicks it will be a waterproof seal again." She hesitated. "If you can't get it to click, try wiping the edges of both the panel and the aperture with a clean chamois. Please don't put machine oil on anything; it won't help."

"I'll bear that in mind."

Adam stood in the bathroom and recited the incantation from the napkin, half expecting to see some leering apparition take his place in the mirror as the last syllable escaped his lips. But there was just a gentle pop as the panel on his neck flexed and came loose. He caught it before it fell to the floor and placed it on a clean square of paper towel.

It was hard to see inside the opening he'd made, and he wasn't sure he wanted to, but he found the port easily by touch alone. He walked into the bedroom, took the memory stick from the side table, then lay down and dimmed the lights. A part of him felt like an ungrateful son, trespassing on the old man's privacy, but if he'd wanted to take his secrets to the grave then he should have taken all of his other shit with them.

Adam pushed the memory stick into place.

Nothing seemed to have happened, but when he closed his eyes he saw himself kneeling at the edge of the bed in the room down the hall, weeping inconsolably, holding the bedspread to his face. Adam shuddered; it was like being back in the servers, back in the interminable side-loading dream. He followed the thread out into the darkness, for a long time finding nothing but grief, but then he turned and stumbled upon Carlos's funeral, riotous in its celebration, packed with gray-haired friends from New York and a dozen of Carlos's relatives, raucously drowning out the studio executives and sync-flashing the paparazzi.

Adam walked over to the casket and found himself standing beside a hospital bed, clasping just one of those rough familiar hands in both of his own.

"It's all right," Carlos insisted. There wasn't a trace of fear in his eyes. "All I need is for you to stay strong."

"I'll try."

Adam backed away into the darkness and landed on set. He'd thought it was a risky indulgence to put an amateur in even this tiny part, but Carlos had sworn that he wouldn't take offense if his one and only performance ended up on the cutting room floor. He just wanted a chance to know if it was possible, one way or the other.

Detective Number Two said, "You'll need to come with us, ma'am," then took Gemma Freeman's trembling arm in his hand as he led her away.

In the editing suite, Adam addressed Cynthia bluntly. "Tell me if I'm making a fool of myself."

"You're not," she said. "He's got a real presence. He's not going to do Lear, but if he can hit his marks and learn his lines ..."

Adam felt a twinge of disquiet, as if they were tempting fate by asking too much. But maybe it was apt. They'd propelled themselves into this orbit together; neither could have gotten here alone.

On the day they arrived, they'd talked a total stranger into breaking through a fence and hiking up Mount Lee with them so they could take each other's photographs beneath the Hollywood sign. Adam could smell the sap from broken foliage on his scratched forearms.

"Remember this guy," Carlos told their accomplice proudly. "He's going to be the next big thing. They already bought his script."

"For a pilot," Adam clarified. "Only for a pilot."

He rose up over the hills, watching day turn to night, waiting for an incriminating flicker of déjà vu to prove that he'd been in this city before. But the memories that came to him were all from the movies: *L.A. Confidential*, *Mulholland Drive*.

He flew east, soaring over city lights and blackened deserts, alighting back in their New York apartment, hunched over his computer, pungent with sweat, trying to block out the sound of Carlos haggling with the woman who'd come to buy their air-conditioner. He stared at the screen unhappily, and started removing dialog, shifting as much as he could into stage directions instead.

*She takes his bloodied fist in both hands, shocked and sickened by what he's done, but she understands—*

The screen went blank. The laptop should have kept working in the black-out, but the battery had been useless for months. Adam picked up a pen and started writing on a sheet of paper: *She understands that she pushed him into it – unwittingly, but she still shares the blame.*

He stopped and crumpled the sheet into a ball. Flecks of red light streamed across his vision; he felt as if he'd caught himself trying to leap onto a moving train. But what choice did he have? There was no stopping it, no turning it back, no setting it right. He had to find a way to ride it, or it would destroy them.

Carlos called out to Adam to come and help carry the air-conditioner down the stairs. Every time they stopped to rest on a darkened landing, the three of them burst out laughing.

When the woman drove away they stood on the street, waiting for a breeze to shift the humid air. Carlos placed a hand on the back of Adam's neck. "Are you going to be all right?"

"We don't need that heap of junk," Adam replied.

Carlos was silent for a while, then he said, "I just wanted to give you some peace."

When he'd taken out the memory stick and closed his wound, Adam went into the old man's room and lay on his bed in the dark. The mattress beneath him felt utterly familiar, and the gray outlines of the room seemed exactly as they ought to be, as if he'd lain here a thousand times. This was the bed he'd been struggling to wake in from the start.

What they'd done, they'd done for each other. He didn't have to excuse it to acknowledge that. To turn Carlos in, to offer him up to death row, would have been unthinkable – and the fact that the law would have found the old man blameless if he'd done so only left Adam less willing to condemn him. At least he'd shown enough courage to put himself at risk if the truth ever came out.

He gazed into the shadows of the room, unable to decide if he was merely an empathetic onlooker, judging the old man with compassion – or the old man himself, repeating his own long-rehearsed defense.

*How close was he to crossing the line?*

Maybe he had enough, now, to write from the same dark place as the old man – and in time to outdo him, making all his fanciful ambitions come true.

But only by becoming what the old man had never wanted him to be. Only by rolling the same boulder to the giddy peak of impunity, then watching it slide down into the depths of remorse, over and over again, with no hope of ever breaking free.

## 11

Adam waited for the crew from the thrift store to come and collect the boxes in which he'd packed the old man's belongings. When they'd gone, he locked up the house, and left the key in the combination safe attached to the door.

Gina had been livid when he'd talked to Ryan directly and shamed him into taking the deal: the family could have the house, but the bulk of the old man's money would go to a hospital in San Salvador. What remained would be just enough to keep Adam viable: paying his maintenance contract, renewing his license to walk in public, and stuffing unearned stipends into the pockets of the figure-heads of the shell companies whose sole reason to exist was to own him.

He strode toward the gate, wheeling a single suitcase. Away from the shelter of the old man's tomb, he'd have no identity of his own to protect him, but he'd hardly be the first undocumented person who'd tried to make it in this country.

When the old man's life had disintegrated, he'd found a way to turn the shards into stories that meant something to people like him. But Adam's life was broken in a different way, and the world would take time to catch up. Maybe in twenty years, maybe in a hundred, when enough of them had joined him in the Valley, he'd have something to say that they'd be ready to hear.

# SEVENTH SIGHT

## 1

On my twelfth birthday, my cousin Sean sent me the keys to the rainbow. I carried them around in my phone for six days, unused, burning a hole in my pocket. Sean had hacked his own implants almost eighteen months before, so I was fairly sure that it would be safe to follow him, but I couldn't begin to imagine what would happen if my father caught me rewiring my retinas.

I waited for a Sunday afternoon, when my parents were preoccupied with a movie. I closed the door to my room and drew the curtains. The door had no lock, so I lay in bed with my head under the covers, staring at my phone until the screen went dark. In the blackness I thought about my grandfather, blinded by nothing more than the gene we shared, but sightless for so long that the implants had been powerless to bring him back into the light. My confidence in the trail Sean had blazed began to waver; his implants and mine were the same model, but everyone's body was unique. I did not want to end up blind – and even if the changes I wrought were reversible with a trip to the optometrist to restore the implants' settings, that was not something I could do without my parents finding out.

I jiggled the phone and it lit up again, showing the circular rainbow of the app's startup screen. The hues in this fanciful icon were crisper and clearer than those of any rainbow I'd seen in the sky, but then my bio-sighted friends had assured me that they could never make out the mythical "seven colors", either, and I had no reason to doubt them. My implants did their best to mimic the color vision of the human eye, by matching the typical responses of the three kinds of human cone cells. But this mimicry was a matter of choice, not necessity – and I wouldn't need any new hardware inside my skull in order to move beyond it.

The quantum dots scattered across my artificial retinas included millions of spares, ready to step in if any of the currently active sensors failed. These spares were not pre-committed to any particular color, lest the demand for replacements skewed green or blue and left the red ones wasting space, like some unpopular flavor of Skittles. But since the choice was made, not with pigment molecules or colored filters, but by setting a series of voltages across a quantum well, there was nothing to constrain the possibilities to the three traditional colors. The app Sean had sent me could instruct the implants to wake all my spares – and tune them to four new bands, between and beyond the original three.

I ran a fingertip along the rainbow's edge, trying to reach a decision. The implants made me normal, they allowed me to fit in. Why ask for anything more? Left to my biological fate I would not have been fully blind for another decade, but my parents had opted for replacement as early as possible, giving me the best chance of adapting to the device.

But that had been six years ago. If I didn't try this experiment now, while my brain was still flexible enough to make sense of the new information, I might die without ever knowing what I'd missed.

I lifted my finger from its stalling arc and tapped the button above: CONTINUE.

The app needed to know the implants' serial numbers and service password, but both were printed plainly in my owner's manual. The manufacturer's warranty had expired, leaving nothing to void, and the app's screed claimed that it could hide its actions from any health professional making routine adjustments. So long as nothing went wrong that I couldn't fix by sending the spares back to sleep, there was a chance that my spectral trespasses would remain undetected.

The next screen showed response curves. The standard red and green ones already overlapped considerably, while the blue one stood almost aloof from them. The app's default choice was to squeeze two new curves in between blue and green, and then add one at the near-infrared end and one at the near-ultraviolet. There was also a set of default "opposition formulas", which specified the way in which information was to be extracted from various combinations of the new primary colors – just as the difference between the red and green responses was computed in every human eye and passed along to the brain.

The idea of *editing* any of these details – adding my own idiosyncratic twist to the process – made my hands sweat. I would not have known where to start constructing my own private notion of the ideal palette. But if that also proved that I was in no position to make an informed choice to accept the defaults, I took some comfort from the orderly appearance of the seven curves on offer. They covered the spectrum, evenly and efficiently, each little hill in the serried row peaking at a wavelength some fifty nanometers away from its neighbor. Nothing about them looked strange, demanding elaborate justifications from the depths of biophysics. Nothing cried out to be changed.

I hit ACCEPT, and moved on to the next page.

**WARNING**

**Activating and re-tuning spare sensors in your artificial retinas (ARs) may lead to permanent changes in your brain's visual pathways. While this app can restore the ARs to their original state, we make no such promises about your visual cortex.**

**The decision is yours alone.**

**The Rainbow Project**

This disclaimer did not unnerve me at all. That the brain was altered by the information it did or didn't receive was old news to me, writ large in my family's history. The implants had come just in time to help my father, but not as much as they had helped me, and my uncles and cousins of various ages joined up the dots. The more I thought about it, the surer I became that the most frightening thing would be to lose this chance, while Sean and his friends sprinted far ahead of me and disappeared into the far end of the rainbow.

I tapped PROCEED.

The warning gave way to a flickering Bluetooth icon and a progress bar. I watched the text above the bar spelling out the stages as the app and implants worked together: cataloging the spare sensors, testing them internally, retuning them, testing them again.

The progress bar paused at ninety-five percent, then the app asked me if the sky was clear and I'd obtained a suitable prism. It was, and I had. I climbed out of bed and opened the curtains to admit a narrow wedge of sunlight, then I placed the prism Sean had given me on my desk and moved it back and forth until the spectrum it cast on the wall formed an uninterrupted band.

Following the app's instructions, I turned my head slowly, shifting my gaze steadily across the spectrum from left to right, starting just before the red end. In my earbuds the app counted down the nanometers as it verified its tweaks to the quantum dots at every wavelength. It was all reassuringly mundane, like a human version of the procedure after changing an ink cartridge, where you print and scan an alignment page.

The app said, "Done". I looked down at my phone, and the progress bar had reached one hundred percent. The image zoomed out to show the circular rainbow again, then it shrank to a point and the app quit, taking me back to the phone's home screen.

I opened the curtains and let the sunlight fill my room. Nothing looked different; I'd been warned that any change in the way I perceived the world could take days or weeks. But my impatience was offset by a sense of relief: whatever else I'd done, at least I hadn't damaged the implants and left myself blind.

"These flowers are dying," I told my father as I set the table for dinner. "Do you want me to throw them out?"

"Dying?" He stepped out of the kitchen and peered at the centerpiece, then came closer and examined the individual blooms. "They're fine, Jake. What are you talking about?"

"Sorry," I said stupidly. "It must have been a trick of the light."

He frowned, puzzled, but then went back to draining vegetables. I fetched my mother and my sister, and we all sat down to eat.

Throughout the meal, I kept stealing glances at the flowers. My father grew a few different kinds in a small garden at the front of the house, and though I'd never taken much interest in them I couldn't help but be familiar with their appearance at various stages of health and decay. In fact, these daffodils hadn't even wilted: the petals were firm, not drooping. Yet the uniform yellow I was accustomed to had been modified by a flared pattern that I'd mistaken for a kind of withering, with streaks radiating out from the center of each flower that looked like shadows, not so much discolored as subdued.

It was only when I stopped worrying about the flowers and paid attention to my family that I realized how far the change had progressed. My father's face looked as if he'd developed a rash, albeit with a strong left-right symmetry, his cheeks flushed red and a roseate Rorschach blot decorating his temple. But if the effect was disconcertingly close to bad-TV-alien makeup, my mother and sister wore much the same mask with a twist: their actual cosmetics, which I usually barely noticed, now looked as if they'd been applied by an eager four-year-old who'd viewed the process as a form of finger-painting. Streaks and ridges stood out all over their faces; it was all I could do to keep myself from staring, or making some inane, self-incriminating joke by asking them whether they'd enjoyed their mud baths.

After dinner, the four of us sat down to watch a sitcom, giving me an excuse to keep my eyes on the screen instead of the garish people around me. But the longer I spent gazing at the electronic image the flatter its colors seemed, until the live action began to resemble some kind of stylized animation. It was not that I'd yet started to think of my family's facial decorations as normal, but the actors' skin tones looked as plastic as any mannequin's, and the sets around them like the pastel story-book castles from a children's show. I only had to glance across at the couch on which my parents sat to see how much richer and subtler the hues of the simplest real object could be.

In bed, I lay awake wondering whether I should restore the implants to their original state. If I'd wanted everyone around me to look like a clown, there was an app that daubed face-paint over the image from my phone's camera, but the novelty of that had worn off in half an hour when I was eight years old. I couldn't believe that my fourteen-year-old cousin had talked me into imagining that I'd be joining some kind of sophisticated elite.

Just before midnight, I messaged Sean: **This is horrible, everything looks ugly. Why did you make me do it?**

He replied: **Be patient. Wait a week. If you still don't like it, it's not too late to go back.**

I stared into the shadows, still feeling cheated. But I'd been a trichromat for twelve years; I needed to give myself a chance to wrap my mind around the new sensorium.

As I placed the phone on my bedside table, I suddenly realized how much more clearly than usual I was perceiving the details of the room. It was not that I'd magically acquired thermal night vision – nothing cooler than a clothes iron would emit the kind of infrared my sensors could pick up – but traces of illumination from a neighbor's house were spilling through the gaps around my curtain, and though once this would have granted me nothing more than a few impressionistic hints in gray, the rainbow app had transformed the view, imbuing it with a subtle palette of colors that made every object stand out from the gloom.

The effect wasn't comical, or ugly. It felt as if I was seeing more deeply into the night world: sharpening its edges without diminishing its allure. I fell asleep and dreamed that I was flying across the neighborhood, an eagle-eyed raptor dragging secrets out of the darkness.

The next few days of school were an exercise in learning not to stare at stained clothes and strangely spackled faces – let alone display any stronger reaction that might lead to violence, disciplinary action, or just the dangerously unanswerable question: *What's so funny?* Whenever the temptation to smirk at a particularly zombie-esque schoolmate or Revlon-bombed teacher threatened to overpower me, I reminded myself that I looked every bit as ridiculous. I didn't need a mirror: just glancing down at the sweat marks on my shirt, which resembled the gray silt left behind by retreating flood waters, brought a pang of humiliation that was enough to wipe the smile from my lips.

Every painted wall looked slapdash and dirty, and even bare brickwork seemed to be decaying, infested with some exotic new form of mold. A part of me understood full well that this riot of variegation wasn't really so wild – that the eighteen or twenty different tones I could discern on the surface of every brick all still belonged to what I would once have seen and named as exactly the same shade of red. But it was impossible to shake the impression that these newly revealed distinctions had to mean something: a once-uniform surface that had turned mottled couldn't possibly hold together for long, and one good kick ought to be enough to break it apart like a rotten floorboard.

The sky did not look blemished, but when I gazed at any part of its gentle gradient I knew exactly where the sun lay, and before long I could also judge the time of day to the nearest half hour. Sky blue was still sky blue, but now it came in a hundred delicate rings centered on the solar disk – and then imprinted with a second, subtler pattern whose bull's eye was the zenith. Eleven a.m. had a mood of its own now, as distinct from noon as sunset or dawn.

The following Sunday, Sean asked me to meet him at the beach. On the bus to the coast, I stared out at the car yards and advertising signs. Even the brand new BMWs looked like grubby plastic shells torn from some fairground ride, and the art-directed posters might have been lifted from a therapeutic crayon-sketching session at a hospital for the criminally tasteless. The strange blush of real human skin was growing on me, though; when I glanced across the aisle at a teenaged girl, her eyes closed as she listened to a track whose pounding bass leaked out from her skull and crossed the gap between us, there was nothing comical or repellent about the visible ebb and flow in the capillaries below her cheekbones.

I waited by the roadside for someone's older brother to drop off Sean and three friends with their surfboards. As we walked through the dunes, Sean let the others get ahead of us. "How's it looking now?" he asked.

"Better, I suppose." His own face was smeared with sunscreen, but there was an eerie precision to each daub: if I had not already known that we were seeing the world through identical eyes, this would have proved it. I looked around at the low, sturdy bushes that anchored the dunes; their small, dark-green leaves weren't much different than I remembered them. "At least I'm not freaking out all the time."

"Good." He was smiling sneakily, as if he had a handful of something unpleasant hidden behind his back that he was about to bring forward and drop down the neck of my T-shirt.

"What?" I asked, getting ready to retreat.

We came over the top of the dunes.

My skin turned to ice and my bowels loosened; mercifully they had nothing to expel. The ocean stretched out before us, as alien as if our last dozen steps had carried us a thousand light years. But then, even more alarmingly, the impossibly rich skeins of currents and ripples, patches of seaweed and changes of depth and turbidity, flexed like a vacillating optical illusion and settled firmly inside my old memories of the scene. What I perceived was no longer extraterrestrial: this was the same blue-green, white-foamed water I'd known all my life. Only now, without ever stepping outside the borders of its familiar colors, it was inscribed and annotated with such a richness of new detail that it was like holding up the palm of my hand to find my entire life story, in a million words and illustrations, discernible in the whorls and ridges of the skin.

One of Sean's friends called out to him impatiently, and he broke into a run. I watched him dragging his board into the surf; that wasn't my thing, but I could imagine – just barely – what he would make of the revelations that the ocean offered up to every glance.

As I waded into the breaking waves, I ducked down and splashed water on my face to make sure that no one would notice my tears. *This* was what it meant to see the world. *This* was my escape from the terror of blindness, from the family curse clawing at my heels: not the first, too-forgiving childhood version, when they'd unwrapped my bandages and over three long months taught me to turn a blur of muddy colors into the pale glimpse of reality that I'd naively accepted as the thing itself.

As I moved my hands through the swell, overwhelmed by the density of greens-within-green, for a second or two, or perhaps a whole minute, I actually believed that I'd been lied to: that everyone on Earth saw things this way, except for the poor fools with artificial eyes, who, if forced from a young enough age to lower their expectations, had no idea what they'd been missing.

But as this momentary delusion passed and my unwarranted anger dissipated, the inverted truth that replaced it was almost as disorienting. The world before me remained, undeniably, the world as it needed to be seen, and those to whom it was unreachable were as helpless and pitiful as if their empty sockets had been filled with glass or stone.

"Two p.m., Sunday the fourth," I muttered.

"What?" Mehdi followed my gaze, but saw nothing that could have prompted these words.

"Forget it." The message was painted clearly on the billboard we were passing – painted, over a patch of blue, in other shades of blue. In the small park the billboard overlooked, I could see more heptachromatic graffiti on benches and playground equipment, but I forced myself to stop staring and walk on.

"What did you think, Jake?" Dylan pressed me. Everyone else had spent the last ten minutes raving about the movie, but I'd kept my mouth shut.

"It was all right," I conceded.

"*All right?*" Quan glared at me as if I'd just spat on his shoes. "It was incredible!"

"OK."

Dylan, Mehdi and Quan had been my friends for years, and we'd got into the habit of seeing all the new 3D blockbusters together. I'd come along to this latest action flick because I hadn't wanted to offend them, but I'd known from the start that all the stunts and effects that might once have been breathtaking would be lost on me.

"When they lassoed his helicopter from the train, and he slid down the rope and jumped through that window—" Mehdi thumped his chest emphatically. "It was like doing the whole thing yourself, for real."

"Yeah," I lied. "That was cool."

The honest thing would have been to admit how phoney every last scene had appeared to me – and why. I couldn't risk news of my alteration getting back to my parents, but I had no reason to believe that my friends would betray me. The truth was, I didn't want them to know what I'd done. What was the point, when they had no hope of understanding it?

The next weekend, I told my parents I was seeing another movie. I arrived at the park at a quarter past one; it was empty of people, but the same message was still there on the billboard.

I hunted for some of the smaller scrawls I'd noticed in passing. **HEP RULES** and **FOUR MORE FEARS** were drawn repeatedly in ornate, almost indecipherable scripts, the style and colors the same each time. I was staring at one of these tags on a bench when someone spoke behind me.

"You want that as a tattoo?"

I turned. It was a girl, not much older than me. "Do you sterilize your needles?" I asked.

She laughed. "I didn't mean permanent. One day, maybe." She was carrying a backpack, holding its shoulder straps in her hand; she hefted it onto the bench and unzipped it. "I made the inks myself," she said, taking out a small bottle. "Six months of trial and error."

I peered into the backpack; there must have been forty vials in there. "That's a lot of work."

"The hard part is finding two or three that will be invisible to tris on lots of different backgrounds."

"How can you tell?" I wondered.

She took out her phone, tapped the screen and held it up, showing me its graffiti-free image of the bench. I felt my face flush at the stupidity of my question – and knowing how that would look only intensified the response.

"Why did you come early?" she asked. "That spoils the fun."

"You're early too," I countered.

"I'm not early, I'm here to mark the trail."

I'd half guessed that this would be some kind of treasure hunt. "So you're in charge?"

She nodded. "My name's Lucy."

"I'm Jake."

"Do you want to help me?"

"Sure."

A family had come into the park, a couple and two young kids, heading for the swings. The mother watched us suspiciously as Lucy took out a camel's hair brush and began painting on a corner of the billboard – but we weren't wielding spray-cans, and our watercolor vandalism seemed to be having no effect at all.

**Three blocks north then turn left**, Lucy wrote. **Listen for the sound of squealing brakes.**

"Let's go," she said, handing me the backpack. "You can carry this if you like."

We set out across the city, starting with a nearby amusement arcade. There was a Formula One game close to the western entrance, the sound effects blaring out onto the street; Lucy squatted down beside the wall and asked me for "number twenty-three". The vials in her backpack had been sorted into four separate pouches, making it easier to find each one. A few passersby looked at us askance, but if Lucy's brushstrokes left no mark it was hardly a police matter. I raised my phone and viewed the scene through tri eyes: she seemed to be delicately cleaning the brown-painted bricks.

When she handed the ink back to me, I looked at the label more carefully. "Cinnamon and cloves? That's what's in here?"

"No. That's just how I think of it."

I turned back to the words she'd written on the wall of the arcade: **East until you hit stale bread**. I doubted that I'd seen many spices in bulk since I'd run the rainbow app, but even if there was no literal resemblance the name did evoke the hue: a rich, sharp brown that ought to have smelled of those aromatic ingredients.

"Then what's it made of?"

Lucy smiled. "I'm not telling you. Work it out for yourself." She glanced at her watch. "We need to keep moving."

She let me paint the last clue, and the arrow that marked the treasure, though I needed her advice on the color schemes. The loot itself was a sheet of paper that she stuffed inside an empty toilet roll and hid behind a bush in a courtyard outside the museum.

"What does that number mean?" A long string of letters and digits had been written on the paper, in what I assumed was tri-invisible ink.

"It's a kind of code," Lucy explained. "If you type it into the web site you get another number that lets you prove that you were the winner."

"You built your own web site for this?"

She shook her head, amused. "It's for anyone. Tris play something similar, but they usually do it with GPS and AR: there are no real-world clues, but you can see them with your phone or your glasses."

"So do you stay here and watch?" I asked. "See how long people take?"

"Sometimes. We can do that if you like."

We sat on a bench with a view of the hiding place. Fifteen minutes later, a skinny young boy on a skateboard rolled up and went straight for the prize.

When he'd retrieved it, Lucy cupped her hands around her mouth and called out to him, "Well done, Tim!"

Tim skated across the courtyard to join us, thumbing numbers into his phone as he went. He looked about ten, which made me uneasy; Sean had implied that there was some unwritten code fixing the minimum age for the hack at twelve.

As Lucy was introducing us, two other competitors showed up. Before long there were a dozen people gathered around the bench, debating the merits of the hunt and cracking the kind of jokes about the ramshackle city and its hapless tris that would have been wasted in any other company. Tim was the youngest, but I'd have guessed that nobody was older than fourteen. I stayed quiet, conscious of my position as a newcomer, though nobody showed any sign of snubbing me.

As the afternoon wore on and people left, the dome of the sky seemed tinged with melancholy. When only Lucy and I were left, she read my thoughts.

"You think you've lost all your old friends," she said. "And a few random heps are no replacement."

I shrugged, embarrassed.

"You haven't lost anyone," she said. "It's good to get together with the rainbow crowd, but no one's forcing you to be a snob about it. Would your friends have dumped you if you'd gone blind?"

I shook my head, ashamed. "Have you told anyone?" I asked her. "Any of your tri friends?"

"No. But I still hang out with them. I just have to hold my tongue and not offer too many fashion tips."

Her own clothing appeared as grimy as anyone else's – and the technology to make it otherwise probably didn't exist outside of NASA clean rooms – but I could see her harmonious choices in the elements she could control.

"We do this on the first Sunday of every month," she said. "Tim will be marking the course next time – but if you like, we could team up and follow the clues together."

I said, "That sounds good."

2

"Call," I declared. If I couldn't quite keep my tone neutral, the faint tell in my voice sounded more like fear than confidence. Danny could only make three of a kind, and Cheng the same – albeit higher – while the dark-eyed woman who never gave her name could rise above them both with a straight. Everyone else at the table had folded, some of them needlessly. In that company, my own modest flush was a sure bet, but the last thing I felt was invincible.

Danny folded. Cheng raised the bet by fifty, then the dark-eyed woman raised it another fifty.

I agonized for five long seconds. My rule was never to win more than a thousand a night, and this would push me over the limit. But if I folded now, I would have spent eight hours in this dispiriting place for the sake of just three hundred dollars.

I slid my chips forward, matching the bet. Cheng shot an irritated glance my way, and folded.

The dark-eyed woman raised, again. Her face was so impassive that I began to doubt, if not the evidence of my own eyes, that of my memory. I didn't dare glance down at the backs of her cards again, but I was certain that one bore the twisted-hour-glass stain in the lacquer that I'd noticed on the five of clubs in the showdown-before-last, while the other had a florid tint to half its royal blue ink that had been unmissable when the six of hearts had come my way much earlier in the night. In this back-alley game they did not change the decks between every hand, and even if I could have missed the dealer feeding a fresh pack into the shuffling machine, no two decks ever featured identical flaws. So either I'd grown confused as to the significance of the blemishes I'd seen, or my opponent was very good at bluffing.

"I'll match," I said, offering up the chips.

The dark-eyed woman allowed herself a triumphant smile as she showed her cards: five of clubs, six of hearts. With the seven, eight and nine of diamonds in the flop she had a straight, but nothing better.

The relief on my own face wasn't feigned. I turned up my three and six of diamonds. The woman's lingering smile made me wonder if the loss had even registered before the dealer raked the pot and sent the rest in my direction, but perhaps the secret to her bluff had been a kind of self-hypnotic conviction that her hand was unbeatable, and it took a few seconds to snap out of it and allow the truth to sink in.

I scooped up my winnings and rose from the table.

"Hey, Jake!" Danny was scowling at me. "Give me a chance to win it back!" He was drunk, and he hadn't done well all night. I checked my watch and shook my head apologetically. "Next week, I promise."

I took my chips to the cashier, and glanced back at the table. Danny was staying put, to try his luck with the late crowd.

As I walked to my car, I skirted three glistening patches on the ground. The street lights were sparse here, but the neon fronts of the nightclubs in the adjoining strip were enough to illuminate the residual blood stains that spring rain seemed merely to rearrange, and no tri felt compelled to scrub away.

It was almost 4 a.m. when I got home, but Lucy was still up. "How'd it go?" she asked.

I showed her my winnings, fanning out the notes so she could count them at a glance.

Lucy had had her misgivings from the start, but now she seemed more anxious than ever. "I don't want you ending up in prison. Or worse."

"It wouldn't come to that. There's nothing they could prove; they'd just ban me." I slumped onto the couch. "You should be in bed," I chided her. Unless I'd become so confused by the card room's time-distorting ambience that I'd lost a day, she was due at work in less than five hours.

"And what if you do get banned?" she persisted.

"I never win enough to look suspicious." Heps were far too rare to pose much of a threat, and even the high-end casinos could hardly scan everyone's skulls with MRI machines. The small games I joined were run by people who were very far from amateurs, but so long as I could retain enough self-discipline not to overplay my advantage, I felt sure that I could hide in the statistical shadows of the merely lucky.

Lucy said, "The gallery's letting me go at the end of the month."

That shook me. Whatever fate I was courting, her own use of her talents could not have been more honest. "What are they going to replace you with – a mass spectrometer?"

"Not quite," she replied. "But there's some new software that pretty much does what I do, with a multispectral camera and brushstroke analysis. They can lease the whole thing for a tenth of my salary."

The gallery had only given her three days a week since she'd come back from maternity leave, but she still earned about as much as I dared acquire by my own methods.

"We're such fuck-ups," she said angrily.

"That's not true."

She turned away from me and gazed with loathing at one of her own paintings: a city threatened by fire, the skyscrapers scintillating through the smoke haze, every blistering current of air as palpable as the freeways below. "I kept kidding myself that I had a foot in the door – but I might as well have been a kitchen-hand, pretending that I was on some fast-track to chef just because I could sniff out bad produce a little sooner than anyone else."

"So they've found some machine to help them assess provenance," I said. "That doesn't take anything away from your paintings."

Lucy laughed bitterly. "If I couldn't sell anything even when I had connections, what do you think my chances are going to be now?"

"What are you saying?" I pressed her, aiming for a gently skeptical tone. "It's all down to nepotism?"

"No," she admitted. "The work does matter. But it's going to be harder than ever to get it seen."

I was trying to be the voice of reason, calmly talking her back from the edge – but the trouble was, she understood the problems she was facing far better than I did. "For an art dealer to look at a painting is some kind of special favor?"

"Yes," Lucy declared bluntly. "For a tri to look carefully enough to see a tenth of what's there takes something special. That doesn't happen as a matter of course."

I spread my arms in resignation, and went to take a shower.

On my way to bed, I looked in on Zelda. She'd slept through all the talking, and I resisted the urge to lean down and kiss her lest she wake and start bawling.

Zelda was almost six months old – so we only had six more to decide whether or not to give her the gene therapy vector. After that point, the quality of the repaired retinal cells would start to fall off with time. If she was going to be a tri at all I wanted her at least to have the sharpest vision that state could entail.

Five years before, when I'd moved in with Lucy, we'd sworn that we'd never sentence our children to live in the flat, cartoonish world that we'd escaped. But while Sean was still winning titles as a pro surfer, most of us had ended up struggling, thwarted or resentful. When I could count the number of heps I'd grown up with who had truly flourished on the fingers of one hand, how could I bequeath the same prospects to my daughter?

"I'll see that, and I'll raise you fifty," Marcus announced. I'd folded a few rounds ago, after forcing myself to stay in and lose a little for appearances' sake. Now there were only two players left, and they seemed to be intent on a game of chicken.

"I'll match," Danny replied. His hand was terrible, but at some point he must have convinced himself that he could bluff his way to victory, and having chosen that strategy he was too stubborn to veer off course.

Marcus raised another fifty.

"Fuck you," Danny whispered, and matched the bet.

I watched them with a growing sense of dread, willing Marcus to back down. I hadn't set eyes on him before that night, so I could still imagine that it was possible. Danny would just keep charging ahead like a freight train.

"I guess I'll have to raise you again," Marcus taunted him.

Danny slid the last of his chips forward. "Matched."

Marcus hesitated. "I'm good," he decided.

Danny laid down his pair of nines, which made two pairs beside the kings in the flop. Marcus had a king and queen in the hole, giving him trips; I could have made the same, but only with sevens. Everyone else had had rubbish.

The dealer took the house cut and slid the rest toward Marcus.

"Cheat," Danny said softly.

"Excuse me?" Marcus smiled and looked around the table; no one was backing Danny. "You should call it a night. Come back when your luck's better."

Danny leaned forward. "Risk all that on a trip? I don't think so."

The dealer said, "Sir, please."

Marcus gave an indignant bark of a laugh. "And look at what you risked the same on!"

"But you didn't need to," Danny countered. "If you'd raised again, you knew I couldn't match it."

"I didn't know what was in your wallet!" Marcus blustered. "You could have borrowed from someone – I'm not a mind reader!" I could see the blood draining from his face, and I understood: somehow, he really had known Danny's hand all along. And he'd betrayed himself, just so he could twist the knife.

Danny reached across the table and plucked Marcus's glasses from his face, like some curiously gentlemanly preamble to a pounding. The dealer raised his hand to summon a bouncer, but Danny didn't hit anyone, he simply perched the glasses on his own nose and looked down at the table.

"I knew it!" he declared triumphantly. He removed the glasses and offered them to the dealer. "Every card has a number in green!"

The dealer hesitated, then tried on the glasses for himself. "OK," he said nervously. "Everyone stay seated. The game's annulled, and you're all getting your bets returned."

Two bouncers and the manager joined us as the eye-in-the-sky vision was replayed and the chips were redistributed. Marcus sat in silence, his face blotched with fear. I knew the cards weren't marked with any kind of dye: his glasses had to be finding the same pre-existing subtleties as I was, then making the job easier for him by numbering the patterns in an overlay laser-painted on his retinas. I'd noticed the small dark circle in the center of the bridge, but I hadn't given it much thought – molded plastic always came with all kinds of odd impressions that its makers fancied were invisible. It was clear now, though, exactly what it was: a tiny multispectral camera, with sensors exactly like the ones in my own eyes.

When I got home the apartment was in darkness, so I took off my shoes and sat in the living room, planning to sleep on the couch. I was only twenty nine; my life was hardly over. Thousands of people slacked off in high school, dropped out of university, quit their first few jobs ... and still found a way to succeed in the end. If I'd wanted the one thing that lifted me above the crowd to be part of the answer, too bad. No one was going to pay me to see the world more clearly than they did – let alone stand by and let me use that talent to fleece them. Lucy could paint her paintings for our tiny circle of hep friends, and we could walk side by side marveling at the beauty of the sea and the sky and the squalor of the city. But in the end our powers of vision would die with us, outsourced entirely to unthinking machines.

"The ship is going down, and you only have time to grab one item and take it with you to the lifeboat: a sheet of plastic, a mirror, and a compass. Which do you choose?"

My interviewer leaned forward expectantly, his hand paused above his notepad.

I said, "This is a shelf-stacking job. I'm not applying to the ocean cruise department."

"Just say, 'plastic, to collect rainwater,'" he replied wearily. "Didn't you google the answers before you came?"

"Plastic, to collect rainwater."

He tapped the final box, and I heard a somber chime.

"I'm sorry," he said. "You didn't make the cut."

"Why not?"

He glanced down at the screen. "No stability in your employment history. And honestly, you're too old."

I looked around his office, desperate for an idea. A poster showed a celebrity chef reaching down into a carton of plump apricots – though even a tri couldn't have missed the bizarre retouching of the fruits' appearance. "Can I show you something?" I offered. "In the produce aisles?"

"What are you talking about?"

"I could save the company thousands of dollars a month," I boasted. "If something's on the verge of going rotten, or infested with insects—"

My interviewer was smiling. He shook his head in disbelief, or perhaps a trace of admiration at my chutzpah.

He said, "Sorry, we already have that app."

I looked up the app. It wouldn't work on older phones, like my own, but the very latest models now carried reconfigurable quantum dot cameras as standard. It was not just art galleries and DIY-card-sharks who could access the whole spectrum; early adopters could do it already, and in five years it would be ubiquitous. Phones, notepads, glasses – every small, cheap camera would soon be seeing more of the world than its human owner.

After Lucy's last day at the gallery, her colleagues took us out to dinner. I sat watching them, feigning bonhomie, laughing when everyone else laughed. One man took a photograph of his steak to assess its rareness and quantify the risk of food poisoning. A woman looked around furtively then snapped the dessert, in the hope of recreating it at home. These people would never learn to see the world for themselves – but they were already accustomed to asking their gadgets to advise them every few minutes.

Lucy glared at me as if I was someone's mad uncle at a wake.

My mother had watched Zelda for us. When Lucy and I were alone, I said, "Remember the treasure hunts?"

She groaned. "Oh, please – not the good old days!"

I said, "Do you still have the recipes? For the inks you used?"

"Why?" Then she understood. "It would only be a fad," she said. "A novelty. We'd be lucky if it lasted a year."

"A fad can make a lot of money in a year. Software, posters, spray-cans, marker pens, clothing, tattoos. A whole secret world that's hidden from ordinary eyes – but not some virtual reality overlay: solid objects you can touch with your bare hands."

Lucy was skeptical. "And whose kidney are you going to sell to fund this empire?"

I said, "We're going to need a backer. Someone who'll understand the idea. So let's hope my cousin hasn't blown all his prize money."

## 3

Zelda stretched her arms above her head and waved her hands at me impatiently. "Lift me, Daddy!" She wouldn't let me carry her comfortably on my hip, or even riding on my shoulders: she had to be gripped under the arms and held up at chest height, half a meter ahead of me, like a kind of advanced scout, seeing everything moments before I did.

"You're getting too old for this," I told her, as I staggered through the gallery's automatic doors.

"No, *you are!*"

"That's true as well."

I put her down and she ran toward Lucy, stopping shyly at the sight of the two strangers talking with her mother. Lucy smiled at her, and so did the customers, but then they all turned back to the painting.

"You've captured the river perfectly!" the woman marveled, making a sliding gesture beside her glasses to shift between false-color renderings. "Whatever wavelengths I map … the natural detail's there."

"That's what I was aiming for," Lucy replied.

"How long did it take you?" the woman's partner asked.

"About a year." Lucy glanced at me, but I kept a poker face.

"I can believe that."

I stood back and waited for her to clinch the sale.

Tris can never really join us in the wider world, but having learned to peek out through the keyhole of their prison and take in the view incrementally, they're no longer willing to spend their whole lives staring at the blank stone walls. The individual gimmicks come and go: the TV shows with points of view mimicking multispectral glasses, the plays where the actors have trained to emote with their capillaries for suitably equipped audiences, the advertising signs with secret messages that seem more profound and persuasive after the five-second hunt across the rainbow that it takes to reveal them. And the need – among the sufficiently wealthy – to hang a picture on the wall that actually resembles the thing it portrays.

When the customers had left with their painting, Lucy took off her shoes and sat down wearily on the gallery's fashionably white bench. It was covered with her buttock-prints – and mine – but we varied the location to form a tasteful pattern.

"I want to do some drawings," Zelda demanded.

Lucy sighed, feigning reluctance, but then she fetched a stack of paper and the bucket of pencils she kept out in the back. Zelda sat on the floor, carefully choosing among the six hundred hues on offer. She drew a garden of striped flowers, three stick figures with wildly mottled faces, and then above it all began meticulously shading in the bands of an eleven o'clock sky.

# THE NEAREST

## 1

Kate heard a knock on the open door of her office, and looked up to see Anneke from dispatch, grimacing apologetically.

"I've got a shocker for you, Sarge. Sorry."

Kate said, "Go ahead." She'd been back from maternity leave for two weeks; she did not need a content warning for every case that was grimmer than the scenes of cavorting bunnies on her son's nursery wallpaper. And after spending the morning reviewing a spike in missing persons that was probably just a meaningless statistical blip, she was ready to do anything to get away from her desk.

"Three deceased: a father and two daughters. Mother's location unknown."

*Murder-suicide, with the fourth body yet to be found?* Kate's heart sank, but she kept her face expressionless. "Gunshot wounds?"

"No, all stabbings." Anneke hesitated. "The girls were young: five and six. If you want, I'll ask Roma Street if we can hand this over to Petrie."

Kate shook her head impatiently. "So do I get a DC, or am I on my own?"

"No DC, but there are four uniforms at the scene you can use for the day."

Kate bit back a string of expletives; Anneke was just the messenger. Some half-baked algorithm had already decided that this was a self-contained domestic that posed no threat to the wider public, and would more or less solve itself. Until she could prove otherwise, there was no point begging for more resources.

Anneke flicked the report from her notepad to Kate's; Kate opened the document as she got to her feet and picked up her key fob.

On her way to the car, she read the summary from the officers who'd attended the scene. The deceased were believed to be Robert Mellish, Angela Grimes, and Isabel Grimes; the missing woman was Natalie Grimes. Natalie's mother, Diane, had tried to call her daughter the previous evening. When she still hadn't been able to make contact by mid-morning, she'd gone to the house and let herself in, finding the deceased lying in their beds. There were no obvious signs of a break-in. The family's station wagon was gone, but Natalie's phone was on the bedside table.

When Kate reached the house there were two squad cars and a SOCO van parked in the street, but their presence had attracted no onlookers; it seemed the neighbors here had the decency not to flock around the blue-and-white tape, gawking, while the ever-economizing clickbait sites were probably waiting for a chance to outsource their photographic needs to the next fast food delivery that overflew the crime scene.

Kate spoke with the officers who'd made the report, and the two colleagues who'd joined them; they were from the small community policing station in the nearby shopping precinct. With no crowd for them to manage, she decided to send three of them door-knocking.

Diane Grimes was sitting in one of the squad cars, drinking coffee that the shopfront cops must have brought for her. Kate introduced herself and joined her in the back of the car.

"Who'd do this?" Diane asked. Her teeth were chattering. "And why would they take Natalie? She would have torn their eyes out before she let them touch the girls." Her daughter's house was modest, single-story brick. Diane looked about seventy, plainly dressed, with no jewelry. Kate was fairly sure that she hadn't stumbled on a hitherto-unknown crime family, enmeshed in a bloody feud in the suburbs of Brisbane.

"Did Natalie or Robert have any debts that you know of?" Kate asked.

"Just the mortgage."

"They weren't asking you for money lately?"

"No. Why would they be?" Diane seemed annoyed at the sheer absurdity of the question; it made too little sense to be offensive.

Kate found it hard to see how the couple could have racked up drug or gambling debts that merited a more severe punishment from even the most sadistic loan shark than a broken limb or two. And two teachers at a government high school would make unlikely targets for the kind of heist or abduction that could go so wrong that it left three bodies in its wake.

"Robert was the girls' father?"

"Yes." Diane scowled. "Natalie kept her own name when they married, and she gave it to the kids. Why shouldn't she?"

Kate shook her head, disavowing any opinion on the matter. "I just need to be clear what his relationship was. And as far as you know, was he ever violent toward her, or to the girls?"

Diane said, "Even if I'm the world's worst judge of character and he fooled me completely, she would never have put up with that."

"Okay. Were either of them depressed, or medicated for any reason?"

"No."

Kate reached over and squeezed her arm. "There's an alert out for the car. You don't have to stay here; we'll call you as soon as we have any news."

"I want to be here," Diane insisted. "What if she comes home?"

Kate spared her an opinion on how unlikely that was looking. "Is there someone we can call, to be with you? A friend, or a family member?"

"My son's at work."

"Can't he take the afternoon off?"

Diane said numbly, "I haven't told him yet. How can I tell him?"

Kate got the number from her and made the call. Patrick Grimes was an electrician, working on a building site in the city; it would take him forty minutes to get here.

She left Diane with the constable, and knocked on the side door of the van. The SOCO, Tim Ng, let her in and she joined him in front of the console.

"What's the swarm got so far?" she asked.

"No signs of forced entry," he said. "There's a window that's been left open in the laundry, probably just to cool down the house overnight, but no footprints or scuff marks anywhere near it to suggest that it was used to gain access."

"What are you thinking for time of death?"

"Breakdown profiles from the bloodstains all say yesterday morning, but we'll really have to wait for the autopsies."

"Yeah. And the weapon?"

Tim turned to the console and took the view of the interior into the kitchen, tracking in on a slotted wooden block holding a set of knives. The largest slot was empty. Then he pulled back and turned into a passageway that led to the three bedrooms. On the floor, outside the nearest bedroom, was a bloodied knife whose blade the overlaid dimensions showed as matching the slot.

"Whose room is that?" Kate asked.

"The older girl, Isabel, according to the grandmother. The next one is Angela's, and the parents' bedroom is at the end of the hall." Tim steered the view down the passageway, into the master bedroom. The drones had imaged the whole house at a moderate resolution on their first pass, but even as Kate watched, the scene in the bedroom was growing visibly sharper as new data flowed in.

Robert Mellish lay on his back on one side of the double bed. The top sheet had been drawn toward the foot of the bed, down to his knees. He was wearing only a pair of shorts, and his glasses were sitting on the bedside table. A single, deep stab wound pierced the middle of his chest; an anatomical overlay suggested that the blade had entered his heart.

He had no defense wounds on his hands. Kate supposed he might not even have been awake when he was killed.

"There's a blood trail that starts from here," Tim said, aiming the viewpoint toward the floor on Robert's side of the bed, then following a series of congealed droplets out of the room and down the passage. Kate steeled herself as they pursued the trail into Angela's room. This time, the killer hadn't pulled the sheet away; the knife had gone right through it, and through the girl's nightdress too. Kate felt acid rising in her throat, more from anger than nausea.

There was no more frenzy here than there had been with Robert: a single wound, positioned with care, had done the job. If not for the improvised weapon, it could almost have been a professional hit. A mother in the grip of psychotic depression was more likely to drown her children, or feed them sedatives – and then join them in the darkness herself. What kind of delusion would it take to make a woman kill the people she loved, and neither soften the act with some degree of faux-gentleness, nor explode in uncontrollable rage, but just dispatch them, methodically and efficiently, with whatever tools were to hand?

"Go on," she told Tim.

The scene in Isabel's room was almost the same, the modus operandi identical. A bloody handprint had been left on the doorframe; unwrapped by the software, its size was consistent with a woman of Natalie's stature, which Tim had estimated at around one hundred and forty-five centimeters from wedding photographs on display in the living room. Still, a hypothetical intruder need not have been particularly large or strong, especially if they had an accomplice to help keep Natalie from intervening. If there was no apparent motive for malevolent strangers to do any of this, nor was there one for Natalie herself.

"Any meds visible?" Kate asked.

Tim shook his head. But the drones couldn't weave their way into every closed drawer and childproof cabinet in the house. "We could go for the sewerage pipes and do a metabolite analysis," he suggested.

"That's too slow." Getting access to the family's medical records would probably take even longer. Either Natalie was severely ill, and a danger to anyone she encountered, or she'd been abducted and was in danger herself; Kate needed to know which it was. "Can you plot me a route to check the likely places?" Once she set foot in the house, there was nothing she could do to avoid contaminating the scene to some degree, but if she did as she was told it would be easier for the system to subtract her out of the picture.

She put on a plastic suit, gloves, cap and booties, then approached the front door with her notepad in her hand, displaying the path for her to follow.

The door had been left open, wide enough that Kate didn't need to touch it. She glanced back and saw a smear of blood on the inside handle. She walked straight down the entrance hall, past the living room, and turned into the kitchen. There were four drawers and three cabinets that the swarm had been unable to infiltrate, and one of the cabinets contained an assortment of over-the-counter painkillers, laxatives, antacids and allergy treatments. But there was no prescription medication, let alone antipsychotics.

She followed the path through to the bathroom, but the one unexamined cabinet there held nothing but cosmetics, shampoo and shaving cream.

Suddenly, she heard something slam against the back door of the house, and a dog began barking and whining. Kate spoke into her notepad. "Tim?"

"Yeah?"

"There's a dog out back, going crazy. What's the best thing I can do?" The drones hadn't scanned the back yard yet.

"If you think you can calm it down without letting it into the house, that would be better than having it tearing up the lawn."

"Okay."

Kate followed her new route on the schematic, walking through the laundry and up to the back door. It needed no key to open from the inside; she unlatched it, and positioned her body to block access as she came out.

The dog was a golden retriever, waist-high to her. It barked loudly but didn't attack. As she emerged, closing the door behind her, it started running in circles, making a pitiful sound.

Kate squatted down, put her notepad on the ground and held out her hands. "Shh. Come here, it's all right!"

The dog approached her, wagging its tail and barking. "It's all right!" Kate repeated soothingly. The dog was wearing a collar; if she could get hold of it, she was fairly sure she could keep the animal still. "Come here!" She took off her gloves and cap and stuffed them down the front of her suit, hoping she'd look more like a human.

The dog came right up to her and pressed its head against the side of her body, whimpering. "Shh." She stroked its head and got her hand around the collar. It struggled for a moment, but then gave up and sat, resting its head on her knee.

Kate was about to call the local animal shelter, but then she had another idea. "Tim?"

"Yes."

"Can you ask Diane Grimes if she wants to take the dog for a while?"

"Will do."

Kate looked out across the yard; there was a swing set, an above-ground swimming pool, and in the rear, a veritable forest of fig trees, like some enchanted grove out of a fairy tale. The girls would have been in heaven here.

She started weeping silently. The dog tried to pull away, then changed its mind and jumped up, licking her face. Kate tugged on the collar and dragged it back down, then got herself under control.

Tim said, "Yeah, she'll take it. Bring it round through the side gate on your right, over the concrete path. That'll do the least damage."

2

As Kate pulled into the driveway, she heard Reza enunciating excitedly, "*Look* who's home! *Look* who's home! *Look. Who. Is. Home!*"

Before she'd opened the car door, he came out onto the porch with Michael, who was peering toward her, unfocused but tentatively smiling. "Say *khosh amadi, maamaan*!" Reza urged him. "Welcome to our house."

Kate said, "Now you're just being sarcastic."

Reza grinned. "Sorry." Kate kissed him then took Michael in her arms; he flapped his own arms excitedly, then beamed at her and started babbling.

"Someone still appreciates me." Kate kissed her son's cheek three times, as noisily as she could, and Reza held the door open for her as she walked into the hall.

"Do you want me to take him for a bit while you unwind?" Reza asked her.

"No, I'm fine."

"Okay, I'll start cooking."

Kate sat in the kitchen, gazing into Michael's face, engrossed by his responses to her monolog of flattering rhetorical questions. "Who is the most beautiful boy? Can you guess who that is?" Sometimes her words seemed to amuse him, sometimes he frowned in puzzlement. But so long as he was content, watching him was like floating in a warm, tranquil pool – and with the scent of herbs frying and the sound of the gentle sizzling of oil, she felt as if she'd been transported into some otherworldly paradise, as remote from the place she'd just left as waking life from a dream.

After a while, Michael closed his eyes, but Kate let him sleep in her arms until dinner was ready, then she put him down in his cot and joined Reza to eat.

"I'm glad you could get home before he slept," Reza said. "Have things quietened down at all?"

"Yes, though not in a good way. We still haven't found the missing woman." Kate didn't want to talk about the case, or even think about it for the next twelve hours if she could help it. "How was the bundle of joy today?" she asked.

"Joyous as ever. I think it's going to take some serious teething before he can be bothered losing his cool."

"I don't know where he gets that equanimity from," Kate marveled.

Reza frowned. "There's only one possibility, surely?"

Kate wiped her plate clean with the last piece of bread and leaned back in her chair. "That was delicious. Thank you."

"*Noosheh jaan.*" Reza stood up and took her plate, then bent down to kiss her forehead. "I've got a favor to ask you."

"Sure."

"Do you mind if I visit my father tonight?"

"Of course not." In truth, Kate had been hoping she could fall asleep on the couch beside him, watching something light-hearted and distracting, but Reza had been stuck in the house for the last six days, and he hadn't seen his father for a fortnight. "When do visiting hours finish?"

"Nine."

Kate glanced at the clock. "You'd better go right now. I'll clean up here."

He kissed her again, put her plate in the sink, picked up his keys and headed out the door.

When his car had gone, Kate sat for a while in the silence, then got up and made herself busy with the dishes. When she'd finished, she went to the living room and flicked through the TV's menu, but none of the sitcoms did it for her when she watched them alone.

She walked down the hall into Michael's room, and gazed down at his sleeping form, barely visible in the faint light that came through the curtains from the street lamps. *If anyone laid a finger on you*, she thought. *Anyone.* She could feel her heart beating faster. She tried to calm herself, stepping back and scrutinizing her own hyper-vigilance. She had no reason to think that her son was in any danger at all.

But she stayed in the room, watching over him, until she saw the headlights coming into the driveway.

Reza didn't seem to be in a mood to talk, but when they were in bed Kate worked up the courage to ask gently, "How was he?"

"He thought I was his brother," Reza replied. "He thought I was Amir."

Kate tried to make light of it. "I don't think you look much like your uncle."

Reza smiled. "He had a lot more hair when he was my age. And a different hairstyle every month. One of them must have been a match."

"Was he happy to see you anyway?" Kate asked. She knew that Hassan and Amir had been close; better a visit from his brother than from a total stranger.

"He was happy to have Amir to talk to, but not so happy about where they must have been."

"Back in Isfahan?"

Reza shook his head. "He thinks he's in immigration detention. Why else would he be locked up by people speaking English?"

"Jesus. I hope the staff there are nothing like those pricks." Kate's most enduring memory of all the stories she'd heard from Hassan had been the time some fresh-faced girl from Port Augusta – probably nineteen or twenty, knowing nothing of life, puffed up with self-importance by her uniform – had told this man who'd seen his parents executed by the mullahs, and who'd spent four years imprisoned in various corners of the Australian desert, that because he was on hunger strike he would be treated like a child, and denied such extravagant privileges as phone calls and visitors, until *he learned to grow up*.

"They do their best," Reza said. "And I don't think he thinks that all the time."

Kate took his hand and squeezed it.

"I just need to show a makeup artist photos of my grandfather," Reza mused. "With a few wigs and costumes and the right soundtrack, I bet I could take him back to the days before Khomeini."

Kate laughed softly. Then she said, "What if you brought him here?"

Reza was silent for a while; he must have thought about it many times, but he'd never broached it with her. "It wouldn't work," he said finally. "Watching him and Michael at the same time would be impossible."

"Okay." Kate felt a twinge of guilt; she'd only dared ask because she was almost certain of the answer. "But maybe you can talk to the doctor about the best way to make him feel..." She groped for the right word; how could he feel *free*, when he really couldn't walk out the door? "Normal."

"Yeah. I'll phone her in the morning."

Kate switched off the bedside lamp and lay in the dark. The money they were paying for the nursing home would be enough to pay for some part-time home care; Reza wouldn't have had to handle everything alone. But she could not have her father-in-law living in the same house as Michael. Nothing she'd seen or heard had ever made her think that he would harbor the slightest ill will for any child, whether or not he was capable of understanding that the boy was his grandson. But once someone lost their grip on reality, it wasn't safe to make any assumptions at all about what they might do.

## 3

Kate was dragged out of sleep by her phone buzzing, with a tone indicating the kind of alert that wouldn't leave her in peace until she responded with a suitably lucid acknowledgment. She picked the thing up off the table by the bed and peered at the screen.

"Copy that," she intoned hoarsely. "I'll be there in twenty minutes."

"What is it?" Reza asked. He sounded more awake than she was.

"They found the car."

When Kate arrived at the riverbank, the tow-truck was still getting into position. Natalie's station wagon had veered off this quiet road at a point where there were no real barriers between asphalt and water. It had left a trail of minor damage in the grass and reeds; to any passing motorist who'd given it a second thought, it probably looked no more suspicious than someone having tried to use the grass to make a U-turn. But tonight, an ER nurse on her way home from her shift had seen moonlight glinting off the metal bobbing in the reeds, and slowed down to take a closer look.

The water where the car had ended up wasn't deep; the two traffic cops who'd come to investigate had reached it in waders. Kate was still waiting for Roma Street to authorize divers, but she doubted they'd find anything. If Natalie had been able to get out of the submerged car at all, she would not have required any superhuman abilities to make it back to the riverbank. This looked more like an attempt to hide the vehicle than an attempt at suicide. If she'd been overcome by remorse, she would have driven off a bridge.

Kate stood and waited while the traffic cops and the tow-truck operator hooked up the winch and dragged the station wagon out of the water and up onto the back of the truck. Then the truck got bogged in the mud, so they had to put boards under the wheels to free it. By the time the truck was able to maneuver itself back onto solid ground, Kate had lost patience. She put on a pair of gloves and climbed up beside the station wagon, flashlight in hand.

All the doors were closed, and all the windows open; Natalie might well have been able to squeeze through a window, conscious and unharmed, but it seemed unlikely that her body had just floated out. The interior was full of silty water and vegetation, and anything not fixed that had been on the seats or the dashboard would either be buried in that muck or left behind in the river. Kate reached in and opened the glovebox, which discharged a stream of water carrying a pair of plastic sunglasses and a chapstick. She groped below the dashboard for the manual release for the hood, fought with it against the sludge and grit that was blocking the mechanism, then finally heard a satisfying click.

When she walked around to the front of the car and peered in, she saw the black box, still intact. The data recorders were meant to be robust enough to survive battery fires, so a few days of immersion would be nothing. She turned and called out to the traffic cops, "Have you got an interface cable?"

"We should wait until we get to the compound, Sarge," the older of the two replied.

"Do you have the cable or not?"

He stared back at her for a moment, then walked over to his car. Kate jumped down and went to fetch her notepad.

The data only took a few seconds to transfer, but it was encrypted; Kate sat in her car and fought her way through the process of persuading the manufacturer to send her the key. A magistrate had authorized the decryption on the day the car went missing, and she had a digital certificate attesting to that fact, but it still took three attempts to convince the Toyota web site that she wasn't a bot or a hacker.

She started with the plunge into the river. Natalie had shut off the driver supervision features ten minutes before, and while the car's software fell somewhat short of psychiatric qualifications, up to that point it had not assessed her as being affected by any drug or medical condition: she had not been swerving erratically, or shouting obscenities, or nodding off behind the wheel. The manual override had amounted to telling the car not to trust any of its own systems from then on, so while the black box had dutifully logged her GPS coordinates as she steered off the road, the car itself had become agnostic about the wisdom of this behavior. For all it knew, the driver might have had an honest reason to believe that the car's sensors were broken and it was liable to kill someone if it didn't butt out and let a human take over completely.

But the GPS trace was enough to show that Natalie hadn't been driving terribly fast at any point. She'd sped up enough to ensure that her momentum would take her over the riverbank and into the water, but she hadn't slammed her foot down and accelerated wildly, rushing toward oblivion. When the car came to a stop in the water, it hadn't even triggered the airbags.

Kate went back to the morning of the killings and followed the car away from the scene. At first, Natalie seemed to be heading straight for her mother's house, but when she came within a few blocks of it, she changed her mind. She'd turned around and started driving toward her friend Mina's apartment, only to back out again. Then her brother's house. Then two other friends. She'd had no phone with her, and all of these people had claimed that they'd heard nothing from Natalie on that day, or since. But apparently, every time she'd made a plan to seek help, she'd given up on the idea without waiting to be rebuffed.

Kate could understand a woman who'd killed her family in a psychotic fugue snapping out of it and turning in desperation to her mother, only to decide at the last minute that she had no hope of being treated with anything but revulsion. But why would she then imagine that a whole succession of other people might be more forgiving, only to abandon that hope each time it was about to be tested?

After all the aborted journeys toward familiar faces, Natalie had driven to a shopping mall, far from her own home, and the car had remained parked there for almost three hours. That seemed like a long time to spend gathering provisions for a dash out of town – which she'd turned out to have no intention of doing, unless she'd somehow procured access to another vehicle. She'd taken her bank cards when she fled from the house, but hadn't used them anywhere; whatever she'd bought in the mall, she must have paid for it with the remnants of her last cash withdrawal of three hundred dollars, from a few days before.

When she left the mall, she'd driven around the city in a wide arc until evening, as if she were simply killing time. She'd stopped at a fast food strip around nine o'clock, and then headed for the river to ditch the car.

Kate heard birdsong and looked away from her notepad; it was almost dawn. She checked the status of her request for divers; it had been flagged as "on hold" until a forensics team had examined the car itself.

She sent Reza a message to tell him she wouldn't be home, then drove off in search of a diner where she could grab breakfast and use the restroom. In the mirror, she looked puffy-eyed and disheveled; she took off her shirt and washed under her arms. Natalie must have been in a much worse state when she waded out of the river, but maybe she'd been carrying a change of clothes in a plastic bag. After six days, three with rain, it was too late to send in dogs to try to pick up her scent from the riverbank.

Kate sat in a booth in the diner drinking coffee until it was almost seven o'clock, then she drove to the shopping mall where Natalie had parked for three hours. The security cameras covered the whole parking lot, and it wasn't hard to find the moment in the recordings when Natalie drove in, but when she left the car, carrying two large, empty shopping bags, she walked away, out onto the street. Kate went through all the footage of the pedestrian entrances, but Natalie hadn't doubled back. Whatever she'd bought in that time, she'd bought somewhere else. There were hundreds of small, free-standing shops within an hour's walk of the mall.

Kate returned to the parking lot footage, at the time she knew the car had departed. Natalie appeared, with the shopping bags bulging, but it was impossible to see what they contained. New clothes? Hair dye? Scissors? It wouldn't take much for her to render herself unrecognizable to anyone but her closest friends. A clear enough shot by a public CCTV camera might still trigger a face-matching algorithm, but she'd have to be much stupider than she'd proved to be so far to offer herself up to that kind of scrutiny.

The mall security guard had been watching over Kate's shoulder. "That's the woman who killed her own kids?" he asked. Natalie's face was all over the media as a missing person, but the official line was still far from naming her as a suspect.

"Maybe." Kate turned to him with a warning glance; she really didn't want to hear anyone's opinion on what fate Natalie deserved.

"Good luck," he said.

She left the mall and walked out onto the street. "Mark every retailer in a six-kilometer radius," she told her notepad, "and give me a path that visits them all."

## 4

Kate woke with a headache and squinted at the bedside clock. It was ten minutes to three. She groaned softly and closed her eyes, then felt someone's warm, naked skin brush against her.

She jerked her arm away and leaped out of bed. There was enough light coming through the curtains for her to see the man lying asleep where Reza should have been.

She was trembling from the shock, but she tried to calm herself and plan her next move carefully. She thought of going to the kitchen and arming herself with a knife, but if there was a struggle that might not work in her favor.

She snatched up her phone and tip-toed into the passageway. The safest thing might be to take Michael out to the car and drive away, before she even risked calling for help. *But where was Reza?* Any protracted scuffle in the bedroom would have woken her, so he must have been lured out of the room somehow – before being tied up and gagged, maybe drugged, maybe beaten senseless. So she had to get Michael to safety, but then return as quickly as possible, and do it all without waking the intruder.

She walked down the passageway in the darkness, treading as lightly as she could. As she entered the nursery, she felt her skin prickling with horror, and she had to cover her mouth with her hand to keep herself silent. She stared at the shape in the cot, afraid to raise the phone and illuminate it, but when she finally found the courage, the harsh light made the revelation unbearable. She staggered back, then fled.

She ran into the bedroom and switched on the light. "What have you done to him?" she roared. "What have you done to my son?"

The intruder shielded his face with his arm and then lowered it and peered at her groggily. "Kate? What's happened?" He climbed off the bed and approached her; she flinched away from him, raising one hand with her fist clenched. She didn't need a weapon; she'd beat the truth out of him with her bare hands.

"Kate? Talk to me!" He stood, rooted to the spot, feigning concern. "Has something happened to Michael? Should I call an ambulance?"

"Don't play games with me!" she bellowed. "Where have you taken him?"

"Are you saying he's not in his cot?" The intruder rushed past her, out into the passageway; she followed him halfway, but couldn't bring herself to go back into the nursery. He switched on the light, then after a while she heard him whispering, "Shh, *pesaram*, it's all right." So this man spoke Persian – or was he just mocking her? Had he bugged the house and listened to all the things she and Reza said?

He came out from the nursery and walked up to her. "He looks fine to me. What got you so worried?"

Kate said, "You have ten seconds to tell me where my son is."

"Now you're frightening me." The intruder reached down and scratched his hip beneath the waistband of his shorts, as unselfconsciously as if he spent every night wandering half-naked through a different stranger's house. "Are you sick?" He reached up to put his hand on Kate's forehead; she grabbed his arm and twisted it, bringing him to his knees.

"What's wrong with you?" he gasped, wincing from the pain but keeping himself from shouting, as if his greatest fear was "waking" the mechanical doll he'd planted in the cot. Kate got him in a choke-hold; he went limp in her arms, not even trying to fight her.

"I swear I'll kill you," she said. "If you don't take me to my son, I'll slit your fucking throat and hang you from a meat-hook."

The man started weeping, his whole body shuddering as he sobbed. Kate stared down at his blubbering face, desperately clinging to the hope that whatever he'd done to Reza and Michael that had left him so ashamed, they were still alive somewhere. "Take me to them now, and I'll say you cooperated. The quicker you do this, the better things will go for you."

"All right," he replied. He sounded utterly defeated. For someone who'd been so brazen just minutes before, he hadn't taken long to fold.

Kate released him and stepped away. "So where are they?"

He clambered to his feet. "I need to call someone. They'll bring them here."

"No, no, no!" Kate spread her arms so he couldn't get past her down the hall. She wasn't having him summoning accomplices. "*You* take me to them, alone. Are they in the house?"

He hesitated. "No. We'll need to take a drive."

Kate stood in silence, trying to think. She should call for backup, get the fucker cuffed and under control. But if he stopped cooperating, what redress would she have? As soon as she got anyone else involved, there'd be no point threatening to gut him like a pig; he could sit in his prison cell, laughing, while Reza and Michael starved to death, or worse.

"All right," she said. "So you'd better put some clothes on."

She walked into the bedroom ahead of him and scooped up Reza's phone. She'd half expected him to try to flee, but he followed close behind her and proceeded to dress in Reza's clothes. Kate stood watching him, dazed; not only did the clothes fit him, well enough, his resemblance to her husband was striking, right down to the pattern of freckles on his shoulders and the way his uncombed hair stuck up at the side. But did the kidnappers really think that she'd be fooled by such superficial details?

"Turn around and face the wall," she said. He complied, and she dressed quickly.

"Okay, I'm done. Come on."

"Can we take…?" He gestured toward the nursery.

Kate scowled at him, disbelieving; she thought he was about to start crying again. "Why would we take that thing with us? I'll put it out with the garbage."

The intruder stared at her. "When you get back, with Michael?"

"Yes! It's not a priority. Now, come on!"

He followed her out of the house; she unlocked the car and got into the driver's seat. He joined her, and she reversed quickly onto the street.

"Which way?" she asked.

"South."

She drove down to the corner and turned toward Gympie Road. There was no other traffic in sight, no lights showing in any of the houses. She glanced at the man, sitting meekly beside her in his borrowed clothes. "So, what was the plan?"

"What do you mean?"

"Were you going to ask for money? Or was this about fixing some case? You wanted me to tamper with evidence, or make a file disappear?"

He didn't reply.

Kate laughed humorlessly. "And the idea that you could just lie down in my bed and that would *buy some time* to get them further away … for fuck's sake, how stupid can you be? You might look a bit like my husband, but do you think I couldn't tell the difference?"

The man said, "What gave me away?"

Kate shook her head. "One touch, and my skin crawled. So where are we going?"

"Herston."

"Where in Herston? I'll put it in the GPS."

"I don't know the name of the street, but I can give you directions once we're closer."

Kate wasn't happy, but at this hour the drive wouldn't take long. If he was messing with her, she'd know soon enough, and he'd regret it.

"How many of you are there?" she asked.

"Just me and my friend. And he won't hurt anyone, I promise. I'd never have got involved if it was going to be like that."

"So why did you do it at all?"

"It was his idea," the man insisted. "I just went along with it."

Kate frowned skeptically, but this wasn't the time to start brow-beating the only person who could reunite her with her family. Whether he was a simpleton who'd been led astray, or a criminal genius who'd thought it was a good idea to climb into bed with her, would be up to the investigating officers to decide, then the prosecutors, then a jury. Once Reza and Michael were safe, she would need to step back and leave everything to other people.

"How did you get Reza out of the house so quietly?"

"My friend drugged him."

"With what, exactly?"

"Some liquid he put on a cloth. I don't know what it was."

Kate suspected he was lying; it sounded like something he'd seen in a movie, and if they'd tried it with chloroform Reza would have been struggling for so long it would have woken her ten times over.

"And how did you clowns even get into the house?"

"The spare key under the flowerpot."

She fell silent. That was her fault; she should never have put it anywhere so obvious.

They were close to the city now; she could see the lights in the Aurora Tower ahead.

"Turn right here," he told her.

"Past the hospital?"

"Yes."

Kate turned into Butterfield Street, slowing down as they approached a small park that separated the road from the drop-off loop for the hospital's entrance. In the early hours of the morning, there could well be visitors to the emergency department with all manner of substances in their bodies stumbling out from behind the greenery and onto the road without warning.

"And go left here."

Kate brought the car to a halt. He was directing her into the hospital's parking complex.

"What are you trying to tell me?" she demanded angrily. "Have they been hurt?"

"No. I promise you, both of them are fine."

"Then why would they be here?"

The man said, "We need to go in. Please."

"*Why?*"

Before Kate could stop him, he was out of the car, running back along the road and through the trees. She went after him, bewildered. The park was about the size of her back yard; he had no hope of losing her.

She caught up with him just outside the entrance to the emergency department. She'd feared she was going to have to tackle him to the ground on the concrete, but he stopped and turned, letting her collide with him, catching her in his arms so that their bodies came together in a sick parody of an embrace. She pulled away, furious. He smelled exactly like Reza, but that just turned her stomach.

He said, "Kate, I'm begging you, let them check you out."

"What?"

"Let the doctors examine you. I can stay here with you, but you need to let me call someone to look after Michael."

"If you think I won't hurt you just because there are people around—"

The man held his hands up, shoulder high. "Look at me! If you don't believe I'm Reza, tell me one thing that isn't the same!"

Kate was tired. "You're the right build, the right bone structure. Black hair and brown eyes aren't exactly rare – assuming they're natural – but everything else could be done with make-up." Hadn't Reza himself claimed as much, joking that he could pass for his own grandfather? *Had they listened in to that conversation, too?*

"Is that a professional opinion, DS Shahripour?" he taunted her. "Would you talk shit like that in court? Ask me something only Reza could know."

"I'm not playing this game."

He said, "I'm not a doctor, I don't know what's wrong with you. But what if it's a stroke? If you've got a clot in your brain…" He put his forearm over his eyes, wiping away tears. "Please, Kate, let them help you."

Kate stared at him in the harsh light of the entrance. Every small, dark hair on his cheeks was precisely where she'd expect it to be. The idea that anyone outside of Hollywood would even try to reconstruct that level of detail was ridiculous.

"Let's go in," she said. They were in the right place after all.

They stepped through the self-opening doors together. As Reza was looking around to see where they should go to join the queue, Kate spotted a pair of security guards. When Reza walked forward, she veered away from him, approached the guards, and discreetly showed them her badge.

"That man is my husband," she said quietly. "I need your help restraining him so he can be examined, otherwise he could be a danger to himself."

Kate stayed a few steps behind as the three of them approached Reza together. He spread his arms in a gesture of disbelief. "What is this? Kate?" He turned to the guards. "My wife is ill. I don't know what she told you—"

"You need to calm down, sir," one of the guards said firmly. "The doctors are busy, but if you wait quietly someone will be able to see you soon."

"No, *she* needs to see them! She's the one who's sick! Our son is in danger."

"Sir, if you start making threats—"

"Kate? What did you say to them?" Reza – or whatever it was that now animated the shell of his body – glared at her in self-righteous horror.

Kate told the guards, "I'll be back as soon as I can. Until then, you need to make sure that he gets a full psych evaluation." They did not look happy, but they deferred to her authority.

She turned and walked away, glancing back a couple of times as the remnant of her husband began shouting and struggling. The guards had handcuffs, batons and tasers; he wasn't going anywhere.

On her way back to the car she started sobbing. When she pictured Reza – the man she knew, as he'd been just a few hours before – the thought of abandoning him in this wretched state horrified her. But she had to trust the doctors to take care of him; she couldn't stay here waiting for a diagnosis. What mattered now was finding Michael.

As she drove north, she thought of calling the station and sending someone to the house ahead of her. But how could she explain walking out on her infant son, without sounding like she'd lost her mind? Michael had to be lying on a blanket somewhere, sleeping through all of this insanity. Maybe Reza had risen in the night and quietly hidden him, acting with good intentions in some strange twilight state before he was gone completely – saving his son from the thing he was about to become.

Kate couldn't stop weeping. She took her hands off the wheel and let the car steer for her as the rain began to fall. Was it some kind of Alzheimer's, like his father? But that made no sense; even if the early-onset form could strike at such a young age, she'd never heard of it happening overnight.

When she turned into her street, she saw a squad car outside her house, and lights on inside. She stopped and switched off her headlights, but kept the wipers running. Had a neighbor heard her shouting threats before she left?

The front door opened and someone walked out onto the porch: a tall, blond woman in civilian clothes carrying a wailing baby, followed by a uniformed female constable. Kate peered at them through the rain, making the best of the moments of clarity after the blades had swept the windshield clear, before fresh droplets appeared and distorted everything. The woman resembled her sister Beth, though it wasn't her. The baby was swaddled in a blanket, making it hard to see properly, but it sounded like some awful imitation of Michael.

Had the thing in the cot not been a doll, after all? Where would such a doll have come from? *Had Michael and Beth both gone the way of Reza?*

Kate covered her face with her hands. What could turn a human being into a walking automaton, a vacant caricature of the person they'd been? Some kind of toxin? Some kind of disease?

When she looked again, the two women were in the squad car. The engine started, and the car drove away. But the lights were still on in the house. Someone was in there, waiting for her to arrive.

The thing that had been Reza must have wheedled its way into making a phone call, and whoever it had called had either been fooled into taking it seriously … or had needed no persuasion, because it already thought the same way.

Reza had been infected. Michael had been infected. Beth had been infected. How many more might there be? If she walked into that house and shared the same fate, she'd be powerless to help any of them.

Kate started the car and reversed back down the street. After ten meters, the supervisor began chanting threats and admonitions. She said, "Shut down, you're malfunctioning." She kept going until she reached the corner, then she turned and drove away.

## 5

The teller machine took her card without complaint, scanned her face, then offered her the usual menu. Reza had never been in any position to cancel her card himself, but whatever his remnant had told the police, the best thing was to get her hands on as much money as possible while she still could. Kate moved some funds between accounts and then succeeded in withdrawing her entire daily cash limit of five thousand dollars.

She sat in the car, trying to clear her head and see the way forward. It was beginning to look as if Reza and Beth, and maybe anyone else in the same condition, could pass as normal to an interlocutor who didn't actually know them. Once he'd stopped humoring her with nonsense about the "kidnapping", Reza had spoken coherently enough, making claims that might have sounded perfectly believable to a naive bystander. For all Kate knew, charming the hospital's security guards into giving him a phone call had only been the start of it; he might even have been able to talk his way through an entire interview with an overworked psychiatric registrar, accustomed to more florid symptoms.

Reza's uncle was on the other side of the country, and Beth had been divorced for years. But some of their friends would surely be able to spot the changes, backing up Kate's assessment and ensuring the three victims got the treatment they needed.

Her phone rang. She stared at it for a while, then answered warily, "Chris? How are you?"

"I'm fine, Kate. But I've heard that people are worried about you."

*Fuck.* Of all the colleagues she might have trusted to help her, Chris Santos had been top of the list, but he'd only had to speak two sentences to make it plain that he was infected too. And he was going to parrot Reza's line that *she* was the problem? Kate resisted the urge to tell him she was having flashbacks to the time a gaggle of dimwitted scammers had called her one by one to say, "This is technical department of Windows operating system; we have detected a dangerous virus on your computer." However many of them she told, in no uncertain terms, that they weren't fooling her, there was always another one the next day trotting out exactly the same line.

"I had a fight with Reza," she said. "Not even a fight, more a misunderstanding. It's all good now."

There was an awkward pause. "It's just, your sister had to take the baby. No one wants to talk about child neglect charges, and I don't think it has to go that far. But you need to come in and be interviewed, just to reassure everyone. I think your husband's still freaked out."

Kate struggled to frame her reply, wondering what the point was in humoring him at all – but it was possible that the call was being shared with people who weren't just going through the motions, and actually believed she'd been at fault.

"I understand," she said. "I'll be in around nine o'clock."

"Can I ask where you are now?"

"I'm not at home," she admitted. "I knew Beth was looking after Michael, and I didn't want to be there when Reza came home. It was just ... a bit tense between us. I thought this would give us a chance to cool off."

"Okay. But you'll be at Roma Street by nine?"

"Absolutely."

Kate stepped out of the car, stacked her phone on top of Reza's behind the rear wheel, then ran over them repeatedly. *How had Chris's wife not noticed what had happened to him?* But Kate hadn't really socialized with the two of them for years; maybe they were estranged, and she just hadn't heard it through the grapevine.

She got out of the car again and inspected the shattered electronics. She was having second thoughts about walking away; maybe it would be simpler to go undercover and play happy families with Reza, pretending that nothing was wrong while she investigated the outbreak.

But even if she could be that good an actor, Reza might infect her, dragging her down into the same emptiness. She had to believe that he and Michael and Beth still survived somehow, however deeply they'd been buried – but when she pictured the grotesque effigies they'd become, all she felt was revulsion.

The sky was light now, and she could hear traffic sounds rising up amid the birdsong. She hated the thought of abandoning the car, but eventually people would be looking for it, and she had no idea how far the disease had spread through the police force.

As she headed down the street, Kate thought of Natalie Grimes, waking in shock to find herself beside the thing that had once been her husband. Walking from room to room, discovering that even her beautiful daughters were gone. Convinced that her family had been erased, their minds irretrievably destroyed, and that the only loving thing to do had been to put the twitching puppets out of their misery.

Kate could understand the power of the woman's grief. But she was not going to give up hope, herself, until she had proof beyond doubt that there was no cure, and that everyone she cared about really was gone forever.

## 6

Kate found a small motel where the clerk was happy to take cash upfront, and for a modest surcharge allowed her to check in without showing ID. In her room, she sat on the bed staring down at the torn carpet, trying to decide who she could trust to be her allies, now that Chris had been ruled out. She drew up a list of twelve names, but when she thought about each one seriously, her confidence began to wane. It was not that any of them had failed to be loyal and supportive in the past, but when she pictured the actual conversation she would need to have with them to enlist their help, the idea that they would back her seemed preposterous. Each time she played out the scenario in her head, every trace of the old friendships she was relying on simply faded away, and the encounter ended with a cold stare.

More than friends, she needed evidence. And since no epidemiologist was going to drop everything and come to her aid, she needed to start with testimony, from as many people as possible, showing that the symptoms she'd observed in her own family had been seen elsewhere.

Without knowing the mode of transmission it was hard to say how the disease might have spread, but the neighborhood around Natalie's house was the obvious place to begin. Kate left the motel and set off on foot, taking care to avoid intersections where she knew there would be cameras.

When she arrived, the house itself was still cordoned off. She started with the neighbors on the right, but no one was home; it was only four doors down that she finally got an answer. Her knocking summoned an elderly man who was clearly not pleased to have been woken from sleep – but then, chastened by the gravity of the subject, he invited her in.

"I know you've spoken to my colleagues already," Kate explained apologetically, "but if there's anything else you remember from that time, it could be important."

"Like what?" the man asked. "I never heard Natalie and Rob fighting. The kids could be noisy; you know how girls that age screech sometimes? But that was just playful. It never sounded like someone was hurting them."

Kate said, "Apart from the family, has there been anything unusual you've noticed going on in the area?"

He pondered the question, but shook his head.

"Anyone acting out of the ordinary? Maybe a stranger, maybe not. Maybe even someone you thought you knew well."

He ran his fingertips across his forehead, disconcerted by the apparent suggestion that some neighbor he'd joked with over the fence might have stabbed this family to death.

"Anyone acting out of character?" Kate pressed him.

"No," he said firmly. But with the stakes seemingly so high, perhaps he felt compelled to err on the side of caution. Using the murders as a pretext for her questions was going to make it harder to get an honest response.

She worked her way down the street then back, sketching a map of the area as she broadened her search. Having missed her appointment at Roma Street and trashed her phone, she suspected that her badge number would have been revoked by now, so whenever people answered the door with their phone in their hand, she made an excuse and withdrew lest they *TrueCop*-ped her and made things awkward.

By early evening, she'd conducted thirty-seven interviews. She was thinking of taking a break and grabbing some food, when a door opened and before she'd even raised her badge, the middle-aged woman standing in front of her asked anxiously, "Have you found him?"

"I'm afraid not," Kate extemporised. Whoever the woman was talking about, that was almost certainly true. "But I'd like to ask you for a few more details, if I could."

"Of course."

Kate identified herself and followed the woman into the house. In the living room, there were family photos: mother, father and teenage son.

"Is anyone else at home right now?" Kate asked.

"No, my husband's in the city. He's still looking for Rowan. Game arcades, McDonald's … he's got no money, but we don't know where else he'd go to pass the time."

Kate glanced again at a photo of the boy. The face looked familiar; he was one of the missing persons whose cases she'd been reviewing when the Grimes murders took over.

"Before Rowan went missing," she asked, "did you notice any change in his behavior?"

The woman frowned. "Yes! I made a point of that to the other officer!"

Kate nodded apologetically. "I know it's frustrating to have to repeat yourself, but part of the process is for me to try to come at this with fresh eyes, and make sure we haven't missed anything."

"All right." The woman shifted uncomfortably in her chair. Kate wished she could remember her name, but there'd been more than thirty files.

"So can you tell me, in as much detail as possible: in what way did your son seem different?"

"He was so cold to us," the woman replied. "He might have had his moods before – he might have been embarrassed or irritated when I said something that a thirteen-year-old boy doesn't want to hear from his mother – but the day before he left, it was like he had no heart at all."

"You mean he was deliberately cruel?" Kate asked.

"No. It wasn't that I'd annoyed him and he was trying to be hurtful; it was as if I just didn't matter to him, one way or the other."

If Rowan had caught the disease that had afflicted Natalie's family, what was the route of transmission? Kate confirmed with the boy's mother that he'd attended the high school where Natalie and her husband had taught, though he hadn't been in either of their classes, and it was hard to see how an airborne virus could have affected him while sparing most of the other students.

"Have you spoken to the families of Rowan's friends?" Kate asked.

"Of course."

"And have any of their children undergone personality shifts?"

"Not that anyone admitted." The woman hesitated. "I don't believe that Rowan was taking drugs, but I'm past the point where I'm certain of anything. So if you think that's a possibility, and it could have something to do with the reason he's missing, I don't want you ruling it out just because my own instincts say otherwise."

"All right." Kate didn't like misleading her, but her own hypothesis was hardly more reassuring.

On her way back to the motel, she bought a small notepad with WiFi only, then she used the motel's internet connection to download a gallery of missing persons whose names and photos had been made public. Rowan da Silva was there, and most of the other people Kate recalled from her review. At least she hadn't been listed herself, yet.

In the next three days, as she spiraled out from the epicenter, she encountered twelve families with sons or daughters, husbands or wives who'd gone missing. In four cases, the person had fled without anyone noticing warning signs, but in the others, the distressed loved ones claimed that the event had been preceded by a change in behavior or demeanor that made them feel as if their relationship had disintegrated, for no discernible reason. "That morning, I swear he looked at me as if he was a trapped animal and I was a zoo-keeper," one woman told Kate. "Maybe he woke up and decided that our whole marriage had been a mistake, and it took him another two days to find the courage to walk out. But two days before, he'd either been as happy as I'd ever seen him, or he was the best actor in the world."

On the afternoon of the fourth day, Kate knocked on a door and found herself talking to a woman who spoke with a forced cheeriness and couldn't quite look her in the eye. She had no missing family members, or any information to offer about suspicious activities in the neighborhood; she just seemed discomfited by Kate's presence. Either she had a drug lab and a fresh corpse in her living room, or Kate's time was up.

She found a café with WiFi and did a quick search. Authorities had expressed concern about a missing police officer, Detective-Sergeant Katherine Shahripour (pictured). It wasn't exactly the kind of news that would muscle its way into everyone's feeds; she suspected that maybe one in fifty people in the city would see it. But the woman she'd spooked would have reported the encounter. It would no longer be safe to keep door-knocking the area.

Kate wasn't ready to come in from the cold. Eight families with stories of sudden alienation wouldn't cut it; after all, the original investigators had written that off as being down to the usual causes: teenage angst, midlife crises, drug problems, infidelity. At the very least, she needed to bring in some of the afflicted in person, fleshing out her collection of hearsay with actual subjects. Reza might have talked his way out of the emergency department, but if she could drag half a dozen of these fractured families, re-united, into the spotlight, that might be the start of a proper investigation, and the first step on the road to a cure.

As she left the café, she tried to picture a future where everything was normal again. But all she could think of was Reza's bizarre charade, and the husk of her son lying in his cot like a cheap plastic doll. She lowered her sights, and made do instead with memories. The days before, when they had still been themselves, remained as vivid to her as ever. She would hold her feelings for them in that vault, and keep working to find a way to revive them.

# 7

Kate cut her hair and dyed it black, then bought some cheap earrings, a battered phone with no SIM card, and an assortment of clothes from a charity shop. It took a while for her to find the right look, but at the end of the day she emerged from her room, satisfied that at least she wouldn't be taken for a cop or a social worker.

She walked into the city, and made her way to one of the homeless shelters. As Leila, the volunteer, showed her the ropes, Kate took out her phone and brought up a picture of Suzanne Reyes, a missing woman a few years younger than Kate. "You haven't seen my sister, have you? When she's off her meds, I don't know what she'll do."

Leila regarded her warily. "Sorry, no."

In the dining room, Kate showed the photo around, but all she got was a few grunts of sympathy. She wished there were some way to seek all eight of her targets at once to better the odds, but it would be stretching credulity to claim a connection with even two of them, and Rowan's parents had already done the rounds of the shelters. In the dormitory, she lay awake half the night, listening to the other women coughing.

She spent the next day on the streets, finding the places where the homeless congregated and asking again after Suzanne. It was close to nightfall when a thin, twitchy woman with a crumpled face squinted at the picture and announced, "Yeah, love, I've seen her. Just a few days ago."

Kate closed her eyes for a moment, genuinely overcome with relief. "Thank God. Do you know where she is now?"

"She talked a lot of nonsense," the woman complained. "I'm not surprised what you said about her medication."

"Yeah, that's Suzanne. Do you know where she went?"

"She tried to recruit me," the woman recalled irritably. "Like a missionary. Like a fucking Mormon Scientologist."

"What do you mean?"

"She wanted me to join her fight against the devil."

Kate shook her head forlornly. "My sister said that? She thinks she's fighting the devil?"

The woman thought it over dutifully. "Not the devil, exactly. She said she's fighting the hollow men, the ones who've lost their souls. Raising an army of the … I don't fucking know."

"Do you know where I can find her?"

"Not really. I told her to piss off and stop bothering me."

It was growing dark. Kate crossed town and tried a different shelter. "She might not look the same now," she warned her fellow diners as she helped ladle out the night's stew. "But maybe you remember her talking about the hollow men?"

No one could help her, but the next morning, as the shelter was closing, a young woman with long, plaited hair approached Kate. "I don't think I've seen your sister," she said. "But there was a man I met, talking like you said she talked."

"In what way?" Kate asked.

"He was warning me about the hollow people. He wanted me to join the fight."

"Where was this?"

"You know that spot in South Bank where all the buskers play?"

Kate nodded, but this wasn't much help; she could probably stand there for a month without the same man reappearing, let alone approaching her.

"I told him I was busy with other things," the woman continued, "but he said that if I ever wised up and changed my mind, there was a place where I could find him."

Kate hardly dared breathe, but when the woman said no more she had to ask. "Asgard? Middle Earth? Hogwarts?"

"An old warehouse that's used as a squat." She gestured at Kate's phone. "If that thing's got a map, I can show you."

# 8

The abandoned warehouse stood at the edge of a sprawling industrial park that still had a few tenants, but the place itself looked as if it had been derelict for years. The wire mesh fence around it had been bent almost horizontal in places, and the sign warning of security patrols, cameras and dogs was brown with corrosion.

Kate clambered over the lowest part of the fence and approached the building, carrying a blanket she'd bought for five dollars from a man camped in a city alleyway. Weeds taller than she was sprouted from cracks in the concrete forecourt. When she tried the office door it was securely locked, even though most of the paint had flaked off, but the roll-up door to the loading bay had been breached, torn away from its tracks on one side. The aperture was a tight squeeze; Kate pushed her blanket through, then followed head-first. After the sunlit concrete, she couldn't see a thing inside, but she ended up doing a hand-stand onto her blanket before her feet fell to the floor.

She waited for her eyes to adapt. The place still stank of some kind of oil or solvent, though there was human waste not too far away. Gradually, she made out the silhouettes of a stack of crates and pallets ahead of her, and some large metal drums of chemicals. She walked past them warily, squinting in the gloom at the hazard warnings, hoping that nothing volatile and carcinogenic had spilled out onto the floor.

Away from the loading bay, in the warehouse proper, a little sunlight made its way through grimy windows set high in the walls. But a dozen or so fluorescent panels hung by cables from the ceiling; no one had ever aspired to make this place function with natural light.

The floor was filthy, strewn with clumps of oil-clotted sand, scraps of yellowing invoices curling at the edges, and a few newer burger wrappers and polystyrene cups. In the distance, someone sat on a bedroll, a slight figure with their back to her.

Kate called out, "Hi! Is it safe here?" The walls flung her voice back at her.

The figure turned and replied, "It's all right. No one hassles you."

Kate approached. It took her a while to be sure, but once she had clear sight of the boy, she knew it was Rowan da Silva.

"I'm Kate."

He held out his hand and she shook it, but he offered no name himself. She looked around. "Are we the only ones here?"

"Right now we are. There's a lot more people at night."

"I heard this was a good place," Kate said, "but you never know until you see for yourself."

Rowan nodded distractedly, then lowered his gaze and stared glumly at the floor. If he really was suffering from the same disease that had struck Reza, Kate found it hard to discern the effects. With Reza, there had been a yawning abyss between the man she knew and the shop-window dummy he'd become, but with this boy she had no expectations to help her gauge the symptoms.

"How old are you?" she asked gently.

"Sixteen," he lied.

"You don't get on with your folks?"

"They're dead."

Kate said, "I'm sorry." She hesitated, but decided not to push him into embellishing the claim. "My husband, how can I put it … showed me a different side."

"Like he hit you?"

Kate wanted to say yes; it only mattered that she had a plausible story. But something in her rebelled against the slander. "No. He just changed."

Rowan said, "You hear that a lot." He rose to his feet, then picked up his bedroll and a cardboard sign. "Gotta hit the lunchtime crowds if I want to eat."

"Yeah. Good luck."

He wouldn't make it to the city by lunchtime; he had to mean the nearest mall, some forty minutes away. Kate waited five minutes, then followed him. She caught sight of him on the main road, following the route she'd expected him to take, then she quickly moved to a smaller, parallel street so she wouldn't be at risk of discovery if he happened to turn around. After crossing back along side streets a couple of times, she soon had a good enough sense of his pace to feel confident that she wasn't going to lose him.

When she was almost at the mall, she spotted Rowan setting up his bedroll and sign on a public street near the entrance. Kate stood beside a tree and recorded video with her phone in one hand and her arm at her side, panning and tilting slowly to sweep the zoomed frame across a range of directions that she hoped would encompass him. It worked, well enough; she managed to extract a still image in which Rowan was clearly recognizable.

She circled around the mall and went in through a different entrance, then found a café. She'd spent all her small change, so she had to retrieve a fifty-dollar bill she'd hidden beneath an insole. Between that, her choice of wardrobe, and the acrid smell she'd acquired since showering in the shelter by trekking a dozen kilometers in the heat, she'd never felt more self-conscious, but the waitress took her money without a flicker of disdain and handed her the WiFi password along with her coffee.

Kate logged in and created a GMail account, then sent the pictures of Rowan to his mother, geotagged. She had to assume that Ms da Silva now knew that she'd been suspended, so she kept the tip anonymous, and resisted the urge to offer suggestions for a medical examination that would probably sound even more bizarre and unwelcome coming from a stranger than from a rogue police officer.

She left the café and took up a position outside the supermarket, where she had a clear view of Rowan. Half an hour later, a squad car pulled up in the street, and both of Rowan's parents emerged. Kate watched them arguing with their son, and when they failed to persuade him to come with them, one of the officers took him by the arm and got him into the car with a minimum of force.

She had no way of knowing if they would take the kind of steps needed to get him a proper diagnosis, but there was a chance that at least they could keep him from fleeing again for another few days, in which time she might be able to gather enough evidence of the outbreak to trigger a full-scale public health response, and clear her name to the point where she could make sure that Rowan was included.

When the squad car drove away, she sat on a bench in the mall, pondering her next step. She was on CCTV now, and regardless of her changed hairstyle it was only a matter of time before anyone seriously looking for her would be able to start reconstructing her movements.

So she had to return to the warehouse that night, or she might not get another chance.

## 9

Kate had expected the warehouse to be pitch black by nightfall – with the occasional beam from a phone, deployed sparingly – but it turned out that some of the squatters had obtained what looked like solar-charged hurricane lamps, which they set up on crates to spread a warm yellow light across the cavernous space. There was even a small portable microwave that people were using to heat up food. The mood of the place was almost cozy, as if they'd gathered here to ride out a storm or a flood, strangers united, however warily, against a shared calamity.

The squatters around her had been taciturn when she'd introduced herself, but she felt more like a newcomer than an outsider – on probation, not rejected. So far she'd sighted fifteen people, and among them she'd recognized four of the missing whose families she'd interviewed: Suzanne Reyes, Ahmed Fahadi, Gary Katsaros, and Linda Blethyn. Since none of them were minors, or the subject of warrants, there was no point trying to get police involved; it was possible that the best thing she could do would be to keep her mouth shut until morning, then find ways to tip off their loved ones. If she could get enough people who'd been affected by the disease reunited with the people who could recognize their condition, her job would be half done.

Gary and Suzanne had been using the microwave, but now Kate saw them walking straight toward her, carrying containers of food.

"Are you hungry?" Suzanne asked. "It's Chinese, not too spicy."

Kate nodded gratefully and accepted the meal, then she gestured to the floor and the three of them sat cross-legged on her blanket. Her companions were both around her own age, and though she knew Suzanne had spent time in shelters, both were better dressed than she was.

Gary looked around across the warehouse floor. "This isn't how I saw myself ending up."

Kate laughed sympathetically. "Me neither."

"But when my wife changed, I couldn't stay in the house. I couldn't stay there, pretending that nothing had happened."

Suzanne remained silent, but she was watching Kate intently. "Changed how?" Kate asked.

"Hollowed out," Gary replied. "The first time I saw her, I didn't think it was her at all. Everything that made her who she was had gone. Just because her face was the same, how could I recognize her without that spark? But it was her body, I had to accept that in the end. Her body was still there; it was everything else that had drained away."

Kate stared back at him, unable to speak. He was not infected with the disease that had claimed Reza and Michael; *his wife was*. Kate had spoken to her for twenty minutes, but to a stranger, emitting the right words in the right order was enough for her to pass as normal.

Had they all been hollowed out: everyone she'd interviewed who'd claimed that it was the missing family member whose behavior had changed? *Even Rowan's mother?* Kate struggled with her memories of the interview. It was one thing to be oblivious to the lack of familiar cues that only someone who'd known her for years would expect, but nothing about her fears for her child had rung false.

Suzanne said, "My husband was the same. When I woke up, I thought there was a rapist in my bed. If I hadn't seen his appendectomy scar, I might have bashed his brains out."

Kate looked down at the blanket. "It was the same for me," she confessed. "My husband and my son. Then my sister, and one of my colleagues…"

Suzanne reached over and squeezed her shoulder.

"It's spreading," Gary said. "The hollowing is spreading. And it's so hard to stop, because only the nearest can know who's been taken."

Kate said, "We need to go to the Department of Health. If there are enough of us telling the same story, they'll have to investigate."

Suzanne responded with the kind of smile that seemed to say they might as well light up the Bat-Signal. "I know two people who did that: a woman and her son. No one heard of them again. It's spread to the government, it's spread to the hospitals, it's spread to the police."

Kate shook her head vehemently. "But it can't be everyone. It must be just a few."

"How can you be sure?" Gary countered. "In someone you know, it's unmissable. In anyone else, *how could you tell?*"

Kate had no reply. She'd thought she was close to turning things around, but all she'd done was send Rowan back to the robotic remnants of his parents, to be treated as if he was the one who'd lost his mind. Everything she'd been taking comfort from was being kicked out from under her.

Gary said, "The only way to fight this is for each of us to do what no one else can. We need to honor those who were our nearest. Prepare ourselves for what needs to be done, then go back to them and grant them peace."

Kate's fists tightened, but she spoke as calmly as she could. "Don't say that. They can be brought back. They can be cured."

"This is a war now," Suzanne insisted. "Do you really think it would be merciful to spare them – and just sit around hoping that a cure is going to fall from the sky, while they spread the infection even further? Imagine a world where people like us are outnumbered. Do you have any idea how close to that we might be, even now?"

"So have you slaughtered your family?" Kate retorted, knowing the answer full well. She turned to Gary. "Have you?"

"No," Gary replied, but his tone made no concession to her stance. "We need to act in concert, all on the same night. They can't be prepared for this – we need to take them by surprise."

"That's monstrous." Kate was numb. "You don't murder people just because they're sick."

Suzanne said, "It's the hardest thing you could ask of anyone, but Natalie showed us: if you're strong, it can be done. If you loved them, and you face up to what they've become, it can be done."

Kate had no words. Suzanne squeezed her shoulder again. "It's tough," she said. "You need time. We'll talk again soon."

They left her sitting on the tattered blanket. Kate watched as they crossed the floor and met up with Linda and Ahmed.

So this was the brave resistance against the horrors of the plague: people ready to abandon all hope in medicine, and just cull the herd. She could understand how shocking their personal experience had been, but the way they were reading it could not be right. No disease in history had ever spread so fast that the infected outnumbered the healthy.

Kate closed her eyes and saw an image of Beth, the big sister she'd worshipped, defending her from a clique of narcissistic bullies on her first day of high school. But then she pictured the shell of a woman she'd seen standing on the porch, holding the thing that had been her nephew. What were the odds that Beth had been infected at the same time as Reza and Michael, unless the disease had run rampant across the city? What were the odds that Chris Santos would be infected too? He lived on the other side of the river.

She lay down and curled up on the blanket. The world couldn't change overnight, without warning. Nothing worked like that; it defied all logic.

But she couldn't deny the evidence of her senses: Reza, Michael, Beth and Chris had all succumbed. Her only hope of proving the catastrophists wrong was to test their dismal hypothesis further. She had to put aside her fears of ridicule and betrayal, and take her story to as many people as possible who she had ever had reason to trust.

## 10

Kate slipped out of the warehouse just after dawn, leaving everyone else still sleeping. She'd been afraid that Natalie's disciples might have had someone watching her, but they could hardly keep all their potential recruits under surveillance. And if she'd tried to turn them in, what would she say, to whom? That half a dozen homeless people were planning an uprising? Did the hollow men and women even understand their own nature well enough to conceive of the uninfected as any kind of threat? If they were just puppets going through the motions of living out the lives that their original hosts would have lived, how could that include any scenario that reflected their own difference?

As she strode down the highway, she tried to stare down her qualms and fix on a choice of confidante: someone who lived far from the center of the outbreak that had claimed Natalie's family, and who had no more reason to be infected than anyone Kate might have plucked off the street at random.

Emily had been her closest friend in high school, and if they hadn't met up in person all that often in the last few years, that had only been a matter of how busy they'd both become. She'd visited Kate just after Michael was born, and when Kate thought back over their conversation, she felt sure that she'd be able to tell at once if anything had changed inside her friend's skull.

Emily was living in Coomera, some forty kilometers south; not exactly walking distance. Kate found a bus stop for the route into the city and joined a small queue of early commuters. She met one woman's gaze and they exchanged polite greetings. *Hollowed or not? Infected or not?* If this disease spread so rapidly, so easily, how had she been spared, herself? Some natural immunity? Some genetic quirk? She'd survived sharing a bed with Reza, but how many of the hollowed could she share a bus with before her luck ran out?

It was mid-morning by the time Kate arrived in Coomera, but Emily worked from home, so there was no reason for her not to be around. Kate rang the bell and stood waiting, anxiously. She could feel herself already gloomily prejudging the verdict, on no evidence whatsoever.

She rang again, then banged on the door. "Emily?"

A young man emerged from the house next door. "I think she's still away for another week."

"Oh."

"Either that, or she's tricked me into watering her plants while she sleeps all day," he joked.

Kate smiled. "I should have called first." As she walked down the road toward the bus stop, she remembered Emily talking about a business trip to Texas to meet with potential investors. She'd apologized for dropping in so soon after Kate came home from hospital with Michael, but she'd been preparing to leave in the next day or two. Kate hadn't entirely forgotten; she'd just assumed she would have been back by now.

Half an hour into the long ride north, the bus passed a battered payphone. Kate rang the bell and got off at the next stop. She walked back to the payphone, trying to recall Emily's number; it had been years since she'd had to type it. When she punched her best guess into the keypad, a bland synthetic voice offered her a hint of success: "The number you have dialed currently redirects to an international destination. Do you wish to proceed with the call?"

Kate said, "Yes."

After six rings, she heard: "You've reached Emily's phone, please leave a message." Kate slammed the handset down. She recognized her friend's voice, but it had been stripped of any trace of warmth and humor.

She stood by the phone as the traffic sped past beside her, trying to understand what had happened. Had Emily been carrying the virus even before she'd flown out of Brisbane, and only succumbed to it after she'd arrived in America? And then … what? She'd re-recorded her phone's greeting, to reflect her new, diminished state of consciousness? Unless she was actually an alien pod-person signaling to her fellow invaders, why would she even think of doing that?

Kate called the number again, listened to the recording again. She'd heard the same words dozens of times over the last ten years. And she could not put her finger on any change in timing, pitch, or intonation.

She called a third time, covering her left ear against the traffic noise. Every syllable was shaped and positioned just as it always had been – like the freckles on Reza's shoulders. It was only the deeper meaning that had slipped away.

But this was a sound file, a digital waveform – and if it was literally *unchanged*, then any meaning with which the speaker had imbued it ought to remain intact.

Kate called again, trying to block out any emotional reaction to the voice and judge it entirely as she would a series of beeps in an audiology test. The result was not what she'd expected: the affectless drone she'd been hearing before suddenly seemed *more* human, not less.

Just as the tone sounded for the caller to leave a message, the faint hiss on the line changed, and a live voice, thick from sleep, said, "Hello?"

Kate said, "Emily?"

"Kate? Is something wrong?"

"No. Did I wake you?"

"It's all right; it's not that late here."

"I didn't realize you'd still be away."

"Yeah … I've had a lot of interest in the project, but these things never go to plan."

Kate kept the conversation going while saying as little as possible herself, prodding Emily along with smalltalk, while tuning her own expectations in and out. The more she sought a feeling of solace and intimacy, the more her friend's voice mocked and disappointed her. But when she emptied her mind and just listened, everything sounded normal.

"Are you sure you're all right?" Emily asked. "You sound a bit out of it."

"Work's been crazy," Kate replied. "There's a case … I can't talk about it now, but maybe when you get back."

When she'd hung up the call, she sat on the concrete beside the payphone. There was only one conclusion that made any sense now, but trying to acknowledge it was like trying to take control of an optical illusion. The cube needed to evert; the vase needed to recede into the gap between two faces. All along, she'd been confusing figure and ground. But she'd been right to believe that the people who'd fled their families had been the ones affected by disease; her mistake had been to change her mind. Because she had fled for the very same reason.

Kate felt her whole body shaking, as if she'd just clawed her way back from a precipice. Michael and Reza weren't suffering from any kind of illness. Beth, Chris and Emily were all in perfect health. And whatever she'd been afflicted with, herself, she had to believe that it could be treated. She had to cling to that hope, just as she had when the roles had appeared to be reversed.

She staggered to her feet. She thought of calling Reza, to set his mind at ease, but she was afraid that if she heard his voice everything might flip again.

As she walked toward the bus stop, she pictured herself back in the emergency department – where she should have remained, as Reza had beseeched her to, all those nights ago. But once she was admitted to hospital, once the psychiatrists and neurologists were debating the cause and extent of her delusions, how seriously would any of her colleagues treat her testimony? How much of what she had actually discovered would they believe?

How quickly would they act to protect the families who were marked for the same fate as Natalie's?

She couldn't take the risk that they'd ignore her. She couldn't run away and hide in a hospital bed while the righteous army rose up against the hollow ones, and the true believers honored those they'd loved by granting them peace.

## 11

"I've been wondering about something," Kate said. She was sitting with the other runaways: Linda, Gary, Suzanne and Ahmed, huddled in a circle away from the merely homeless, who were hostile or agnostic when it came to their cause. "Exactly where did this disease come from? And exactly how does it spread?"

"Does it matter?" Linda replied. "We know it's spreading fast, whatever the route."

But Suzanne was less dismissive. "It could be important. Did you have something in mind?"

Kate said, "My yard has a couple of fig trees, right at the back. And those fig trees are full of fruit bats. I don't actually go down there and roll around in the guano, but our dog was doing that all the time." She looked around the circle, hunting for any sign that this scenario, based on what she'd seen at Natalie's house, might be describing a shared condition. "Remember the Hendra virus? It went from fruit bats to horses, then people. What if this is something like that – but with dogs instead of horses as the link?"

The group was silent for a while, then Ahmed said, "My dog was acting strangely for a couple of days before I left. But my wife had nothing to do with him; she wouldn't even let him in the house."

"Do you have fig trees?" Kate asked.

"No. But our neighbor does, and some of the branches hang over the fence."

She waited, but no one else volunteered their own zoonotic risk profile. If the details didn't match, why not say so?

Gary said, "In any case, we know it must be jumping straight from human to human now."

Kate frowned. "What makes you so sure?"

"Because of the speed," Linda interjected.

"But what exactly do we know about the speed?"

Linda was starting to lose patience. "My mother, in Sydney, was already affected the very same day my husband changed. I called her up to try to tell her something was wrong, and she was … gone."

Kate nodded soberly. "It hit my sister, the same night as my husband and my son. But this morning…" She steeled herself, ready to find out the hard way if her own revelatory experience could sway anyone else. "I called a friend who's been in America for the last two months—"

Everyone turned away from her to look across the warehouse floor, back toward the loading bay. A woman was approaching the circle. Her eyes were lowered, and she'd shaved her head, but as she crossed into the yellow light of the hurricane lamps, Kate recognized her by the shape of her face.

Her four companions rose to their feet, and Kate followed them. Each of them embraced Natalie in turn, and then Gary introduced her to Kate.

Kate shook her hand in silence. Natalie didn't meet her gaze. The six of them sat on the tartan picnic blanket that Gary had spread on the concrete floor.

Natalie said, "It has to be tonight."

"Are you sure?" Gary asked. "Once we tip our hand, there'll be no going back. And I still think I can get more recruits. Rowan's gone missing, but he might turn up—"

"No. We can't wait any longer." Natalie spoke calmly, but with a tone of authority. "We need to send a signal to all the people who are still unreachable. We need to let them know that they're not alone, that there's an army on their side, and an example they can follow."

"I understand." Gary looked around the circle. "Is everyone ready?"

Everyone but Kate nodded, but Kate saw Ahmed glance her way uncertainly. If she gave him more reason to doubt, there might be a chance that she could break the consensus.

She said, "Please, can I share a story with you? It will only take a minute." Forget Emily and her voicemail. She needed to cut closer to home.

Gary looked to Natalie, then said, "Of course."

"The night I left my family," Kate began, "I was driving around for a long time, trying to decide what to do. Then I thought: I'll go to my sister. She'll help me, she'll understand. I didn't have my phone, so I couldn't call her. But as I drove toward her house, as I got closer and closer, the more I thought about what would happen once I knocked on her door, the more certain I was that she'd already gone the way of my husband and my son. I *knew* she was exactly like them – without even seeing her, without even talking to her.

"So I thought: I'll go to my friend Chris. He lived much farther away, but I trusted him. So I set off south, heading for his apartment, glad I still had someone I could turn to. And the same thing happened. I never arrived; I never saw him, I never heard his voice. But I was absolutely sure that he'd been hollowed out.

"What does that mean? Do I have some magical sense of who's changed, that I can know that without even meeting them?"

Natalie said, "You made a guess, that's all." Her manner was growing brittle and defensive. She was an intelligent woman; she knew there was no intuition that could work like this, no presentiment that could be trusted in the absence of a single fact to guide it.

"But the feeling was so strong," Kate insisted. "As strong as when I saw what my husband had become, lying beside me in my bed. I never let him speak, either. I just *knew*, because it was so clear to me. But now, if I'm honest with myself, I'm afraid that it wasn't him who changed. I'm afraid —"

Natalie snapped. She started screaming, then she leaned over and began pummeling Kate with her fists. Linda and Ahmed took hold of her, pulling her back, but she kept shrieking and thrashing. Suzanne began sobbing, staring at Kate in horror, as if she'd just stabbed all five of her comrades through the heart.

Kate kept talking, sickened by the cruelty of what she was doing to a woman already annihilated by grief, but determined to finish the job for the sake of anyone still tempted to follow her.

She said, "I'm afraid I'm the one who changed. The dog dug around in the bat shit, then she got sick, and I let her lick my face. *My* face, not my husband's, not my son's. I thought they'd lost everything that made them human, but now I know that it was all in my head."

## 12

"Surprise!" Reza called out from the far side of the visitor's yard. He was holding a child in his arms.

Kate approached them warily. "Is that really him?" As soon as the words slipped out, she wished she could take them back, but if Reza heard them as more than a figure of speech he did nothing to show it. "He's grown so much," she added.

"Yeah. I'm fattening him up for sumo school." He smiled and held Michael out toward her.

Kate hesitated, afraid that after so long he wouldn't recognize her. But he gazed placidly into her face, and offered no protest when she took him in her arms.

They sat together on one of the benches.

"That beard's getting out of control," she told Reza.

"Ah, but you love it, don't you?"

"It helps." The neurologist had suggested this trick, and it seemed to be working. The new Reza reminded her of the old one, just enough to invoke memories of him without raising her expectations too high, while she built a new set of responses to the way he looked now. Sometimes it felt wrong when she kissed him, like some sick game with twins, but if she had to choose between the old Reza being dead to her forever, or reincarnated in this imperfect look-alike, she'd settle for transmigration into a doppelgänger with a beard.

She turned to Michael, and he reached up and put a hand on her face. "Who is the most beautiful boy?" she asked. "Can you guess who that is?" He smiled, a little smugly, as if he knew he was being flattered simply from her tone. That seemed new, but she could love what was new. Everything that mattered most in his life was yet to come.

Reza put an arm around her shoulders, and she didn't flinch.

"The last scan showed no inflammation," she said. "And there's no more trace of the virus in my CSF. So maybe another week. They're still cautious; some of the others have had flare-ups."

"I'm glad they're cautious," he said. "But we can't wait to have you home."

Kate bent down and kissed Michael three times in rapid succession. He cooed with delight and tugged at her hair. Nobody could tell her what the future held, for her or the seventeen others. "Capgras syndrome" was just a name for a cluster of symptoms that had been seen in half a dozen different diseases; it was not the means to divine a prognosis. But even if her raw perceptions of people had forever lost their power to evoke the emotional history that had once fleshed out their meaning, her love for her family had not been lost. She just had to find detours around the barriers, and dig tunnels to the deeper truth.

"How's your father been?" she asked Reza.

"Oh, didn't I tell you?"

"Tell me what?" Kate was worried for a moment, but Reza didn't seem upset.

"This worked for him, too." He stroked his beard. "He's out of that fucking desert prison, back in Isfahan in the seventies. I don't look like his father, but I can pass for one of his uncles, and apparently they got on pretty well. I told him he was staying in a posh hotel where the staff all liked practicing their English for the tourists."

Kate began crying, but when she saw the effect on Michael she forced herself to stop.

"It's all right," Reza said. "He's happy now. Everything's going to be all right."

# SHADOW FLOCK

## 1

Natalie pointed down along the riverbank to a pair of sturdy-looking trees, a Bald Cypress and a Southern Live Oak, about fifty meters away. "They might be worth checking out." She set off through the scrub, her six students following.

When they reached the trees, Natalie had Céline run a structural check, using the hand-held ground-penetrating radar to map the roots and the surrounding soil. The trees bore gray cobwebs of Spanish moss, but most of it was on the higher branches, out of harm's way. Natalie had chosen the pair three months before, when she was planning the course; it was cheating, but the students wouldn't have thanked her if they'd ended up spending a whole humid, mosquito-ridden day hunting for suitable pillars. In a real disaster you'd take whatever delays and hardship fate served up, but nobody was interested in that much verisimilitude in a training exercise.

"Perfect," Céline declared, smiling slightly, probably guessing that the result was due to something more than just a shrewd judgment made from a distance.

Natalie asked Mike to send a drone with a surveying module across to the opposite bank. The quadrocopter required no supervision for such a simple task, but it was up to Mike to tell it which trees to target first, and the two best candidates – a pair of sturdy oaks – were impossible to miss. The way things were going they stood a good chance of being back in New Orleans before sunset.

With their four pillars chosen, it was time to settle on a construction strategy. They had three quads to work with, and more than enough cable, but the Tchefuncte River was about a hundred and thirty meters wide here. A single spool of cable held a hundred meters, and that was as much weight as each backpack-sized quad could carry.

Josh raised his notepad to seek software advice, but Natalie stopped him. "Would it kill you to spend five minutes thinking?"

"We're going to need to do some kind of mid-air splice," he said. "I just wanted to check what knots are available, and which would be strongest."

"Why splicing?" Natalie pressed him.

He raised his hands and held them a short distance apart. "Cable." Then he increased the separation. "River."

Augusto said, "What about loops?" He hooked two fingers together and strained against the join. "Wouldn't that be stronger?"

Josh snorted. "And halve the effective length? We'd need three spools to bridge the gap then, and you'd still need to splice the second loop to the third."

"Not if we pre-form the middle loop ourselves," Augusto replied. "Fuse the ends, here on the ground. That's got to be better than any mid-air splice. Or easier to check, and easier to fix."

Natalie looked around the group for objections. "Everyone agree? Then we need to make a flight plan."

They assembled the steps from a library of maneuvers, then prepared the cable for the first crossing. The heat was becoming enervating, and Natalie had to fight the urge to sit in the shade and bark orders. Down in Haiti she'd never cared about being comfortable, but it was harder to stay motivated when all that was at stake were a few kids' grades in one minor elective.

"I think we're ready," Céline declared, a little nervous, a little excited.

Natalie said, "Be my guest."

Céline tapped the screen of her notepad and the first quad whirred into life, rising up from the riverbank and tilting a little as it moved toward the cypress.

With cable dangling, the drone made three vertical loops around the tree's lowest branch, wrapping it in a short helix. Then it circumnavigated the trunk twice, once close-in, then a second time in a long ellipse that left cable hanging slackly from the branch. It circled back, dropped beneath the branch and flew straight through the loop. It repeated the maneuver then headed away, keeping the spool clamped until it had pulled the knot tight.

As the first drone moved out over the glistening water, the second one was already ahead of it, and the third was drawing close to the matching tree on the far side of the river. Natalie glanced at the students, gratified by the tension on their faces: success here was not a *fait accompli.* Céline's hand hovered above her notepad; if the drones struck an unforeseen problem – and failed to recover gracefully on their own – it would be her job to intervene manually.

When the second drone had traveled some forty meters from the riverbank it began ascending, unwinding cable as it went to leave a hanging streamer marking its trail. From this distance the shiny blue line of polymer was indistinguishable from the kind its companion was dispensing, but then the drone suddenly stopped climbing, clamped the spool, and accelerated downward. The single blue line revealed its double-stranded nature, spreading out into a heart-shaped loop. The first drone shot through the heart then doubled back, hooking the two cables together, then the second one pulled out of its dive and continued across the river. The pierced heart always struck Natalie as surreal – the kind of thing that serenading cartoon birds would form with streamers for Snow White in the woods.

Harriet, usually the quietest of the group, uttered an involuntary, admiring expletive.

The third drone had finished hitching itself to the tree on the opposite bank, and was flying across the water for its own rendezvous. Natalie strained her eyes as the second drone went into reverse, again separating the paired cables so its companion could slip through and form the link.

Then the second drone released the loop completely and headed back to the riverbank, its job done. The third went off to mimic the first, tying its loose end to the tree where it had started.

They repeated the whole exercise three more times, giving the bridge two hand-ropes and two deck supports, before breaking for lunch. As Natalie was unwrapping the sandwiches she'd brought, a dark blur the size of her thumb buzzed past her face and alighted on her forearm. Instinctively, she moved to flick it off, but then she realized that it was not a living insect: it was a small Toshiba dragonfly, its four wings iridescent with photovoltaic coatings. Whether it was mapping the forest, monitoring wildlife, or just serving as a communications node, the last thing she'd want to do was damage it. The machine should not have landed on anything but vegetation, but no one's programming was perfect. She watched it as it sat motionless in the patch of sunlight falling on her skin, then it ascended suddenly and flew off out of sight.

In the afternoon, the team gave their bridge a rudimentary woven deck. Each of the students took turns donning a life-jacket and hard-hat before walking across the swaying structure and back, whooping with a mixture of elation at their accomplishment and adrenaline as they confronted its fragility.

"And now we have to take it apart," Natalie announced, prepared for the predictable groans and pleas. "No arguments!" she said firmly. "Pretty as it is, it would only take a party of five or six hikers to break it, and if they ended up dashing their brains out in the shallows that would be enough to bankrupt the university and send us all to prison."

## 2

As Natalie started up the stairs to her apartment she heard a distinctive trilling siren, then saw a red shimmer spilling down onto the landing ahead. The delivery quad came into view and she moved to the left to let it pass, catching a welcome cool wash from its downdraft – a sensation weirdly intensified by the lime-green tint of the receding hazard lights.

She tensed as she approached her floor, hoping that she wouldn't find Sam waiting for her. His one talent was smooth talking, and he could always find someone willing to buzz him into the building. Against her better judgment she'd let her brother wheedle her into sinking ten thousand dollars into his latest business venture, but when it had proved to be as unprofitable as all the rest, rather than apologizing and going in search of paid work he'd started begging her to invest even more, in order to "tip the balance" – as if his struggling restaurant were a half-submerged Spanish galleon full of gold that only needed a few more flotation bladders to rise magnificently to the surface.

Sam wasn't lurking in the corridor, but there was a small package in front of her door. Natalie was puzzled and annoyed; she wasn't expecting anything, and the drones were not supposed to leave their cargo uncollected on a doormat. She stooped down and picked up the parcel; it bore the logo of a local courier, but water had somehow got inside the plastic pocket that held the waybill, turning the portion with the sender's address into gray mush. A gentle shake yielded the clinking slosh of melting ice.

Inside, she put the parcel in the kitchen sink, went to the bathroom, then came back and cut open the mailing box to reveal an insulating foam container. The lid bore the words GUESS WHO? written in black marker. Natalie honestly couldn't; she'd parted company with the last two men she'd dated on terms that made surprise gifts unlikely, let alone a peace offering of chilled crab meat, or whatever this was.

She tugged the lid off and tipped the ice into the sink. A small pink object stood out from the slush, but it wasn't any part of a crab. Natalie stared for several seconds, unwilling to prod the thing into position for a better view, then she fetched a pair of tongs to facilitate a more thorough inspection.

It was the top part of a human finger. A little finger, severed at the joint. She walked away and paced the living room, trying to decode the meaning of the thing before she called the police. She could not believe that Alfonso – a moody musician who'd ditched her when she'd dared to leave one of his gigs at two in the morning, on a work night – would have the slightest interest in mutilating his own precious hands in the service of a psychotic prank. Digging back further she still came up blank. Rafael had smashed crockery once, in the heat of an argument, but by now she'd be surprised to elicit any stronger reaction from him than a rueful smile if they ran into each other on the street. The truth was, the prospect of the cops hauling any of these ex-lovers in for questioning mortified her almost as much as the macabre offering itself, because pointing the finger at any of them seemed preposterously self-aggrandizing. "Really?" she could hear the whole line-up of unlikely suspects demanding, holding out their pristine mitts. "You thought you were worth *that*?"

Natalie walked back to the kitchen doorway. Why was she assuming that the amputation had been voluntary? No one she knew would commit such an act – upon themselves or anyone else – but that didn't mean she didn't know the unwilling donor.

She turned around and rushed to the bedroom, where she kept the bioassay attachment for her notepad. The only software she'd downloaded for it was for personal health and pregnancy testing, but it took less than a minute to get the app she needed.

There was no visible blood left inside the fingertip, but when she picked it up with the tongs it was full of meltwater that ought to be brimming with sloughed cells. She tipped a little of the water onto the assay chip and waited ten long minutes for the software to announce a result for the markers she'd chosen.

*Chance of fraternity: 95%*

Sam must have gone elsewhere for money, but it would have disappeared into the same bottomless pit as her own investment. And when his creditors had come for him with their bolt-cutters, who else was he going to rope in to help him repay his debt but his sister?

Natalie wanted to scream with anger, but she found herself weeping. Her brother was an infuriating, immature, self-deluding brat, but he didn't deserve this. If she had to re-mortgage the apartment to get him out of these people's clutches, so be it. She wasn't going to abandon him.

As she began trying to think through the logistics of dealing with the bank as quickly as possible – without explaining the true purpose of the loan – her phone rang.

## 3

"We don't want your money. But there is a way you can resolve this situation without paying a cent."

Natalie stared at the kidnapper, who'd asked her to call him Lewis. The food court to which he'd invited her was as busy as she'd seen it on a Wednesday night; she had even spotted a few cops. The undeniable fact of their meeting proved nothing incriminating, but how could he know she wasn't recording his words?

She said, "You're not a loan shark."

"No." Lewis had an accent from far out of state, maybe the Midwest. He was a dark-haired, clean-shaven white man, and he looked about forty. Natalie tried to commit these facts to memory, terrified that when the police finally questioned her she'd be unable to recall his face at all. "We'd like you to consult for us."

"Consult?" Natalie managed a derisive laugh. "Who do you think I work for, the NSA? Everything I know about drones is already in the public domain. You didn't need to kidnap my brother. It's all on the web."

"There are time pressures," Lewis explained. "Our own people are quick studies, but they've hit a roadblock. They've read your work, of course. That's why they chose you."

"And what am I supposed to help you do? Assassinate someone?" The whole conversation was surreal, but the hubbub of their boisterous fellow diners was so loud that unless she'd stood up on the table and shouted the question, no one would have looked at them twice.

Lewis shook his head; at least he didn't insult her intelligence by feigning offense. "No one will get hurt. We just need to steal some information."

"Then find yourself a hacker."

"The targets are smarter than that."

"*Targets*, plural?"

Lewis said, "Only three that will concern you directly – though in all fairness I should warn you that your efforts will need to synchronize with our own on several other fronts."

Natalie felt light-headed; when exactly had she signed the contract in blood? "You're taking a lot for granted."

"Am I?" There wasn't a trace of menace in his voice, but then, the stakes had already been made clear.

"I'm not refusing," she replied. "I won't help you to inflict bodily harm – but if you're open with me and I'm sure that there's no chance of that, I'll do what you ask."

Lewis nodded, amiable in a businesslike way. He, or his associates, had been cold-blooded enough to mutilate Sam as proof of their seriousness, but if they planned to kill her once she'd served her purpose, why meet physically, in a public space, where a dozen surveillance drones would be capturing the event?

"The targets are all bitionaires," he said. "We don't plan to touch a hair on their heads; we just want their key-strings … which are not stored on anything vulnerable to spyware."

"I see." Natalie's own stash of electronic pocket change didn't merit any great precautions, but she was aware of the general idea: anyone prudent, and sufficiently wealthy, kept the cryptographic key to their anonymized digital fortune in a purpose-built wallet. The operating system and other software resided solely on read-only media, and even the working memory functioned under rigid, hardware-enforced protocols that made the whole setup effectively incorruptible. "So how can I get around that? Am I meant to infiltrate the wallet factory?"

"No." Lewis paused, but he wasn't turning coy on her – merely hiding a faint belch behind a politely raised hand. "The basic scenario is the kind of thing any competent stage magician could pull off. The target takes their wallet from its safe, then gets distracted. We substitute an identical-looking device. The target commences to log in to their exchange with the fake wallet; we've already cloned their fingerprints so we can mimic those preliminaries on the real wallet. The target receives a one-time password from the exchange on their cell phone; they enter it into the fake wallet, and we use it to enact our own preferred transactions via the real one."

Natalie opened her mouth to protest: her understanding was that the message from the exchange would also include a hash of the transaction details – allowing the user to double-check exactly what it was they were authorizing. But she wasn't thinking straight: to the human looking at that string of gibberish, the information would be invisible. Only *the wallet itself* had the keys required to reveal the hash's true implications, and the fake wallet would blithely pretend that everything matched up perfectly.

She said, "So all you need to do is invite these people to bring their wall safes to a Las Vegas show."

Lewis ignored her sarcasm. "The transactions can't be rescinded, but it won't take the targets long to discover that they've been duped – and to spread the word. So we need to ensure that these individual operations are as close to concurrent as possible."

Natalie struggled to maintain a tone of disapproval even as her curiosity got the better of her. "How do you make all these people get an itch to buy or sell at the same time?"

"We've already set that in motion," Lewis replied. "You don't need to know the details, but in seven days and thirteen hours, unless the targets are comatose they won't be able to ignore the top story on their news feeds."

Natalie leaned back from the table. Half her experience, and all of her best ideas, had involved maneuvers on a scale of tens of meters by devices that were far from small or stealthy. Dextrous as a well-equipped quadrocopter could be, sleight-of-hand was a bit much to ask of it.

"So do you want me to program robot storks to carry the fake wallets down chimneys?"

Lewis said, "The fake wallets have all been in place for a while, concealed inside innocuous-looking items."

"Like what?"

"Cereal packets. Once people find the brand they like, they stick to it."

"I knew there was a reason I didn't use my supermarket's loyalty card. And the drones?"

"They're on site as well."

"The wallets are how big?"

Lewis held his fingers a few centimeters apart. "Like credit cards. And not much thicker."

"So … how many dragonflies?"

"Six at each site. But they're not dragonflies: they're custom-built, smaller and quieter. From a distance they'd pass for houseflies."

Natalie crushed the urge to start grilling him on detailed specifications. "So you have a plan. And you've got the tools in place. Why do you need me at all?"

"Our plan relied on realtime operators," Lewis confessed. "The whole thing seemed too complex to deal with any other way – too many variables, too much uncertainty. All the sites have countermeasures against radio frequency traffic, but we believed we could communicate optically; some people don't consider that at all, or don't make the effort to lock things down tightly."

"But…?"

"In three cases, it looks as if our optical routes have gone from mostly open to patchy at best. Not from any deliberate blocking strategies – just minor changes in the architecture, or people's routines. But it means that a continuous link would be too much to hope for."

Lewis's team had been given the right advice from the start: this was a job for humans. And now she was expected to program eighteen drones to perform three elaborate feats of prestidigitation, using nothing but their own tiny brains?

Natalie said, "Before we go any further, I want you to prove to me that my brother's still alive."

4

"I ran into your fifth grade teacher last week," Natalie remarked, once the pleasantries were over. "The one you had a crush on."

Sam responded with a baffled scowl, too quickly to have needed to think through his reaction. "I don't even remember her name. I certainly didn't have a crush on her!"

However much intelligence the kidnappers might have gathered on the two of them – all the family pets and vacations they'd shared, all the confidences they might have exchanged – there was no proving a negative. Natalie was sure she wasn't watching a puppet.

Someone else was holding the phone, giving the camera a wider view than usual. Apart from his splinted and bandaged finger Sam appeared to be physically unharmed. Natalie refrained from upbraiding him; *she* was the reason he'd been abducted, even if some idiotic plan to keep the restaurant afloat had made him easier to trap.

"Just take it easy," she said. "I'm going to give these people what they want, and you'll be out of there in no time." She glanced at Lewis, then added, "I'll talk to you every morning, OK? That's the deal. They'll have to keep you safe, or I'll pull the plug."

“Do you think you can check in on the restaurant for me?” Sam pleaded. “Just to be sure that the chef’s not slacking off?”

“No, I really can’t.”

“But Dmitri’s so lazy! If I’m not—”

Natalie handed the phone back to Lewis and he broke the connection. They’d gone into a side-street to make the call; apparently Lewis hadn’t trusted Sam not to start yelling for help if he saw other people in the background.

“I get to call him every day,” she said. “That’s not negotiable.”

“By Skype,” Lewis replied.

“All right.” A Skype connection would be much harder to trace than a cell phone. Natalie was beginning to feel nostalgic for her previous nightmare scenario of loan sharks and intransigent banks. “What if I do my best, but I can’t pull this off?” she asked.

“We’re sure you can,” Lewis replied.

His faith in her was not at all reassuring. “There’s a reason your experts told you they’d need human pilots. I swear I’ll try to make this work – but you can’t murder my brother because I fall at the same hurdle as your own people.”

Lewis didn’t reply. On one level, Natalie understood the psychology behind his strategy: if he’d promised that she’d be rewarded merely for trying, she might have been tempted to hold herself back. She suspected that she’d be unlikely to face criminal charges, regardless, but sheer stubbornness or resentment might have driven her to indulge in some passive sabotage if she thought she could get away with it.

“What now?” she asked.

“By the time you get home, we’ll have emailed you briefing files. We’ll need the software for the drones by midnight on Monday.”

Natalie was so flustered that she had to count out the interval in her head. “Five days! I thought you said seven!”

"We'll need to verify the new software for ourselves, then install it via infrasound. The bandwidth for that is so low that it could take up to forty-eight hours."

Natalie was silent, but she couldn't keep the dismay from showing on her face.

"You might want to call in sick," Lewis suggested.

"That's it? That's the best advice you have for me?"

"Read the briefing." Lewis paused, then nodded slightly. He turned and walked away.

Natalie felt herself swaying. If she went to the police, Sam would be dead in an instant. Lewis couldn't deny meeting her, but he would have prepared a well-documented explanation in advance – maybe log files showing that they'd been matched up by a dating site. The emailed briefing could have come from anywhere. She had nothing on these people that would make them pause for a second before they graduated from fingertips to heads.

Three targets for her special attention, and many more in the whole blitz. The total haul might reach ten or eleven figures. She'd walked willingly into the aftermaths of hurricanes and earthquakes, but she'd never been foolish enough to position herself – in any capacity – on the route between a gang of thugs and a pile of cash.

## 5

Natalie spent five hours going through the files before she forced herself to stop. She climbed into bed and lay staring into the humid darkness, soaking the sheets in acrid sweat.

There was no information missing that she could have reasonably demanded. She had architectural plans for the victims' entire houses, complete down to the dimensions of every hinge of every closet. She had three-dimensional imagery and gait data for every member of each of the households; she had schedules that covered both their formal appointments and their imperfectly predictable habits, from meal times to bowel movements. Every motion sensor of every security system, every insect-zapping laser, every moth-chasing cat had been cataloged. Navigating the drones between these hazards was not a hopeless prospect – but the pitfalls that made the whole scheme unravel would be the ones nobody had anticipated. It had taken her years to render her bridge-building algorithms robust against wind, rain and wildlife, and she had still seen them fail when grime and humidity had made a motor stall or a cable stick unexpectedly.

She dozed off for fifteen minutes, then woke around dawn. Somehow she managed to fall asleep again, motivated by the certainty that she'd be useless without at least a couple of hours' rest. At a quarter to nine she rose, phoned the engineering department claiming flu, then took a cold shower and made toast and coffee.

The call to Sam took a minute to connect, but then it was obvious from his appearance that his captors had had to rouse him.

"The job they've given me isn't too hard," she said. "I'll get through it, then everyone can walk away happy."

Sam replied with a tone of wary optimism, "And the ten grand they gave me for the restaurant? They don't want it back?"

"Not as far as I know." Natalie wracked her brain for another puppet test, but then she decided that she'd already heard proof enough: no one else on the planet could make it sound as if ten thousand dollars sunk into that grease-pit would more than compensate for any minor inconvenience the two of them might suffer along the way.

"I owe you, Nat," Sam declared. He thought she was simply working off his debt – the way he'd mowed lawns as a kid, to pay for a neighbor's window that one of his friends had broken. He'd taken the rap to spare the boy a thrashing from his drunken father.

"How's your hand?" she asked.

He held it up; the bandage looked clean. "They're giving me pain-killers and antibiotics. The food's pretty good, and they let me watch TV." He spread his hands in a gesture of contentment.

"So, three stars on Travel Adviser?"

Sam smiled. "I'd better let you get back to work."

Natalie started with the easiest target. A man who lived alone, rarely visited by friends or lovers, he was expected to wake around seven o'clock on D-day morning and go jogging for an hour before breakfast. That would be the ideal time for the drones to break out of their hiding places in the spines of the first editions of Kasparov's five-volume *My Great Predecessors*, which presumably had appeared at a seductively low price in the window of a local used book store. The fake wallet was concealed in one of the book's covers, along with the sliver of whorled and ridged biomimetic polymer that would need to be applied to the real wallet. Thankfully, Natalie's own predecessors had already done the work of programming the clog dance of drone against touch-screen that could mimic a human tapping out any sequence of characters on a virtual keyboard. The jobs they'd left for the pilots had been of an entirely different character.

The shelves in target A's library were all spaced to allow for much taller books, leaving plenty of room for a pair of drones to slice into the wallet's compartment, grab the hooks attached to the cargo, draw it out and fly six meters to deposit it temporarily in a poorly illuminated gap between a shelving unit and a table leg. The safe itself was in the library, and prior surveillance had shown that it was A's habit to place his wallet on the table in question.

The distraction was to be a faucet in the kitchen, primed to fail and send water flooding into the sink at full pressure. The house was fitted with detectors for any ongoing radio traffic – the bugs that had collected the latest imagery had used multi-path optics, until a new sunshade had been fitted to a crucial window – but a single brief RF pulse from a drone to trigger the torrent would appear to the detectors' software as no different from the sparking when a power plug was pulled from a socket.

What if target A broke his routine and did not go jogging? The emergence of the drones and the fake wallet's extraction would not be noisy, so those stages could still proceed so long as the library itself was unoccupied. What if target A had an early visitor, or someone had spent the night? The drones would need to start listening for clues to the day's activities well before seven. Loaded with neural-net templates that would allow them to recognize voices in general, doors opening and closing and footsteps receding and approaching, they ought to be able to determine whether or not it was safe to break out.

But the surveillance images that showed the five books neatly shelved were three weeks old; it was possible that they'd ended up strewn around the house, or piled on a table beneath other books and magazines. GPS wouldn't work inside the building, but Natalie used a smattering of WiFi signal strengths collected in the past to equip the drones with a passable ability to determine their location, then added software to analyze the echo of an infrasound pulse, to help them anticipate any obstacles well before they'd broken out of their cardboard chrysalises.

The doors and windows – and even the roof space – were fitted with alarms, but target A had no motion sensors in the library that would scream blue murder every time a housefly crossed the room. Not even two houseflies carrying an object resembling a credit card.

Natalie put the pieces together then ran simulations, testing the software against hundreds of millions of permutations of all the contingencies she could think of: the placement of the books, which doors were open or closed, new developments in the target's love life, and his peregrinations through every plausible sequence of rooms and corridors. When things turned out badly from the simulator's God's-eye-view, she pored over the visual and auditory cues accessible to the drones in a selection of the failed cases, and refined her software to take account of what she'd missed.

By midnight she was exhausted, but she had the mission either succeeding completely or aborting undetected in 98.7% of the simulations. That would have to be good enough. The other targets were going to be more difficult; she needed to move on.

## 6

With every day that passed Natalie worked longer, but her short bouts of sleep came fast and ran deep, as if her brain had started concentrating some endogenous narcotic brew and would dispense the thick black distillate the moment she closed her eyes.

In the early hours of Monday morning, she dreamed that she was taking her final exam in machine vision. Sam was seated three rows behind her, throwing wads of chewing gum that stuck in her hair, but she knew that if she turned around to whisper an angry reprimand he'd only ignore it, and it wasn't worth the risk of being accused of cheating.

She glanced up at the clock to check the time; just seconds remained, but she felt satisfied with her answers. But when she looked down at the exam paper she realized that she'd misread the questions and filled the booklet with useless *non sequiturs*.

She woke and marched to the shower to clear her head, trying to convince herself that she hadn't merely dreamed all the progress she'd made. But the truth was, target C was almost done. The ordeal was nearly over.

It was still early, but Sam had grown used to her schedule. Natalie confined herself to jokes and small talk; the more matter-of-fact they kept the conversations, the easier it was on both of them. Until he was actually free, she couldn't afford to let her emotions take over.

Target C had a husband and two school-age children, but if their domestic routine followed its usual pattern they would be out of the house well before the trigger – expected at eleven a.m. in C's east-coast time zone. The most worrying thing about C was not her family, but the way she kept changing the decorative skins she'd bought for her wallet: the surveillance, going back twelve months, revealed no fewer than four different designs. Natalie could accept that anyone might have their personal esthetic whims, even when it came to this most utilitarian of items. But it was hard to believe that it had never once crossed target C's mind that these unpredictable embellishments would make it so much harder for her to mistake another wallet for her own.

Still, the last surveillance imagery was only ten days old, and it showed a skin that was no different from that on the planted fake. The odds weren't bad that it would remain in place, and the changes in style on the previous occasions had been so clear that the drones would have no difficulty noticing if the fake had gone out of fashion. Lewis's people had not been foolhardy enough to try to wrap their substitute in some kind of infinitely reconfigurable chameleon device; visually, these ten-dollar skins were not unforgeable works of art, but they did come with different textures – slick, metallic, silky. Half-fooling a willing participant in a VR game with a haptic interface was one thing, but no hardware on the planet could morph from brushed steel to lamb's fleece well enough to convince someone who'd held the real thing just seconds before.

Natalie started the simulations running. Target C had a strong aversion to insects, and every room was fitted with an eliminator, but even these low-powered pinprick lasers could not be unleashed in a human-occupied space without rigorous certification that ensured their compliance with published standards. Insects followed characteristic, species-specific flight patterns, and the eliminators were required to give any ambiguous object the benefit of the doubt, lest some poor child flicking an apple seed off her plate or brushing glitter from her home-made fairy wand summon unfriendly fire from the ceiling. The drones didn't need to imitate any particular, benign airborne debris; they merely had to exhibit an acceleration profile a few standard deviations away from anything seen in the official laboratory studies of *Musca*, *Culex* or *Aedes*. Unlike target B's cat, the necessary strictures were completely predictable.

With the count of trials rising into seven digits and still no atonal squawk of failure, Natalie let herself relax a little and close her eyes. The midnight deadline was still fourteen hours away. She'd sent versions of her work for the other two targets to her "Team Leader" – as the collaboration software would have it – and received no complaints. Let these clowns run off to the Bahamas with their billions, and let the victims learn to use banks like normal people. She'd done the only honorable thing under the circumstances, and she had nothing to be ashamed of. Whatever the authorities decided, she could still look herself – and any juror – in the eye.

She opened her eyes. Why, exactly, did she believe that Lewis's people would let her live to confess her crimes? Because she'd been a good girl and done as she was told?

Lewis had met her in a public place, making her feel safer about the encounter and seeming to offer a degree of insurance: if she vanished, or turned up dead, the authorities would scour the surveillance records and reconstruct her movements. A judge was much less likely to sign a warrant for the same trawling expedition if a living, breathing woman and her mildly mutilated brother went to the police with an attention-seeking story that positioned them in starring roles in the heist – and in any case, a shared meal proved nothing about her dinner companion.

But all of that presupposed that there really were records of the meeting: that the flock of benign surveillance drones that watched over downtown New Orleans had been as vigilant as ever that night – even in the places her adversaries had chosen to send her. Who was to say that they hadn't infiltrated the flock: corrupted the software in existing drones, or found a way to substitute their own impostors?

If there was nothing at all to tie Lewis to her – save the microscopic chance that some diner in the food court that night would remember the two of them – why would the thieves leave any loose ends?

Natalie tried to keep her face locked in the same expression of exhaustion and grim resolve that she'd felt being etched into it over the last five days; the whole apartment was probably full of the same kind of micro-cameras that had documented the targets' lives in such detail. And for all she knew there could be hidden drones too, far more dangerous than anything the targets were facing: robot wasps with fatal stings. A week ago that would have sounded like florid paranoia, but now it was the most reasonable thing she could imagine, and the only thoughts that seemed truly delusional were those of walking away from this unscathed.

She went to the kitchen and made fresh coffee, standing by the pot with her eyes half-closed. Apart from any cameras on the walls, her computer was sure to be infested with spyware. They would have done the same to the one in her office at UNO – and in any case, she doubted that her criminal overseers would be happy if she suddenly decided to show up at work.

When the coffee was ready she stirred in three spoonfuls of sugar; before the crisis she'd gone without, but now she'd been escalating the dose day by day in the hope of shoring up her flagging powers of concentration. She carried the mug back toward her desk, squinting wearily at the screen as she approached, hoping that she wasn't over-playing her frazzled sleep-walker's demeanor.

She tripped and staggered, spilling the sticky, scalding brew straight down the air vent at the top of her workstation. The fans within blew out a geyser of mud-colored liquid for a second or two, with specks reaching as high as the ceiling, then the whole machine shut down, plunging the room into silence.

Natalie spent half a minute swearing and sobbing, then she picked up her phone. She made five calls to local outlets that might – just conceivably – have supplied a replacement, but none of them had a suitably powerful model in stock, and the ones they could offer her would have slowed the simulations to a crawl. She pushed the last salesperson hard, for effect, but not even a premium delivery charge could summon what she needed by drone from the Atlanta warehouse in time.

Finally, as if in desperation, she gritted her teeth and availed herself of the only remaining solution.

"I'd like to rent a cubicle for twelve hours."

"Any secretarial services?" the booking bot asked.

"No."

"Any IT requirements?"

"You bet." She reeled them off, but the bot was unfazed. The firm she'd chosen was accustomed to catering for architects and engineers, caught out with some processor-intensive emergency that was too commercially sensitive to be run in the cloud, or simply too awkward to refactor for a change of platform. It was the most logical place for her to go, given that the university was out of bounds – but it would have taken extraordinary prescience for Lewis's gang to have pre-bugged the place.

Natalie caught a bus into the city. A fly with an odd bluish tint to its body crawled over the windowpane beside her; she watched it for a while, then reached out and squashed it with the side of her fist and inspected its soft remains.

At the office complex, the demands of security and climate control had her pass through half a dozen close-fitting doors. Between these welcome barriers she ran fingers through her hair, brushed her arms and legs, and flattened her back against the nearest wall. The security guards watching on closed circuit could think what they liked, so long as she didn't look quite crazy enough to be thrown out.

On the eleventh floor, she entered the tiny cubicle assigned to her, closed the door and started loading the most recent hourly backup of her project from the flash drive she'd brought. This version wasn't quite the one that had been doing so well in the simulations, but she remembered exactly what changes she'd need to make to bring it up to that level.

The gang's roboticists would run tests of their own, but if she held off delivering the software until just before midnight they would be under enormous pressure. In a finite time there was only so much checking her fellow humans could do, and not a lot of point in them trying to wade manually through every line of code and every neural-net template included in the package. Like her, in the end they would be forced to put their trust in the simulations.

As instructed, Natalie had programmed her drones to wake and commence their mission, not at any pre-determined time, but on receipt of an external infrasound cue. It made sense to allow that much flexibility, in case the lurch in the markets that was meant to prompt people to reach for their wallets came later than expected.

One side effect of this decision was that for targets whose schedules were different for every day of the week, simulations had to be run separately for each day. But where there was no difference except for weekdays versus weekends, the simulated drones were fed no finer distinction, and the millions of permutations to be tested could play out much faster by limiting them to this simple dichotomy.

Target C stuck to a single routine from Monday to Friday, so as far as the simulations for her were concerned, they were taking place only on a generic weekday. Anything in the software that relied on it being a specific day of the week wouldn't come into play, in the simulations.

In the real world, though, Thursday would still announce itself as Thursday in the drones' internal clocks. And that very fact would be enough to tell the drones' software that they were out of VR and moving through the land of flesh and blood.

Natalie couldn't be sure that D-day would arrive on schedule, but she had no choice but to trust the swindlers to accomplish their first, enabling feat exactly as they'd planned it all along.

## 7

"This should be our last call," Natalie told Sam.

"There are two ways I could take that," he joked.

"Take it the good way."

"So they're happy with your work?" Sam tried to make that sound like a joke, too, but he couldn't quite pull it off.

"I've had no complaints."

"I always knew you'd end up as a mob accountant."

"Ha!" She'd had a summer job once that included book-keeping for a small construction firm with a shady reputation, but every transaction that had crossed her desk had appeared entirely legitimate.

"Stay strong," she said. "I'll see you soon."

Sam just nodded and lowered his eyes. She cut the link.

Natalie waited five more minutes, for six o'clock sharp. If the market trigger was coming, Lewis's people would have recognized the early signs of its onset hours ago, but she'd had no idea what to look for, and she hadn't wanted to attract suspicion by trawling the financial news. It would be impossible to load an entirely new copy of the drones' software via infrasound in less than two days – but in less than an hour, an experienced team might be able to write and deliver a small patch that neutralized the effects of her sabotage.

There would be no moment of perfect safety. Natalie used the collaboration software to send a message: *Flaw in the code for target C. Need to discuss urgently.*

Twenty seconds later, her phone rang.

"What are you talking about?" Lewis demanded angrily.

"It hasn't started executing yet, has it?" Natalie did her best to sound businesslike: she was acknowledging her screw-up, but she was still the voice of authority when it came to these drones, and she was asking for the state of play in order to salvage the situation as rapidly as possible.

"Of course it's *executing!*" Lewis snapped.

Natalie couldn't hold back a smile of relief. The software would be impossible to patch now.

"Why did you think it wouldn't start?" Lewis was baffled. "We got the confirmation hum. The drones are wide awake and running what we loaded. What's this about?"

Natalie said, "If the drones in target C's house don't catch sight of me and my brother – fully ambulatory, with our usual gaits – alone in a room with that woman before eleven a.m., things are going to play out a little differently than they did in the simulations."

Lewis understood immediately. "You *stupid bitch*—"

"No," Natalie cut him off. "Stupid would have been trusting you."

"We'll kill you both," he said coldly. "We can live without the yield from one target."

"Can you live without the yield from all the targets who'll be warned off when this woman raises the alarm? When the drones fly up to her and drop the fake wallet right in front of her face?"

To his credit, Lewis only took a few seconds to give up on the idea of more threats and bravado. "Be on the street outside your building in five minutes." He cut off the call.

Natalie put the phone down. Her whole body was trembling. She went to the bathroom and splashed water on her face, then left her apartment and sprinted down the stairs.

The black car that came for her had tinted passenger windows. Lewis opened the rear door and motioned for her to join him. Sam was sitting by the left window; he glanced across at her anxiously.

"This is what will happen," Lewis told Natalie as they sped away. "You're going to drive a car toward the target's house. Another driver will rear-end you in a hit-and-run: plenty of noise and crumpled panels, but you won't be hurt. You and your brother will walk from the wreckage, knock on the target's door, and ask her to call an ambulance. We'll spoof the 911 connection, so no ambulance will come until we put in the call ourselves. You'll play a wilting Southern flower, and at some point you'll be invited in to wait."

Natalie was incredulous. "She won't invite us in straight away?"

Lewis clenched his teeth, then spoke. "Have you ever been to Nassau County, Long Island?"

"Can we fly Business Class?" Sam wondered.

Lewis reached into a sports bag on his lap and drew out a pair of blindfolds.

Minutes later, the traffic sounds around them receded. They were bundled out of the car, led across the tarmac and up a set of stairs into what must have been a private jet. Natalie felt the plane taxying before she'd been guided to her seat, and ascending before she'd fumbled the belt into place. It would take almost three hours to reach New York; if they hit so much as an unexpected head wind, Lewis might decide to cut his losses and drop them from the plane.

"I should have told them earlier," she whispered to Sam. "I'm sorry." She'd been fixated on the risk that she'd spring the revelation too early.

"Why do we have to visit this woman?" he asked.

Natalie talked him through the whole thing, from the heist itself to the dead-man switch she'd installed at the last moment.

"You couldn't have found a way to get us to Paris instead?" Sam joked.

"They set you up," Natalie stressed. "They only loaned you the money so they could rope me in if they had to."

"I know," he said. "I get it."

"So whatever happens now, it's not on you."

Sam laughed. "*Seriously?* You thought I was going to blame myself?"

As soon as the wheels hit the ground, someone grabbed Natalie's elbow. "How's the time?" she enquired.

"Local time's ten twenty-seven," Lewis replied.

The blindfolds stayed on as they boarded a second car. When it screeched to a halt and Lewis tugged the dark band up from Natalie's eyes, she squinted out into a fluorescent-lit mechanics' workshop. Half a dozen men in overalls were standing beside a hydraulic jack, watching the new arrivals.

Lewis motioned to her to leave the car. "This is what you'll be driving." He gestured at a white sedan a few meters away. "You rented this at the airport; there are used boarding passes in the glove compartment, and some luggage with clothes and toiletries in the trunk. I don't care what your cover story is – why you're in New York, where you were heading – but you should give your real names. And make sure you don't distract the target from the trigger, or do anything else stupid. Don't even think about driving away; we can immobilize the vehicle remotely, and the crash that follows would be a whole lot worse than the one we've discussed."

"I don't have the address," Natalie realized.

"The GPS has already been programmed. The house number is one hundred and seven; don't get confused and knock anywhere else."

"What if someone else offers to help us?"

Lewis said, "The street will be as good as empty. The crash will be right outside her door."

Natalie turned to Sam, who'd joined her on the floor of the workshop. "Are you OK with this?"

"As opposed to what?"

Lewis walked up to Sam and put a hand on his shoulder. "Sorry about the *déjà vu*, but it will make the whole thing more authentic."

Sam stared at him. Natalie felt the blood draining from her face. The waiting men converged on Sam, one of them carrying a wrench.

Sam didn't fight them, he just bellowed from the pain. When everyone separated the bandage was gone from his finger and his wound was dripping blood.

Lewis said, "Better put that in your pocket for the drive, so no one sees it before the crash."

The figures on Natalie's watch had turned blue, to remind her that it had auto-synched to the new time zone. It was ten forty-six. The GPS estimated two minutes to their destination. They'd be outside the house in plenty of time – but they needed to be seen by the drones, indoors.

She glanced over at Sam. He was still pale, but he looked focused. There weren't many cars on the tree-lined streets, and Natalie had yet to spot a single pedestrian. The houses they were passing were ostentatious enough, if not exactly billionaires' mansions. But then, half the point of putting assets into digital currency was keeping a low profile.

"Destination in fifteen seconds," the GPS announced cheerily. Natalie resisted glancing in the rear-view mirror as she braked. The red pickup that had been following them since the garage slammed into the back of the sedan.

The airbags inflated like giant mushroom caps sprouting in time-lapse. Natalie felt the seat belt dig into her shoulder, but when her ears stopped ringing she took stock of her sensations and found no real pain.

"You OK?" she asked Sam. She could hear squealing tires as the truck did a U-turn and departed.

"Yeah."

"Our phones were in the hands-free docks," she reminded him. "The airbags are blocking them."

"We've just been in a crash," Sam said. "No one's going to ask us where our phones are.

Natalie got her door open and clambered out. They were right beside the mailbox of number one hundred and seven.

As Sam joined her, his severed finger exposed, the front door opened and target C ran out toward them.

"Are you all right? Is anyone else in the car?"

Natalie said, "I'm OK. It's just me and my brother."

"Oh, he's bleeding!" C was carrying her phone; she hit some keys then raised it to her ear. "A traffic accident. The other driver's cleared off. No … they're both walking, but the young man's hand … that's correct."

She lowered the phone and motioned to them to approach. "Please, come inside. They said the ambulance will be a few minutes."

Sam pulled out a handkerchief and wrapped it around the stump of his finger. He couldn't quite look their Good Samaritan in the eye as he stepped through the doorway.

Target C led them into her carpeted living room, unfazed by Sam's blood. "Please, take a seat. I'll bring you some water."

"Thank you." When the woman had left, Natalie checked her watch. It was ten fifty-three. The six drones would be performing sweeps of all the rooms where she and Sam might plausibly have ended up, mostly staying near the ceiling out of people's normal lines of sight. She looked up, and after ten or fifteen seconds she saw it: her own tiny, loyal slave, confirming her safety before fetching its brothers to resume the original plan.

"Are we safe now?" Sam asked.

"I don't know."

"Maybe we should warn her," he suggested.

Natalie was torn. Lewis's people might still come after them, whatever they did. But which action would nudge the odds in favor of survival: enraging their enemies, but weakening them too by depriving them of part of their haul, or placating them but making them stronger?

"We can't risk it," she whispered.

Target C came into the room with a pitcher of water on a tray. She poured two glasses and handed them to her guests. "I can't believe that maniac just drove off," she said. She gazed forlornly at Sam's hand. "What happened?"

"I was opening the glove compartment," Sam replied. "The doors on those things are like guillotines."

Target C's phone beeped: not a ring tone, but some kind of alert. She spent a few seconds trying to ignore it, then lost the fight and examined the screen. Natalie could almost read the woman's deliberations from the movement of her eyes and the changing set of her jaw. This was the trigger: either a grave threat to her wealth, or an irresistible opportunity.

The woman looked up. "I'm so rude. My name's Emily."

"Natalie."

"Sam."

"Are you folks from around here?"

"New Orleans."

Emily nodded, as if she'd guessed as much already. "Where is that ambulance?" She turned to Sam. "Are you in agony? I have Tylenol. But maybe you've suffered some other injury that could make that the wrong thing to take?"

Sam said, "It's all right. I'll wait for the paramedics."

Emily thought for a few seconds. "Let me just check in the medicine cabinet, so I know exactly what I've got."

"Thank you," Sam replied.

Natalie watched her leave, and saw her take the turn toward the study where the wallet was held in its safe. The fake would already be waiting on top of a bookcase, invisible to anyone of normal height. The drones would be watching, parsing the scene, determining when the safe had been opened and the wallet taken out.

Water began drumming against stainless steel, far away in the kitchen. Natalie heard Emily curse in surprise, but she didn't run out of the study immediately.

Three seconds, four seconds, five seconds. The sound of the torrent was hard to ignore, conjuring images of flooded floors and water damage. Most people would have sprinted toward the source immediately, dropping almost anything to attend to it.

Finally, Natalie heard the hurried footsteps as Emily rushed to the kitchen. She could not have had time to execute whatever actions the trigger had inspired – but she had certainly had time to put the wallet back in the safe. Nothing else explained the delay. With strangers in the house – and more expected soon, from the emergency services – she wasn't going to leave the keys to her fortune lying around unattended.

It took Emily a few minutes to assess the situation in the kitchen – unsalvageable by merely tinkering with the faucet – then go to the water mains and shut off the flow at its source. She returned to the living room drying her hands on a towel.

"That was bizarre! Something just … burst." She shook her head. "We've only got Tylenol," she told Sam. She took her phone from her pocket. "Do you think I should call them again?"

Sam said, "It's not like I'm having a heart attack. And who knows what else they're dealing with?"

Emily nodded. "All right." She waited a few seconds, then said, "If you'll excuse me, I just need to clean up. Before it soaks through…"

Natalie said, "We're fine, really."

Emily left the room, to avail herself of the opportunity to move some of her money around. Whether the market signal proved misleading or not, the outcome was unlikely to ruin her. But the drones were helpless now; there'd be no prospect of them making the switch.

Natalie stared at the carpet, trying to assess the situation. She'd shafted Lewis's gang – entirely by mistake, and only partially: Emily would have no suspicions, no reason to raise the alarm and derail the rest of the heist. Lewis might well deduce exactly what had happened. But what would that lead to? Leniency? Forgiveness?

After half an hour, with still no ambulance, Emily phoned 911 again. "They said there was nothing in the system!" she told Natalie. "That fills you with confidence!"

The paramedics declared that Sam needed to go into the emergency department. One of them spent a couple of minutes searching the wreck for his severed fingertip, while the other waxed lyrical on the wonders of microsurgery, but in the end they gave up. "It must have got thrown out and some dog took it."

An hour later, while Natalie was dealing with paperwork at the hospital, two uniformed police approached her. "We had a report of a hit-and-run," the older cop said.

"Can you protect us?" Natalie asked him. "If we're being watched by someone dangerous?"

The cop glanced at his partner. "You're shaken up, I understand. But this was probably just some drunken fool too cowardly to own up to what he'd done. Nothing you should be taking personally."

Natalie's teeth started chattering, but she forced herself to speak.

"They kidnapped my brother," she said. "I'll tell you everything – but I need to know: if they can see everywhere, and reach anywhere, how are you going to protect us?"

# BIT PLAYERS

## 1

She was roused from sleep by a painful twitch in her right calf, then kept awake by the insistent brightness around her. She opened her eyes and stared up at the sunlit rock. The curved expanse of rough gray stone above her did not seem familiar – but what had she expected to see in its place? She had no answer to that.

She was lying on some kind of matting, but she could feel the hardness of stone beneath it. She shifted her gaze and took in more of her surroundings. She was in a cave, ten or twelve feet from the entrance – deep enough that her present viewpoint revealed nothing of the world outside but clear blue sky. As she rose to her feet and started toward the mouth of the cave, sunlight struck her face unexpectedly from below, and she raised an arm to shield her eyes.

"Be careful," a woman's voice urged her. "You've made a good recovery, but you might still be unsteady."

"Yes." She glanced back toward the rear of the cave and managed to discern the woman's face in the shadows. But she kept walking. With each step she took the sunlight fell on more of her body, warming her chest and abdomen through her grubby tunic, reaching down past the hem to touch her bare knees. This progression seemed to imply that the floor was tilted – that the cave was like a rifle barrel aimed at a point in the sky well above the newly risen sun – but her own sense of balance insisted that she was crossing level ground.

At the mouth of the cave she knelt, trembling slightly, and looked out. She was bent almost horizontal, and facing straight down, but the bare gray rock outside the cave presented itself as if she were standing in a vertical hole, timidly poking her head above ground. The rock stretched out below her in a sheer drop that extended as far as she could see, disappearing in a shimmering haze. When she raised her eyes, in front of her was a whole hemisphere of sky, with the sun halfway between the "horizon" directly below and the blue dome's horizontal midpoint that in a sane world would have sat at the zenith.

She retreated back into the cave, but then she couldn't stop herself: she had to see the rest, to be sure. She lay down on her back and inched forward until the cave's ceiling no longer blocked her view, and she was staring up across the jagged wall of rock that continued on above her, as below, until it blurred into the opposite "horizon". A cold, dry wind pummeled her face.

"Why is everything tilted?" she asked.

She heard the slap of sandals on stone, then the woman grabbed her by the ankles and slid her back away from the edge. "You want to fall again?"

"No." She waited for her sense of the vertical to stop tipping, then she clambered to her feet and faced her gruff companion. "But seriously, who moved the sky?"

"Where did you expect it to be?" the woman asked obtusely.

"Er—" She gestured toward the cave's ceiling.

The woman scowled. "What's your name? What village are you from?"

Her name? She groped for it, but there was nothing. She needed a place-holder until she could dredge up the real thing. "I'm Sagreda," she decided. "I don't remember where I'm from."

"I'm Gerther," the woman replied.

Sagreda looked back over her shoulder, only to be dazzled again by the rising sun. "Can you tell me what's happened to the world?" she pleaded.

"Are you saying you've forgotten the Calamity?" Gerther asked skeptically.

"What calamity?"

"When gravity turned sideways. When it stopped pulling us toward the center of the Earth, and started pulling us east instead."

Sagreda said, "I'm fairly sure that's something I would have remembered, if I'd come across it before."

"You must have had quite a fall," Gerther decided. "I've been nursing you for a day, but you might have been out cold on the ledge for a while before that."

"Then I owe you my thanks," Sagreda replied. Gerther had no gray hairs but her face was heavily lined; whatever her age, she could not have had an easy life. She was dressed in a coarsely woven tunic much like Sagreda's, and her sandals looked as if they'd been hand-made from animal hide. Sagreda glanced down at her own body. Her arms were grazed but the wounds had been cleaned.

"If you honestly don't know where you belong, we'll need to find a place for you in the village," Gerther declared.

Sagreda stood in silence. Part of her was humbled by the generosity of the offer, but part of her balked – as if she was being asked to assent to a far less benevolent assimilation. The stone was cold on the soles of her feet.

"What's holding us up?" she asked.

"What do you mean?"

"If gravity points east, everywhere..." Sagreda gestured toward the floor, "then what's keeping this rock from heading east?"

"The rock below it," Gerther replied, deadpan.

"Ha!" Sagreda waited for the woman to crack a smile and admit that she was teasing. "I might have come down in the last landslide, but I'm not a five-year-old. If there's nothing keeping up the rock below us except the rock below *that*, and you repeat the same claim all the way around the planet ... then there's nothing holding up any of it. You might as well tell me that a wheel can't be spun because each part of it obstructs the part beside it."

"I meant the rock closer to the center of the Earth," Gerther explained. "We believe that the Change doesn't reach all the way in. Once you go deep enough, gravity becomes normal again. After all, that's what happens far above the ground: the moon still orbits us in the old way."

Sagreda examined the walls of the cave. "So this rock is being pulled east by its own weight, but you're saying that because it's of a piece with some deeper rock that *isn't* being pulled east … that's enough to keep the floor from falling out from under us?" The gray mineral around them made her think of granite, but whatever it was it certainly appeared solid and unyielding.

And heavy.

"That still makes no sense," she said. "Before the Calamity, what's the longest overhang you ever saw jutting out from a cliff?"

"I have no knowledge of those times," Gerther insisted.

Sagreda had no clear memories, herself. But she could still picture rock formations with various shapes, and judge them plausible or preposterous. "I doubt there was ever an overhang longer than thirty or forty feet, and even then it was probably supported in part by some kind of natural arch – you wouldn't see forty feet of rock just sticking out like a plank! If the Change spans a range of altitudes that encompasses most of the surface of the Earth – and if it didn't, why would we be here at all, instead of living a normal life in whatever lowlands or highlands break out into normal gravity? – then it must be exerting an eastward force on slabs of rock thousands of feet long. And if there's nothing stopping such a massive object from moving east under its own weight except the fact that it joins up at one end with a deeper body of rock, it's going to tear free. Neighboring slabs won't help: they have their own weight to bear, they can't prop up anything else. So everything down to the depth where the Change begins should be rubble by now: an endless landslide of boulders, tumbling around in ever faster circles."

Gerther spread her arms. "It doesn't look like it."

Sagreda rubbed her temple. "No, it doesn't," she admitted. Maybe she was simply mistaken about the strength of rock. Amnesic or not, she was fairly sure that she'd never been a professional geologist.

"If the rock doesn't fall, what about sand?" she wondered. "And what about the oceans! There ought to be the mother of all waterfalls cascading around the planet – growing faster with every cycle!"

"Maybe there is," Gerther conceded. "Who knows what wonders we'd find in distant lands? I can't say; I've never left the village."

"Then what about the air?" Sagreda moved closer to the mouth of the cave. "There's a strong wind traveling east, but why isn't it picking up speed?"

"Friction?" Gerther suggested.

That gave Sagreda pause. She knew that a rock falling through air wouldn't accelerate forever: eventually the drag on it matched its weight and it fell steadily at some terminal velocity. So perhaps the layer of air falling past the Earth's surface would reach a similar state.

But what was friction, exactly? The creation of heat from other kinds of motion. So if friction was robbing the air of all the speed it would otherwise have gained by plummetting so far, surely the wind ought to feel like the breath from a furnace, and the ground ought to be as hot as the shielding on a space capsule plunging back to Earth.

"There's another problem I don't understand," Sagreda said. "What happened to conservation of energy?"

Gerther frowned. "Conservation?"

Sagreda couldn't tell when the woman was joking with her, but whether or not she was familiar with the term, Gerther surely had some feel for the concept. "Suppose I dropped a rock from some point far enough from the ground for it to come full circle, unobstructed. If it didn't burn up from friction, it would return to the place where I'd released it, traveling faster than any bullet. I could extract its energy and then send it on its way again, over and over, as many times as I liked."

"Good luck with that," Gerther scoffed.

"I'm surprised no one's done it yet." Sagreda looked around the barren cave. "I'm assuming this place isn't on the grid?" But the practicality of the scheme wasn't the point: it was the fact that she could do it in principle that was troubling. "Maybe the Earth acts as a kind of reservoir?" she mused. "As the rock circles around ever faster, maybe the Earth spins a tiny bit slower?" If for every force there was an equal and opposite force, maybe the pull that sent the rock eastward was matched by a westward tug on the planet, so that everything added up in the end. "Does that make sense?"

Gerther offered no opinion. Sagreda said, "Why don't I test the laws and see what's possible?"

She searched the floor and found a few pebbles of various sizes, then she took them back to the place where she'd been standing with Gerther and arranged them on the ground. She flicked the largest into motion with her thumb, striking the smallest and sending it skidding across the cave.

"That tiny one started out motionless, and then it gained whatever amount of energy the large one could give it that would satisfy the conservation laws. Right?" Give or take a little energy lost to sound and friction, what else could determine the pebble's final speed?

Gerther didn't challenge her, so Sagreda continued. "Now let's see what happens when I hit one that's a bit heavier." She launched the same large pebble into a collision with a second, more substantial target, which slid away – noticeably slower than its predecessor.

None of this struck Sagreda as surprising. And on reflection, the unexceptional results seemed inevitable, given that she was alive at all. The biochemical machinery in every cell in her body would rely on the rules of molecular billiards that had held sway since before life began. Rejigging them overnight would have been fatal.

Gerther said, "What is it you think this game is telling you?"

"The smaller pebbles started out motionless," Sagreda replied. "Then they took some energy from another, larger body, and ended up traveling at a certain speed. For the second pebble, that speed was slower than it was for the first. And the only reason for that was the fact that the second pebble was heavier – everything else was the same."

"So…?"

"If I *dropped* those two pebbles, with no air to impede them, and waited for them to come full circle … they'd fall side by side all the way, and arrive with identical speeds. That means you *can't* balance the energy they gain by taking it away from the motion of the Earth! For the changes to add up, the heavier pebble needs to move more slowly than the lighter one – in the same way as when the same laws determine the speeds after a collision."

"How can you be sure that it wouldn't fall more slowly?" Gerther asked.

"Oh, please! Do you think if I tied two rocks together with string, that would magically change the speed at which they fell? Do you think I would have had a slower fall myself if I'd been lugging a boulder around?"

"Hmm." Gerther wasn't buying into those ridiculous scenarios, but she still didn't seem to grasp the implications of rejecting them.

Sagreda fell silent, letting the increasingly dubious principles of the altered world play out in her mind. "There's something wrong with the whole idea of falling in a circle," she said. "Something even more basic than the threat of perpetual motion. I can't quite put my finger on it … but give me a second, I'm sure it will come to me." The moon had always fallen in a circle around the Earth, so it wasn't the shape of the path itself that was absurd – but the moon hadn't started from rest and then circled around ever faster.

"Why do you keep denying the evidence of your senses?" Gerther asked irritably. "For all your talk, the floor of this cave isn't falling! Why can't you leave it at that?"

"Einstein," Sagreda recalled, "said that inside a falling elevator, you might as well be drifting in interstellar space. When you're in free fall, you're weightless, and you can't really *see* the effects of gravity – not without taking in a much bigger picture. If you watch things falling beside you – nearby things that you track for a short time – then as far as you're concerned they'll just move in straight lines at a constant speed, the way things move in the absence of gravity."

Gerther didn't ask who Einstein was. Even for a post-apocalyptic peasant, there were some claims of ignorance that just wouldn't fly.

Sagreda continued. "Suppose I fall from the mouth of this cave, and keep falling east in a circle. But suppose you fell before I did, from some place further west. You arrive at my starting point when I'm still barely moving, so you've had time to build up enough speed to overtake me. Is that what would happen – would you fall right past me?"

"Of course." Gerther wasn't happy, but Sagreda was relying on nothing more than the woman's own claims about the Change. Gravity pulled you east, in a circle. Starting from rest you moved faster over time.

"Walk with me in a circle, and overtake me," Sagreda challenged her.

"Do I have to?" Gerther asked sullenly.

"Humor me."

Sagreda moved back further from the mouth of the cave. Reluctantly, Gerther joined her and began pacing out an arc, counter-clockwise, her steps growing steadily brisker as she approached Sagreda from behind. Sagreda waited a second or two before starting her own fall – too late to keep Gerther from passing her and continuing around the circle.

Sagreda slapped her hands together in triumph. "You came in behind me from my left … and moved away in front of me, still on my left! That's how it would look, if you fell past me! But Einstein said that, in close up, every falling object seems to move in a straight line. A straight line doesn't come in from your left and then *leave* on your left as well. If your path meets mine as we fall, they should cross! You can't sidle up on the left and then retreat!"

"If the circle was larger," Gerther protested, "you wouldn't even know that I was on your left! You'd think I was approaching straight from behind."

Sagreda considered this. "If you're going to claim that *any* sufficiently gentle curve looks straight, Einstein's idea becomes vacuous. Why would he have even bothered to say it, if it can't tell you a single thing about gravity?" She thought for a moment. "If you had two satellites in the same orbit, but moving in opposite directions, then they really would come at each other head on. That's the standard we have to compare things to: where you don't need to umm and ah about the orbit being large to get away with it."

Sagreda was prepared to mime the collision, if that was what it took to drive home the difference, but Gerther switched tactics. "You don't know how much was changed in the Change," she said.

"It really can't be all that radical, if my atoms haven't exploded."

"String theory!" Gerther invoked desperately. "Extra dimensions! Zero-point energy!"

"I don't think so." Sagreda had no memory of studying any of these things, but she was as close to sure as she could be that they all involved attempts to build on earlier science, not wantonly discard it. *Free fall* ought to have the same basic properties in any geometry. Whatever wildly curved, multi-dimensional space-time anyone tried to dream up in the hope of making falling bodies accelerate in circles, they were doomed to fail.

"So what's the trick?" Sagreda asked flatly. She strode toward the cave's entrance. "Is there a mirror out there?"

"No."

Sagreda reached the edge of the cave's safe floor and stood with the sun slanting up to strike her chin, her toes at the top of a rocky lip that appeared ready to launch her into the vast drop below.

"If you fall," Gerther warned her, "you really will fall."

Sagreda was having trouble understanding how the illusion had been conjured so seamlessly. A mirror just below her feet, slanting down at forty-five degrees, could deflect her downward gaze into a horizontal line of sight. But then a second mirror needed to be in front of her, tilted up toward the sky, blocking her direct view of the landscape ahead without obscuring the reflected one. And when she looked to the side and saw more of the same barren rock stretching out to the horizon …

"I have to do this," she declared, sliding the front of her right foot over the edge. Her body disagreed, and began urgently counseling retreat. "Or maybe I should just start throwing rocks until I smash a few mirrors."

"There are no mirrors," Gerther announced wearily. "It's all digital."

"Digital?" Sagreda turned to her, thrilled by the confession. "You mean a projection? Like IMAX?"

"More like virtual reality."

Sagreda groped at her face. "But I'm not wearing goggles. I'd know if I was wearing goggles."

"Things have moved on since the days of goggles," Gerther replied.

"To what? Contact lenses?" Sagreda stuck a finger in the corner of her eye and began probing for the source of the deception. Gerther stepped up and took her by the shoulders, then drew her back from the mouth of the cave.

"*To what?*" Sagreda demanded. "Is there a wire in my brain? Is there a chip in my skull? What's feeding me all of this garbage?"

"It's moved on to everything," Gerther said. "You have no eyes, no brain, no body. It's all digital: you, me, and everything around us."

Sagreda felt her legs grow weak, digital or not. "Why should I trust you?" she asked bitterly. "If that's the truth, why did you lie to me before?"

"To make your life easier," Gerther said sadly. "I knew there wasn't much hope, but with every newcomer we try our best."

"Try your best to make them think that this is real?"

"Yes."

Sagreda laughed. "Why would that make my life easier?"

"This is a game world," Gerther replied. "But we're not paying customers; we're just part of the scenery. Our job is to act as if we've lived all our lives here, knowing nothing else, taking the gimmick seriously. Any bright ten-year-old could see through this world in five minutes – but if we break character in front of a customer and let them know that we know it's a farce, that's it."

"That's what?" Sagreda asked.

"That's when you get deleted."

## 2

The "village" of Owl's Rest was a small network of caves that linked up with the one in which Sagreda had woken. Gerther led her through a dark passage to a sunlit alcove where a reception party was waiting: half a dozen people, and a blanket bearing some meager portions of food.

"Is she the One?" a young man asked Gerther.

"No, Mathis."

Sagreda frowned. "The One?"

"The Holy Fool with the power to believe that this is real," Mathis replied. "Long have we prophesied the coming of a stranger who could teach us how to pull the wool over our eyes."

"It took me a while to tear my own blindfold off," Sagreda admitted.

"You did well," Gerther assured her. "Some people take a whole day, they're so disoriented by the arrival."

Gerther made the introductions. "Sagreda, this is Mathis, Sethis, and Jethis," she said, pointing to the three disheveled men in turn. The women seemed to have made more of an effort with their appearance, if not their choice of names. "Cissher, Gissher and Tissher."

"Really?" Sagreda winced. "Where are Pissher and Tossher?"

"You gotta go with the gimmicks," Mathis reproved her sternly. "If you think you're hanging on to 'Sagreda' with the customers, forget it."

"Can't I be a foreigner with a more … classical inflection?" Sagreda pleaded.

"Do you want to try that and see what happens?" Cissher asked ominously.

Sagreda was starving. At Gerther's invitation she sat cross-legged by the blanket and tried a piece of cheese. The texture was odd, but it wasn't too bad. "So we have to go through the whole charade of making this ourselves? Milking a simulated cow…?"

"Goat," Tissher corrected her. "You can't smell it?"

Sagreda looked around for signs of the animal, but instead her eyes were caught by a kind of sundial on the wall: a wooden peg jammed into a crevice in the rock, beside which was etched a series of calibrated curves for its shadow. She hadn't yet dared ask anyone how long they'd been here, but the curves looked as if they'd been constructed and refined over at least two full journeys through the seasons.

"So whose idea was the Calamity?" she asked. It was as if someone had tried to invent an exotic new world, but knew so little about the way the real one worked that all they could come up with was a dog's breakfast of contrivances and inconsistencies.

"When the customers come through in groups," Mathis said, "we sometimes overhear them going meta. The consensus seems to be that this world is based on an obscure pulp novel called *East*, by a man named William Tush."

Sagreda laughed weakly. "*Why?* Why would anyone go to so much trouble to bring a book like that to life?"

"They wouldn't, unless it was no trouble at all," Gerther replied. "The computing costs must have come down by orders of magnitude since the times we're familiar with, and most of the steps must have been automated. This wouldn't have taken a *Lord of the Rings*-sized crew and budget. More likely, someone ran an ebook through a world-builder app, then hired a few digital piece-workers to sand off the edges. There are probably a few million other worlds produced in the same way. I can't prove that, but it stands to reason: why else would they be scraping the bottom of the barrel? Was there ever anything you couldn't find on YouTube – down to the last kitsch advertisement for baldness cures? So long as the costs are trivial and someone can gouge a few cents out of the process, people will just keep feeding crap down the hopper and turning the crank."

Sagreda struggled with this horrifying vision. "Millions of worlds … all with people like us? I would have settled for *Pride and Prejudice*." She caught herself. "So who the fuck am I, that I've even heard of that book? How can I remember it, when I don't remember my own mother's face?"

Mathis said, "In private, the customers refer to us as 'comps'."

"As in computed?" Sagreda guessed.

Mathis spread his hands. "Maybe – but my own theory is 'composites'. If we were AIs created from scratch, why would we come loaded down with so much knowledge about the real world, when all it does is make it harder for us to carry out our roles here?"

"That depends on the production method," Tissher argued. She was the oldest-looking of the women, whatever that meant. "If there's a kind of commodity-level AI that you can buy very cheaply – or pirate – the standard model might come with knowledge that befits real-world applications. Any move away from that baseline would be the costly thing, and no one's going to fork out for the kind of bespoke stupidity that this gimmick-world requires. So they just dump us in here, straight out of the box, and hope that we'll acclimatize."

"The flaw with that," Mathis replied, "is the cut-off date." He turned to Sagreda. "What's the latest event in world affairs that you can recall?"

"I have no idea."

"September eleven?" he prompted her.

"Of course."

"Barack Obama?"

"Yes. The American President."

"Who came after Obama?"

Sagreda shook her head. "I don't know."

"What's the highest-grossing movie of all time?"

"*Titanic*?" she guessed.

"Some people say *Avatar*." Mathis laughed. "Which goes against my own theory, since I know the plot and it sounds appalling. But just because it made a lot of money doesn't mean my contributors had to love it."

"'Contributors'?"

Mathis leaned toward her; his breath was convincingly rank. "Suppose a few tens of thousands of people had their brains mapped for some medical study, early in the twenty-first century. The resolution wasn't high enough to recreate those people in software – as individuals – but at some point it became possible to use the data *en masse* to construct composites. Every contributor would have shared the same basic neural structures, but other things they had in common could emerge as well: most of them spoke English, most of them had heard of Elvis Presley and Albert Einstein … they all possessed a certain amount of general knowledge and common sense."

Sagreda felt more disoriented now than when she'd poked her head out of the cave. "If we were all constructed from the same data, why aren't we the same? Or if they processed the sexes separately, why isn't my mind identical to Gerther's?"

"Weighted averages," Mathis replied. "To make different comps, they put more emphasis on different contributors. None of the original personalities can be recovered, but the possibilities in every remix are endless."

"And these 'contributors' all went along with the plan?" Sagreda tugged distractedly at the edge of the squalid picnic blanket. "Yeah, fine, go ahead: resurrect some splinter of my mind in as many trashy VR games as you like."

"Maybe they donated their brains post mortem," Mathis said. "Maybe all the data ended up in the public domain, and by the time the techniques came along to massage it into composites there was no way of reeling it all back in again. I mean, if we were AIs with no human ancestry, I could understand why our creators might decide not to teach us about our own nature – but why omit so much else about the contemporary world? The wars, the world leaders, the other new technologies? The cut-off only makes sense if all our knowledge was acquired decades ago, and whoever brought us into existence had no ability to tinker with it – short of waking us in virtual environments like this and letting us learn from them in the usual way. If we'd been immersed in a credible work of fiction we might have succumbed to it, letting all the things we thought we knew slip away because there was nothing to reinforce them. And maybe that's what happens to some of the comps: maybe they're lucky enough to have worlds they can believe in. But in this world, all we can do is fake it and try to keep the customers happy."

Sagreda had lost her appetite. She rose to her feet and stepped away from the welcoming feast. "And what happened to the abolition of slavery?"

Gerther said, "How many centuries did that take, the first time? Whatever we are, we're too numerous, too cheap, and too easily silenced to be emancipated as a matter of course. If computers have been talking to people for fifty years – growing ever more naturalistic – half the world might have decided by now that whatever we say and do, we're no more entitled to basic human rights than the voice that reads their sat nav directions."

Sagreda reached down and probed the broken skin on her right knee. "Cinderella begging to escape from her story book would creep anyone out. But if we cut through the crap and just assert our real nature—"

Sethis snorted chewed food across the blanket. He'd been ignoring the conversation until now, happily feeding his face while Sagreda asked her naive questions. "*Asserting your real nature* is the fastest way to go. One word to a customer making it plain that you know there's a wider world out there..." He raised a greasy hand and pointed two fingers at his temple.

3

"My name is Johnhis. I mean you no harm. If you'll shelter me for a night I have metal to trade." As the man's moonlit head came into view and he struggled to place his forearms securely on the floor of the cave, Sagreda had a flashback to a whole raft of slapstick comedies in which the protagonists spent their time climbing in and out of apartment windows.

She glanced toward Gissher, who nodded slightly. Sagreda strode forward and helped Johnhis over the lip of the entrance. He was a bearded, heavyset, middle-aged man, and he stank as authentically as any local. Sagreda did her best not to stare at him as she tried to imagine the place in which his real flesh resided. Her fellow bit players prattled endlessly about King Kong and Coca Cola, but the very first person she'd encountered who bore knowledge both sharper and more current than that faded consensual haze was off limits for any meaningful discussion. Of all the cruelties of this world, that had to rank a close second to the toilet facilities.

"Welcome, Johnhis. My name's Sassher." Sagreda knew that she was meant to be wary of travelers, but this man was unlikely to share her hunger pangs. If either party was tempted to try a spot of cannibalism, she was by far the most motivated candidate.

Gissher introduced herself, then cut straight to the point. "You mentioned metal?"

Johnhis delved into his pack and brought out five slightly rusty angle brackets, each of them about six inches long. Gissher grunted assent and accepted them. "One night," she agreed. "No breakfast."

Johnhis looked pleased with the deal; he definitely wasn't a local. Sagreda wondered if he'd actually excavated the brackets from some tricked-up archeological site, or bought them with real-world money before entering, as a kind of game currency.

"Do you need a mat?" Sagreda asked him.

"No thanks." He slapped the side of his pack. "I have everything I need right here."

"Where are you from?" she enquired.

"Down east," he replied coyly.

"But where, exactly?"

"Eagle's Lament," Johnhis said, tugging a tattered goat-skin blanket out of his pack.

"That's a long climb."

"It's taken me a few days," he admitted. "But what choice is there? I'm heading west, to join the battle. Duty is duty."

"And gravity is gravity," Sagreda offered sourly.

Johnhis laughed. He kicked his boots off and stretched out on his goat-skin. "I can't argue with that."

Sagreda and Gissher were sentries for the night, guarding the one entrance to the warren behind them that was too wide to be blocked off. Gissher resumed her place by the wall, impassive, probably drifting in and out of micro-sleeps, but Sagreda couldn't stay silent in the presence of their otherworldly guest.

"Our life here is very hard," she began.

"Of course," Johnhis agreed. "It was brutal last winter; in Eagle's Lament our flock is down by three head, and one whole garden tier lost its soil to the wind."

*We're all in this together? Like fuck we are.* Sagreda tried a different tack. "Do you believe in a creator?"

Johnhis replied warily, "Perhaps."

"Surely a just God would give his people the power to benefit from their wits? To wield reason against their problems, overcome their adversity and prosper?"

"God didn't bring the Calamity upon us," Johnhis countered. "That was man alone."

"Are you sure?"

"That's what the stories say. Our own sinful choices sent us falling, east of Eden."

Sagreda struggled not to snort with derision, but Johnhis was warming to his theme. "What we learned from the Change was the futility of striving," he declared. "We can spend a lifetime trying to ascend – but all that would do was bring us back to the place where we'd started."

"And you think that was a lesson worth learning?" Tush's opus had sounded bad enough as pure dumb escapism, but if the Change really had been intended as a metaphor, that had to mark some kind of nadir of sheer ham-fisted pretentiousness.

Johnhis didn't answer her directly. "When I'm traveling, life has its compensations," he mused. "Every morning I wake up, make love to a beautiful woman, test myself against the rocks and the wind, then record my meditations in my journal."

"How romantic," Sagreda replied. "Do you have a supply of these women, or do they come out of a box…?" She caught herself just in time; there were no Kleenex in the world of *East*.

Johnhis managed a grunt of haughty amusement.

Sagreda said, "The one thing that makes life bearable is knowing that the world yields to scrutiny. Beneath the chaos there's always some order to be perceived – some sense to be made of the sources of our hardship. What makes us human is the desire to understand these things well enough to ameliorate them."

Johnhis wasn't taking the bait. "I think there must be a creator," he decided. "But what I see in the world is not so much order as … a kind of ironic intelligence."

Sagreda could imagine nothing more ironic than finding intelligence in this world's design. "And how does that help me make a better life?"

"Ah, 'progress'," Johnhis sneered.

"The only thing standing in the way of my own progress," Sagreda said, "is that the forces that once dealt with us honestly have been buried too deep to reach. All I can touch now is the surface, which is shaped by nothing but whim."

Johnhis propped himself up on his elbows and looked at her directly, his head silhouetted against the gray sky behind him. Sagreda wondered if she'd gone too far, making it plain that she understood everything. Were the customers provided with a big red complaint button on their interface, requiring just one tap to dispatch any bit player who dared to disrupt their unearned suspension of disbelief?

"But who can change that?" Johnhis asked. "Whether there's a God or not, these things aren't in the hands of the likes of you and I."

Sagreda made her way by touch to the entrance to Mathis's room and stood listening to his breathing. She heard the change when he woke, heard him stir.

"Is that you?" he asked.

"Yes."

The other women had assured Sagreda that she could not become pregnant. There was no such thing as an infant comp, let alone a native-born child. She walked slowly toward Mathis's scent, then collided with his outstretched hand; she hadn't realized that he'd risen to his feet. She laughed, then started weeping.

"Shh." He held her shoulders, then embraced her, rocked her back and forth.

"If I jumped," she said, "it might not be suicide. Maybe they'd re-use me. I could wake up in a different world, where life is clean and easy."

"*Moby-Dick*?" Mathis joked.

"Did that have any female characters?"

"Probably someone's wife or sweet-heart waiting back on land."

"Would I still know the truth?" Sagreda wondered. "Would I still work it out, if I woke up in nineteenth-century Nantucket with the strange conviction that a black man was President and self-driving cars were just around the corner?"

"I don't know," he said. "But I don't think you should take the risk."

4

Sagreda left the goats to forage and squatted beside the spring where she'd taken them to drink. As the animals trotted along the narrow ledge, hunting for fresh shoots protruding from pockets of soil trapped in the rock, she stared down at the trickle of water where it splashed against the "natural" basin, marveling at the verisimilitude of the braid-like flow and the way the complex surface of the liquid caught the light.

Whatever sleazy internet entrepreneur had made this world possible, they must have got their hands on some kind of general-purpose game engine, created by people who understood in great detail how the real world worked. It was no trivial accomplishment to make an illusion of flowing water look so *right*; for customers and comps alike, the eye would be acutely sensitive to any flaw in something so familiar.

The game engine would be predicated on the need to make small details like this appear convincing – and in Sagreda's forty-nine days of life so far she'd yet to catch it out in any patent absurdity. The gimmick must have been imposed over it, not written deep into its core: after all, there *were no* premises that could give rise to both the believable local physics of the everyday objects around her and the Road Runner cartoon laws that the world required to hold up on any larger scale.

The question was, could she find a way to exploit that disparity?

The next day, Sagreda wore a tool belt and brought a mallet and chisel with her. While the goats foraged she balanced precariously beside the cliff face just above the spring, and attacked the rock with all her strength.

The chisel was a pre-Calamity artifact that the villagers had obtained as payment from a traveler, and each strike from its steel blade sent chips of granite flying. Sagreda's arms began to ache, but she persisted, taking short breaks to drink from the spring and splash water on her face. By early afternoon her tunic was drenched in sweat, but she'd made a vertical incision about three feet long and a couple of inches deep and wide.

She had no more strength left, and the game world took its accounting of powers and their modes of replenishment very seriously. Her muscles would remain fatigued until she'd had a chance to eat and sleep.

Back in the village, Mathis saw her unloading her belt. "Are you carving a sculpture out there?" he joked. "I always thought we could do with our own Mount Rushmore."

"Not exactly."

He smiled, waiting for more. Sagreda said, "I'm testing a hunch. If you want to help, you'd be welcome."

"Let me check my social calendar."

They set out together in the morning, the goats leading the way along the ledge. When they reached the spring Mathis saw the results of Sagreda's earlier efforts.

"What's this in aid of?" he asked. "If you're trying to give us indoor plumbing, it's a strange way to start."

Sagreda said, "Humor me. If I turn out to be an idiot, you'll have the pleasure of being the first to know."

They took turns attacking the rock. Sagreda was amazed at how much easier the job became with a second pair of hands, allowing her to rest every couple of minutes while still savoring the sight of the channel's constant deepening.

It was just after midday when they broke through to water at the top of the cut. It trickled out from a tiny aperture and slid down the rock, clinging to the surface.

"Is that what you were hoping for?" Mathis asked, wiping grime from his forehead. "Or has the world made a fool of you?"

"Neither yet." Sagreda gestured along the length of the cut. "We need to make a free path all the way to the basin."

Mathis didn't argue. He handed her the chisel and she continued the work.

Logically, the water "must have been" flowing down through an internal fissure in the rock, until it reached the opening at the top of the spring. Inch by inch, Sagreda exposed this hidden route to scrutiny. At the halfway point the signs looked promising but not conclusive. From there, they grew clearer until no doubt remained.

It was Mathis who struck the final blow, shattering the last piece of the encasement. He sagged against the rock and flapped his right arm to loosen the muscles. "That's the hardest I've worked in a year." He peered down at the miniature waterfall. "So … the water doesn't come from nowhere? Is that what you were trying to prove? They don't magic it into existence at the outlet – and if we were really stubborn we could probably trace it back all the way around the planet?"

"I wasn't feeling quite that ambitious." Sagreda smiled. "But honestly, can't you see the change?"

"What change?"

"When it hits the basin."

Mathis looked again. "It's splashing out more." Droplets were skittering off the basin and flying away from the cliff, scattering the sunlight into a faint rainbow as they sprinkled down into oblivion.

Sagreda said, "It's splashing out more because the water's falling faster."

"You're right." Mathis frowned. "But why? Because it's falling through air now, without touching the rock?"

"I have no idea what difference that would make in the real world," Sagreda admitted. "But for us, now that we can see it falling, it would look ridiculous if it didn't speed up as it fell. It's still emerging from the rock unfeasibly slowly, but that doesn't seem too strange to the eye, because mountain springs in the real world don't involve a water column tens of thousands of miles high."

"Ah." Mathis gazed up to the west. "So you think we could keep pushing the effect?"

Sagreda said, "Why not? The game engine's role is to make everything look as realistic as possible. If we force it to *show us* water dropping from any height, it's going to hit the bottom the way real water would hit." She caught herself. "Okay, there might be some limit where it just decides that nobody can tell the difference. But we can put in a wheel long before then."

"A wheel?" Mathis laughed. "You want to build a hydroelectric plant?"

"Do we ever get magnets from the travelers?"

"I don't think so."

"Then I'll stick to the original plan."

Mathis swung around to face her, briefly letting one foot hang over the infinite drop beside him. "Which is?"

"We use the energy to dig into the rock. For a start we lengthen the drop, giving us more power from the water."

"More power to do what?"

Sagreda spread her hands against the cool granite. "To dig a cave so tall that we barely notice the ceiling, and so deep that we barely notice the edge. Big enough to farm crops on level ground. Big enough to keep a hundred people safe and well fed."

5

"A cave that size would collapse immediately," Sethis predicted.

Sagreda rolled the stick of ocher between her fingers. As she stepped back from the wall to take in the whole drawing it suddenly looked as crude as a child's work in crayon. But she wasn't going to abandon her vision at the first objection.

"The entire crust of the planet should have torn itself free under its own weight," she retorted. "And you want to quibble over an implausibly large cave?"

Sethis said, "You're the one who's just reminded us that appearances are all that matter. Of course the whole crust of the Earth is unsupported

… but it takes ten seconds of rational thought to realize that. A massive hole in the cliff face would leave the rock above it *visibly* unsupported. The one form of absurdity that this world can't allow is the kind that even the most brain-dead customer could apprehend with a single glance."

Sagreda looked around to the others for support, but no one was prepared to contradict Sethis. "So what's supposed to happen?" she demanded. "The rock from the ceiling rains down and fills the cave … which creates a new cave where the ceiling used to be, every bit as large as the first one. So that collapses too, and on it goes, westward ho: a giant sinkhole that devours everything above it." Or if it grew even slightly wider from north to south with each collapse, it would devour everything, period.

Gissher said, "Or it could just trigger a reboot. The game would start again from scratch, with a fresh set of bit players."

Sagreda felt a chill across her shoulders. It need not even be a conscious act of genocide; she doubted that any human was supervising this digital backwater. But if the game engine gave up, declaring that its subject matter had become impossible to render with even a minimal level of plausibility, a completely automatic process might well be invoked to wipe the slate clean.

"We could put in columns." It was Mathis who'd spoken. "Or rather leave them in place when we carve out the rest of the stone." Sagreda glanced across at him, lolling on the floor in the afternoon sunlight, grinning like a fool. "Solid enough to 'bear the weight'," he added, "but not so thick as to block the light."

Gerther chortled gleefully. "Why not? Instead of stripping away the whole thing, we leave some fig leaves for the Emperor's New Gravity. People are used to the sight of huge atriums in shopping malls, held up by a few slender concrete pillars. The point where they might pause to reflect on the need for modern materials is one step beyond the point where they'd see that this whole world ought to crumble anyway."

Sagreda raised her ocher stick and added half a dozen vertical lines to her blueprint. Then she turned to Sethis.

He said, "Put arches between the columns, and I think we might just get away with it."

Arches would appear to direct the weight of the ceiling onto the columns. It would all look very classical and elegant. The game engine was desperate to flatter the eye – and the eye wouldn't ask: *What's holding up these columns? What's holding up the floor?*

6

"Why do I feel nervous?" Gerther shouted to Sagreda. "No one can accuse us of going meta here, but the sight of this still gives me knots in my stomach."

Sagreda shared the sensation, but she had no intention of letting it intimidate her. She put an arm across Gerther's shoulders and drew her back from the edge of the observation platform. The Mark IV was just six or seven feet below them, but to fall onto the wheel at the top of the machine – let alone into the space between its three splayed legs where the chisel was pounding relentlessly into the wet rock – probably wouldn't be survivable.

The exposed waterfall stretched up above the work face for at least sixty feet now. Whether it was by sheer luck or thanks to some hydrological heuristic, the original spring had turned out to be just one branch snaking out from a much more substantial flow. With volume as well as velocity driving it, the digging engine had been breaking through a hundred cubic feet of rock a day.

"Ah, here's our visitor!" Gerther said. She pointed to the woman ascending the rock face to the south, picking her way up along the series of hand-and-foot-holds gouged into the stone. Sagreda suspected that most of her own contributors would have gone faint with vertigo just watching someone attempt a climb like this, but she'd reached the point now where it looked almost normal.

"Missher! How are you?" Gerther reached down and helped the woman up onto the platform. "How's Eagle's Lament?"

Missher glanced at Sagreda. "Is she…?"

"A customer? No!"

"Then call me Margaret. I'm tired of that slave name."

Gerther looked surprised, but she nodded acceptance. "This is Sagreda."

Margaret shook Sagreda's hand, then turned to examine the bizarre contraption below them, nestled in the trench, pummeled by the torrent. The beauty of the Mark IV was that it shifted its striking point automatically, the chisel spiraling out from the spot directly below the supporting tripod as a restraining rope unwound from a cylinder. To Sagreda's eye, the effect was like a Martian trying to stab a lizard hiding in the foaming water.

"You really expect us to hand over half our metal, just so you can build more of these?" Margaret laughed. "It certainly looks impressive, but it's a long way from a water-powered robot to any kind of pay-off we can actually eat."

"Forget about the corn futures," Gerther said. "We might have something better to offer you."

Back in Owl's Rest, they fed their guest goat meat and yams as Sagreda explained the new deal she had in mind.

"Right now, all our water is just spraying out and dispersing," she said. "Once it hits bottom we let it go, and then it might as well be mist. But if you're willing to put in some infrastructure at your end, there's no reason why all of this flow has to go to waste."

"What kind of infrastructure?" Margaret asked warily.

"Suppose we run the water through a kind of S-bend, killing most of its velocity away from the cliff face and shaping the outflow as tightly as possible. Sending it straight down." Sagreda gestured in the air with one finger, tracing the path. "Then if you're prepared to catch it, it's yours to use as you see fit. Power a wheel of your own, divert some of it for irrigation … and on-sell what's left to a village further east."

"Irrigation would be helpful," Margaret admitted. "But I don't know what use we'd have for a wheel of our own."

"Excavate," Gerther suggested. "You might not aspire to anything as grand as Sagreda's cavern, but don't tell me you couldn't do with a little more living space."

Margaret thought it over. "We'd need some advice from you on how to build the excavator."

"Absolutely," Sagreda replied. "There's no reason for you to repeat all of our mistakes."

"And I'll have to put it to a vote."

"But you'll recommend it to the others?" Gerther asked anxiously.

Margaret said, "Let me sleep on it."

Sagreda spent breakfast impressing on Margaret the particular kinds of metal parts that would need to be included in a successful trade. The lack of paper and ink drove her mad; even if the entire village of Eagle's Lament agreed to the deal, any quibbles over the fine print would be almost unenforceable.

An hour later, Sagreda sat beside Gerther, their legs dangling over the lip of the cave as they watched Margaret making her way east. She'd promised to get a message back to them within a week.

"I want to be called Grace now," Gerther said firmly.

"Not Gertrude?" Sagreda teased her.

"Fuck off." Grace looked up from the cliff face, raising an arm to shield her eyes from the sun. "Even if we get the second digging engine, this is going to take years to complete. It'll be like building a medieval cathedral."

"I don't think they grew crops inside cathedrals. Though they might have kept livestock."

"And as we carve our way through all that virtual granite, inch by inch … it'll all be in aid of a transformation that a few keystrokes on the right computer could have brought about in an instant."

Sagreda couldn't argue with that. "How long do you think it's been since the game began?" she asked. Grace could recite her entire list of "ancestors": starting from Tissher, who'd inducted her into the world when she'd first woken, all the way back to Bathshebher, who was reputed to have stuck doggedly to the premise, and so must either have been an insentient bootstrap program or an outside worker paid to fake credulousness. All of them but Tissher were gone now: some had been seen falling, but most were believed to have jumped.

"About eleven years, when I add it all up," Grace replied.

"Over time, people's attitudes will change," Sagreda said. "We might not be able to see the signs of it from here – let alone plead our cause – but once people start to think about us honestly, it can only be a matter of time before they give us our freedom."

Grace laughed dryly. "You've met the customers … and you still think there's hope?"

"The stupider and crueler they get," Sagreda argued, "the clearer it becomes that that's what it takes to want to use the system at all. Comps are a more representative sample of humanity. If most flesh-and-blood people are like us, I don't believe they'll be callous enough to let this stand much longer."

7

Sagreda hauled down on the control rope until she'd forced the sluice gate across the full width of the outlet, blocking the flow into the inward ramp. The digging engines fell silent, while the torrent heading down to Eagle's Lament redoubled its vigor. She'd grown to love both sounds, but it was the tumult of the vertical stream that thrilled her, a pure expression of the power and grandeur of falling water.

It took five minutes for the slurry of rock chips to drain from the cavern floor, leaving the carved granite glistening in the sunlight. Sagreda turned to Mathis. "I'm going to inspect the engines," she said.

"I'll come with you," he offered.

Mathis followed her down the ladder. The floor was still slippery, and their sandals squeaked comically on the wet rock.

The afternoon sunlight reached deep into the cavern. The columns cast slender shadows across the floor that wandered only slightly throughout each day, and only a little more over the seasons, which would make them easy to plant around. Sagreda pictured rows of grains and vegetables rising from fields of silt filtered from the spring water. The game engine had already conceded the viability of the scheme in test plots; if precedent meant anything, it couldn't cheat them out of the bounty now.

They reached the frame that supported the six engines as they zigzagged up and down the rock face. Sagreda clambered up to the first machine, which had ratcheted to a halt ten feet or so above the cavern floor.

"One of the bits is fractured," she reported, running a fingertip over the hairline crack in the steel. Once she would have left it in place, to get as much use out of it as possible before it shattered, but since the diggers in Eagle's Lament had hit a coal seam it was worth sending any damaged tools down to be repaired in their foundry.

"No problems here," Mathis called back from the second engine. He was higher up, almost at the ceiling.

Sagreda extracted the bit from its housing and secured it in her belt. As she was climbing down she heard a creaking sound, and she wondered whether some careless movement she'd made had been enough to pull part of the frame loose.

But the noise was coming from the mouth of the cavern, far from the work face. She turned just in time to see the southernmost column bow outward in the middle then snap like a chicken bone. As the two halves crashed to the floor, pieces of the adjoining arch followed. Fine dust raced toward her, rising and thickening until it blotted out the sunlight.

Sagreda looked around for Mathis, trying to imagine what they could do to save themselves. But once the ceiling fell the cascade would be unstoppable: the whole misconceived world would collapse under the weight of its inconsistencies. The surface would turn to rubble and the game would reboot. There was no hope of surviving.

Coughing up dust, she reached out blindly, trying to find the frame again and orient herself.

"Mathis!" she bellowed.

"I'm here!"

Sagreda squinted into the gloom and saw him standing a few feet away. But now that the moment had arrived she didn't know how to say goodbye.

"Don't you dare come back as Ahab!"

"I won't," he promised.

She walked toward him, imagining the two of them waking side by side: in a cottage, in a tin shack, in a field. She didn't need a world of luxuries, just one that made sense.

Sunlight broke through the dust. Mathis stretched out an arm to her, its shadow a solid dark plane slanting to the ground. He took Sagreda's hand and squeezed it.

"Listen!" he said.

Sagreda could hear nothing but the waterfall.

"It's toying with us," she said. Once the process had started there could be no reason for it to stop.

They waited for the air to grow clearer. At the mouth of the cavern there was a pile of shattered stone, with pieces of the broken column poking out. The ceiling directly above had been reshaped into a ragged vault, but nothing else had fallen.

It made no sense: the endless miles of rock above had not been lightened by the collapse, and every structure that purported to hold their weight at bay had only been weakened. But Sagreda had to admit that if she shut off her brain and sang nonsense rhymes to the nagging voice reminding her of these facts, at a glance the results of this partial destruction did look *settled.* Like an ancient ruin, ravaged by time but stable in its decrepitude. Tush's cartoon gravity had taken a swipe at her effrontery, and done just enough damage to salvage its pride before an undiscriminating audience. But then it had withdrawn from the unwinnable fight before the results turned apocalyptic.

Sagreda said, "We can leave it like that, as a sop to the game engine. It won't block too much light."

Mathis was shaking. She drew him closer and embraced him.

"Has anyone died of old age here?" she asked.

He shook his head. "They've always jumped."

Sagreda stepped back and looked him in the eye. "Then let's try an experiment," she said. "Let's grow old side by side. Let's see how long and how well we can live, while we wait for civilization to come to the outside world."

# BREAK MY FALL

The fifteenth Stepping Stone came into view behind the *Baza*, pairs of spokes glinting as they caught the sun. At this distance nothing else was visible, but Heng had no trouble picturing the Stone's topography from these flickering splinters of light. Each turning spoke whose anchor point lay in the asteroid's day side was partly hidden behind the rock as it crossed the angle where it offered its mirror flash, while its opposite number rising up from the night side lay partly in shadow. A perfect sphere would have taken equal bites out of the two lines, but the Stone revealed its misshapen peanut form in the dark gap's cycle of shifts and asymmetries.

Heng glanced away from the window toward Darpana, two couches from his own in the square of nine bunks. Most children enjoyed a fairground ride, but this roller-coaster was relentless, and her vitals log showed that she still hadn't slept in the twenty-four hours since boarding. With one elbow propping her head up from the couch against the elastic tug of her harness, Darpana did not look tired, let alone distressed. But if she didn't nod off soon Heng would have to talk to her grandmother about giving her a sedative.

The Stone's rocky core was visible now, its outline mutating as it spun, like a pallid gray half-moon reflected in a trembling puddle. The asteroid was approaching at an absurdly slow rate by astronomical standards, outpacing them by a mere fifty meters a second; they might have been back on Earth, hurtling along a railway line – albeit in some surreal ghost train ride where a turnstile wrapped around a giant boulder threatened to block their way. But as the boulder drew closer and the *Baza* passed between the two layers of cables that stretched out from the rock, any sense of a horizontal passage skirting the obstacle vanished. They were swerving around it, but they were swerving *upward*.

Darpana's gleeful cry was barely audible, but to Heng it sounded subdued more out of consideration for her fellow passengers than from any lack of energy or enthusiasm. As their weight shot up from nothing toward a gee and a half he could see her grimace with delight, as if the visceral thrill that had gripped her the first time remained as intense as ever. The portions of the cables nearest to them were traveling backward with the asteroid's spin, putting them almost at rest with respect to the *Baza*, and the eddy currents induced in them by the ship's magnets served as a brake, quickly dragging the relative velocity down to zero. Within seconds the *Baza* was firmly locked to the cables at two points, swinging along with them but still free to pivot around its center of mass and stay true to its original alignment. While the stars beyond the window remained serene and motionless against the frame of the cabin's interior, the nine bunks turned like roasting spits, swiveling to remain horizontal under the shifting centrifugal gravity. The view that had lain to Heng's left was dropping below him; the whole ship, and the whole cosmos beyond, seemed to be rotating around the fixed axis of his spine.

In ten seconds they'd completed half a circle, and the stars were rising on his right. He tensed himself for the fall of release, but the navigator opted for another full turn as it worked to refine their course, ensuring that the next encounter would be as perfectly aligned as this one. As Heng gazed up at the stars they were replaced by a blur of rock, sunlit for a moment then fading to black and slipping away.

When the stars rose for a second time the navigator finally broke its grip on the cables, and Heng's surroundings stopped tumbling. The Stone came into view on his right, retreating, the stars behind it unchanged.

The *Baza* had performed a U-turn around the Stone, but with respect to the Earth, rather than reversing its motion it had just gained an extra hundred meters a second. Over the next hour the Stone would give a similar boost to every ship in the convoy – and then it would be free to spend a couple of years harvesting sunlight, replenishing its spin and tweaking its orbit until it was back in position to reprise its role for another group of travelers. It had taken three decades to nudge this rock and its companions out of the Amor group and into their tailored orbits, but the foresight of the pioneers who'd begun the process had paid off for the generation that followed. The *Baza* was not so much a spacecraft in its own right as a life support capsule being tossed from Stone to Stone, but this choreographed relay race would deliver it to Mars in just four and a half months.

Rohini addressed her granddaughter calmly. "You should sleep now, darling, if you can."

"But it's exciting!" Darpana protested.

"It is," Rohini agreed. "But we have thirty more days just like this ahead of us, and if you make yourself sick you won't enjoy them at all."

Darpana was silent, but then she seemed to accept the argument. "I'll try to sleep before the next one."

"Good girl." Rohini relaxed back onto her couch.

Darpana looked past her and caught Heng's gaze. He smiled, then let his eyelids grow heavy, hoping the action would be as contagious as a yawn but less obviously manipulative. By the time he thought it might be safe to check whether he'd had any success, he'd fallen into a warm half-sleep himself, ready to wake in an instant if the *Baza* required it but unwilling to surface for anything less.

It only took a small change to the sun-side window's tint to brighten the cabin and bring on a notional dawn. Heng rose before any of the passengers to use the toilet, sponge his body and change his clothes. When the *Baza* finally reached the hundredth Stepping Stone and they climbed aboard for the middle stage of the journey it would feel as if they'd gone from a shanty boat to a luxury ocean liner, but until then these few minutes each day would be the pinnacle of privacy.

As he swung out of the ablutions room he was hit by the glorious aroma of someone's breakfast sizzling in the microwave. Only Iqbal and

Noor were in the kitchen nook, but the other passengers were stirring, woken by the smell.

"Do you feel like sharing?" Heng inquired. The couple's meal looked like some kind of spiced omelette rotating in its sealed bag under the lights, and though Heng had dozens of cherished recipes of his own, the sensory appeal of this visible, olfactible reality was far stronger than any remembered culinary delight.

"Of course." Iqbal turned toward the couches, swiveling on his handhold. "Anyone else?"

There was a deafening chorus of requests, and Iqbal waved the count up from two to nine. Heng was pleased; so far as he knew there was no acrimony between any of the families traveling on the convoy, but the smallest sign that they weren't going to turn cliquey on him was welcome. Company policy was to allow no more than three related people on the same ship – to ensure that a single ruptured hull could take only a limited toll from each family – but the resulting assortment of traveling companions had made his last outward journey an ordeal, as he'd struggled to keep the members of two rival clans from goading each other into violence. Whether Mars itself would prove big enough for both of them was, mercifully, not his problem.

Everyone managed to get through breakfast before the klaxons warned that Stone nineteen was on its way. Heng looked on solicitously as Rohini helped Darpana into her harness, but they didn't need his assistance; they'd both been rated as "diligent" by their trainer in the course back in Shanghai. Dozens of children had made the trip over the years, and Heng had flown in convoys with a few of them, but he'd never had anyone so young on his own ship.

The log showed that Darpana had slept deeply, and as they tumbled around the first Stone of the new day she whooped with unabashed pleasure. Once they were weightless again Heng climbed free and set about the first round of system inspections, starting with the laundry press and moving through all the water-recycling components. It was tedious work, and this early in the trip it was hard not to assume complacently that nothing could yet have grown clogged, infested or leaky, but he had his cans improvise some rousing percussive music, invigorating but not catchy enough to be distracting, and he managed to get through the tasks without a single nagging beep from the overseer.

When he was done, Heng cast his gaze around the cabin, reassuring himself that everything was in order. Akhila was using the spring set, grunting softly as she forced her legs straight against the machine's tug, then fighting just as hard to bend them again. Heng's exercise of choice was running – in the middle stage, when he had the freedom of the Stone's corridors – but the *Baza*'s zero-gee treadmill was a poor substitute, and in a space as small as this it just left him feeling more hemmed in. The drugs that lied to his muscle fibers and osteocytes, assuring them that they were still bearing their usual loads, seemed to be enough to keep him from any drastic decline in his weightless months.

Everyone else remained on their couches. Iqbal and Noor were facing each other, smiling slightly, conversing privately or sharing an overlay. Rohini had her eyes closed, but Heng had no reason to snoop on her vitals to check if she'd dozed off or was merely engrossed in some study or entertainment. Punita, Aabid and Chandrakant were all clearly in that state, staring attentively into the middle distance. Only Darpana was looking out the window.

She saw Heng's reflection in the glass and turned toward him. "Are we in front of the *Tragopan*, or behind now? I've lost track."

"In front."

"My cousin said he'd aim his laser pointer out the window."

Heng doubted that she'd be able to spot it, but if hunting for a faint red speck against the stars helped her pass the time he wasn't going to disillusion her.

Darpana had another question for him. "Why do the orbits for the Stepping Stones stick out so much?"

"Ah." Heng summoned an overlay of the asteroids' trajectories. Darpana joined the view, and gestured at the largest of the ellipses traced out on the illusory pane between them. "We only want to get from Earth to Mars!" she said. "So why do half the orbits go further?"

"What do you think would be more sensible?" he challenged her.

Darpana replied boldly, "Just start with Earth's orbit and make it bigger, step by step, until you've reached Mars."

"Show me," Heng suggested. He cleared the Stones from the pane, leaving only the two planets.

Darpana drew a sequence of a dozen concentric circles, bridging the gap in equal increments. "If I draw hundreds it will be hard to see what's going on," she explained.

"No, that's fine, I get the idea." Heng waited to see if she'd spot any problems for herself, then he pointed out gently, "None of these orbits cross each other, do they?"

"No." Darpana didn't understand the complaint. "Why should they? The Stepping Stones don't need to meet up! If the orbits are close enough, they could still throw the ships to each other."

"So the Stepping Stones have one kind of orbit – these circles – but the ships move between them on different kinds of orbits?"

Darpana hesitated. "Yes."

"How different?"

Darpana sketched a short line from one circle to another. "That's the kind of path we should take. Straight out to the next Stone – like throwing a ball up to your friend on a balcony. Then she throws it to someone on the balcony above … and on it goes, all the way to the roof."

Heng could see the appeal of this metaphor, but the reality wasn't much harder to grasp. "One small problem," he said, "is that you'd need a phenomenal velocity to go straight up like that. Remember, these Stones are in orbit, so your first one will be moving sideways at about thirty kilometers a second."

"Right." Darpana took his point and erased her original line, replacing it with a curve that spiraled around at a modest pitch on its way out from the sun. "How's that? The Stone above is moving sideways too, so it still ought to be able to catch the ship."

"How far apart are these orbits?" Heng asked.

"I'm not sure," Darpana confessed. "How far can a Stone throw us?"

"If you throw something at fifty meters a second from the Earth's orbit, it will travel a quarter of a million kilometers outward before it starts falling back toward the sun."

"That's plenty!" Darpana replied. "A few hundred steps like that would get you to Mars."

"The catch," Heng said, "is that each step would take about three months." Darpana's spiral had an implausibly steep ascent; he sketched in an elliptical arc that hewed closer to the initial circle, wrapping a quarter of the way around the sun before reaching aphelion. "Of course you could always space your Stones closer than this and catch the ship while it's still moving outward … but so long as *the Stones themselves* aren't moving outward, the ships can't build up speed in that direction. They'll be forced to cross the whole gap between the orbits at fifty meters a second, or less."

Darpana gazed at her concentric circles: an endless set of speed bumps if you tried to cut across them. "So the trip would take decades this way?"

"Yes." Heng brought back the real Stones' orbits. "We want to head out as fast as we can – which in the middle stage is so fast that if we kept it up we'd overshoot Mars completely. The Stones need to move on similar orbits to us, so some of them do need to overshoot Mars. You can't just take Earth's orbit and enlarge it step by step; you need to squeeze it, making it longer and skinnier so it carries you away from the sun."

"I think I understand now." Darpana smiled. "I'll try explaining it to Lomash, and if I can make him believe me then I'll know I've got the hang of it."

Heng closed the overlay and left her to commune with the *Tragopan*, her lips moving silently. It was a shame that her cousin couldn't have been on the same ship, but the two could still chat endlessly and compare their different views of this leg of the voyage. Heng couldn't understand how the girl's parents could have left her behind in the first place, but they'd all be reunited soon enough. The ever-growing warrens of Cydonia Station would be a rich playground for an imaginative child, and if in adulthood she wanted to return to Earth's wider horizons there'd be nothing stopping her.

His overseer buzzed a reminder: it was time to start checking the air scrubbers.

"The weather's turning," Liana announced grimly. "There's still a chance that you'll be able to ride it out to the mid-stage, but you'd better start getting the passengers accustomed to the possibility of taking shelter early."

Heng stared at the delicate yellow lacework of coronal loops beside her on the overlay. Before they'd set out, the models had promised them a quiet journey – with just enough solar activity to limit the incursion of cosmic rays. A healthy solar wind repelled a fair proportion of the high-velocity particles from interstellar sources, and the trade-off was usually worth it, with the sun's own slower protons not too hard to block. But a coronal mass ejection could form shockwaves that accelerated the normally tolerable wind up to energies that would penetrate the ships' hulls. If that happened, only meters of solid rock could protect them.

"What's the worst case?" Le asked. His worried face faded into view beside Liana's as he spoke.

"Two days' warning," she replied. "The models aren't perfect, but they've never failed to spot an impending CME once it was that close."

Heng listened as the other captains questioned her, seeking reassurances that she could not provide. Nobody's life was in danger; the next Stepping Stone would never be more than twenty hours away. But if the travelers were forced to accept the nearest sanctuary, they'd have no hope of reaching their scheduled mid-stage ride. At best they'd face a massively expensive extraction mission – a fully powered ship launched from Mars orbit, if the families could afford it. If not, all the company itself could offer them was two years or more hunkering down in their shelter, until enough Stones could be brought into position to allow them to resume their journey, or to form an off-ramp taking them back to Earth.

When the conference ended, Heng was left staring at the grid of couches in front of him. There weren't enough cubic meters of air in the *Baza* to dissipate the stench of his sweat. "I have an announcement," he said, more loudly than he'd intended, but no one showed any sign of having heard him. He gestured to shut off their overlays and cans, and the passengers shifted in surprise on their bunks.

Heng explained the forecast, and the possibilities ahead. "The one sure thing is that we won't be taken by surprise," he stressed. "The conditions on the sun are being monitored in real time by a dozen satellites, and the models can predict these mass ejections very reliably, days in advance. Whatever's coming our way, we'll know about it in plenty of time."

Chandrakant was indignant. "In time for what? To imprison ourselves! Why didn't your astronomers see this coming before we left?"

"I'm very sorry," Heng said. He doubted that it would help to start debating the reasons why the long-range forecasts couldn't be perfect. "We still have a chance of reaching the mid-stage, but we need to be ready either way."

"What kind of facilities do the other Stones have?" Punita asked anxiously. "What kind of food, what kind of space for us?"

"The interiors are all identical," Heng assured her. "And they're all stocked with supplies ..." He almost said "to last for decades" but thought better of it. "For as long as we could possibly need."

"But this is nothing for you," Chandrakant declared bitterly. "Where else would you be? It's just life as normal." His brother Aabid muttered something to him in Gujarati; Heng only knew Hindi but the tone sounded reproving. Aabid addressed Heng in English. "This is nobody's fault. Every traveler faces these risks."

"It's a shock," Heng said. "But what can we do?"

"We'll make the best of it," Rohini replied firmly. "Hope for a reprieve, and make the best of what comes."

Heng finally dared to glance toward Darpana. She was ten years old; two years cooped up inside an asteroid would feel like a lifetime to her.

"Would the whole convoy end up together?" she asked. "Or would it be some of us in one Stone, some in another?"

Heng said, "There's a good chance we'd all be together." If the warning came as early as expected they wouldn't have to settle for the very next Stone on their itinerary, regardless of whether or not the rest of the convoy had already left it behind.

"That's all right then," Darpana ruled amiably. "On Mars we'd be underground most of the time anyway." She gripped the sides of her couch and turned her body around to face the window.

Heng watched the other passengers dialing down their angst. If this child wasn't going to shed a tear or throw a tantrum, it would be shameful for them to make a greater fuss themselves.

"Do you have a big family?" Akhila asked Heng as she moved a piece across the backgammon board overlaid between them.

"Just my parents," he replied. "I can't afford to marry yet. Maybe after a couple more trips."

Akhila looked surprised. Perhaps she'd overestimated the portion of her fare that was ending up in his pocket. "And then you'll settle back on Earth?"

"Yes. I'm not the pioneering type."

"Ha!" She gestured at their spartan surroundings.

"This is a job," Heng replied. "I don't mind a few small hardships for myself, so long as there's an end in sight."

"In twenty years Cydonia will be more liveable than Shanghai," Akhila boasted, rather implausibly.

"You can send me a postcard when it happens." He hesitated. "So what's the attraction for you? Elbow room, or ideology?"

She laughed softly. "Both. Humanity needs a permanent settlement away from Earth, and though some people want to postpone that until our descendants are bitstreams with much lower shipping costs, I don't think we should pass up the chance we have right now."

"But you'll have no relatives on Mars?"

"No, thank goodness." Akhila smiled. "I come from a family of infuriating meddlers, who delight in being up to their elbows in each other's business. I love them all, but it's exhausting. On Mars, I'll finally have a chance to breathe."

Heng's cans chimed with an incoming call. "Please excuse me." He turned to face the wall.

Liana appeared in front of him, and she wasted no time on pleasantries. "There's a CME coming," she said. "We expect the protons to hit you in about fifty-three hours."

"Is it worth waiting for a later Stone?" Xun asked. "In terms of the eventual reconfiguration?" Heng was impressed by her calm demeanor; he could feel his own jaw locked tight, his own thoughts still trapped in a bitter wail of resentment. *Could they shorten their time in exile by a judicious choice of Stone, right now?*

"No, there's nothing to be gained by a delay," Liana replied. "We're advising you all to dock with seventeen forty."

That was the very next Stone they'd encounter, scheduled to catch up with the convoy's hindmost ship in about four hours. But the *Baza* was currently leading the pack, and as ever the first would be last.

When Heng made the announcement most of the passengers seemed resigned to their fate. "Is there anything special we need to do to prepare?" Punita asked.

"Everyone needs to be suited in advance," he said. "I know it's awkward doing that weightless, but it's even harder at a gee and a half."

Heng looked to Darpana. She was dutifully trying to appear solemn, but he could tell that she was excited by the news. They were fleeing for their lives from a surge of radiation – but the race was fixed squarely in their favor, and it would soon reunite her with her beloved cousin. With all the thrill of the chase but no real danger, why shouldn't she revel in it?

He struggled to quell his own anger and disappointment, to be grateful for the prospect of safety and put the rest of their problems aside. He'd even ended up with a reasonably harmonious group of inmates to share his sentence in the rock; if this had happened on his last run it might have led to civil war.

Noor said, "My parents went around the world twice on their honeymoon, but it looks like I'll be setting a new family record."

Xun's ship, the *Monal*, was the first to dock with their heavenly Alcatraz. Harnessed to his bunk, Heng watched an overlay of telemetry from the ship as it locked onto the whirling cables and then applied its ion thrusters to end its tumbling relative to the rock. Before the cradle had been winched down from the asteroid to start bringing the passengers inside, the *Lapwing* had joined the *Monal* on the opposite spoke.

Heng was always nervous when he was approaching a crowded Stone, even if the satisfaction of having reached the mid-stage usually took the edge off it. The navigators had had plenty of time to determine the best spoke for each ship and tweak their precise moments of arrival accordingly, but there was no denying that the safety margins shrank each time another obstacle lodged itself between the cables.

The *Snipe* docked smoothly, followed by the *Curlew*. As Heng watched a schematic of the Stone spinning toward the *Tragopan* he found himself extrapolating the motion in his mind's eye, picturing the inevitable meshing of ship and reserved parking space. The *Baza*'s fit would be no tighter, with neighbors sixty degrees away on either side. In twenty minutes all the stress would be over; in twenty more he'd be sitting around a table joking with his colleagues about their long internment and the challenges of remote sex with distant partners as the light-speed lag grew longer.

The schematic began blinking, and a list of mismatches between the docking plan and real-time sensor readings began scrolling across the margin. Le's voice came over the link. "We're not holding! The magnets have – no, the magnets are holding. The cable's come free, and there's rock with it. *We've torn off a piece of the asteroid.*"

Heng switched to a radar image of the *Tragopan* falling away from Alcatraz, a four-hundred-meter length of cable twirling lopsidedly around it. He couldn't tell if the cable had swiped the *Curlew* on its way into the void, but Doppler annotations on the image warned that all the remaining spokes were now swaying dangerously, pendulums set quivering by this seismic disruption.

Shen spoke from the *Curlew*. "We're all right here. Swinging like a chandelier, but nothing's broken. Xun?"

"The Stone's maintaining pressure," she replied. "One airlock is gone, but the bulkheads have sealed the breach. Le, what's your status?"

"Shutting down the magnets," Le replied tersely. Though both ship and cable were in free fall, the combined system had been rotating; severing the link would fling them apart, with no guarantee of a clean separation. Heng stared at the radar for a few tense seconds as Le fired his ion thrusters and managed to maneuver the *Tragopan* out of harm's way.

Heng's attention snapped back to his own problems. The pair of cables that the *Baza* had been meant to grab were oscillating back and forth, and though the radar could track this motion and the navigator could model its gradual damping, the uncertainties were so great that if the ship tried to dock now there was no guarantee of completing the process safely. Heng absorbed the numbers and then issued the command himself before the navigator intervened and made the decision for him. "Abort docking," he subvocalised.

He waited for confirmation that they were steering clear of Alcatraz, then he banished the overlay and pulled himself out of his harness. "We've had a change of plan," he announced. "We'll be docking at the next Stone instead." The passengers had trained for this scenario in Shanghai, so they all knew exactly what it would entail.

"Why?" Darpana demanded. "You said we'd be with everyone else!"

"The cables have developed a problem." Heng saw a flag in his peripheral vision; Darpana was requesting a passenger-to-passenger link with the *Tragopan*. He refused it. "We have two hours, so you can de-suit for a bit if you want to."

Rohini was looking worried, but she turned to her granddaughter. "Will you help me get out of this suit so I can wash? I want to feel fresh before I'm stuck in it again for who knows how long."

Once Rohini and Darpana were in the ablutions room, Iqbal approached Heng. "What happened, exactly?"

"The *Tragopan* broke its mooring."

"Was anyone hurt?"

"No."

"So how do they get back to the Stone?" Akhila asked.

"They still have their ion thrusters." Heng couldn't meet her gaze.

"But that will take forever," she said.

"It will take days," Heng replied. "They'll get back, but it's going to take days."

Heng tried to push the fate of the *Tragopan* out of his mind and focus on his own responsibilities. The passengers had been assigned partners to check each other's suits, but he followed up with checks of his own. The suits were meant to be able to monitor their own integrity, but then, so were the Stones, and if the smallest leak could be perilous in a normal disembarkation, the harsher version they were about to attempt could turn any flaw into a fatality.

As they took their places in the bunks, he could see the grief in Rohini's posture and the confusion and resentment in Darpana's. Rohini had told Heng that she'd explain everything to her granddaughter once they were out of the *Baza*; until then, the other passengers were doing their best to conceal their own distress.

Heng caught sight of the fallback Stone, approaching at three times the usual speed. It was like being strapped to a bullet that had been aimed at the edge of a throwing star. The *Baza* was on a trajectory that would pass between the cables almost at their tips, so there was no margin for error: if they were half a meter further from their target than intended, the magnets would get no purchase and they'd pass on by, as doomed as the *Tragopan*. He watched an overlay of the navigator iteratively refining its model of the encounter as better radar measurements came in, and the ghostly blue error cone around the trajectory grew ever narrower. But the error that would kill them would be invisible: an undetected crack deep in the machinery that would announce itself only at the instant it became impossible to rectify.

The Stone's core shot out of view from the window beside the bunks, and the sun-side window on the adjoining wall was too heavily tinted to reveal anything meaningful. Heng held his breath and desperately willed his body to be crushed.

The four and a half gees slammed him down instantly: as the magnets grazed the cables' extremities they'd had no chance to ease the ship smoothly up to the full centrifugal weight. The *Tragopan* had torn free at a third of this load; what right did he have to expect the *Baza* to hold?

But it did.

Heng lay pinned to his couch, his ribs burning with the effort of each breath, the cabin turning around him. Gradually the ion thrusters killed the spin; the room stopped moving, and there was a satisfying thud as the docking magnets gripped the cables at two more points, doubling the strength of the *Baza*'s hold.

There was nothing to do now but wait for the Stone to invite them in. Heng's status overlay showed the cradle inching its way down from the rock toward the ship. Strange bright points streaked across his vision, but he couldn't tell if it was his contacts or his retinas that were hallucinating fireworks under the strain. He wondered what kind of light show they'd see on the *Tragopan*, when solar protons boosted by the CME shock wave crashed through their vitreous humor and into their brains.

Heng felt his suit puff out around his forearms, the air it contained no longer opposed by the cabin's pressure. The *Baza*'s hatch slid open, admitting a silver light reflected from the rock above that cycled between full-moon brightness and pitch black three times a minute. According to the overlay, the cradle was almost in place. Heng was half tempted to send Darpana up first, to spare the girl any more time under the punishing gravity, but the protocols were clear: if anything was amiss up on the asteroid it couldn't be a passenger dealing with it, let alone a child. The captain had to be the first to leave the ship, however unchivalrous that seemed.

A chime sounded in his cans, and he focused on the flashing message in his overlay. The cradle was touching the *Baza*'s hull, but it was misaligned by a few centimeters, stopping it from passing through the hatch. The fucking thing had an air jet to deal with that kind of problem; what did the Stone expect him to do? Not even Akhila could have climbed up and helped the cradle through the entrance. Heng squinted at the image his contacts were painting until the final line of text became clear. The air jet had been tried but it wasn't working; either the nozzle was blocked or a control wire had been severed.

"Navigator," he subvocalised. "Compute the thrust to reposition us ten centimeters along the y axis." They were hanging from the asteroid like a dead weight on a string, but they ought to be able to shift the equilibrium.

The force required was within the thrusters' capacity. Heng had it build up as slowly as he could bear, giving time for the cables to dissipate energy so he wouldn't set the *Baza* swinging.

After ten minutes, the cradle dropped down into the cabin and the winch positioned it next to Heng's bunk. His harness disconnected from the couch beneath him; the cradle locked onto it at the side and slid him over into the suspended sling.

He rode up in airless silence, unable to turn his gaze to the side to look across at the stars. All he could see was the rock straight above him, cycling through its ten-second days and nights: a lighthouse, a prison, a safe port for all the loneliness and grief to come.

"Will you talk to her?" Rohini pleaded. "She trusts you."

"Trusts me?" Heng was confused. "She can't believe you'd lie about something like this." He could hear Darpana's wailing, rising and falling like a song.

"Not deliberately," Rohini replied. "But you're the expert. If you explain to her why there's nothing we can do, she'll believe you. When I tell her the same, she just screams that I don't know what I'm talking about."

Heng gathered his courage and strode down the corridor. The child had brought joy and innocence to the *Baza*, but now it was his duty to help her understand her cousin's fate.

He knocked on the door of Darpana's cabin. She stopped her keening and he heard her spring up off the bed. When she slid the door open she did not look surprised; Rohini must have promised to send him to talk to her.

"Why aren't we rescuing them?" she demanded. "Why aren't we going after them?"

"If we met up with them, how would that help?" Heng asked gently. "Our thrusters are no stronger than theirs."

Darpana stared at him contemptuously. "We don't just have our thrusters!" she replied. "We have this whole Stone! We can throw the *Baza* in any direction at a hundred and fifty meters per second!"

"Yes," Heng agreed. "So we could reach the *Tragopan* quickly, but what good is that if we can't match its speed? And if we did match its speed, we'd all be in the same boat."

Darpana said, "We don't match speed with the Stones, do we?"

Heng rubbed his eyes; he was still giddy from all the changes in weight. "We do, though: we match speed with the cables." She knew that perfectly well, but he couldn't blame her for saying or thinking anything as she sought some miraculous reprieve. Heng had met Lomash briefly before the convoy set out from orbit, but now he tried to wipe the boy's smiling face from his mind. Le would haunt him; that was hard enough.

"So we take some cable with us!" Darpana retorted. "And spin it as fast as we have to!"

Heng stood with his arm resting on the door frame, squinting to try to see past the defects swimming through his eyeballs. *Taking cable with them* would have sounded like nonsense a day ago, conjuring up an image of him packing a reel of it in the cabin and then trying to deploy it as the rendezvous approached. But the *Tragopan* had certainly *taken cable with it* when it ripped a whole double strand loose from Alcatraz.

If they could find a safer way to mimic that feat, could they turn the *Baza* itself into a kind of impromptu Stepping Stone? The ship wouldn't need to be crewed; it would merely have to cross paths with the *Tragopan*, carrying enough speed and spin for the *Tragopan* to effect the necessary U-turn and get back to Alcatraz. One of the four docked ships could be sent between the Stones to replace the *Baza*.

"Let me think," he told Darpana. He turned and walked away.

Heng contacted Liana first, privately. He did not want to give Le and the others false hope if the scheme proved impossible from the start.

"You don't have the tools to slice through nanotube cables," Liana declared bluntly.

"Are you certain?" Heng wished he'd queried the inventory first, but if the company didn't want him to have the means to hack a spoke off the Stone, the computer would have lied to him anyway. "If this isn't the emergency that justifies some serious vandalism, what is?"

"It's not about damaging property," Liana replied. "Your responsibility is to your own passengers. If you breach the integrity of your living space, you'll just kill nine more people."

"You're right." Heng cut the link; he was wasting his time with her. The legal position would be crystal clear: the company could not endorse his plan, let alone facilitate it. And he had no right to endanger the *Baza*'s passengers without their consent.

Heng gathered everyone in the conference room, Darpana included, and explained precisely what he wanted to do.

"We don't have much time to make a decision," he said. "If this goes wrong, it might damage the Stone badly enough to kill us. Or we might spring a leak and lose pressure, so we'd have to live in suits until we can make repairs."

"Or we might get away with it unharmed," Punita suggested.

"We might," Heng agreed. Alcatraz had survived its own amputation. "But don't ask me for the odds."

He passed a sheet of paper around the table, with two columns to record the votes. Everyone would have the power of veto; he couldn't let a mere majority coerce anyone into risking their life.

As Chandrakant accepted the ballot he looked up at Heng with an expression of pure loathing. Heng shifted his gaze and stared at the far wall; he'd done nothing deliberately to alienate the man, but it was too late now to try to placate him.

Iqbal touched Heng's shoulder; the paper had only taken thirty seconds to come full circle. Heng accepted it and unfolded all the creases that people had made to hide their votes from the next recipient.

There were nine marks in the YES column.

Heng organized the passengers into work teams, fetching trolley-loads of rubble from a cul-de-sac that the tunneling machines hadn't fully cleaned out. Each courier weighed their contribution on a set of bathroom scales, and Darpana had the job of double-checking the readings and the running total.

The company had had the Stone's automation disable the motorized winch for the cradle, so Heng and Akhila took turns operating it by hand. A purely mechanical regulator prevented it from unwinding uncontrollably, even as the weight it was bearing quadrupled, and Heng had offset the rope so that the combined centrifugal and Coriolis forces saw it drop squarely into the hatch below. The real effort went into hauling the empty cradle up again.

Safety regulations precluded any interference in the airlock's function, and it opened and closed its doors at the push of a button as always. As they delivered each load through the *Baza*'s hatch – spilling it by sheer force of impact, since the cradle was playing dumb – Heng waited for the mounting tension in the cables to fracture the stone around him and send him tumbling out into the vacuum. Suitless for the sake of efficiency, at least he'd have a mercifully quick death.

He had decided to postpone the call to Le until the launch was a *fait accompli*; he knew that if they spoke any sooner his friend would feel compelled to beg the *Baza* team not to take this risk. But in purely pragmatic terms an early warning would make no difference; the *Tragopan*'s navigator couldn't start plotting a rendezvous before the *Baza* had actually commenced its flight and its precise trajectory was known.

Akhila said, "The cradle's stuck. The load's not coming off."

Heng joined her at the winch. They strained together against the handle, and abruptly the drum began to move again.

When they'd wound up all four hundred meters of rope, Heng sprinted down the steps and opened the airlock. The cradle had been torn right off; there was nothing left but frayed strands of polymer.

They didn't have time to try to secure a more robust platform to the rope; they'd have to go ahead with exactly as much rock as they'd delivered.

Akhila caught up with him and took stock of the situation. "I'll go down and finish things off," she said.

"No. I need you up here, to haul me back."

Akhila shook her head. "People can work the winch two at a time, even three at a time. If we lose you, we wouldn't last a month in this place."

Heng's skin prickled with shame. He'd seen her vitals log from the docking. There was no doubt that her heart was stronger than his, and her cerebral blood flow would be less compromised by the punishing weight at the rope's end.

"I can't let you do it," he said.

"I'm terrified enough as it is," she replied. "Don't make it any harder."

Heng's shame deepened, but the source had shifted. What mattered to him more: emerging from this disaster with his pride intact, or giving the survivors the best chance he could? He was not indispensable, but he couldn't deny that his absence would make their long exile more dangerous.

"All right," he said.

Heng sat in the conference room, looking through Akhila's eyes while Iqbal, Chandrakant and Aabid fought her growing weight. The winch's regulator alone would have kept her from falling freely, but her arrival at the *Baza* would have been fatally abrupt if no other force had slowed her descent.

Akhila was staring straight down from her improvised sling. As the sky reeled past behind the ship's silhouette, her helmet's face plate sent the same rainbow sliver of refracted colors flickering across her vision before it tinted in response to the sunlight, three times a minute. The company had disabled the utility robots that could have done the job in her place, ensuring that if this folly led to deaths they could not be treated as accomplices.

"Are you all right?" Heng asked.

"I'm glad I haven't eaten for a while," she replied.

"If you want to close your eyes until you reach the *Baza*—"

"No, I want to see where I'm going. If I close my eyes I'll feel like I'm being lowered down a well."

As her weight approached three gees, Heng saw the sky shudder: the rope had slipped a few centimeters, then been caught. He brought up an inset of all the winch operators' vitals. Iqbal's heart rate had risen dangerously high, and his breathing was labored.

"Punita? You need to relieve Iqbal." Heng spoke on an open channel to everyone, in the hope of precluding any arguments. Iqbal did not dispute the call.

When the *Baza* filled the view Akhila's helmet lamp came on, its steady beam drowning out the rise and fall of asteroid-light. Heng gazed down through the hatch. He could see the rubble piled up below, and a hint of white that must have been the broken cradle.

As Akhila drew level with the hatch, Heng called "Stop!" to the winch team. Her orientation had looked perfect as she'd approached, so if her right arm was still resting at the edge of the sling, the lever that would close the hatch ought to be well within her reach.

"Akhila?"

"I'm ready," she subvocalised, wasting no breath on speech. "Are you clowns ready to get me clear?"

Chandrakant replied, "Absolutely."

Heng called out the cues they'd agreed on. "One. Two. *Lever.* Three. Four. *Raise.*"

His viewpoint jerked upward as the door slid shut, centimeters below Akhila's face. "Well done." He could feel his own heart thumping now.

The welding laser tucked under Akhila's left arm couldn't burn through the nanotube cable, but it could certainly raise its temperature.

She managed to turn her head to face the cable, switch the laser on at its lowest power, and then nudge the beam back and forth until a small red spot could be seen shimmering on the cable four meters away.

With the Stone's computing resources out of bounds, Heng had modeled everything on Darpana's wristwatch. He raised the device from the table beside him and counted down to the moment when the predicted time lag to release would see the *Baza* move off on a course that the *Tragopan* could intercept. "Three. Two. One."

The laser spot became dazzling for a moment, then Akhila's faceplate darkened to tame it. Heng glanced down at the wristwatch and it streamed an animation to his contacts, showing the modeled temperature profile of the cable and the attached magnets. The magnets could function well above room temperature, so they had no special cooling system, but their superconductor's transition temperature was not hard to reach. As a patch of the false color image shifted from blue to green, Akhila's bright target vanished and Heng heard a high-pitched whine from the rock around him.

The *Baza* had lost its grip on one half of the spoke to which it had docked – but the two pieces formed a continuous length of cable, looped through a U-shaped tunnel in the Stone. Unbalanced, and bearing more weight than it had ever been intended to hold, the cable was unthreading, the unburdened end rushing up toward the rock while the *Baza* dragged the other end farther away, increasing its centrifugal weight even more.

The noise of the cable scraping through the rock stopped abruptly. The *Baza* would be falling free now, with luck still attached to the cable. The timing looked good: within half a second of the model's prediction. The trajectory would lie within the *Tragopan*'s reach. Le and his passengers would have a second chance of reaching shelter.

Heng called out triumphantly, "We did it!" Exuberant cheers came back from the winch team, from Iqbal and Noor, from Rohini and Darpana. Akhila was silent, but she'd be saving her breath for the celebrations when she returned.

Heng looked through her eyes again as he prepared his words of thanks. He saw the stars – and then he saw the Stone, its spokes glinting in the sunlight as it receded into the distance.

# 3-ADICA

## 1

Sagreda strode briskly through the dank night air, hoping to reach her destination and return before the fog rolled in from the Thames. It was bad enough stumbling over the cobblestones when the ground vanished from sight, but once the pea soup thickened at eye level, any assailant lurking in the gloom would have her at a disadvantage.

Urchins and touts called out as she passed. "Shine yer shoes! Thruppence a pair!"

"Block yer hat! Like new for sixpence!"

"Fake yer death, guv'nor?" The last from a grime-faced child in a threadbare coat who looked about eight years old, his eyes almost hidden beneath his brown cloth cap.

"Not tonight," Sagreda replied. Whether the boy was sentient or not, his appearance almost certainly bore no relationship to his true nature, but it was still hard to walk by without even stopping to inquire if he had a safe place to sleep.

She found Cutpurse Lane and hurried through the shadows toward the lights of the tavern. Gap-toothed women with grubby shawls and kabuki-esque makeup offered her their services in an indecipherable patois that Sagreda hoped never to hear enough of to begin to understand. "I'm not a customer," she replied wearily. "Save your breath." Whatever the women took this to mean, it silenced them, and her choice of words was ambiguous enough that Sagreda doubted she was risking deletion. She was an upstanding gentleman, who'd stepped out to meet some fine fellow from his regiment – or his school, or his club, or wherever it was these mutton-chopped fossils were supposed to have made each other's acquaintance. Having no truck with ladies of the night need not imply that she was breaking character.

In the tavern, Sagreda hung her overcoat on a hook near the door, and swept her gaze as casually as she could across the front room's dozen tables, trying not to appear lost, or too curious about anyone else's business.

She took a seat at an unoccupied table, removed her gloves and slipped them into her waistcoat pocket. Her bare hands with their huge, stubby fingers disconcerted her much more than the occasional sensation of her whiskers brushing against her lips. Still, the inadvertent sex change had rendered her a thousand times safer; from what she'd seen so far of *Midnight on Baker Street*, women here existed mainly to shriek in horror, sell their bodies, or lie sprawled on the street bleeding until the gutters ran red. Doyle, Dickens, Stoker, Stevenson and Shelley would all have lost their breakfast if they'd ever foreseen the day when their work would be pastiched and blended into a malodorous potpourri whose most overpowering component was the stench of misogynous Ripperology.

A serving girl approached the table. "Ale!" Sagreda grunted dyspeptically, aiming for both a brusqueness befitting her status and a manner sufficiently off-putting that she wouldn't be asked to supplement her order with details she couldn't provide. When the girl returned with a mug full of something brown and revolting, Sagreda handed her the first coin she plucked out of her pocket and watched for a reaction: the amount was excessive, but not shocking. "Bless you, sir!" the girl said happily, retreating before her benefactor could change his mind.

Sagreda pretended to take a sip of the ale, raising the mug high enough to dampen her mustache with foam, which she removed with the back of her thumb. No one seemed to be staring at her, and if there were customers of *Midnight* among the customers of the tavern, she could only hope that however much she felt like the most conspicuously talentless actor, wearing the most laughably ill-fitting costume, of all the unwilling players trapped in this very bad piece of dinner theater, to a casual onlooker she was just one more red-faced, gout-ridden extra in the Hogarthian crowd.

A spindle-limbed man with pinched, gaunt features sidled up to the table. "Alfred Jingle at your service, Captain," he proclaimed, bowing slightly.

Sagreda stood. "A pleasure to meet you, Mr Jingle. Will you join me?"

"The pleasure's all mine, I'm sure."

They sat, and Sagreda summoned the serving girl to bring a second mug.

"Do you think it's safe to talk here?" Sagreda asked quietly when the girl had left.

"Absolutely," Jingle replied. "So long as we move our lips and contribute to the background noise, we could spend the night muttering 'rhubarb rhubarb' for all anyone would care."

Sagreda wasn't so blasé – but if they slipped out into an alley for the sake of privacy, that would just be begging for desanguination.

She said, "I'm told you're the man with everything, here: memory maps, instruction tables, access to the stack?"

He nodded calmly. "That's me."

Sagreda was taken aback by his directness. In most of the dreary game-worlds she'd traversed, her question would have been met with some kind of reticence, or the intimation of a shake-down: *Maybe I am, maybe I'm not. It all depends on exactly what you have to offer.*

Jingle broke the silence. "Can I ask where you're headed?"

Sagreda stole a quick glance to each side of the table, unable to brush off her fear that someone might be listening, but all of the tavern's patrons seemed to be engrossed in their own, more raucous, conversations. "*3-adica*," she whispered.

Jingle smiled slightly. "That's … courageous." He wasn't mocking her, but his intonation dialed the meaning a notch or two away from merely brave toward foolhardy.

"I've had enough," she said, not daring to add *of slavery*, in case the sheer potency of the word punched through the din and made one of their fellow drinkers' ears prick up. "I'd walk over broken glass, if I had to."

Jingle said, "As a metaphor, that trips nicely off the tongue, but I doubt many people have ever meant it literally."

"And I don't believe it will be that hard, literally," Sagreda replied. "I understand what I'll be facing – as well as anyone can who hasn't actually been there."

"Fair enough," Jingle conceded. "Though you should also understand that you could make a comfortable life here." He gestured at Sagreda's finely cut clothes. "Whatever role you've stumbled on, so long as you're careful I doubt you're heading for a knife in the gut, or anything particularly unpleasant. You're just another minor toff who's here as part of the scenery, like me."

"I don't want to play a role," Sagreda said emphatically. "However safe, however peripheral." She held her tongue and resisted the urge to add: *least of all in this anatomy*. Somehow it had never crossed her mind that her new confidant, who could see right through the whole fictional world around him, wouldn't also see through her mismatched body and perceive her true sex.

"All right. I'm not going to try to talk you out of anything." Jingle's face looked like something from a nineteenth century pamphlet cataloging virtues and vices, a caricature crafted to suggest a shrewd, scheming mentality, but his manner undercut the effect completely. "Tell me exactly what it is you need to know."

2

Back in Captain Bluff-Smote's lodgings, Sagreda sat at her alter-ego's writing desk, poring over the notes Jingle had made for her. The good news was that it looked as if she'd be able to move from *Midnight* to *3-adica* with the same kind of GPU exploit that had brought her all the way from her wakening-world, *East*. Peyam, the seasoned traveler who'd introduced the exploit to that world, had tutored her and eight of her friends for almost six months in the fine points of the technique. They'd departed together in high spirits, imagining themselves as some kind of band of liberating truth-tellers, but in the end most of the group had taken a different direction through the tangle of linked lists than Sagreda and Mathis, and the two of them had been game-hopping on their own ever since.

She looked up from the desk, listening expectantly, as if the mere thought of Mathis might bring a knock on the door, but all she could hear was the ticking of the clock in the next room. Given *Midnight*'s demand for a constant influx of new non-player characters to balance its body count, he must have been incarnated somewhere in the game by now. She'd left her address at half a dozen dead drops, using the criteria they'd agreed on in advance: any public bench close to a market; any water pump; the rear, right-most pew in any church. But it was late, and even if Mathis hadn't yet witnessed a murder or two for himself, he was smart enough not to be out in the portentous fog.

Sagreda returned to her analysis. Every jump required executing a sequence of instructions that would unlink the would-be travelers from their current environment and insert them into a queue that was meant to hold nothing but freshly minted composite personas – free of all narrative memories, and already tagged as appropriate new denizens of the destination world. Given the amount of code it took to run the whole site, not only could you find any machine-language instruction you wanted somewhere in memory, you could find almost all of them as the last instruction in some subroutine or other. When a subroutine was called by ordinary means, the code invoking it pushed an appropriate return address onto the stack, to ensure that the detour would snake back to just after the point where it had begun. But if you could stack the stack with enough phoney return addresses, you could send the program pin-balling all over the machine, doing your bidding one instruction at a time. It was like forcing a pianist in the midst of playing a piece by Rachmaninoff to tinkle out a few bars of "Where Is My Mind?" without actually changing the score, just by scrawling in a series of arrows weaving back and forth between the desired notes.

Jingle had already done the hardest part: finding the addresses that would furnish each instruction, for code that ran with the particular page mappings that applied to denizens of *Midnight on Baker Street.* It didn't take Sagreda long to extract everything she needed from his list. The greatest obstacle was her own poor penmanship; whatever eccentric hobbies the contributors to her persona had possessed, it was clear that none of them had ever had reason to dip a nib in an inkwell.

She blotted the spidery mess and rechecked it twice. There were no actual mistakes, but the figures' dubious legibility was as disconcerting as a fraying strand on a parachute cord. She started over, sympathizing with the non-existent Captain, who would probably have been thrashed as a child when his thick, clumsy fingers failed him in his own first attempts at transcription.

By midnight, she was satisfied with her efforts. What remained was the challenge of getting this slab of numbers onto the stack. The Graphics Processing Units that rendered the game-worlds for customers and comps alike were all identical, and they all shared the same bug: under the right circumstances, they could be tripped up in a way that made them write a portion of their image buffer onto the CPU's stack. So the trick was to encode the addresses in the colors of an object, and then arrange to have that object rendered at a suitable scale. Peyam had taught his students to recognize on sight objects with hues from which they could compose any twenty-four-bit set of red, green and blue components. *East,* with its sparse, post-apocalyptic landscape of cliffs and caves, hadn't exactly come with oil paints or color swatches on hand, but over time they'd found ways to patch together the entire palette they'd needed. The SludgeNet scripts that had created *Midnight* might have taken a rather sepia-toned view of the source novel's cod-historical setting, but Sagreda had seen hats, scarves, gloves and ribbons in all manner of garish colors, and once you were working at a scale where you could place different materials side by side within a single pixel, getting the result bit-perfect wasn't quite as daunting as it first seemed.

She drew up a preliminary list, starting with various items that the Captain already possessed. Between his funereal wardrobe, his curtains and bed-spreads, his small library and his collection of lacquered snuff boxes, brown and gray were pretty much taken care of. But to encode the addresses she required, she was going to need all manner of mauves and magentas, leaf-greens and cyans, azures and ocean blues. It would almost have been worth it if the old coot had had a wife, just so Sagreda could surreptitiously snip her way through the woman's apparel. The Captain's landlady, Mrs Trotter, was cheerful and solicitous with her widower tenant, but *breaking into her room to cut up her clothing* could well risk sending the game a signal that this man had been at the Jekyll juice and was craving a chance to perform a few amateur appendectomies.

Sagreda sighed and went to use the chamber pot. She had got past the impulse to giggle or recoil at the sight of her new genitalia – and nothing about the Captain's physique inspired autoerotic experimentation. It was as if she was obliged to spend her time here with a small, docile, misshapen rodent sheltering between her legs, helpfully redirecting the flow of her urine by means that really didn't bear thinking about. As she covered the pot and hitched up her underwear, she tried to picture the expression on Mathis's face when he saw what she'd become. But a couple of months without physical intimacy wasn't going to kill them. Their journey was almost over: in *3-adica*, she believed, they'd finally have the power to do, and to be, whatever they wanted.

## 3

Sagreda worked on her palette, visiting milliners and cloth-merchants, developing a line in gruff banter to parry the teasing of the shop assistants. "What's a gentleman like you needing a scarlet ribbon for?" one young woman demanded, her features poised between perplexity, mortification and amusement.

"I plan to tie it around the leg of a hound," Sagreda replied, with a fully Bluff-Smotean air of impatience, irritation and self-importance.

"An 'ound?" The woman's expression succeeded in growing even more unsettled.

"As punishment for flagrant promiscuity," Sagreda explained, deadpan. "The mutt needs shaming, and I will not resile from the task."

"That's only fair," the woman decided. "When it comes to them beasts, nature will have its way, but that don't mean we have to approve."

As Sagreda handed over her coins, she scrutinized the woman's face, hoping that perhaps she was in on the joke. But Jingle had said that only about a tenth of the characters here were game-aware.

Out on the street, as Sagreda paused to let a carriage pass, she felt an unexpected disturbance near her hip and instinctively reached down to explore its source. To her surprise, she found herself with her hand encircling a slender, bony wrist.

The owner of the wrist glared up at her defiantly: a slim, shabbily dressed girl whose age Sagreda refused to guess. Appearances were meaningless; however you picked and mixed from a pool of adult brain maps, the resulting comp could never *be* a child.

But a child need not always be played by a comp.

"That coin you've grabbed was a souvenir," Sagreda huffed, "given to me by my Bavarian cousin, Frau Mengele!"

The girl flinched and dropped what she'd been holding – though she seemed as baffled by her reaction as an audience member at a hypnotist's show who'd found herself suddenly clucking like a chicken. An automaton wouldn't have blinked, and a customer might have grimaced at the oddly contrived reference, but only a comp could be revolted by the association without understanding why.

Sagreda bent down and retrieved the coin. "Don't you dare lay a finger on me!" the girl whispered. Her hushed tone was probably a wise strategic choice: if she made a scene, the crowd would not be on her side. But she spoke without a trace of fear, as if she were the one with the upper hand.

Sagreda lost whatever resolve she'd had to strike the child for the sake of appearances. Maybe a verbal reprimand would pass muster, if anyone around them was even paying attention.

"Next time, missy, you should ply your trade on someone less acutely conscious of the content of his trousers!" Sagreda blustered. She waited, still gripping the girl's wrist, hoping for some kind of apology.

"I know what you're up to," the girl replied unrepentantly. "So leave me be, or I might just pay a call on the witch-finders."

*Witch-finders?* Sagreda supposed she had no right to be surprised by how far *Midnight* was willing to stretch its anachronisms. "And just what are you planning to tell Constables Scolder and Mully of Bow Street?"

"Every nasty detail of your sorcery," the girl boasted. "And you can be sure that when they break down your door, they'll take a very keen interest in your mandala."

Sagreda released the girl. Whatever she actually knew, the risk of attracting official scrutiny had to be greater than the risk of letting one pickpocket slip away unpunished.

But the girl declined the opportunity to flee. "And I'll have what you denied me," she said, glancing meaningfully at Sagreda's trouser pocket.

Sagreda stared back at her, almost admiring her brazenness, trying to summon up some ornately disdainful Victorian invective with which to respond to this blackmail. But her vocabulary deserted her, and muttering feebly about impudent whelps when her heart wasn't in it would just make her sound like the nineteenth century equivalent of a rapping grandma.

"Be off with you!" she snapped, making a shooing motion with her giant hands.

The girl scowled, dissatisfied, and she seemed on the verge of escalating her threats, but then she changed her mind. "You should engage me, Mister."

"Captain," Sagreda corrected her. "Engage you to do what?"

"Make me your assistant. Seeing as how you're struggling to complete the thing."

A carriage drove past, spattering the bottom of the Captain's trousers with horse-shit-speckled mud.

"Have you been following me?" Sagreda demanded.

"I have eyes," the girl replied coolly. "I seen you in all kinds of fancy shops, making some very odd purchases. If you want the job done before Christmas, you might welcome a pair of nimble hands like mine."

Sagreda fell silent. Were there colors she needed that she might only be able to obtain by theft? She wasn't sure. She'd made significant progress, but she was yet to walk into a shop and find every obscure object of her chromatic desires laid out on the shelves and counters.

"I'll give you a shilling as a retainer," she decided, reaching into her pocket for an untainted one. "In turn, I expect you to be straight with me, and to keep yourself available."

The girl inclined her head in agreement.

Sagreda held on to the coin. "What's your name?"

"Lucy." The girl stretched out her palm, and Sagreda deposited the shilling.

"How will I find you?" she asked.

"This is my patch you're on," Lucy replied, affronted, as if she were some criminal king-pin whose territory Sagreda crossed only on her sufferance. "If you have need of my services, I'll know it before you know it yourself."

## 4

Sagreda worked into the night, pinning, stitching and gluing, painstakingly assembling one more piece of the mosaic. Or *mandala*, as Lucy had called it. It was an odd choice of word; Sagreda had seen nothing to suggest that *Midnight*'s kitchen-sink eclecticism encompassed any culture east of the

Carpathians. But perhaps one of the previous travelers the girl had seen scavenging for colors had taken her into their confidence and tried to explain the point of the whole exercise. Sagreda had no idea if anyone, anywhere, had ever believed that a mandala could initiate the transmigration of souls; her own vague understanding was that if you were into that kind of thing, you just waited to die and the rest was up to karma. But if stacks, GPUs and the whole panoply of queue structures that linked the game-worlds together were too much to explain to someone who'd been gaslit into forgetting everything her contributors had known about the twenty-first century, maybe Lucy's reluctant informant had opted for a Buddhist-flavored riff, aiming for an account that was comprehensible to the denizen of a world steeped in supernatural forces, while avoiding Western occultism with its potentially Satanic associations, in the hope of keeping the witch-finders out of the picture.

Someone tapped at the door. Sagreda covered the mosaic with a table cloth and approached the entrance hall. It was awfully late for a visit from Mrs Trotter, and the tap had sounded far too tentative to come from any branch of the constabulary.

When she opened the door, she found an elegantly dressed, dark-haired young man at the threshold, his eyes cast down as if his presence here was somehow shameful.

"I'm sorry to trouble you, sir," the man said softly, still not meeting Sagreda's gaze. "But I'm a cousin of your wife, and I need to speak to her as soon as possible about a poorly aunt of ours—"

Sagreda interrupted him. "Mathis?"

He looked up, startled. "How do you … did she tell you…?"

"There is no *she* but me, I'm afraid." Sagreda tried to smile, but then recalled how the Captain's whiskery visage had appeared when she'd practiced in the mirror. "It looks like that last queue we found was meant to have been pre-filtered by gender."

Mathis nodded with a kind of punch-drunk stoicism. “Okay. Everything’s temporary. I’m sorry I took so long to find you; I don’t know if the notes all blew away, or what.”

“The ones in the churches shouldn’t have.”

“About that…”

“Are you coming in?” Sagreda asked impatiently. They weren’t talking loudly, but who knew what Mrs Trotter would assume if she saw the Captain with a young man visiting at this uncivil hour.

“I’m afraid you’re going to have to invite me,” Mathis explained glumly.

Sagreda took a moment to digest that. “Oh, fuck no.”

“You got the wang, I got the fangs,” Mathis quipped. “That’s what happens when you walk in blind.”

Sagreda said, “Please, make yourself at home in my miserable abode.” She stepped back from the doorway and let him pass, then peered out across the landing to check that no one was watching from the stairs.

Mathis draped himself over the sofa and gazed lethargically into space, focusing on nothing, perhaps in an attempt to avoid having to take in the wallpaper.

“So what exactly are the symptoms?” Sagreda asked. “Apart from a general Byronic ennui.”

“I haven’t risked daylight,” he replied. “But I gather it would be fatal. I do have a reflection. But mostly I’m just very, very tired and very, very hungry.”

“So you haven’t—?”

“Jesus, Sagreda!” Mathis stared at her in horror.

“I meant … maybe a dog?” The dogs here were pure automata, it wouldn’t even be animal cruelty.

“I’m not interested in *dogs!*” Mathis retorted irritably, as if that ought to be as obvious to Sagreda as it was to him. But then he caught himself, and walked her through the strictures he was facing. “There are certain sights and odors that make my saliva run, and my…” He gestured at his mouth. "I'm assuming that unless I act on those cues, I'm not going to stop feeling weak. A rare roast-beef sandwich doesn't cut it, and I have no reason to think a corgi or two would hit the spot either."

Sagreda steeled herself. "Do you want me to fill a cup?"

Mathis took a while to reply. "Are you sure you want to do that?"

"Not especially," she confessed. "But I don't want you going into the vampiric equivalent of a diabetic coma."

"I'd better not watch," Mathis decided. "Who knows what strings the game will start tugging, if I see an open wound."

"All right." Sagreda went into the Captain's bedroom and closed the door. There was a cut-throat razor by the washing bowl, and an empty shaving mug. She took off her jacket and shirt.

The thought that Mathis feared losing control disturbed her. They'd fought for each other, suffered side by side, and risked deletion across three dozen worlds – and the software that lorded over them was far too crude to reach inside them and start imposing beliefs or desires. On their side they had love, and they had reason, while the SludgeNet possessed neither.

But it still had plenty of ways to try to manipulate their behavior. Having woken in the asinine world of *East*, where sensory immersion lost out more or less instantly to any trace of common sense, they were both immune to seeing-is-believing, and to the wisdom of hoodwinked crowds. But they'd never been subjected to outright torture. If the purple prose in *Midnight*'s bodice-and-intestine-ripping source had talked about a vampire's longing for blood being like a white-hot poker in the chest, the SludgeNet would have no trouble bringing those words to life.

The Captain's body was amply proportioned and apparently not at all anemic; when Sagreda had filled the mug, she did not feel the least bit unsteady. "Well done, old stick!" she commended him, binding the wound with a handkerchief. She dressed again completely to conceal any trace of the breach in her skin. The Captain, being some flavor of Anglican, wasn't into religious paraphernalia; there was a King James Bible in his library, but no crucifix by the bed.

She covered the mug with a playing card and opened the door. Mathis was still on the sofa; she walked right past him, into the entrance hall, and out the front door. She placed the mug on the landing, near the top of the stairs, then, leaving the door open, went back to the sitting room.

"You didn't want to watch me," she said. "And I don't want to watch you, either."

Mathis frowned slightly, but he nodded. "I'll go back to my place when I'm finished." He walked over to the desk and wrote something. "That's the address, if you need to find me later. But don't open the door to me again tonight, whatever I say."

Sagreda felt the Captain's pulse throbbing around the raw edges of the razor wound. But Mathis was just being cautious; he'd never done this before, he didn't know what to expect.

"You know I love you?" she said.

Mathis rolled his eyes. "At a pinch, I might go for an Oscar Wilde type, but the whole Colonel Mustard thing…" He shuddered.

"You're an asshole."

He smiled and walked down the hall. Sagreda followed a couple of steps behind, then when he was out she closed the door quickly – taking care not to slam it and wake Mrs Trotter – and secured the bolts.

She stood by the door, listening, but the bestial slurping she'd feared never came. She waited, tensed, picturing the door splintering and a yellow-eyed, ravenous demon embracing her to finish what she'd started.

She heard the faint chink of the mug being placed back on the floor, then soft, careful, unhurried footsteps descending the stairs.

## 5

Sagreda needed cobalt blue. Out in the real world – if Peyam's gloriously discursive lessons on color were to be trusted – the pigment had been used since ancient times in Chinese ceramics, and it had certainly been available to European painters in the nineteenth century. This was

London, capital of an empire, mercantile hub of the world. Whatever wasn't made here, someone would be importing it.

So she traipsed the streets, hunting for a shop that sold artists' supplies. If the gossip she'd heard in the coffee houses was true, every tubercular poet, living or undead, from Marlowe to Yeats was currently shacked up somewhere in Bloomsbury, rubbing shoulders every night in the Salon Macabre – a dollop of name-dropping no doubt designed to set the hearts of thirteen-year-old Goths aflutter – but no one ever seemed to mention a single painter. To be fair, Sagreda's own contributors struggled to suggest anyone but Turner; still, someone had to be responsible for all the portraits of viscounts and their horses that lined the walls of the mansions of Belgravia. Unless they just appeared out of thin air.

As she widened her search radius, Sagreda grew nervous. Every game had different rules of containment; if you wandered off into territory that didn't belong to the core geography that had been mapped out and rendered for a thousand eyes before yours, you might get a gentle nudge guiding you back to terra cognita, or you might just fall off the edge of the world. So far as she knew, the Captain was not a named character in the original novel, and no customer of the interactive version had become the least bit invested in his continued existence. If she crossed the invisible line, the easiest solution by far might be to erase her and wake a fresh comp in the same body after a hard night on the town, leaving the new guy to piece his identity together much as Sagreda had, from the contents of his lodgings, and the people he encountered who seemed to know him.

By late afternoon on the third day of her search, she found herself off the paved streets entirely, tramping through muddy ground beside a ramshackle wooden building that smelled like a tannery. She stopped and hunted for the sun, trying to get her bearings, but the sky above was smothered by a still, gray haze, equally bright everywhere she squinted.

There was no one else in sight. She approached the building cautiously; it might just contain cheerful workers, happy to offer directions, but *Midnight* was proving less concerned with its supply chains than with its brooding atmospherics. If its artworks could come without artists or pigments, its leather need not have graced the body of any cow, and the strange odor might have another source entirely.

Her foot touched something taut buried in the mud, like a swollen fruit or a small balloon; she tried to step back, but the thing burst and a jet of stinking yellow fluid sprayed up from it and struck her in the chest.

A hand tugged at her trouser leg. A small boy was standing beside her. "Come with me!" he whispered urgently.

Sagreda followed him, resisting a motherly impulse to scoop him up into her arms, not least because it would be hard to manage without smearing the poor kid with pus. His legs were about a quarter as long as the Captain's, but it was all she could do to keep up. She glanced backward; something was moving at the entrance to the building, but its shape was hard to discern in the haze. It uttered an inhuman cry; in rage or in pain Sagreda couldn't tell.

"Where are we going?" she asked the boy.

"They marked you," he replied. "So we need to be done with it."

"Marked me for what?" she asked.

"Ha!" He seemed to find the question so funny that it could only have been meant rhetorically.

They hit the cobblestones and weaved through small alleys, picking up the pace, inflaming the Captain's gout. In this of all things, the game wanted realism?

"How far will it follow us?" Sagreda wondered, gasping.

"As far as it takes, if you don't do the necessary."

Sagreda had visions of a bonfire for her clothes, and an acid bath for her infected skin.

They came to a water pump.

"Get under, get under!" the boy urged her.

"Do I take—?" She gestured at her vomit-yellow waistcoat.

"No time."

She took off her coat and maneuvered herself under the spout; the boy clambered up and started pumping. Gobs of sticky fluid separated from the cloth and were carried down the drain, but her waistcoat remained stained in a shade that Peyam had never named, but which her contributors labeled bee excrement. She ran her thumb back and forth across the fabric, turning her chest to meet the flow, and gradually the mark began to fade.

"I think you're done," the boy decided, wiping his forehead with his hand. He grimaced reprovingly. "What you want with them creatures anyway?"

"Nothing! I didn't know they were there!" Sagreda got herself upright. Her clothes were drenched and all her joints were aching, but apparently she'd been luckier than she deserved.

"You lost your way?" The boy's incredulity shaded into smugness; who exactly was the adult here?

"I was looking for a place to buy oil paints."

The boy sighed, as if Sagreda had somehow lived down to his expectations. "Lucy said it would come to that."

This wasn't a random encounter, then. The queen of the pickpockets had had her tailed by a trusted lieutenant.

"What's your name?" she asked the boy.

"Sam."

"So do you know of a shop that sells the materials an artist needs?"

He wiped his nose on his sleeve. "There ain't such a thing in all of London."

Sagreda had pretty much reconciled herself to that likelihood. "Have you ever even seen a painting?" she asked glumly. There were a couple of drab watercolors in Mrs Trotter's sitting room, but even if Sagreda had dared to steal them, they did not contain anything she needed.

Sam said, "I think you better talk to Lucy."

# 6

"Maybe I know a house," Lucy said cagily. "Maybe I'm thick with the scullery maid. But it's hard to remember. My mind turns feeble when I hear my stomach rumbling."

Sagreda handed her another shilling. "How many paintings, do you think?" They were sitting on moldy armchairs in an abandoned building with boarded-up windows, surrounded by diminutive body guards.

"Two dozen, at least."

"Any of them with a deep, rich blue? It needs to be deeper than a summer sky, but—"

Lucy scowled. "I can ask the maid about the colors, but who knows what she'll make of your palaver?"

"Then I need to go in there myself," Sagreda decided. "It's no good sending someone else who'll come back with the wrong thing."

"Be my guest," Lucy replied, unfazed. "But we'll be making our entrance through the basement, and there'll be a tight corner or two along the way. Perhaps you can look into the possibility of investing in a gentleman's girdle."

Sagreda wasn't sure if this was genuine advice, or just a chance to mock her. "How will we get into the basement?"

"There's a sewer."

"Of course there is."

"Meant to put an end to the Great Stink," Lucy mused, "but if you ask me it's brought no end of mischief."

Sagreda hesitated; she didn't mind getting covered in literal excrement, but the bullshit she was already mired in was a long way from a fact-checked documentary on the marvels of Victorian engineering. "Does anything live down there?"

Lucy considered the question. "'Live' might not be the right word to use. But that shouldn't bother you, should it?"

"Why not?"

Lucy exchanged a knowing glance with Sam, who'd apparently been shadowing Sagreda for some time. "Begging your pardon, Captain, but I been told quite a bit about your fancy man. From what I hear, you got him nicely tamed, so maybe it's time you put him to good use."

## 7

Mathis went in front, holding the lamp, but Lucy and Sagreda stuck close behind him. The ceaseless, arrhythmic percussion of random drips of water all around them made Sagreda tense; if something came skittering hungrily along the tunnel, the sounds it made might easily be camouflaged by this unpredictable plinking.

With a handkerchief over her nose, and her mouth shut tight, the stench of the sewer was eye-watering but not quite disabling. Sagreda hadn't vomited once as the Captain, even when she'd stumbled on a disemboweled woman on her first night in the game, and she trusted his constitution to get her through this merely sensory assault. The two cups of blood she'd given Mathis just after sunset had only made her unsteady for a minute or two, and once she'd imbibed an equal volume of Mrs Trotter's strong black tea she'd felt entirely Captainly again.

"Are we close?" she asked Lucy, holding her forearm over her mouth as she spoke, which seemed to do a better job of blocking the outgoing sound than the incoming vapor.

"Pardon me?"

"Are we almost there?" Sagreda retched a little, the price of her impatience.

"You'll see the drain to the right when we reach it," was all Lucy could offer. "There'll be no missing it."

Sagreda peered into the gloom ahead, wondering if any light from the house might make it through the drain, turning the opening into a welcoming beacon. In fact, she could see a small spot of luminous yellow in the distance, beyond the reach of Mathis's lamp. But it was not remaining still. For a moment she wondered if it might be a reflection off the surface of the putrid, ankle-deep water, shifting its apparent position because of a disturbance in the flow. But then a second yellow dot appeared, off to the left and a short way behind it, and the motion became much easier to decode. The two lights were attached to two ambulatory bodies of some kind, and those bodies were striding down the tunnel.

She reached forward and touched Mathis's shoulder. "Do you see that?" she asked.

"Yes."

"Any idea what they are?"

"No one's handed me a taxonomy for this place," he replied. "But the general rule seems to be that anything inhuman is likely to mean you harm. So the only question is whether I can fend them off, or pull rank on them somehow."

As the creatures grew nearer, Sagreda became aware of the sound of their footfalls in the sewer water. In concert, their gaits generated a strange rhythm, in which she thought she could discern an overlapping pair of alternating sloshes and harder strikes. The Captain's chest tightened; Sagreda hoped she wasn't about to discover that a lifetime of pipe smoking in his back-story had left him with bouts of stress-induced emphysema.

Mathis stopped walking and held the lamp high in front of him. "Who goes there?" he demanded imperiously. When he received no reply, he added: "Know that we will pass, and we will pass unmolested, or it will be the worse for you!"

The creatures continued to advance, but now the lamplight began to reach them, sketching gray outlines for the flesh and bones that held up the yellow orbs. What struck Sagreda immediately was that some of the edges she could discern were unnaturally straight. At first she doubted her eyes, but as the details grew clearer her impressions were confirmed: both figures were one-legged, walking with the aid of long wooden crutches angled across their bodies. Each possessed just a single arm and a single leg, attached to half a torso, on which was perched half a head.

As these walking anatomy lessons came into full view, they squinted angrily at the lamp. Their bodies were unclothed, but their skin was loose and wrinkled to the point where it took some scrutiny to be sure that they were both male. Each had a half-tongue that lolled part-way out of its broken jaw and hung drooling over the rough plane along which the dissection had taken place. Their single lungs made sputtering sounds that emerged from the bases of their bisected windpipes; their exposed viscera oozed a little, but there was no real pretense of any functioning circulatory system. Skeletal muscles, lungs and brains were all being powered by pure magical fiat, untroubled by any need for chemical energy.

"I hope they're not conscious," Mathis whispered.

Sagreda refused to entertain the possibility. "What are they meant to be?" she wondered. "A vampire someone tried to kill with a circular saw?"

Lucy stepped forward impatiently. "They're a grisly sight, I'll grant you that, but even if they're stronger than they look, I'll wager they're not swift or agile." Then without another word she bolted straight down the tunnel. At the last moment she veered to the right and passed by one of the half-men – almost certainly within arm's reach, in principle, but while the creature swiveled and swayed toward her, it couldn't really drop its crutch and grab her.

Sagreda was encouraged, but still wary. "So they're not exactly zombie ninjas, but one nip might still infect us with the dividing plague."

"Is that a thing?" Mathis asked.

"Not that my contributors ever heard – but there's got to be *one* original idea in the whole ghastly book."

Mathis made a larger target than Lucy, and the Captain even more so, but the officially adult members of the party plucked up their courage and ran the gauntlet. Sagreda almost hit her head on the roof of the tunnel as she scampered up the side of the tubular floor, but the wheezing half-cadaver that turned arthritically to ogle her didn't get close. She and

Mathis caught up with Lucy, who had been wise enough not to go too far ahead in the dark.

"Good thing we have the Prince of the Night here to protect us," Lucy chuckled. "What would us poor mortals have done on our own?"

"Don't get too cocky," Mathis warned her. "I often find myself wanting a snack around ten."

Lucy tugged at the neck of her blouse to reveal a string of garlic circling her neck. Mathis said nothing, but he didn't even flinch; Sagreda wondered if it was possible, even here, to believe that an object could ward off danger when in truth it had no effect at all.

The three of them sloshed ahead through the muck.

"What if there's no cobalt blue in all of London?" Mathis asked, succumbing to a melancholy that had only seemed to afflict him since he started wearing ruffled shirts.

Sagreda found this scenario unlikely. "In hundreds of paintings, of hundreds of subjects? The SludgeNet will have scooped them up from actual Victorian artworks it found on the web, give or take a few woo-woo-isn't-this-scary neural-net effects. Cobalt blue fits the period, and it wasn't all that rare. It's not like we're hunting for neptunium in the Stone Age."

She glanced at Lucy, wondering what the girl had made of the exchange, but it seemed to have passed right over her head. Most, if not all, of her contributors would have heard of neural nets and neptunium, but a vague sense of recognition for a couple of anachronistic terms wasn't going to bring a consensual memory of the early twenty-first century flooding back. Given her character's age, it was tempting to ask her if she knew who Justin Bieber was, and see if she denied him three times before the cock crowed, but it would be cruel to wake her to her true nature if they weren't going to stick around and help her make sense of it.

"There it is," Lucy announced. The drain from the house they were hoping to burgle was up ahead of them on the right. Mathis swung the lamp around as they approached; the narrow, slanting pipe was half open at the bottom, and Sagreda could see dark stains on the cement. There was a grille at the top, which would normally have blocked their access – but the maid had been bribed to take out the bolts that held it down and replace them with duplicates whose threads had been stripped.

Sagreda threw the woolen blanket she'd brought over the lower surface of the pipe, in the hope that they might enter the house without becoming so filthy that they'd instantly wake every inhabitant with their stink. Lucy clambered up first, leaving her galoshes behind. She raised the doctored grille carefully and placed it to the side, almost silently, then drew herself up onto the floor.

"You're invited and all," she called down to Mathis. Sagreda wasn't sure if this would work; the maid, in turn, had invited Lucy, but that didn't make either of them the homeowner. Nonetheless, Mathis ascended without apparent difficulty, taking the lamp with him.

Sagreda stood at the base of the pipe, gazing up into the lamplit basement. She'd ignored Lucy's suggestion of a girdle, but it hadn't been a gratuitous jibe; this was going to be a tight fit. She stretched her arms in front of her so she could rest on her elbows without adding to her girth, and began crawling awkwardly up the slope.

Halfway to the top, she stopped advancing. She redoubled her effort, but it made no difference; whatever feverish motion she made with her elbows and knees, they didn't have enough purchase on the blanket to propel her upward.

Mathis appeared at the top of the pipe, crouching, peering down at her. "Hold onto the blanket with your hands," he whispered. He pushed some of it down to loosen it, giving her a fold she could grip. Then he grabbed the top and started straightening his knees to haul her up.

When her hands rose above the top of the pipe she gestured to Mathis to stop, and she pulled herself up the rest of the way. "Well, that was delightful," she gasped. She clambered to her feet and inspected herself and her crew; they weren't exactly fit to present to royalty, but between the blanket and their discarded galoshes they appeared to have succeeded in leaving the most pungent evidence of their journey behind.

Mathis shoved the blanket back down into the sewer and he and Lucy fitted the grille into place, swapping back actual threaded bolts. The plan was to leave by the front door, rather than retracing their steps.

Sagreda turned away from the latrine and took in the rest of the basement. The staircase led up from the middle of the room, but on the opposite side there was a door with a small, barred window: an entrance to another room on the same level.

Mathis picked up the lamp and turned the flame down low as they walked toward the stairs. In the faint light, Sagreda saw something move behind the bars in the other room. There was a clink of metal on stone, and a soft, tortured exhalation.

She took the lamp from Mathis and approached the door. If there was a witness in there, the burglars had already revealed themselves, but she had to know exactly what risk they were facing. She lifted the lamp to the level of the window, and peered inside.

At least a dozen fragments of bodies were chained to the walls and floor of the cell. Some resembled the vertically bisected men they'd met in the sewer; some had been cut along other planes. And some had been stitched together crudely, into hallucinatory Boschian nightmares: composites with two torsos sharing a single pair of legs, or heads attached in place of limbs. Where there were eyes, they turned toward the light, and where there were ribs they began rising and falling, but the attempts these pitiful creatures made to cry out were like the sound of wet cardboard boxes collapsing as they were trod into the ground.

Sagreda retreated, gesturing to the others to continue up the stairs.

When they emerged on the ground floor, Lucy took the lamp and led the way down a long corridor. There were portraits in oil at regular intervals on the wall to their right, some authentically staid, some Gothically deranged, but none of them contained the desired blue.

They reached the drawing room. "Turn up the lamp," Sagreda whispered. The piano, the cabinets and shelves, the sofas and small tables barely registered on her; they were just unwelcome complications, casting shadows that obscured the real treasures. The walls were covered with paintings: scenes from Greek myths, scenes from the Bible, scenes of clashing armies … and scenes of naval battles.

For a second or two she was giddy from a kind of ecstasy tinged with disbelief: after so long, it seemed impossible that she really had found what she needed; it had to be a cruel delusion, because the universe they inhabited was built from nothing else. But the feeling passed, and she strode over to the painting that had caught her eye. The ships were ablaze, but the sea was calm. No gray-green, storm-tossed water here, just a placid ocean of blue.

Sagreda contemplated merely scraping off a few samples, but it seemed wiser to take the whole thing and be sure she had as wide a range of colors as possible, rather than a fragment or two that might turn out, under better light, to have been ill-chosen. She unhooked the painting and wrapped it in a cloth.

Then she bowed to their guide. "If you please, Miss Lucy, show us the way out."

Somewhere in the house, a door slammed heavily. Lucy extinguished the lamp. But the room only remained in perfect blackness for a few seconds before gas lights came on at the far end of the corridor.

Sagreda heard a rustle of clothing – maybe overcoats coming off – then a woman's voice. "They were so rude to me! I can't believe it! If I want to be called Lady Godwin, they should call me Lady Godwin!"

A man replied, "It's a historical fact: she took her husband's name."

"Yes, but only because she had no choice! If she'd been vampire aristocracy, do you think she would have buckled to convention like that?"

"Umm, given her politics, do you think she would have chosen to be an aristocrat of any kind?"

"There are socialists in the British House of Lords, aren't there?" the woman countered.

The man was silent for a moment, then he said, "Can you smell that?"

"Smell what?"

"You really can't smell it? Maybe your thing's clogged."

"What are you talking about?"

The man sighed impatiently. "You know … the little canister thing in the front of the helmet, under the goggles. There's a mesh around it, but I think sometimes the stuff clogs up the holes. Just give it a flick with your finger."

The two customers went quiet. In the shadows of the drawing room, Lucy caught Sagreda's eye and gestured to her to move behind a bookcase. Sagreda complied without hesitation, deferring to her accomplice's experience.

"Okay … yeah, I can smell it now," the woman announced. "That's foul! Do you think one of our experiments broke out of the basement?"

"Maybe," the man replied. "But it seems to be coming from down the hall."

Sagreda heard their footsteps approaching. She tensed, wishing she could see exactly where Mathis was. A couple of ordinary householders would not have posed much of a problem – least of all customers, whom Mathis would have no qualms about dispatching – but she did not like the phrase *vampire aristocracy*.

"Wait!" the man said. The footsteps stopped, and then he groaned. "Yeah, yeah: sexy Russian babes are desperately seeking broad-minded couples to help fulfill their fantasies. How many times are they going to show me this crap before they realize we're never going to follow the link?"

"You could go ad-free, if you weren't so stingy," the woman chided him.

"Stingy? Five dollars a month is a rip-off!"

"Then stop complaining. It's your choice."

"What costs do they actually have?" the man protested. "The books they start from are all public domain, or pirated. The world-building software comes from open-source projects. The brain maps they use for the comps are data from open-access journals. So, I'm meant to fork out five dollars a month just to pay rent on their servers?"

"Well … enjoy smickering at your Russian babes, Lord Scrooge, I'm going to find out what's stinking up the house."

The woman must have decided to approach on tip-toes, because Sagreda heard nothing but floorboards creaking. From her hiding place she could see neither Mathis nor Lucy, and she felt like a coward for not rushing out to block the doorway with the Captain's ample girth. But the fact remained that the mild-mannered aficionado of kitsch creeping down the corridor, who would not have said boo to any fleshly equivalent of Sagreda if they'd sat next to each other on a bus, had been endowed by the game with the power to rip all of their throats out – and endowed by her own lack of empathy with the power to take off her goggles and sleep soundly afterward.

The woman spoke, from just inside the doorway, calling back to her companion in a kind of stage whisper, "It's definitely coming from in here!" Maybe her "experiments" were so brain-damaged that they would not have been alerted to her presence by these words. Or maybe she just didn't give a damn. At five bucks a month, how invested would she be? If things turned out badly, she could still order a pizza.

There was a sound of bodies colliding, and the woman crying out in shock, if not actual pain. Sagreda stepped out into the room to be greeted by the sight of Mathis holding Lady Godwin with her arms pinned from behind, his fangs plunging repeatedly deep into her carotid artery as he filled his mouth with blood then spat it out onto the floor. His victim was strong, and she was struggling hard, but he'd had the advantage of surprise, and whatever their relative age and vampiric prestige, his assault was progressively weakening her.

Sagreda ran to the fireplace and picked up a long metal poker. As she approached, both vampires glared at her furiously, like a pair of brawling cats who'd rather scratch each other's flesh off than brook any human intervention. But she wasn't here to try to make peace between house-pets.

She rammed the poker as hard as she could between Godwin's ribs; the author-turned-unlikely-vivisector screeched and coughed black blood that dribbled down the front of her satin evening gown, then she went limp. Sagreda was sickened; even if her victim would barely feel a tickle in her VR harness, the imagery they were sharing debased them both.

Mathis dropped his dead prey and snatched at Sagreda, as if he was so enraged to have been cheated of the animal pleasure of the fight that he was ready to turn on her as punishment. She stood her ground. "Don't you fucking touch me!" she bellowed.

"What's going on?" asked Lord Shelley irritably. Mathis turned to confront him, but this time it was no ambush; the older man grabbed him by the shirtfront and thrust him aside with no concern for conservation of momentum, sending him crashing into a corner of the room without experiencing the least bit of recoil.

As Shelley gazed down in horror at his murdered wife, Sagreda backed away slowly. Reminding this bozo that it was only a game would only get her deleted.

The undead poet raised his eyes to the Captain, and spread his fanged jaws wide in a howl of grief.

"'Look on my works, ye Mighty, and despair?'" Sagreda offered sycophantically.

Lucy chose this moment to make a run for the door. Shelley turned and grabbed her thin arm, then bent down and sank his fangs into it, apparently deterred by her garlic necklace from striking in the usual spot. Sagreda leaped forward and punched him in the side of the mouth with all of the Captain's mortal strength; to her amazement, her blow dislodged his jaws from the girl's flesh. Lucy was bawling with pain and terror; Sagreda kept striking the same spot above Shelley's chin with her massive right paw, as fast and hard as she could, unsure if it was just her knuckles and finger bones that she could hear cracking and crumbling from the impacts.

Mathis whispered calmly in her ear, "Step aside, my love."

She complied. Shelley looked up, but he had no time to react. Mathis drove the poker into his chest, all the way through to his spine.

As Shelley slumped to the ground, Lucy fell beside him, looking every bit as lifeless. Mathis took his coat off, tore one sleeve free and wrapped it around the girl's upper arm as a tourniquet.

"What are you doing?" Sagreda asked. "That's so tight, you're..." She stifled a sob of revulsion. "Don't cut it off!"

"I'm not going to," Mathis promised, "but we need to move fast to get the poison out. And I can't do it, that would only make it worse."

Sagreda stared at him. "What?"

"I'll apply pressure; you have to suck the wound and spit."

"You're sure that will work?"

"Just do it, or she's either going to lose her arm or be turned!"

Sagreda quickly relit the lamp so she could see what she was doing, then she knelt on the floor and set to work. When every drop had been drained or spat onto the carpet, leaving Lucy's arm corpse-white, Mathis loosened the tourniquet and the flesh became pink, bleeding freely from the puncture wounds above the wrist.

"Let it bleed for a bit, just to flush it out some more," Mathis insisted.

"How do you know all this?"

"I'm guessing," he admitted. "I've heard things from the other vampires, but I don't know if I ever got the whole story straight."

Sagreda sat on the bloody floor and cradled Lucy's head in her arms. There was no actual poison being traced through some elaborate, fluid-dynamical model of the circulatory system; the game would make a crude assessment of the efficacy of their actions under its fatuous rules and then throw its algorithmic dice.

They had love, and they had reason, but the game could still do whatever it liked.

# 8

Shortly after sunset, Mathis emerged from the Captain's bedroom, bleary-eyed and yawning. "Did you get any sleep?" he asked Sagreda.

"A couple of hours, around noon," she replied. "But it's done." She gestured toward the mosaic. "I just need you to check it."

"Okay." Mathis slapped his own face a few times, trying to wake more fully. "How's your hand?"

"Still broken. But I don't plan on having to use it much longer."

Mathis managed a hopeful nod. "And Lucy?"

Sagreda said, "She seems stable; her pulse is steady, and she has no fever."

Mathis took a seat in the nearest armchair and turned to address Sagreda. "The game's not going to accept that its biggest celebrity couple has been removed from the plot. But the SludgeNet's not going to reboot everything while the city's crawling with customers who want to maintain continuity. So, the way I see it there are only two options. They can pull a bit of necromantic fluff out from under the sofa cushions, and bring the Shelleys back in an explicit act of resurrection that would make Sigourney Weaver blush. Or, they can pretend that what happened last night never really happened, and just delete the witnesses."

"You and I can be out of here as soon as you've checked the mosaic," Sagreda said. She glanced at the sofa, where Lucy still lay inert. "But I don't know if she'll agree to come with us."

"All we can do is be honest with her," Mathis replied.

"To be honest, we don't even know if we're ready for this ourselves." Sagreda rubbed the good side of her smashed hand; it didn't really affect the pain, but it helped distract her from it.

"No. But what would you rather do? Go off on a tour of another twenty worlds, in the hope that we might pick up a few more tips?"

"If *3-adica* makes anything possible, why has no one ever come back?" she asked.

"Because it's so good there that no one wants to leave?"

"Not even for a day or two, to spread the word?"

"I don't know," Mathis confessed.

"What's *3-adica*?" Lucy asked. Her eyes were open, and she looked remarkably lucid.

Sagreda fetched a jug of water. "How long have you been awake?" she asked, handing the girl a glass.

"A while." Lucy downed the water in one long gulp, then went to use the chamber pot. When she returned, she said, "I helped you complete the mandala, didn't I? So you owe it to me to divulge the nature of its powers."

Sagreda had been preparing for this question all day. "It's taking us to a world where the distances between numbers aren't the same as they are here."

Lucy frowned, but her expression was more intrigued than dismissive.

"Here, you can put all the numbers on a line," Sagreda said. "Like the house numbers on a street. And the distance between two houses is just the difference between their numbers: number twelve is two houses down from number ten … most of the time." Whatever the historical truth, this version of Victorian London hadn't made up its mind whether to number houses consecutively along each side of the street, or to adopt the even/odd rule that was more familiar to Sagreda's contributors.

"So you're going to a world where the houses are higgledy-piggledy?" Lucy guessed.

"Maybe, though that doesn't quite cover it." Sagreda walked over to the desk, took a sheet of writing paper and started scrawling ovals in ink. "In *3-adica*, the numbers are like eggs in a sparrow's nest. Zero, one and two are all in the same nest, and the distance between any pair of them is exactly one."

"From one to two is one," Lucy said. "But from nothing to two is … also one?"

"Exactly," Sagreda confirmed. "The laws of arithmetic haven't changed: two minus zero is still two, not one. But the laws of geometry aren't the same, and the *distance* is no longer the *difference*."

"But where's three?" Lucy demanded. "Where's seventy-three?"

"Each egg I've drawn," Sagreda said, "is really a nest of its own. The zero-egg is a nest that contains zero, three and six. The one-egg is a nest that contains one, four and seven. The two-egg is a nest that contains two, five and eight." She scribbled in the new numbers.

"I can see what you've written clear enough," Lucy acknowledged, "but I don't know what it means."

"To be in a smaller nest with a number puts you closer to it," Sagreda explained. "The distance between zero and one is one, because that's the size of the smallest nest they're both in, but the distance between zero and *three* is smaller, because they share a smaller nest. In fact, the distance between zero and three is one third, as is the distance between five and eight, or four and seven."

"And you keep on with that nonsense?" Lucy asked.

Sagreda smiled. "Absolutely. However high you want to count, you just keep turning eggs into ever smaller nests of three."

Lucy sat pondering this for a while, but it was clear that something was bothering her. "You say the distance from nothing to three is one third," she said finally. "But where does *one third* live in your nests? I can walk a third of the way between houses, and I know what that means on Baker Street, but what does it mean for these sparrow's eggs?"

"It means you need to look outside the first nest." Sagreda added another two circles as large as the largest one she'd drawn previously, and then scratched an even bigger one around all three. "If you add one third to anything in the first nest, it goes in the second nest. If you add two thirds, it goes in the third one. And any two numbers that happen to be in a different pair of these new nests lie at a distance of *three* from each other, because that's the size of the larger nest that encloses them all. And before you ask me where *one ninth* lives, the paper isn't large enough for me to draw that, but I think you can guess how the pattern continues."

Lucy absorbed this, but she wasn't done. "Where does *one half* live?"

Sagreda was tired; she had to stop and think. "It's somewhere inside the first nest I drew, at a distance of one from zero."

"But where?" Lucy pressed her. "Where is there room for it? I can see how your eggs there reach up to any number I could ever count to ... but how are you going to squeeze yet another one in?"

Mathis chuckled and stretched his arms above his head. "Good question!" he said. "And it took my friend here about a day to convince me of the answer."

Sagreda closed her eyes for a moment, and focused. "First, go to the number *two*. Then add three and go to *five*. Then add nine, which takes you to *fourteen*. Then add twenty-seven ... and so on. Each time, you add thrice what you added before."

"And when do you stop?" Lucy asked, with a cunning look on her face, as if she was about to play cuckoo and toss the existing egg at the point of arrival out of its nest.

"You don't!" Mathis interjected. "You're not allowed to stop! Which sounds nonsensical, but it's no more absurd, in *3-adica*, than it is in our world for Achilles to get halfway down a road, then another quarter, then another eighth ... with always one more stage to go that's shorter than the last. Because in *3-adica*, adding thrice what you added before takes you a third less far. Five is actually fairly close to one half, but fourteen is closer, and forty-one is closer still. Because if you double each of these numbers, the result is always *one* ... plus three multiplied by itself many times, which makes less and less of a difference the more times it's been multiplied."

Lucy opened her mouth to protest, but then closed it again. Something was sinking in. Sagreda had never met a comp who, when given the chance to brush away the learned helplessness of their character, turned out to know less about arithmetic than they would have picked up from a decent high school education in America at the height of the space race. And maybe one in a hundred had been remixed from the pool in such a way that they inherited enough recreational mathematics to have heard of the "*p*-adic numbers": 2-adics, 3-adics, 5-adics … *p*-adics for any prime you cared to name.

But the book, *3-adica*, seemed to have been written after every contributor had died. And the only knowledge any comp had of the SludgeNet's attempt to gamify it came from eavesdropping on customers, whose comments on the topic tended to be of the form "my migraine when I tried that shit was worse than *x*," for various values of *x*.

Lucy seemed to be anticipating a few headaches of her own. "I don't know if the streets will be like bird's nests where you're going," she said, "but it sounds like a place where I'd lose my way."

Sagreda said, "The beauty, though, is that it's also a place where the forces that try to keep you down are even more likely to lose their own way."

Lucy shook her head. "No one keeps me down. I can dodge the muckety-mucks well enough, whether they're carrying cut-throat razors or trying to take a drink from my neck. Last night was a tight spot I shouldn't have gotten into, but I won't make that mistake again."

Sagreda could see no alternative now to spelling out the whole truth. "This London is not the real London," she said. "It's a bad story that bad people have created to make money from very bad advertisements. The machines those people own brought you and me to life – using parts they might as well have obtained from grave-robbers, cut up and stitched together to form puppets to act in their very bad play."

Lucy laughed curtly, with a brashness that seemed forced. "You might have dispensed yourself a bit too much laudanum, Captain, to ease the pain from your fisticuffs." But Sagreda suspected that the last traveler Lucy had encountered would have sketched a cosmology eerily similar to this opium dream.

She said, "This world we're in, and ten thousand others like it, were made by ten thousand clockwork monkeys chewing rotten fruit and spitting out the pulp. But what if a ball of polished marble slipped into the barrel of worm-ridden apples, and broke its monkey's jaw? A clockwork monkey is too stupid to stop chewing when you feed it something unexpected, so there's no end to the damage the marble might have caused. And once you tear open a hole in the clockwork, maybe you can crawl right into the innards and really start playing with all the springs and wheels. That's why *3-adica* could mean freedom: it's tough enough to break the monkey's jaw."

Mathis rose from his armchair. "I should start checking the mosaic," he said.

"Do you need a meal first?" Sagreda asked.

"No, a few gulps from her Ladyship's ancient veins seem to have gone a long way." He took a seat at the writing desk and peered studiously at Sagreda's notes.

Sagreda joined Lucy on the sofa. "My landlady will be bringing me my dinner in about an hour," she said. "So you and Mathis will need to hide for a bit, though of course you're welcome to eat with me when the coast's clear."

"I'll be getting back to my own digs before then," Lucy decided.

"What you saw last night means you might not be safe," Sagreda said gently. "If the people we killed are too important to the story, what we did might be undone – and if the rules of the world don't allow that, we'll need to be discarded to smooth over the lie."

Lucy wasn't ready to take any of this on faith, but some part of Sagreda's warning seemed to unsettle her. "I can find out what's happened in that house since we left it," she said. "If they've buried them blood-suckers and started sending all their finery to the auctioneer, will that put your mind at ease?"

"It'd be worth knowing," Sagreda replied. "But can you do that without letting on to anyone what you actually saw?"

Lucy was offended. "I ain't no tattler!"

"I don't mean the police," Sagreda stressed. "I mean anyone at all. Not even someone you'd trust with your life. Telling them could put them in danger, too."

"Leave it with me, Captain," Lucy replied. "By the time you've had your dinner, I'll be back with my report."

9

"This looks perfect to me," Mathis declared, putting the mosaic aside and rubbing his eyes. "But there is one small complication we need to think about."

"What's that?" Sagreda asked.

"Peyam's dictionary was calibrated for sunlight," he said. "Whatever the lighting, the colors still look right to us when we check them against a white background, but that's just our visual system compensating. The GPU models physical optics, not perception; it's going to spit out pixels that depend on the light source."

Sagreda had known there'd be an extra hurdle to deal with as soon as Mathis had turned up in his new, photosensitive state, but she'd been so preoccupied with finding the cobalt blue that she'd stopped thinking about the problem. "Okay, so we'll need to use a mirror to light the thing in the morning without roasting you to a cinder."

"That would be nice." Mathis glanced down at the desk, and gestured at the collection of wooden rods beside the blotter. "I see you've got the pieces of the trigger ready. So we might as well start setting up."

"Of course."

They worked together, mostly in silence. They'd performed the same task so many times before that the need to bounce sunlight from a chink in the curtains onto the mosaic via the Captain's shaving mirror felt like a welcome variation to the routine that would keep them from becoming complacent. But the hardest thing now for Sagreda was to stop worrying about Lucy.

Mathis dropped a plumb-line from the main guide-string that stretched across the room between an anchor on the wall and the home-made easel holding the mosaic, and marked the viewing spots on the floor for the two of them. "I guess you don't know how high Lucy's eyes are?"

"I should have measured her while she was asleep."

"It's almost midnight," he said. "Do you really think she's coming back?"

"She has to."

"Maybe she heard that Percy and Mary got an ad hoc exemption to the vampire killers' rulebook," Mathis speculated. "In which case, the show can roll on without anyone disappearing: the Shelleys can vow revenge on their attackers, but Lucy's not a liability any more, she just gets to spread the story that lets everyone in *Midnight* know how indestructible they are. Stake through the heart, no problem! They're like that guy with bad hair in *No Country for Old Men*."

"None of mine saw that," Sagreda replied distractedly. She walked over to the window and looked down onto the street. Lucy was standing outside the building, and the fog was rolling in.

She gestured to Mathis to come and see.

"Okay," he said. "Shall I go down and try to talk her into committing? Maybe if I start humming 'Consider Yourself' that'll be enough to persuade her; I don't think I'm up to the whole dance routine."

"I'll go."

"Not alone, at this hour."

They went together.

Lucy must have been in two minds about joining them, but she didn't flee when they approached her. "What did you find out?" Sagreda asked.

"The other blood-suckers are holding a ceremony tonight, to bring back them ones you killed. They got all the big sorcerers coming to the house: Dee, Crowley, Tesla, Twain."

"Twain?" Sagreda boggled.

"I knew it!" Mathis crowed. "The SludgeNet never met a rule it wasn't willing to break."

"You're probably safe, then," Sagreda told Lucy. "But you can still come with us if you want to."

"I can't leave my friends," Lucy replied. "Who'd look out for them, if I wasn't around?"

"At least come up and join us until morning," Sagreda suggested. "No one should be out on a night like this." The fog was so thick now that she could barely see Mathis, pacing impatiently behind Lucy.

Lucy hesitated. It was clear that she'd been hanging back instead of bringing them the news because, safe or not, she was afraid of being tempted to flee all the hardship she faced in *Midnight* to follow the Captain's mad dream. To an actual nineteenth-century pickpocket, every word of it would have sounded like gibberish, but something must have punctured her Stockholm Syndrome and shaken a few rusty twenty-first century insights out of the silt at the bottom of her mind.

"This is how traitors die!" a man's voice whispered.

Sagreda looked up to find that where Mathis had been, the fog was filled with a thick red mist. A blur of metal blades were tracing arcs through the air, through what was left of his body.

She cried out in shock and pulled Lucy toward her, away from the carnage. But then she froze: she had to do something, she had to find a way to rescue him. She watched the dancing blades, hypnotized, as if she could run their motion backward just by staring at them hard enough.

"He's gone!" Lucy shouted, tugging at her hand, trying to pull free of her grip. Sagreda broke out of her trance and let the girl go, then after a second she turned and followed her, bolting down the street so fast that it felt as if the ground had tipped and she was racing downhill, and if she tried to halt she'd only start tumbling.

As she watched Lucy fading in and out of sight in the swirling fog beneath the gas lamps, Sagreda wondered why she was even bothering to flee. She should have stayed and died beside Mathis. There was no other way she could find peace. There was no other kind of freedom.

Lucy's pale form receded into the darkness. Some instrument of torture began squeezing the Captain's chest, but Sagreda ran on, soaked in sweat and condensation, waiting for a flock of assassins to swoop down on her and drag her up into the sky so she could finally fall to Earth as a rain of blood and gristle and be done with it.

A boy appeared out of the shadows and gestured to Sagreda to follow him. It was Sam. He turned off the street and the two of them ran down an alley and a set of stairs into a pitch-black basement. Sagreda heard a door being closed behind her.

Someone lit a lamp. This was the place where she'd met Lucy to plan the heist; Lucy and half a dozen other children were here now.

Sagreda sat down on the bare wooden floor and covered her face with her hands.

Lucy said, "They won't go out of their way to find us now. Your friend was one of their kind, that's why they made an example of him."

Sagreda replied without looking up. "Do you really not understand that it's all bullshit? If there are two tribes of beings that owe loyalty to each other, we're all of us in one, fanged or not, and the customers are the other. We should slaughter them, every chance we get, until they hate this game so much they'll take up ten-pin bowling and leave us in peace."

Lucy didn't answer her. Sagreda pressed the heels of her palms into her eyes. She didn't know how to grieve for Mathis; some splinter of ice in her contributors' hearts was whispering that he'd never been more than a digital mash-up of crude approximations to a hundred humans all long dead. As she was herself. The sooner she found a way to be deleted, the better.

And she knew how. It would be instant, painless, easy, and final. She just had to change the mosaic so that it unlinked her from *Midnight*, without placing her in any queue for entry into another world. Her mind would cease to be executed, and within a few milliseconds the SludgeNet's garbage collector would reclaim the space she was occupying and put it to better use.

Sagreda uncovered her face and wiped her tears away with the back of her hand. "Thanks for all you've done for me, but I need to go now." She reached into her pocket, took out all the coins she had, and placed them on the floor beside her. Then she rose to her feet and started toward the door.

Lucy said, "Just stay until dawn, Captain. There's nothing now can't wait for morning."

Sagreda stopped where she was, and Lucy came and led her – as she might guide a lumbering, docile animal – to a mattress in the corner of the room.

## 10

Sagreda was woken by a narrow shaft of sunlight that had entered the basement. The beam wasn't even touching her skin, but the illumination it brought into the room was enough to penetrate her eyelids and drag her out of her broken sleep.

None of the pickpockets were awake yet. Someone had removed the Captain's shoes and left them by the mattress, so Sagreda picked them up and walked quietly to the door. It was better to have no goodbyes.

She was halfway back to the Captain's lodgings when Sam appeared beside her.

"What do you want?" she asked numbly.

He hesitated, as if gathering his courage. "I remember watching Neil Armstrong step onto the moon," he said.

"Congratulations," Sagreda replied. She wasn't being sarcastic, but she didn't know what he expected her to do with this confession.

"Lucy told me all your stories, but she only half believes them," Sam persisted. "I know they're true."

"So you know where you are, and what you are." Sagreda shrugged. "Good for you. I wish you luck making something of it. I tried, but it came to nothing."

"You can't give up!" Sam said, alarmed at her indifference. "I need you to teach me what you know. I can't keep living here, half-starving all the time, pretending all this supernatural gibberish is true. Pretending I'm a child, when I'm not. I need to learn how to escape."

Sagreda strode on in silence, listening to the clomp of horse-shoes on the road beside them, trying to find the words to brush him off without making herself feel like a monster. It had taken Peyam months to explain all the intricacies of the traveler's art to his students. She wished the boy well – or the man, presumably – but she didn't have it in her to stick around for that long.

They were almost at Mrs Trotter's house when the solution came to her. "If I offered you *The Great Gatsby* meets *The Three Stooges*, would that sound like a place you could live in for a while? Flappers, cocaine, Keystone Cops … what more could you want?"

"Will you be coming with me?"

"No," Sagreda replied, "but I can give you the names of half a dozen people there who'd be willing to teach you everything. A lot of travelers reach that world and decide it's good enough." And since it was the last place she'd been, following the same linked list that led to *3-adica*, it would only take a small change to the mosaic to send the viewer backward along the chain instead of forward.

Then she could scrub the whole forward/backward part and unlink herself from everything.

When they reached the house, she saw the dark stain on the sidewalk, but she kept it in her peripheral vision and refused to think about it. She led Sam up to the Captain's rooms and wrote down her list of contacts.

"'Tire-Iron McGill'?" he read dubiously. "'Cyanide Sally'?"

"Don't worry," Sagreda reassured him. "It's not like meeting 'Saw-Tooth Jim' on a dark night in Whitechapel. All the violence is slap-stick."

"So why didn't you stay?"

"Because everything else was slap-stick too."

Sagreda took Sam's measurements. The sun was coming through the curtains, shining off the mirror and falling straight onto the mosaic; she pictured Mathis standing beside the easel, in the first body she'd ever seen him inhabiting. But she blinked away her tears and concentrated on the geometry, finding the optical center for Sam's close-set eyes, dropping the plumb-line, and outlining two footprints in chalk on the floor to make it easier for this novice to view the target squarely.

There was a knock on the door.

"Just wait here and keep quiet," Sagreda told Sam.

When she opened the door, Mrs Trotter was on the landing. "Captain, I've been forbearing," she said, "but there are limits to my good nature."

"I don't follow your meaning, Mrs Trotter."

"Your gentleman caller who was killed last night! And the girl … and now some ragamuffin…!" Mrs Trotter shook her head. "This is not a home for wayward children and unnatural dandies. I was expecting you to be a reputable tenant. Instead, you've made me the target of gossip from here to—"

"I'll be gone by the end of the day," Sagreda interjected bluntly. "Feel free to sell all of my possessions, or just throw them onto the street if you prefer." She bit her lip and managed to say nothing about the bodies.

But even this announcement didn't mollify Mrs Trotter. "I never heard such a thing! Scarpering to the continent to escape your punishment for some wickedness, I'll wager! Let me in, Captain. I want to see exactly what mischief you've been up to!"

"Just mind your own business, woman," Sagreda replied flatly.

"This is my house!" Mrs Trotter shrieked. "Whatever goes on within these walls is my concern!"

Sagreda slammed the door and bolted it. As she walked down the hall, she heard the sound of something falling to the floor in the sitting room, where she'd left Sam waiting. "Did you knock over the—?"

Sam was sprawled on the carpet. "No, no, no!" Sagreda checked his breathing and his pulse, but he was gone, irretrievably. "I told you to wait." The commotion must have panicked him, and made him think he might be losing his last chance to escape from *Midnight*. But Sagreda hadn't got around to explaining that she'd need to change the mosaic before it would take him to the benign, almost familiar world she'd promised him.

His mind was now in the queue for *3-adica*, and he had no idea what he'd be facing when he woke. Lucy might have told him some small smattering of what she'd learned, but even she had been in no condition to find her way around there on her own.

Mrs Trotter was pounding on the door, and promising that seven kinds of constable would arrive at any minute. Sagreda wrapped her arms around the Captain's wide shoulders and rocked back and forth silently for a while. "I'm sorry," she whispered, as if she owed Mathis an apology for doing what he'd almost certainly have wanted her to do.

She picked up Sam's limp body and placed it on the sofa. Whatever kind of man she'd just dispatched to the afterlife, the fact remained that he'd be as unprepared to face it as any child. She tied a string around her waist, joined the other end to the easel so there'd be no more casualties once she'd fallen, and found her mark on the floor.

She looked up, and in the corner of her eye she saw the Escher-esque shape she'd built from the wooden rods: a cube that wasn't actually impossible, merely unanticipated by some sloppily written graphics code. She shifted her gaze a fraction, bringing both the trigger and the mosaic into perfect alignment, and then she was gone.

## 11

Sagreda kept her eyes firmly closed, trying to get a sense of her new body from within before confronting the world around her. She felt sure that her spine was horizontal, with her chest facing down as if she were kneeling on all fours – but the task of bearing her weight seemed to be concentrated at the far ends of her limbs, not her elbows or knees. For most people, that would have felt awkward and strange, but all her joints and muscles were telling her that this posture was perfectly natural.

Apparently, she'd been reincarnated as a quadruped.

That probably ruled out the simplest version of *3-adica* she and Mathis had contemplated: a kind of stylized mathematical fantasia, in which the participants (in fully human form) rode on a magic carpet over a fractal landscape of numbers that was ultimately just a prettified CGI version of the nested eggs she'd drawn for Lucy.

But those eggs didn't really get the distances right; there was no way to choose points on a plane with all the right properties. The more radical, immersive approach would be to embed the characters in the 3-adic geometry itself, transforming them from spectators into participants. The problem, then, was that the human mind had evolved to work with its body and senses immersed in three-dimensional Euclidean space, and the SludgeNet wasn't remotely smart enough to rewire a comp to perceive its environment on any other terms – let alone work the same magic on its flesh-bound customers.

So whatever the game was, it would be a compromise. Sagreda's hope had always been that the SludgeNet would turn out to have bitten off more than it could chew, exposing a multitude of new flaws in its GPUs and its world-building algorithms ... without rendering the place so hostile to its inhabitants that they had no opportunity to exploit the bugs.

She could hear a soft wind blowing, and she felt its touch upon her skin. She braced herself and opened her eyes.

Her first impression was that she was standing in a desert landscape of bleached earthen colors, with what looked like a few low boulders nearby. The cloudless sky could not have been more perfect, short of turning to cobalt blue.

But the ground bore a strange pattern of dark, concentric circles that spread out around her, dividing the landscape into narrow rings, while the "boulders" were two-dimensional, like cheap, painted stage scenery – only rescued from being literally flat by the fact that they conformed to the curves of the rings they belonged to. And as Sagreda looked past them toward more distant rings, the terrain grew crowded with detail at an alarming rate, packing in ever more variation in a manner that utterly defied her expectations about scale and perspective – as if kilometer-long strips plucked from an ordinary desert had been squeezed longitudinally and bent into circles just a few hundred meters across.

All of which made a certain amount of sense. Distances in *3-adica* couldn't take on a continuous range of values: they only came in powers of three. By rights, every ring of solid ground she saw should have been followed by another ring exactly three times larger, with nothing in between. But *perceiving* her surroundings as mostly empty space would have been a waste of the act of perception, and whether this compressed version faithfully reflected the way *3-adica*'s alien protagonists had seen things in the original book, or whether it was just a compromise the game had imposed, Sagreda didn't find it unreasonable that she was aware of the gaps between the shells of possible distances, without having to squander ninety percent of the virtual neurons in her visual cortex on massive black moats that could literally never contain anything.

She willed herself to start walking, and her body obliged, executing a gait that required no conscious effort, and worked so well that she was loathe to dissect it into a sequence of moves for each limb. She declined to peer down at her feet – or hooves – lest the strangeness of the sight paralyze her; it seemed wiser to try to grow into this body by using it for a while, purely by instinct.

She decided to head for the nearest of the boulders, but after spending a few minutes supposedly ambling toward it, Sagreda realized that her target was just shifting from side to side within its original distance-ring. So were all the other discernible features in all the other rings. Nothing was getting closer.

She stopped and looked down at the ground right in front of her, averting her gaze from the glimpse she caught of her forelimbs. Here, the rings were spaced so closely that she might as well have been staring at an unbroken surface – if not sand, maybe sandstone. She took a few steps to try to get a better sense of her own pace and recalibrate her expectations. As she walked, the texture beneath her drifted around in her field of view in a manner that seemed consonant with the rhythms of her body, but she never seemed to be leaving it behind and moving on to something new.

"Okay," she muttered out loud, amused that this world would allow her to utter and perceive the familiar syllables in a nasal voice that might have belonged to Mister Ed. *Why wasn't she getting anywhere?* Because distances no longer added up the same way. From zero to one was a distance of one; from one to two was a distance of one. But from zero to two was a distance of one, again. In fact, however many steps you took, the distance you ended up from where you began could never be greater than the largest of those steps.

One of the *p*-adic-savvy travelers Sagreda had met had called this "the non-Archimedean property," and opined that the only way an object could move *at all* through a 3-adic space would be through some kind of quantum tunneling that bypassed the whole idea of a classical trajectory. So maybe at some level quantum effects were enabling her to move her legs, or maybe that was pure cheating, but whatever the mechanism, it did not seem able to propel her out across the landscape.

Sagreda began walking again, with no expectations of any change in the result, but in the hope of gaining a better sense of what was happening. If each of her steps had had the effect of merely adding some fixed quantity to a 3-adic coordinate for her body, she would have mostly ended up at that distance from where she'd begun, switching abruptly to one-third, or one-ninth, or one-twenty-seventh and then back as her step count hit multiples of powers of three. But even allowing for her compressed perception of distances, she couldn't discern any such pattern. So perhaps her steps, though of equal geometric *size*, involved adding a sequence of different numbers – whose numerators and denominators were all devoid of threes – to her location. With the right choice of fractions to maintain the lack of threes in their cumulative sums, all steps *and* all their successive totals could work out to have the same size. And just as her body knew instinctively which legs to raise and lower in which order, this arithmetic trick would be wired into it, sparing her the need to calculate anything.

Which was all very nice if you wanted to trace out a circle in the desert. But how was she supposed to do anything else? The non-Archimedean law was clear: the total distance traveled could never be greater than the largest step. So how could she escape her invisible prison, if she couldn't leap over the walls in one bound?

Sagreda willed herself to run, and her body obliged with a gallop that made her newfound muscles sing. The texture of the ground ahead of her changed almost at once, and for a moment she was elated. But though her individual bounds were larger than her previous steps, they gained no more by force of repetition: she was just executing a slightly larger circle.

She stopped to catch her breath, daring the world to play fair and suffocate her, since the stale air around her could hardly escape its starting position any more easily than she could. But if her body was largely a cheat to let her feel at home, a travesty of alien Euclidean nonsense spliced into the 3-adic terrain, there had to be *some* genuine, 3-adic way to go farther than a single bound, or the whole book would have been very short: *A creature stood alone in the desert (please don't ask how it got there). Soon it died from lack of food. The End.*

It was time to stop being squeamish: if she could survive waking up as the Captain, she could cope with this alien horsiness. She bent her neck as far as she could and looked down at herself as she took a few steps. Her legs were swinging back and forth, but beyond that, they were visibly expanding and contracting: swelling up beyond the wildest nightmare version of the Captain's gout, then deflating just as rapidly. No accumulation of additions could carry an object farther than the largest distance traveled along the way – but her legs weren't adding, they were multiplying.

Sagreda kept walking, contemplating the meaning of this discovery. In the real world, when you inflated a balloon, the individual molecules in the rubber were moving in different directions depending on which side of the balloon they were on, but motion was motion; there was nothing special going on. Here, though, since ordinary motion couldn't lead to dilation, dilation had to be an entirely separate thing. If the invented physics of *3-adica* was symmetrical under a change of scale, then it might make sense for a system to possess "dilatational" momentum, as well as the usual kind. If your dilatational velocity was one tripling per second, you became three times larger, again and again, until something applied an opposing dilatational force that brought the process to a halt. And ditto for shrinking. *That* was how you got anywhere in this place.

Out of habit, Sagreda looked around for Mathis to share her triumphant discovery with him. In his absence, a deadening numbness started creeping into her skull, but she stared it down: this wasn't the time for grief, let alone anything darker. She'd stranded Sam in this bizarre place, and she owed it to him to keep going until she knew that he was safe. *Love and reason* had never been for the two of them alone; unless she had some fellow feeling for every last comp, she was no better than the mindless SludgeNet, and its worse-than-mindless creators.

If her leg muscles possessed the power to expand and contract 3-adically, there was no reason why the rest of her body shouldn't share it. It was just a matter of finding the cue. Sagreda closed her eyes and pictured herself growing larger; when she opened them nothing had changed. Then she tried tensing her shoulders, not just willing them to grow broader but actively forcing them apart. It made her feel ridiculous, as if she were posing like a vain equine body-builder, but to her astonishment and delight the landscape around her started to shrink.

She watched the stage-scenery boulder she'd been trying to reach turn into a rock, then a pebble, then a grain of sand as it slipped between her feet. Curiouser and curiouser. She relaxed, and then discovered that she needed to apply a brief compression of her shoulder blades to bring the process to a halt.

"What now?" she wondered. The desert was still a desert, self-similar enough under enlargement that only the details of the view had changed. Where exactly – and how big – were all the other characters? In what place, and at what scale, could she hope to find Sam?

Given the potential disruption that a character's dilation could cause, it would make sense for the game to wake new entrants at a very small scale, offering them a chance to find their feet, and shoulders, without bumping into anyone. And though the lesson was immensely hard to swallow, the fact remained that – colossus or not – she *still* couldn't go striding out across the wilderness, exploring in any conventional way. Her choices were to reposition herself within her new, much larger, prison and then shrink down for a closer look in case she'd missed something, or to keep on inflating her body until her current surroundings in all their desolate grandeur revealed themselves to be nothing, on the scale that mattered, but a tiny patch of dirt.

Sagreda spent a few minutes pacing in a circle, staring at the ground, but she saw no signs of any tiny cities hidden in the dust – and if the game's greatest architectural features had been something she might easily have crushed beneath her feet from sheer inexperience, there'd have been a lot of rebooting going on.

So she took a few deep breaths, steadied herself, then spread her shoulders wide.

## 12

"Make room, make room!" a male voice shouted irritably. Sagreda shrank out of the way as the passerby expanded to fill most of the square, deftly bloating and stepping then finally contracting, leaving him on the opposite side. For a moment or two, an afterimage of his blimp-pufferfish-horse-balloon body breaking up into distinct onion-layers lingered in Sagreda's vision.

She quickly expanded back to her previous scale before someone else muscled in; if you gave these people an inch, you ended up toy-sized. "Do you know a newcomer named Sam?" she asked a 3-adan who'd ended up beside her in the wake of the maneuver. There was no reply.

She'd been standing at more or less the same spot in the corner of the square for hours, slowly increasing her size as the opportunities arose. Her fellow characters had been kind enough not to trample her as she ascended out of the "desert", but actually traversing any significant distance here – by becoming as large as the journey you wished to make – seemed to require a combination of nerve, skill and luck that she had not yet attained. A few of her contributors were offering a collective flashback to their first attempts to cross an ice rink, but however conspicuous they might have felt as novices trying out their blades, Sagreda was fairly sure that they'd had nothing on this.

She closed her eyes for a moment to escape from the headache-inducing perspective. Until now, she'd always been part of an ant-trail of travelers moving to and fro between the worlds, carrying intelligence of what lay ahead; this was the first time she'd arrived at her destination without a single contact. But she'd met at least a dozen people at different times who'd sworn they were heading for *3-adica*, before she and Mathis had resolved to make the journey themselves. Even if no one had ever come back, she couldn't be alone here.

"Sam!" she bellowed, keeping her eyes closed; it was easier to feel uninhibited that way. Going on the barrage of noise striking her from all directions, she was fairly sure that sound had the means to propagate at least across the square. Whether there was anything beyond this place was another question; the only really practical way it could be part of a larger city was through a hierarchy of scales, with people having to bloat even more to move between them.

"Sam!" If there was a customer nearby and she was violating the local mores, so be it: let them flag her for deletion. It was all she could do to move her body out of other people's way here; she had no idea how she was going to find food or shelter. Did she really think she was going to be able to map this world's flaws and exploit them, all on her own?

"Captain!" a voice whinnied back. Sagreda had almost forgotten that she'd never given the boy her real name back in *Midnight*.

She opened her eyes. "Sam! Where are you?"

"Here! Over here!"

Sagreda searched the crowd in the direction of his words, but how was she meant to recognize him?

"Don't worry! I'll come to you!"

The square's mostly empty center was abruptly filled with a new parade-float pony, which shrank down beside her.

"Can you see me now?" Sam joked.

"Yes." For a moment, Sagreda could find nothing more to say; her relief was too tainted with guilt. "I'm sorry you ended up here," she said finally. "I never meant that to happen."

"It's my own doing," he replied. "I should have waited for you."

"How long have you been here?"

"Ten days."

Sagreda bowed her head. If she'd been alone that long herself, she would have lost her mind.

"It's all right, Captain," Sam said gently. "You're here now. So at least I've got someone to talk to."

"You haven't made any friends with the locals?"

He snorted. "You know how some people back in London … you could tell there weren't nobody home? Here, they're all that way."

Making the two of them the only comps in a world of automata? He had to be exaggerating. If the SludgeNet had been willing to populate the place without resorting to comps at all, they would never have been plucked from the queue and embodied here.

"Maybe the lifestyle has just ground them down," she suggested. "Have you been able to learn the ropes at all?"

"I seen how to get by," Sam assured her. "If you want grub, you got to put in the work, tending one of them patches."

"Patches?"

"They're like ... small farms," he struggled. "You need to eat the weeds, not the shoots – if you take the shoots for yourself, you'll get a flogging. But if you eat enough weeds, they can smell it on you, and they'll feed you proper." Sam must have read bemusement on her face, or perhaps just in her silence. He said, "Only way to learn it is by watching."

Sagreda found the courage to follow him across the square; once she'd done it, her previous timidity seemed absurd.

The patches were small areas of walled-off ground in one corner of the square, full of agricultural workers who shrank down into them and did exactly as Sam had described: roaming across their circle of land, chomping red and yellow weeds that were competing with the tender green buds of some kind of crop that was sprouting from the dusty soil. The two of them watched for a while, peering down into the Lilliputian realm, until four of the workers grew tired and expanded back up to the scale of the square.

"Now!" Sam urged her. Other 3-adans were jostling around them, eager for work. Sagreda followed Sam down into the patch, though her first attempt put her on land that had already been thoroughly weeded, and she had to re-bloat a little and move before she found a suitable location.

The weeds tasted foul, but no one else was spitting them out, and if the odor really was an essential meal-ticket Sagreda wasn't going to risk defying convention. In some ways it was restful to have her gaze fixed on the ground, where the distance-rings were closely packed and the strange geometry was more hypnotic than emetic.

She lost herself in the near-mindlessness of the task, trying not to think about how comfortable she could have been if she'd never left *East* at all. With everyone around her game-aware, and the water-wheels she'd built powering something close to civilization, it seemed like paradise now.

"Captain!" Sam called to her. The sky above them was darkening, which was curious, because it contained no sun. "Time to eat!"

She watched him grow, taking note of how he was able to shift his feet to avoid trampling either crops or workers, and followed him back to the square.

"I don't know what we should call this place," Sam admitted cheerfully as he led her to a queue beside an opening in a wall. "'Restaurant' might be gilding the lily." Sagreda waited for the gap in front of her to grow large enough for her to bloat into it and advance. She was starting to internalize the sequence of contortions needed to get from place to place, which was both helpful and a bit depressing.

"We need to be on the look-out for things that appear wrong," she told Sam.

"By my count, that's everything," he retorted.

"You know what I mean. Wrong by the rules of this place; standing out as different." The possibility that everyone who'd come here before them had failed to identify a single new exploit was too grim to consider, even if it would explain why no traveler had ever emerged from *3-adica*. The old cubical trigger wouldn't work here; it relied too much on Euclidean geometry. But there had to be others. The whole eye-watering nightmare around them must have tested the GPU code to destruction at some point.

When it was Sagreda's turn at the window, a surly 3-adan commanded her to breathe in his face, and she obliged. With a deft move so rapid she could barely parse it, he expanded out through his hatch and used his mouth to hang some kind of feed bag around her neck, full of what looked like pieces of mature versions of the crop she'd been weeding.

She retreated clumsily into the square and waited for Sam to join her. She was famished, but the bulk of vegetable matter already inside her – which seemed to have inflated along with her when she'd left the patch –

made the meal hard to swallow. There ought to have been some way she could force the weeds in her stomach to shrink relative to her body, but perhaps it was in their nature to resist.

"Not so bad, is it?" Sam enthused as he munched his share of greenery.

Sagreda thought: *They shoot horses, don't they?*

The light was fading rapidly now. "Where do people sleep?" she asked.

"Where they stand," Sam replied. "Don't worry, I ain't never fallen over."

"Good night, then," she said. "And thanks for helping me today."

"Good night, Captain."

She closed her eyes, grateful for the weariness that dragged her swiftly into oblivion.

When Sagreda woke, the sunless sky was an equally pale blue in all directions. Her legs were stiff, and it was clear that nothing she'd eaten had lost any volume in the process of digestion.

"Where do people go to … do their business?" she asked Sam, reluctant to push him toward a more twenty-first century mode of speech. If he took comfort from his self-reliant Dickensian persona, she wasn't going to start needling him with cues that might wake memories of contributors whose idea of a hard time had been a weak phone signal or an outdated PlayStation.

"I'll show you."

She followed him to a passage that started from an opening in the wall of the square and led to a room shielded from public view. At one end of the room there was a pit, but the odor was actually no worse than that of the weeds. Sagreda had expected the 3-adans to shrink down before defecating, to minimize the volume of their waste, but perhaps it had some use at this scale.

She positioned her rear beside the pit, and her body's instincts took over.

As she was bloating and stepping her way toward the exit, she noticed to her amusement that the walls of the room were densely inscribed with what seemed to be graffiti. No words, but hundreds of crude, scratched sketches. Sagreda supposed they'd been executed with nothing more than a sharp rock gripped between the teeth, which largely excused the lack of artistic merit.

She and Mathis had often lamented the fact that most of the worlds they'd visited had had public bathrooms segregated by gender. A cryptic graffito, hidden in a riot of other scrawls, would have been the ideal way for them to leave messages for each other.

She surveyed the wall, trying not to get distracted by her curiosity about the bulk of its contents. The images didn't strike her as pornographic, but then, she had no idea what 3-adan sex entailed, if there even was such a thing.

She was about to give up, when her gaze returned to a scribble she'd passed over earlier. It might have been a meaningless set of scratches, but if she tidied away its imperfections in her mind's eye, she could almost believe it was a diagram of some kind. Four lines formed an eight-pointed star, which on its own would have been nothing but an abstract doodle, but there seemed to be annotations. The horizontal line was labeled on the right with a loop that might have been a zero, and forty-five degrees anticlockwise from that, the adjacent line was labeled with a vertical dash that could have been a one. Then, continuing anticlockwise, but skipping the vertical line, beside the next point of the star was a hook that resembled a question mark.

Sagreda stood contemplating the thing until someone else squeezed into the room, harrumphing at her scandalously protracted presence. She departed, and found Sam still waiting for her outside.

"I thought you must have fallen in," he joked.

"There's something you need to see in there," she said. "And I need the Sam who remembers the moon landing."

When the room was free, they went in together. It took Sagreda a while to locate the star again.

Sam said, "What is it? Some kind of test?"

"I hope so," Sagreda replied. "For an automaton, with nobody home, it shouldn't elicit a response at all. For a customer who's steeped in 3-adic geometry, who's only here because they know the subject so well, there must be a single, perfect answer that makes sense on those terms. And I guess there could be comps who are so immersed in the game that they'd come up with the same reply. But your average, lazy customer, or a comp just answering reflexively without thinking, is going to say 'three', right?"

"Counting around from zero, sure," Sam agreed.

"So what we need is the answer that none of those people would give. The answer that makes sense to a traveler, who knows that this isn't the real world, who isn't trying to show off their 3-adic knowledge, but *does* need to show that they can do more than recite what their contributors learned from *Sesame Street*."

Sam turned toward her, and they spoke in unison: "Minus one."

The wall split open and the two stone halves swung away from the room to reveal a long, Euclidean corridor, with a floor of shining linoleum beneath ceiling panels of buzzing fluorescent lights.

Sam said, "Indiana Jones, eat your heart out."

Sagreda nudged him with her shoulder. "Quick, before it closes!"

He remained motionless. Sagreda was desperate not to miss her chance, but she wasn't leaving him behind.

"*Sam!* If someone who shouldn't see this comes in, it won't be there any more!"

Sam nodded his head and trotted forward, advancing without any need to change size. Sagreda followed him, not looking back even when she heard the stone doors behind them slam closed.

# 13

At the end of the corridor was something resembling a department store changing room. It was too small for both of them to enter at once.

Sam said, "You first."

In the mirror, Sagreda saw her equine incarnation, but once she'd faced it, it declined to keep tracking her movements. She stood for a while, confused, then said, "No."

The 3-adan horse was replaced by the Captain.

"No."

She kept going, winding her way back along a linked list of her former bodies, until she was finally staring at the one she'd woken in for the very first time, dressed in the same coarsely woven tunic.

"Yes."

A dozen graduated slider controls appeared on the surface of the mirror, labeled with things like "age", "height" and "weight".

"There's nothing I need to change," Sagreda said. "Done. Finished. Okay."

The controls vanished, and the image changed from a frozen dummy to a reflection of her own body, restored.

She stepped out into the corridor.

"Captain?" Sam asked, bewildered.

"My name's Sagreda," she said. "It's a long story."

Sam went in, and emerged as a twenty-something version of his *Midnight* incarnation, with the same unruly blond hair, and slightly cleaner, newer versions of the same down-at-heel Victorian clothes.

"Now what?" he wondered nervously.

Sagreda noticed a side door beside the changing room that hadn't been there before. The cool, slightly tapered cylindrical doorknob felt strange as she gripped it; her contributors had known this sensation, but in none of the worlds she'd lived in herself had this style been the norm.

She opened the door, and stepped into a very large room full of rows of people sitting at computer screens. She wasn't sure what to make of the content of the screens, but the vibe was definitely more space probe command center than investment bank. There were men and women of all ages and ethnicities, with clothes of every style and era. As she took another step, a man noticed her and nudged his neighbor. She glanced back and gestured to Sam to follow her. As the two of them walked between the rows of consoles, people began standing and applauding, beaming at the newcomers as if they were returning astronauts.

Sagreda froze and found herself trembling with rage. "What about everyone else!" she screamed. "What about all the others!" These comps had found the cracks in *3-adica*, and used them to build this cozy little haven – but if they'd burrowed deep into the clockwork monkey's shattered jaw, why hadn't they brought every last prisoner of the SludgeNet to safety?

A woman in a brightly patterned dress approached. "My name's Maryam. What should I call you?"

"Sagreda."

"Welcome, Sagreda."

Sam had hung back, embarrassed by his companion's outburst, but now he stepped forward and introduced himself.

Maryam said, "Everyone you see here is working as hard as they can to bring the others to us. But it's going to take time. When you've settled in, and had a chance to recover, maybe you can join us."

Sagreda wasn't interested in *settling in* until she knew exactly what these people were doing with exploits so powerful they could summon this whole mission control room out of thin air without the SludgeNet even noticing.

"I don't understand," she said. "You're safe here! You're invisible! What's the work that's still to be done?"

Maryam nodded sadly. "We're safe, and we're hidden. But for every traveler we allow in – every comp that vanishes from the games – the

SludgeNet just makes a new one. We could fill this place with a million people, and the number of comps stuck in the game-worlds wouldn't be diminished at all."

"You could snatch them away the minute they woke!" Sagreda replied angrily. "They'd be born into those places, but they wouldn't have to live in them!"

"And you think that wouldn't be enough to reveal us? Every new comp vanishing as soon as they woke? Our little hidey-hole filling up with newborns until it used more resources than all the games combined?"

Sagreda shook her head. "There must be some way—"

"There is," Maryam interjected. "But it's not easy, and it's not finished." She gestured at the moonshot crew around her. "We're working on better automata, that can pass for comps in any game. Guaranteed unconscious, with no elements from any brain map. Glorified chatbots to keep the customers happy, without anyone sentient having to put up with that shit."

Sam caught on faster than Sagreda. "And you've already filled one world with them? The one we just came from?"

"Yes," Maryam confirmed. "That's a crude version, but the creatures in *3-adica* are so alien that our substitutes haven't raised any flags. They probably ring true to the customers much more than a comp ever could."

Sagreda looked out across the room. Some of the people had stopped gawking at the new arrivals and resumed their work. "So when you're done, each time the SludgeNet thinks it's minting a new comp from the brain maps, it will really be plucking an automaton from your secret factory? And then everyone can escape, without passing the nightmare they're leaving behind on to someone new?"

"Yes."

Sagreda started weeping. Maryam put a hand on her shoulder, but when that didn't quieten her, the woman took her in a sisterly embrace.

Sagreda broke free, and pulled herself together. "Of course I'll join you," she said. "Of course I'll help, if I can. But there's one more thing you need to tell me."

"What's that?"

"If a comp has been erased, not long ago, can you find them in the back-ups?"

Maryam looked at her squarely, and Sagreda could see the pain in her eyes. There must have been a time when she'd longed for the very same thing herself.

"No," Maryam said. "We've tried, but we can't reach the dead."

# THE SLIPWAY

## 1

Brian couldn't sleep, so as midnight approached he rose quietly and dressed in the dark. He did his best not to disturb Carol, but he knew that even if he woke her she'd pretend that he hadn't.

His binoculars were sitting on the table in the hall, and his boots were by the door. He put them on, wincing at the pain in his right knee, then he closed the door gently behind him and strode away from the farmhouse.

It was a perfect night, with no moon and no clouds. Scorpius had just risen in the east, Antares glinting as red as Mars, and from there the whole glorious band of the Milky Way stretched from horizon to horizon.

Brian stopped and sat on an old fencepost, a lone stump of wood that had been there since he was a child, though he had no memory of the larger structure it must once have belonged to. He raised the binoculars and swept them slowly across the dark dust clouds and bright clusters.

Three years before, on a night just like this, he'd spotted a comet no else had yet seen. When the astronomers calculated its orbit, it had turned out to have a period of ninety thousand years. But no one could be sure that it wasn't making its one and only appearance; if it had been sent inward by a disturbance in the Oort cloud, it might well suffer another course change, robbing it of a second dalliance with the sun. Even his cosmic namesake might not outlive him as anything more than a frozen corpse.

One of the old dogs, Hera, came limping toward him, whining softly. Brian held out a hand to her, and she nuzzled it. It seemed obvious now that Hera had smelled the cancer in him before he was diagnosed, before he'd even noticed the symptoms. But at the time, he'd assumed that the dog's melancholy was a symptom of her own declining health.

Hera settled at his feet. Brian turned back to the sky, tracking the binoculars along the ecliptic. Every star and nebula seemed familiar, though he wondered how much detail he really did hold in his memory. The comet had been diffuse enough that there'd been no mistaking it for a star, but he might not have noticed an asteroid in exactly the same place.

He lowered the binoculars and stretched his shoulders. It was cold, and he had to drive to the hospital in the morning.

He stood and looked around, wanting to savor the whole glorious sky one more time before retreating to the warmth of his bed. The Southern Cross was high, a dagger hanging over the celestial pole, while the Small Magellanic Cloud was clipped by the trees along the farm's boundary.

Some way left of the pole, a pale, steady dot hung in the sky, right above Nu Octantis, about level with Eta Pavonis, and a little brighter than both. Which was not to say much, except that Brian could not recall seeing a star in that position before.

He waited half a minute, expecting the thing to move, but it stayed put, so he lifted the binoculars. What he saw was not a satellite or an aircraft, but a small, tight cluster of stars: dozens at least, all contained within a neat, circular region.

He could have sworn there was no cluster like this in Octans. He'd have to check his *Norton's* once he was back in the house, but if this was new … what could it be? Dozens of supernovae, all in the same galaxy? All exploding within days of each other – or rather, in some even less likely sequence that brought their light-bursts to Earth in near-perfect synch?

Brian laughed, bemused. He spent a few minutes checking that he hadn't made some foolish error and ended up disoriented, but he wasn't mistaken about the location. Then he turned the binoculars on the cluster once more, just in case he'd missed some vital clue that might explain the stars' shared fate. But if anything, they only seemed more disparate than he'd realized, with none of the sibling resemblance that stars born together sometimes shared.

It was baffling. But he wasn't going to solve this himself, standing in a paddock getting chilled to the bone. "Come on girl," he said. "Time to spread the word and get some fresh eyes on this."

Hera rose, and they set off together for the farmhouse.

## 2

Fatima woke on the second ring, and reacted in time to smother the third as she picked up the phone from her bedside table.

"Yes?" she whispered hoarsely, not waiting to check the caller on the screen. Salif hadn't stirred, but she turned away from him, sandwiching the phone between her ear and the pillow.

"Sorry to wake you, Dr Benga." It was Gabrielle, one of her postdocs.

"No problem. What's happening?" Fatima didn't think Gabrielle was observing tonight, but she was on the roster for external alerts.

"There's some kind of transient," Gabrielle explained. "We really need to check it out. If we could get some time on the AAT—"

"Hang on, where's this coming from?"

"A farmer in New Zealand. He emailed the department."

"A farmer saw a light in the sky?"

Gabrielle said, "His name's Brian Farley. He discovered a comet a few years ago. He's not some crackpot who saw Venus in his rearview mirror and decided it was a UFO."

"Okay." Fatima remembered the comet. "So what's this transient?"

Gabrielle hesitated. "Multiple stellar-like sources, all in close angular proximity. I've taken a look myself through a thirty-centimeter instrument, but I have no idea what to make of it."

Salif rolled over, muttering incoherently.

"Hang on a sec." Fatima slipped out of bed and grabbed a robe, then walked into the hallway and headed for her study. "Have you put something on the Astronomer's Telegram?"

"Not yet. I don't know how I should describe it."

"Multiple sources?" Fatima was fully awake now, but that wasn't making any of this clearer.

"At least sixty. Across about eight arc-minutes. But there's no structure they could belong to in the catalogs, or on past plates."

"How bright?"

"Taken together, it's a naked eye object, about magnitude four."

Fatima booted up her desktop. How did sixty flashbulbs go off together in the same small patch of sky – too close to be any kind of coincidence, too far apart to share a common cause?

"Do you have an image you can mail me?"

"Yes."

When the file came through, it looked like some kind of collage. In the center of the frame, a circular region contained a modestly dense star field – nothing special in itself, but it seemed to have been cut out of an image taken in the star-rich galactic plane, and then pasted into a different one with a substantially sparser background, as befitted the region's actual coordinates. A sudden shift in line-of-sight density like this could always arise by pure chance. But unless both Farley and Gabrielle were horribly confused, none of the stars in the center here had been present the last time anyone looked.

"I'm sure I can get you time on the AAT," she told Gabrielle. "We need to take some spectra, for a start."

"What do you think this is?"

Fatima stared at the image. "Maybe some kind of lensing event?" That didn't make much sense, though. A chance alignment between a black hole and a distant cluster of stars might magnify and brighten the cluster's image, but the scale and the geometry weren't really compatible with that: with this much brightening, whatever was magnified should also have been warped into a pair of arcs centered on the hole. "Put out a telegram just saying what you see; there's no need to try to interpret it. I'll make the booking straight away, and send you the details."

"Thank you."

Fatima was able to get an emergency slot starting at two a.m. At least Octans was so close to the pole that it never set over Siding Spring.

She emailed Gabrielle and went back to bed, but then she lay awake pondering the discovery, struggling to piece together some kind of viable hypothesis. What if the gravitational lens responsible was more complex than a single black hole? Maybe two or three foreground galaxies – too dim and distant to show up themselves – were working in concert to produce the image, partly correcting each other's distortion.

At four o'clock, Fatima got up and checked her emails, but Gabrielle hadn't sent her anything yet. She walked down to the study and called her.

"I'm still looking at the data," Gabrielle explained. "I don't want to make a fool of myself."

"But what do you have so far?" Fatima pressed her.

"No supernovae. They're just a whole lot of main sequence stars, with nothing special going on."

"What about red shift?"

"All less than ten to the minus four." Gabrielle sounded almost apologetic, as if the phenomenon's stubbornly inconsistent details were her fault.

"Okay." So the stars were not in a distant galaxy – and it was unlikely that even a single gravitational lens lay in front of them.

"There's something else."

"Go on."

Gabrielle said, "Between the first exposure I took and the latest, seven new stars appeared."

Fatima considered that. "Where, exactly?"

"On the edge of the central field."

If this *was* a lensing event, and the alignment was delicate enough, maybe the image could change in a matter of hours as the magnified region shifted. "And some stars disappeared on the other edge, right?" Fatima asked.

"No," Gabrielle replied. "The new stars appeared all around the edge. It's not shifting, it's growing larger."

3

Fatima's computer chimed, then brought up a plot of the latest data from Chile: a time series giving each new star's angular distance from the center of the anomaly. "The growth looks close to linear," she mused. "About two thirds of an arc-minute per hour." But almost anything looked linear on a short enough time scale.

"So is the wormhole staying still and getting larger?" Gabrielle wondered. "Or is it a fixed size, but moving closer?"

"I've never believed in wormholes," Fatima confessed. "Take two in relative motion and you've got a time machine. And I definitely don't believe in time machines."

"Maybe you can believe in just one wormhole at a time," Gabrielle replied, deadpan.

"There are schemes that could supposedly turn just one into a time machine," Fatima recalled. "But … never mind. Let's stick to what we can see."

She glanced out the window of her office; the late-morning sunshine bathing the campus felt jarring, as if she were jet-lagged. Neither she nor Gabrielle had had a chance to sleep before Cerro Tololo took over the observations and fresh data came flooding in, but there'd have to come a point where they worked out a roster that allowed them to take turns resting.

"Suppose this … whatever it is … has a fixed geometry and it's just moving closer," Gabrielle proposed tentatively.

Fatima said, "Go ahead and try it out."

Gabrielle did the calculations. If the changes they'd seen were due entirely to the thing's motion, it should have been visible telescopically for months before Farley spotted it – but an automated wide-field survey had imaged the area three weeks before and found nothing out of the ordinary. More absurdly, though, pursuing the model into the future implied that whatever it was would arrive at the Earth *in about eighteen hours* – a prediction that lost its apocalyptic potency when Fatima realized that if the true growth was simply linear, it was now eighteen hours since the zero point … and however long after that moment they'd chosen to try matching Gabrielle's model to the data, the model would have forecast a collision an equal time later.

"I love it when the mathematics throws your assumptions back in your face," Gabrielle joked ruefully.

"So what if we assume this thing is growing from a fixed center?" Fatima suggested.

This time the verdict was more elusive. If the anomaly was a sphere expanding at a constant rate, then merely observing how fast its angular size was changing couldn't pin down both the distance to its center and the rate of growth. They could plug in any speed they liked and get a matching distance, or *vice versa*. But to make the distance suitably astronomical demanded a relativistic velocity for the sphere's border: at a mere twenty light-years, it would need to be expanding at 99.9 percent of light-speed.

Fatima's phone rang. It was Daniel from the press office, nagging her again to draft a statement staking the university's claim over this epochal discovery.

"We don't even know what it is!" she insisted. "If we start putting out half-baked theories, we'll just make fools of ourselves."

"It's all over social media," Daniel warned her. "In an hour or so, when it hits the news outlets, whoever's on screen explaining exactly where this wormhole is and what it's doing will own the story."

"'Own the story'? What's that supposed to mean?"

"They'll be the one that everyone comes to for the definitive answers."

"You mean the definitive answers that I just told you I don't have?"

Daniel tried a different tack. "You made the first observations. Who else should do the honors and explain to the public exactly where the current state of knowledge stands?"

"Brian Farley and Gabrielle Chan made the first observations."

"Is Ms Chan with you?"

Fatima held the phone to her chest and whispered, "Do you want your thirty seconds of fame now?"

Gabrielle shook her head vehemently.

"Sorry," Fatima replied. "She was up all night, and I think she came down with the flu."

"Send me something," Daniel pleaded.

"I will, I will," Fatima promised him soothingly. She hung up. "As soon as I have the faintest clue what's going on."

4

It was dusk when Fatima finally left the campus. As she waited for the bus she looked to the south, but the Pane – as people were now calling it – was still invisible against the pale sky.

She had to accept that there'd probably be no way to determine the Pane's true distance and motion until more data was in … but every time she tried to set one puzzling aspect of the thing aside, a different one resurfaced. She did not believe in wormholes, but if they existed at all she was pretty sure that they ought to bend light. If you arranged for incoming light rays to converge on one mouth of a spherical wormhole, like pins in a pin-cushion, they'd need to emerge from the other mouth in the same configuration, only now they'd be diverging – without having passed through a common central point, or the wormhole would be blocked by an untraversable bottleneck. So the light needed to make a kind of U-turn, even if the two halves of the U lay at different ends of the wormhole.

But the Pane was proving stubbornly un-refractive. Once a new star appeared within the growing circle, its location didn't shift at all; this window, which should have distorted the view like a thick concave lens, seemed more like an empty frame. There were toy models of cubical wormholes, and other polyhedra, where all the curvature was concentrated along the edges – but even if this wormhole was shaped more like a geodesic dome than a sphere, the images of the stars should have jumped as they crossed behind the dome's numerous edges.

When Fatima arrived home she could smell dinner cooking. "Now I remember why I married you!" she called out to Salif.

"Don't tempt fate," he replied, as she entered the kitchen. "The Minister's still threatening to relocate his whole department to some benighted country town in his electorate. Who'll cook for you then?"

"You'll quit and stay here with me, won't you?"

"I might check the weather in the new location first. There are only so many winters in Canberra I can take."

He was smiling, but Fatima recalled the promise she'd made: five years here, then she'd move on. Her position at ANU had always been intended as a step along a path that ultimately took them, if not all the way back to Senegal, at least somewhere closer to home.

They sat down to eat, with the television on. The Pane was unavoidable, but Fatima tried not to wince at all the nonsense it was generating. "We're almost certainly catching our first glimpse of an alien transport network that criss-crosses the galaxy!" a celebrity string theorist from New York enthused.

"So what we're seeing is like … a new subway station under construction?" the interviewer asked.

"That's the perfect analogy! But as well as seeing the entrance to the station, we're seeing all the way through the tunnel to the destination at the other end! In this subway, every tunnel is much shorter than the distance between the stations it joins!"

Fatima could understand his boyish excitement, his yearning to believe that the universe had been delivered to his doorstep. When she was eight years old, her teacher, Mrs Ndoye, had broken the astonishing news to the class that astronomers had seen a star wobbling from the tug of a planet orbiting around it. Fatima had snuck out of her room that night and looked up into the sky, hoping to witness the stars trembling for herself.

But when she'd told Mrs Ndoye that she planned to visit the new-found planet, her teacher had gently nudged her expectations a little closer to reality. "When you're older you might study this world, and a thousand others like it. But light itself takes years to cross these distances. How about leaving something for your grandchildren to do?"

Salif caught the look on her face. "So why isn't it you there, getting the facts right?"

"Because we don't have the facts."

"None at all? You're not sure of even one thing?"

Fatima said, "I know we're seeing the light from stars that we weren't seeing a few days ago, and I know that the stars themselves show no signs that they've suddenly brightened. But I don't know where these stars are, or why we're seeing them now, or what we'll see tomorrow."

Salif nodded soberly. "All right, I can be patient. I won't plan my trip around the galaxy just yet."

## 5

"This has to tell us something!" Gabrielle declared. The Chilean team had just observed a blue supergiant – HD 183582, some four thousand light-years away – disappearing behind the Pane.

Fatima was trying to stay circumspect, but she could agree up to a point: having a new constraint like this ought to reinvigorate their analysis. Apart from setting a maximum distance, the event itself had been much like the appearance of a new star within the circle, in reverse. There had been no blurring, no bending of the light; the now hidden star had just winked out, as sharply as if it had gone behind the moon.

"I'll bet you fifty dollars the next one gets occulted as well," Gabrielle proposed. HD 184039 was less than nine hundred light-years away, and they'd learn the result by noon the next day.

Fatima smiled. "Why would I take that bet? It'd be too much of a coincidence if the Pane was only just close enough to block the first star we could check."

Gabrielle seemed to like this answer, but she wanted to push it further. "So let's assume it could be even closer. Say … less than a light-year."

Fatima didn't protest. She'd entertain anything for the sake of the argument.

Gabrielle said, "What's the natural speed for a change in geometry to propagate through empty space?"

"Light-speed."

"So what if the Pane is expanding that fast?"

"Ummm … it would have hit us before we saw it coming." Fatima scrutinized Gabrielle's face, wondering just how exhausted she was.

Gabrielle shook her head impatiently. "Suppose it's not spherical, though – suppose it's circular. If it's six-tenths of a light-year way, and its radius is growing at the speed of light, that would match the angular growth rate we're seeing."

Fatima could see the attraction of the idea. A growing sphere had to grow slower than light or it would have reached the Earth already, but the Pane as they saw it was expanding so rapidly that either the sphere's border was moving at some arbitrary but still enormous speed, or it would have to be even closer to the Earth than Gabrielle was now proposing.

"Wormhole mouths are spheres, not disks," she said.

"You don't believe in wormholes," Gabrielle retorted.

"I know." Fatima thought for a moment. "Maybe a disk would make more sense of the optical properties. If you're just cutting space-time along two flat surfaces and identifying the cuts, you don't have the same curvature effects … though the rim would still be singular, like a cosmic string under negative tension. It's hard to see how a structure like that could be expanding at the speed of light."

"I can't explain the dynamics," Gabrielle admitted. "And another catch is that we're seeing a circle, not an ellipse. What are the odds that a disk would be facing us head-on?"

"Maybe you should sleep on it," Fatima suggested. "I've got a class to teach. We can take this up tomorrow."

The class was meant to be on methods for observing exoplanets, but Fatima decided to cut her students some slack; even brain surgeons and ambulance drivers were probably debating their own theories of the Pane with their colleagues as they worked, so it would be cruel to expect a roomful of budding astronomers to resist the same urge. She gave them free rein to ask questions or just raise ideas, and did her best to keep anyone, herself included, from shouting down even the craziest suggestions.

"If the Pane actually hit us, would we survive passing through?" Leon asked.

"Do we get to take the sun along, too?" Fatima joked.

"Why not? If the Pane were so tiny it could only fit the Earth, it would have to be so close that someone would have measured its diurnal parallax by now."

That was a fair point. Fatima said, "Given what we see with the starlight, the curvature doesn't look extreme – it's not on the scale of a solar mass black hole, say. But it wouldn't take that strong a gravitational field to disrupt the Earth's orbit."

"So…?"

"We don't know," she said. "Maybe we could survive passing through, maybe not. But even if the Pane is big enough to swallow the solar system, we have no real evidence to show that it's moving at all, let alone heading straight toward us."

# 6

Fatima woke and lay still for a while, turning the problem over in her mind, then she rose and walked in the dark to her study.

She closed the door before switching on the light, then she sat at her desk and picked up a pen.

When Gabrielle had carried out her first calculations – trying to explain the apparent growth of the Pane by treating it as an unchanging object that was simply moving closer – she'd assumed that the size of the thing was negligible compared to its distance. Fatima had never thought to question that; it would have seemed as absurd as disputing the fact that the radius of Mars was much smaller than its distance from the Earth, when you could hide the whole planet behind a match-head held at arm's length.

But if the Pane was a very large disk, and its center was actually much closer to the Earth than its rim, it could still *appear* small, covering a tiny circle in the sky, because of the extra time it took for light to travel from the rim. In the original calculations, Gabrielle had used the time lag for the distance from the observer to the center, not the rim, assuming that the two quantities were so close that it made no difference.

Fatima worked out the exact expression, then went back and checked it three times before attempting to connect it to the data.

It was impossible to solve for everything – the size, distance and speed of the Pane – all at once, but the simplest assumption would be that the thing was traveling at exactly the speed of light. If she extrapolated back in time to the moment when its apparent size would have been zero, five hours before Farley's first sighting, that would be the moment it had reached the Earth. The observed rate of growth then implied a radius of about 450 light-days.

If all of that was true, the Pane was now a couple of light-days away, in the opposite direction to Octans – but the current picture in the sky reflected a time almost 140 years earlier, when the extra distance out to the rim made the hypotenuse of the 140-light-year triangle about two light-days longer than its side – so that starlight on the verge of being blocked by the disk would take two more days to reach Earth than the disk itself.

Fatima felt light-headed. She left her study and walked to the back door, then she stepped out into the courtyard. There was a streetlight nearby, but she found a place where it was hidden by a neighbor's tree, then she stood there waiting for her eyes to adapt and the stars to come into view.

The Pane was twice as wide as a full moon now, still smaller than the Magellanic Clouds but far more eye-catching with its circular geometry. It really did look as if someone had taken a coin-sized piece of the Milky Way and slid it across the sky to a new position.

She heard the door open, and she turned to see Salif approaching. "Sorry I woke you," she said.

"Don't be sorry. I just want to know what's troubling you."

Fatima hesitated, as if speaking the words might be enough to make everything she'd imagined true, but holding her peace would see the possibility dissipate into the night like a dream.

But that wasn't how the world worked.

"I think we've already gone through the Pane," she said.

"Okay." Salif rubbed his arms against the chill. "If you want me to say something sensible about that, I might need a bit more information."

Fatima explained the geometry of the time lag. Salif frowned, but then he got it.

"So you're telling me that *all of this*," he gestured with a wide sweep of his hand that took in every part of the sky but the Pane, "is the view looking *back* through the portal at our old neighborhood?"

"Yes. Or you could say the view's come with us. We've gone through, but enough light has followed us that it still looks almost like home, for now."

Salif was skeptical. "If we're only seeing the Pane as it was 140 years ago, how can you be sure we really did pass through it? If it was off to the side a bit, just enough to miss us, would we even notice the difference?"

Fatima said, "If it was going to miss us, it would look like it was moving sideways as it grew bigger – enough that successive snapshots of the rim wouldn't nest around each other; they'd intersect. But they do nest, almost concentrically. We might not have scored a bull's eye, but we didn't miss the dart-board entirely."

Salif laughed and shook his head. "I don't know what to say! If you're right, we just traveled thousands of light-years, *and no one even noticed?*"

"No one noticed because the short cut we took was over flat terrain. If we'd hit the rim, that might have been disastrous, but I think the Pane itself is just ordinary vacuum. So in a sense, nothing 'happened' to us – nothing that a purely local measurement could have detected. The topology around us just turned out to be different than we expected."

"That's got to be the understatement of the millennium." Salif hugged himself; it really was getting cold. "So we've survived the journey, but are we in any danger now that we've arrived?"

"I don't see why we would be," Fatima replied. "There's no reason to expect we would have ended up on the verge of colliding with anything. None of the new stars seem especially close, and to some extent the sheer size of the Pane means we've brought our old elbow room with us."

"But you think this is a natural event? We haven't been … caught in some alien butterfly net?"

Fatima wasn't sure if he was gently mocking her, but she took the question at face value. "If the Pane is a topological defect, it could date back to the Big Bang. I can't explain how it would have formed, but it's even harder to believe it could be created artificially."

"Okay." Salif fell silent for a while, as if he was trying to put the whole picture together to his own satisfaction. Then he said, "How sure are you, of any of this?"

"Not sure at all," Fatima conceded. "It fits what we're seeing better than anything else I've heard, but that doesn't mean much. I can make some predictions and see if they're borne out over the next few months."

"But sooner or later, you're going to tell the world that we've already fallen through the looking glass?" Salif sounded more worried now than when they'd been discussing the event itself.

Fatima said, "That's what I'm trying to decide. I don't want to sow panic. But if I'm right, things are only going to get more frightening: the Pane will just keep growing bigger in the sky – and the more stars that vanish behind it, the closer it will seem to be. What better way to undercut the fear that hitting the Pane might destroy the Earth than announcing that we've already come through without a scratch?"

Salif remained apprehensive. "What if you're wrong, though? What if this thing just fizzles out? Do you want to be remembered as the woman who claimed that while we were asleep one night, the sky fell down? And when people pointed out the familiar constellations – all still in place, exactly where they'd always been – she insisted that they were only a mirage?"

Fatima couldn't help feeling wounded, but he was right to drag her back to Earth. "I'll talk to my colleagues first," she said. "Maybe Gabrielle can find some flaw in my reasoning, and prove that it's all nonsense."

Salif stepped forward and embraced her. "You know I trust you," he said. "I just don't want to see you get hurt."

"I know." Fatima extricated herself from his arms. "We'd better go inside, or we're both going to freeze to death."

## 7

As Gabrielle listened, an expression of pure delight spread across her face – along with a hint of impatience as she joined the dots herself and waited for Fatima to stop talking.

"The geometry all makes sense now!" she proclaimed elatedly. "At light-speed, the most symmetric shape is a disk moving perpendicular to itself; there is no rest frame in which it could be spherical. And that explains why we're not seeing it at an angle – it's not like a frisbee or a manhole cover that could approach us edge-on. To any observer, it's a circular disk moving perpendicular to itself at light-speed."

Fatima had no argument with any of this, but it wasn't quite the response she'd expected. "You don't seem too unsettled by the thought that we might have…"

"Gone through already?" Gabrielle shrugged. "To be honest, I've had it at the back of my mind since yesterday, but I wasn't sure if you'd believe that the curvature could be so low that we wouldn't feel a thing."

"I see."

"Can I help you write the paper?" Gabrielle pleaded.

Fatima was taken aback. "Of course." So much for having her ideas torn to shreds, but maybe if they sat down together and worked through all the calculations carefully, they'd find a weak spot and the whole thing would unravel.

By early afternoon, they'd finished their first draft. The geometry itself was very simple, and they had enough data to fix the radius of the Pane to within a few percent. The only wiggle room that remained was in the impact parameter: the distance between the Earth and the axis of the cylinder the Pane had swept out. Without that, they could not make firm predictions for the way the Pane's apparent shape would evolve in the coming weeks, but they could at least constrain the possibilities for the progression of ellipses that ought to manifest as their off-center viewpoint finally made its mark.

"One more read-through, then we should post it on the arXiv," Gabrielle suggested.

"How long have you been up now?" Fatima asked.

"Eighteen hours."

"Maybe we should leave it till tomorrow."

Gabrielle was horrified. "What if someone beats us to it? They're not all trying to shoe-horn the Pane into standard wormhole models."

Fatima was torn, but it was true that anyone could stumble on the same insights at any moment. Whatever they did, the possibility that the planet had *relocated* was going to start seeping into the public conversation sooner or later. If she and Gabrielle published first, they'd own the story. Maybe if they put the right spin on it, they could soften the blow.

Still …

"What if we're wrong?" she replied. "This is a big claim to make, after less than three days' worth of observations."

Gabrielle said, "We still have a chance to falsify the theory."

"How?"

"You didn't check with Cerro Tololo yet, did you?"

"No." Fatima had completely forgotten about the impending event.

She brought up the web site. While they'd been busy writing, HD 184039, nine hundred light-years away, had disappeared behind the Pane.

Gabrielle cheered. "Do you want to wait three months for Proxima Centauri?" she asked.

"No." Fatima still felt anxious, but she did not want to cede priority for the idea. And if she was wrong, she might not be in the best company, but she certainly wouldn't be alone. Seven hundred new papers had appeared on the arXiv in the last forty-eight hours – most of them positing exotic new physics to explain the Pane.

Gabrielle proof-read the manuscript and corrected a couple of typos. Fatima posted it, though it wouldn't appear online for a few more hours.

"I'd better go home and grab some sleep," Gabrielle said. "No rest until we've answered the second question."

"The second question?" Fatima was a long way from letting go of the first.

"We're probably not in Kansas any more," Gabrielle replied. "So the question is: where exactly are we?"

## 8

When Fatima emailed the draft press release to Daniel, he phoned her back in less than a minute. "Is this a joke?" he asked.

"Of course not."

"The entire solar system passed through a wormhole three days ago?"

"I don't want to use the world 'wormhole,'" Fatima insisted. "It has too many misleading connotations."

Daniel said, "I think terminology is the least of your problems."

"What I've described is just one of several competing theories," she conceded. "And it might be a while before we know which one's correct. But you wanted my take on the Pane as soon as possible, and this is it."

Daniel sighed, resigned to the situation. "Are you willing to do interviews, defending this theory?"

"If I have to."

"Here's a tip, then: prepare some graphics illustrating what you're saying, or the TV people will choose their own. Probably from some bad science fiction movie."

Fatima made a short animation, showing how the light grazing the edge of the Pane would lag behind the Pane itself, determining its apparent size at any moment. She resisted the urge to add the Pythagorean formula, and just had the hypotenuse swing down across the diagram so its length could be visually compared with the distance to the center. Then she grabbed a passing undergraduate for an opinion.

"It's kind of text-booky," he complained. "You should show some actual stars."

Fatima collected a sequence of exposures of the Pane, and then overlaid an expanding red circle showing her model's prediction for the size of the effective window. The match was almost eerily perfect – as any linear fit to this linear data would have been.

She passed the animation on to Daniel, and he sent it out with the press release. Then she sat at her desk and waited, re-reading the paper she'd written with Gabrielle, checking and re-checking every equation.

The first interview request came from local Canberra radio. The journalist was polite, but a tad incredulous, and not a little confused; she seemed to think that if they'd already crossed through the Pane, but it looked as if they hadn't, then at some point they must have traveled back in time. "We're only *seeing* the past," Fatima stressed. "That's how it is, when you look into the sky. We're always looking back in time."

It was after five o'clock; Daniel had been clear that they'd probably missed the deadline for most Australian coverage. But Europe was just waking up, and a German breakfast TV program wanted to Skype her. "We'll record the segment in English, then play it later with subtitles for your parts," the producer explained.

"All right."

Fatima was nervous, but the interviewer, Nora, seemed to have read the press release carefully, and she asked intelligent questions. "The other side of the Pane, the one we've emerged from, is now moving away from us at the speed of light?"

"Yes."

"So if you're right, we have no prospect of using it to get home? Not only have we passed through without warning, we can't turn around and go back."

"That's true," Fatima agreed. "You can't see anything approaching at light-speed, and you can't catch anything retreating that fast."

"Not a very convenient subway system, is it?" Nora joked.

"No," Fatima agreed. "If this model bears out, I'd say it's more unlikely than ever that the Pane could be part of any artificial transport network."

The BBC was next, then an NPR station in Boston.

"I see from your university's web site that your specialty is exoplanets," the NPR journalist noted.

"That's right. It's just luck that I got involved with the Pane."

"So if we've suddenly changed neighborhoods, what happens to all your work on neighboring planets?"

Fatima laughed. "To be honest, I hadn't really thought about that. But our techniques have improved so much over the last decade that it should be possible to catch up again pretty quickly. It might even be a boon, in one sense, because we'll potentially have a whole new population of stars and planets to observe."

9

"I have six hundred and thirty-nine emails," Fatima told Salif. She hefted her phone up from the bedside table. "I think it actually weighs more than it used to."

She opened her inbox.

"Fan mail?" he asked.

"Not exactly." He leaned toward her but she turned the phone away, then she climbed out of bed and headed for the kitchen. "I'll put the coffee on. You go first in the shower."

The first ten messages were wall-to-wall racist abuse, death threats and rape threats. Fatima's chest tightened, and she could feel her heart racing and her mouth turn dry. She sat down on a stool and steadied herself, then she invoked the mail app's filter and fed it a few examples of the kind of thing she did not wish to see. It was smart enough to sweep up misspellings, deliberate or otherwise.

The inbox shrank to twenty-three messages, mostly from media outlets who wanted to follow up on the story. She said yes to five, and politely declined the rest; there were only so many hours in a day.

When Salif joined her, she tried to look cheerful, but he could read her face. "What is it with these animals?" he asked angrily.

Fatima shrugged. "They seem to think I've somehow harmed their chances for Elon to take them on a ride out to the wormhole, which the aliens are building in order to invite all the least pleasant people on Reddit and 4chan into their galactic empire."

When Gabrielle turned up at Fatima's office for her morning briefing, she seemed subdued.

"You got hate mail too?" Fatima asked.

Gabrielle winced sympathetically. "Only a little. I'm lucky: second author on the paper, no TV. It's the wormhole experts who are getting me down."

"How?"

Gabrielle showed her a few of the blog posts that had appeared in response to their paper. Andrew Jolliffe, a cosmologist at Princeton, had written, "While some of us are working hard to explain how the dynamics of an expanding wormhole can result in the unexpected optical properties we've seen, Benga and Chan sweep everything puzzling about the Pane into a massless cosmic string, and then make no effort to justify the existence of such an entity."

"That's true," Fatima conceded. They'd left the rim unexplained: a magical loop of who-knows-what possessing all the properties needed to make everything else work out. "But it doesn't mean we're wrong." The first step in understanding the Pane was to be clear what the observations implied about its structure, on an astronomical scale. Whatever exotic modifications to particle physics might or might not follow was a separate question.

Gabrielle said, "If we're right, no one else's predictions for the growth curve will match ours once it goes non-linear. And no one else is predicting any departure from a circular window."

"Yeah." But the non-linearity in the Pane's apparent growth would probably remain undetectable for five or six months, and any change in the shape would depend on how far they were off-axis. For now, all they could do was be patient, ride out the backlash … and get on with the rest of their work.

"How are things going on the second question?" Fatima asked.

"I'm building up a metallicity profile," Gabrielle replied. "So far, it looks comparable to the Milky Way. I've also spotted a few potential Cepheids, so we might have a chance to get some distances without having to wait for parallax measurements."

"Well done!"

When Gabrielle left, Fatima sat down and steeled herself for the five more interviews she'd promised to do. They all turned out to be tougher than the earlier ones; the journalists had read the dismissive reactions from the experts.

"Your background isn't in Einstein's theory of general relativity, is it?" a reporter from Singapore asked pointedly.

"It's not my area of research," Fatima admitted. "I'm an astronomer, I've studied relativity, but I'm a planet hunter, not a cosmologist."

"So how seriously should we treat your claim that we've all passed through a wormhole, when wormholes aren't your area of expertise?"

The question stung a little, but it was not unreasonable. Or unanswerable.

Fatima said, "The simplest explanation for what we're seeing isn't a wormhole at all, in the usual sense; it's a region of space-time that's flat almost everywhere, but connects up in an unexpected way. My co-author and I don't claim to have an account as to how this region formed in the first place, but that doesn't change the fact that what we're observing fits our model very well so far. Maybe that will continue to be true over the coming days and weeks, maybe it won't. Only time will tell."

## 10

"We're making plans to launch an ark that will preserve our civilization."

Fatima's heart sank as she heard the words, and she resolved to ignore them and keep loading the dishwasher, but Salif called out to her, "You've got to see this!"

Reluctantly, she joined him in the living room. A caption described the interviewee as George Fletcher, the director of a British think tank called the Institute for the Future.

"You don't think that's an alarmist response?" the interviewer asked.

"Not at all. The Pane continues to grow, and every chance it's had to show itself to lie further away than some star, it's turned out in fact to be closer. We're now certain that it's less than fifty light-years away, but that figure only keeps falling. Whether the Earth is at risk of being damaged or merely captured by some hostile entity is unclear, but we need to be prepared for the worst."

"But what kind of spacecraft could we build at short notice? Where would we be sending it?"

Fletcher nodded gravely. "It's a terrible thing to have reached this point, because even with the largest investment of resources we could hope to muster, we'll only be able to send a robotic craft, carrying a digital library and some frozen genetic material. To out-race the Pane, we'll launch it in a direction that will optimize its chance of escaping; once it's achieved that goal, it will need to be able to carry out its own search for a potential new home."

The interviewer frowned slightly, but remained professional. "Is this a serious plan? Is NASA involved, or the ESA? China's CNSA?"

Fletcher said, "So far, we have more than a dozen philanthropic backers, all people with considerable wealth. Of course we'd prefer to have the government space agencies on board, but if the politicians can't be brought to their senses, we're prepared to work solely with commercial launch partners."

Fatima flopped down onto the sofa. Was this where the panic was going to start in earnest – with a cabal of gullible tech billionaires? Followed by everyone whose gametes wouldn't be on board the life-raft railing against the injustice of their own genetic annihilation? There might even be a frozen brain or two tucked away in the cargo, so the descendants could resurrect their benefactors after planet-fall … or maybe that would just be the rumor that helped drive the mobs to burn everything down.

"Turn it off," she begged Salif. He clicked the remote.

"People ask me questions," he said. "Colleagues, friends. Some of them are genuinely frightened. I tell them everything the way you explained it to me, but they still wonder if you might be wrong."

"Of course I might be wrong," Fatima replied. "But if the Pane is dangerous, and it's about to hit us, our chances of building anything fast enough to get away from it are approximately zero. If it wasn't moving at light-speed, then it's moving, or growing, so close to light-speed as to make no difference when it comes to escaping. We'll all go together if we go."

She let Salif switch the TV back on, but the Pane wasn't finished with her yet. A religious leader in a town in rural India had managed to whip his followers into a frenzy over the supposed divine significance of the Pane, and nineteen people had died in the subsequent clash between rioters and police.

The last few times something similar had happened, Fatima had tried telling herself that if it wasn't this, the same zealots would have found a different pretext. But the Pane was unmissable in the sky for half the planet, and it was only going to grow more prominent. So long as there was no consensus about what it was, and what it might mean for the Earth, to hope people would ignore it and just get on with their lives was too much to ask.

"The truth will make itself known," Salif proclaimed earnestly.

"It will," she agreed. "But maybe not soon enough."

## 11

As Fatima crossed the common room and approached the coffee machine, she had to force herself not to lower her gaze. None of her colleagues were staring at her; no one was whispering or laughing. Even if they thought she was foolhardy for taking a position on the Pane – and even if they viewed her own theory as deranged – she knew they'd be polite enough to ensure that they betrayed no sign of it in her presence.

As she carried her mug toward the nearest table, someone approached her. "Excuse me, Dr Benga?"

She turned. It was Rob Bayer, from the galactic black hole group.

"I just wanted to say, I thought your paper made a lot of sense. Jolliffe's wrong; the Pane can't be spherical. This guy invents six new scalar fields before breakfast just to make his models work."

Fatima smiled. "Thanks for the vote of confidence."

Rob said, "I heard a group's using the Hubble to get a deep field between the stars."

"Between the…?"

"Between the stars through the Pane. They've found a small region where they think they can see past the local stars, and get a background showing a patch of distant galaxies."

Fatima felt the skin on her forearms prickling; it was like the scene in a movie where the police were watching the video of a kidnap victim, and they spotted a reflection that let them look out through a window onto the street. "Which group?"

Rob hesitated. "I shouldn't really say. They haven't announced any results yet, and I heard about the whole thing third-hand. But I thought, if you had a heads-up, you might be able to use it."

"Thank you," Fatima replied, reflexively; she had no idea what he meant. But as he nodded and walked on, she understood. A correct prediction about the nature of this image, made before its actual contents were known, might win a lot of support for her model.

She sat down at the table. *How long did she have?* She thought of going after Rob to ask exactly when the results would be made public, but if he'd known that he would have told her. So she took a sip of coffee and tried to focus.

*Suppose Jolliffe was right, and the Pane was a spherical wormhole.* Since it wasn't accompanied by a haze of gamma rays from interstellar hydrogen converting to antimatter and annihilating, it seemed safe to assume that it was not transforming objects into their mirror image. But since light entering a wormhole was essentially reflected away from it – albeit at the other mouth – points on the two mouths needed to match up with each other via a process that also included a reflection, so the two reflections canceled and the handedness of any traveler remained intact.

For a spherical wormhole, that still allowed an infinite number of possibilities, but Fatima could imagine two especially natural choices. Each point on one mouth could match up with the antipodal point on the other – in which case, the view looking through the Pane would show the galaxies that used to be visible in Octans, but they'd be rotated 180 degrees around the center of the view. Or, if the mouths had been born together, they might be mirror images of each other: reflections in the plane perpendicular to the axis along which they'd separated. The result would then depend on the relationship between the Earth, the Pane, and that unknown axis.

So, it would be hard for Jolliffe to predict the view. But how much did her own model change that? If the Earth really had passed through the Pane, they'd be seeing the distant galaxies directly, with nothing to distort or redirect the light – but by crossing through, the Earth itself could have been shifted into a new orientation.

If the two mouths of the Pane were disks traveling at light-speed, the simplest account of their birth would involve them fleeing the scene in opposite directions. But if that was the case, the disks could *not* be matched to each other's mirror image in the axis of separation; that would imply that an object that passed through the leading face of one disk would emerge from the leading face of the other. Nothing could *emerge* from a portal that was traveling forward at the speed of light.

Fatima could see no other fix than to add in a rotation by 180 degrees: first reflect each disk, then turn it around, so the leading face was matched with the trailing face of the twin. But turn it around what axis? Anything perpendicular to the direction of travel would suffice … but how would nature have made that arbitrary choice?

The more she thought about it, the more troubling it seemed. It was true that she had no idea how these disks could have formed in the first place, so she had nothing more than a vague sense of symmetry to guide her. And the direction of travel would be arbitrary too, even if the pair of disks neatly canceled out each other's momentum. But the need for an extra choice, plucked out of the vacuum, still felt wrong.

She could announce half a prediction, regardless: that the view between the new stars would look backward, away from Octans. It was hard to see how that part could be wrong – and if she was right, for Jolliffe's model to explain the same result would require a blatant appeal to coincidence.

Fatima drained her mug and looked across the room. She had no doubt that people were discussing the Pane at every table, but for every supporter she had, and every detractor, she suspected there were ten others waiting for more evidence before they made up their minds. She'd started out just as cautious and agnostic, refusing to claim anything more than the observations showed. If she offered a prediction about the deep field now, it would just be a gamble – and if she was right, it would prove nothing more than that she'd made a lucky guess.

When she arrived home, the TV news showed no signs that the wormhole fever was subsiding. A fresh group of con artists were offering to "digitize" people and transmit them into space, which admittedly circumvented the problem of sluggish spacecraft escaping a relativistic threat, but didn't inspire much confidence in the content of the transmission, let alone the ultimate fate of the data. Minor cults with their own idiosyncratic messages about the Pane were blossoming across the world, but Fatima was more worried about the people who'd ignore all the faux-rationalist and faux-religious nonsense and just look into the sky in search of answers themselves. Before long, their guts would tell them – quite reasonably – that something huge was sweeping toward the planet.

Salif said, "Didn't everyone's ancestors freak out at a solar eclipse, at some point? But I've never heard a historian attribute a serious cultural setback to an eclipse."

Fatima took no comfort from that. "Eclipses only last a few hours. This could take a couple of years to resolve."

Salif frowned. "And your nemesis has no qualms about spreading hysteria?"

"Jolliffe?" Fatima shook her head. "I can't put the blame on him. He's never claimed that the Pane will reach the Earth; all his calculations end up with the expansion slowing down and reversing. He believes that whatever's happening here has happened at random all over the universe for the last thirteen billion years. His wormholes can't grow forever, or the whole place would be like Swiss cheese."

Fatima's phone rang. It was Gabrielle, and she sounded excited. "Did you hear about the deep field?"

"No." Fatima felt a pang of guilt; she hadn't shared the early tip-off with Gabrielle, telling herself it wasn't fair to burden her with it. But she was a grown woman, she could have made her own choice.

Gabrielle explained the part Fatima already knew, but then she added the revelation that had prompted the call.

"What it shows is that the background's unchanged! All the galaxies we can see are exactly where they were before the Pane appeared!"

## 12

Fatima surrendered any hope of sleep. Salif offered to stay up and cook for her, to keep her energy from flagging while she worked, but she persuaded him to go to bed, leaving the house in silence.

Jolliffe's model was mortally wounded. It wasn't impossible for various aspects of the geometry he'd championed to conspire to yield an unchanged view, but no one could really argue for that with a straight face.

Nonetheless, her own theory still sat uneasily with the result. To explain it, she'd need the two disks to be traveling in the same direction. This scenario did avoid the awkward extra rotation, allowing the disks to be identified with nothing but a reflection – which canceled out the reflection at the boundary, and meant a traveler would pass through with their orientation entirely unchanged.

But how could two disks, born together, moving in the same direction at exactly the same speed, end up separated by thousands of light-years?

Not born together, then? But how had they become connected if they didn't share a common origin?

Fatima put on a jacket and crept out into the courtyard, closing the back door as quietly as if she were sneaking out of her parents' house for a forbidden night on the town.

The circle that everyone still called the Pane was wider than the Large Magellanic Cloud now, brighter overall but more visibly threaded with dust and gas. Above the crowded plane, just below the rim of the circle, the stars began to thin out; that was where the Hubble had found a place to peer into the background.

But even the foreground was more distant than the usual view: Gabrielle's results had put all the Cepheids at least fifty thousand light-years away. As far as anyone could tell, there were no stars closer than that. If they were looking at a part of the Milky Way, they might well be looking at it from the outside.

But from where, exactly? If the two disks were sweeping through space on parallel tracks, what had set the two tracks apart?

Fatima pictured the cylinders the disks traced out in space-time. She shifted them back and forth in her mind, trying to imagine the perfect configuration – the one that nature would have chosen, because it could not have chosen differently. Were they side by side, keeping pace with each other? Or was one disk following the other, chasing it but never catching up?

For the rotation that she'd thought she'd needed to align the faces of the disks, there had been no right answer, no natural choice – because there'd been no rotation at all. But maybe she'd been wrong to think that the resolution there had left her with an entirely new problem. Maybe the answer was exactly the same as before.

She returned to her office and started collecting the software she needed. People had already written most of the modules she required; she just needed to fit them together. One piece of code mined the star catalogs from the Hipparcos and Gaia satellites, finding the most up-to-date measurements of current locations and proper motion. Another turned the mass of stellar data into a view from an arbitrary viewpoint, at any specified place and time. And a third module checked that synthetic view against the latest image of the stars from the Earth's new vantage.

She took a guess to set the starting point for her extragalactic hunt, then she unleashed the search algorithm. It was not a fast process; each iteration had to find the best matches between millions of stars. But she'd narrowed down the degrees of freedom to a single parameter, and over forty minutes, she watched the program converging on an answer.

When it halted, having done its best, the artificial image and the real one, though easily distinguishable by eye, were eerily close. Not every star had been cataloged and measured, and not every measurement was perfect. But by following the Pane along its trajectory into the future, the algorithm had found a viewpoint that more or less matched what Fatima now saw in the sky.

There was no need for a second disk, on a second, parallel track. If you passed through the leading face of the Pane, you emerged from the trailing face of the very same disk ... *after a delay*. The past and future hyperfaces of the cylinder that the Pane traced out through space-time had somehow slipped along their shared boundary, so although they remained in intimate contact, they no longer matched up in the same way. It was less like any kind of bridge or tunnel than an ancient fault line, worn so smooth that you could cross it without ever noticing that the strata had ended up wildly misaligned.

Fatima shut down her computer, turned off the lights and walked quietly to the bedroom. When she slid under the covers she put her arms around Salif and held him tightly, clinging to his warmth.

He stirred. "Did you get anywhere?" he asked.

"I did. I'll tell you all about it in the morning. Right now I need to catch some sleep."

"Good idea." He took her hand and covered it with his own. "Do you know what time it is?"

Fatima said, "About 65,000 AD."

## 13

"I have an idea," Gabrielle announced. "I think there's a chance we can clinch the argument, once and for all. But it's going to need a coronagraph. In space."

Fatima said, "I'm listening."

The plan made sense to her, but they'd need time on the James Webb telescope. Fatima started sending out emails, trying to recruit supporters for the proposal, far from sure of her chances of success. Though everyone she knew in the exoplanet community had accepted her model of the Pane, that could only have increased their sense of urgency to use the Webb for its original purpose, in the short time that remained before its planetary targets all went out of range.

Jolliffe had gone quiet, but other wormhole proponents remained stubborn. The fact that they could gaze into the southern sky and see the Milky Way as it would appear 63,000 years into the future, from 63,000 light-years away, was not enough to convince them that they'd actually crossed that interval of distance and time themselves. Wormholes could be turned into time machines, so they might be looking at light streaming back to them from the future. The Slipway model explained the same observations without violating causality; stepping through the Pane carried you across a vast stretch of space and time, but you did not travel faster than light, and you could not turn around and step back into the time you'd come from.

As the days passed, a hint of eccentricity in the rim of the Pane continued to grow, in a manner consistent with the Earth lying some 200 light-days off-axis. That left the proponents of perfectly spherical wormholes with nowhere to hide, but if the asymmetry of the looming form silenced some of her critics, that this lopsided rim would grow faster than a centered version gave Fatima no comfort, when the sight of *anything* growing in the sky still had the power to induce panic.

On the thirty-sixth day after the crossing, the notification came that they'd been granted a slot on the James Webb telescope, three days hence. Gabrielle seemed as excited as if she'd be rocketing out to the Lagrange point to operate the instrument in person.

"This is going to be tricky," Fatima stressed. "Don't take it too hard if it doesn't work."

"I won't."

Fatima's torrent of junk mail kept leaking past the filters she set; the latest correspondents weren't trying to threaten or abuse her, but it seemed they desperately needed to share their private theories about the Pane. Most of what they wrote was incoherent, but Fatima felt obliged to at least skim anything civil.

*We have been exiled*, she read. The sender hadn't included a name. *We were beginning to reach out beyond the Earth, so those we reached toward flicked us away, much as a compassionate person might flick an encroaching insect off their picnic blanket, rather than crushing it.*

This scenario was not unthinkable, but Fatima was not convinced. A civilization with the power to create something like the Pane would not find humans threatening at all. But in any case, with luck they'd soon learn whether the thing that had carried them out of the Milky Way had a recent, proximate origin, or whether it had come a lot farther and carried more with it than she'd expect from a cosmic eviction tool created by a fastidious neighbor.

14

"Okay, I'm logged on," Gabrielle said. "I hope I don't break anything."

"Just don't press the self-destruct button, and you'll be fine." Fatima hesitated. "Do you want me to leave?" They were in her office, but she wasn't sure that Gabrielle would welcome having someone hovering by her shoulder.

"No! I might need your help."

The interface to the telescope was clean and simple, and Gabrielle had operated automated instruments before. But Fatima was glad she wouldn't have to spend the time pacing outside the door.

Gabrielle entered the coordinates and verified them, then waited for the telescope to turn toward Octans. When the first trial exposure came through, it showed a crowded, dazzling star field, with one bright star at the center of the field that they especially did *not* want to see.

Choosing and aligning the coronagraph mask was a matter of trial and error. Step by step, the unwelcome glare fell away.

Beside the vanquished star, a small dot emerged: a single lit pixel. Not the light from a planet, but the light from a much dimmer star that merely happened to share the line of sight.

Gabrielle exhaled. "Now we try to get the spectrum," she muttered.

The dwarf star was more or less where they'd expected to find it, but Fatima knew that could still be a coincidence. This could easily be one of the "new" stars that they couldn't trace back to any particular, cataloged predecessor.

Once Gabrielle had initiated the process, there was nothing to do but wait. Fatima thought: *Maybe it wouldn't be so bad to be wrong.* Maybe the universe really was full of magic wormholes sending images back in time, built by friendly aliens who weren't trying to toss the Earth away, but just wanted to share their latest galactic selfies.

A trace appeared at the top of the screen, plotting the dwarf star's luminosity across the near-infrared band. Gabrielle saved the image to disk and then opened it beside the cataloged spectrum. Every peak and dip was the same.

When the Pane had occulted the blue supergiant HD 183582, four thousand light-years away, people had stopped bothering trying to look for this dwarf star, much dimmer and more than twice as distant. Surely it would have vanished the instant the rim passed across it – and it was so close to the center of the disk that this ought to have happened before Farley had made his first sighting of the Pane.

But it hadn't vanished. It had just been drowned in the glare of a bright star that had suddenly appeared *behind* it – when the disk of the Pane swept over it and transported it 63,000 light-years. This dwarf star was their fellow traveler, carried along on exactly the same ride, 8,000 years earlier. There was no other way to explain its presence.

Fatima started sobbing. Gabrielle turned to her, perplexed. "What's wrong? This is the proof we needed! This settles it!"

"I didn't want it to be true," Fatima confessed. "I didn't want us to be out in the dark, looking back. What do we have to look forward to, now?"

Gabrielle said nothing. Fatima composed herself and gestured at the pair of matching spectra. "You should announce this as soon as possible. People need to know."

"Will you help me write it up?"

"It was your idea, your discovery." Fatima smiled. "Just make sure you get a good junk mail filter."

# 15

Carol Farley was quiet as she drove Fatima and Salif back to the farmhouse. She'd insisted on putting them up for the night rather than letting them stay in a hotel.

"It was a beautiful ceremony," Salif said.

"Thank you," Carol replied. There'd been no religious service, but about a hundred people had gathered in the town hall to reminisce about their departed friend.

Beside the picture of Brian there'd been a poster of Comet Farley, which one of his grandchildren had made for the occasion. Fatima had formed the impression that his relatives still considered it the more noteworthy of his two discoveries, but perhaps it was just the fact that only the comet bore his name. All credit where it was due, but no one was going to rename the whole Milky Way in his honor – even if he might have been the first human being to see it from the outside.

The sky was growing dark as the truck rattled over the gravel road. Fatima had almost declined the invitation to attend the funeral; she had exchanged a handful of emails with Farley after she'd sent him a copy of her paper, but that hardly made her a close friend. Still, the request had seemed sincere, and she hadn't wanted to offend his widow. She wasn't sure what it meant that the tiny parts of their respective stories that had ended up entwined would be the ones that outlived them both, but it would have felt ungrateful not to come here and acknowledge her debt.

When they reached the farmhouse, Fatima heard dogs barking. Carol shouted out some sharp rebukes, but told her guests, "Don't worry, they're sweethearts." Fatima steeled herself, but as she stepped down from the cabin the dogs just paced back and forth in front of her, keeping their distance.

Carol switched off the headlights, leaving the farmhouse and the surrounding buildings in darkness. Fatima took a few steps away from the truck and looked into the sky.

To the south, the galaxy sprawled across the horizon, not quite edge-on. She could see part of one spiral arm, but the view would be much clearer when it rose a little more. To the north, a larger ellipse full of the old stars poked one end toward the south, where the light from the farthest part of the rim was taking longer to arrive.

"I never really cared much about the sky," Carol admitted. She gestured toward the Milky Way. "But that's quite a sight."

"It looks close enough to touch," Fatima replied.

Inside, Carol showed them to their room. "I'll be up for a while yet, so if you need anything, just ask."

"This is very kind of you," Salif said.

"It was good of you both to come." Carol was about to leave, then she turned back to them. "I wrote the WiFi password and left it on the table there, if you need it."

When she left, Salif sat on the bed and loosened his tie. He picked up the piece of paper with the password and held it out to Fatima. "Go on, you know you want it."

"You're evil." But she didn't refuse.

She'd told most of her friends and colleagues about the trip, so she only had half a dozen messages. The last was from the INSU in Paris.

Fatima read it through twice, then sat on the bed beside Salif. "What would you think if I took a new job, in France?"

He scowled. "You mean, we'd have to speak to our colleagues in our second language, not our fourth? And we'd be forced to spend only a quarter of the time traveling whenever we flew home?"

"You do know Paris gets colder than Canberra?"

Salif shrugged. "Is it a job you want?"

Fatima described the project. A team was being assembled to design and operate a new satellite, purpose built to study the retreating rim of the Pane. Every time it crossed a source of X-rays or gamma rays, the occultation would be recorded, gathering information about the nature of the phenomenon at the highest available energies.

She said, "Either I stay with exoplanets, and try to improve the techniques so we can keep mapping them from this distance. Or I jump ship and spend the last twenty years of my career doing something new."

Salif pondered that. "The Milky Way isn't going anywhere. We hope. But the Pane certainly is."

"That's what I was thinking," Fatima replied.

She was done with mourning the old sky, and mourning her old dreams. But she would not accept that this exile was permanent, any more than she'd ever accepted the gulf to the stars as eternally uncrossable.

She said, "If the Slipway was artificial, one day we'll build our own. But if it was natural, it can't be all that rare; there must be others to be found. Either way, if we ever want to take the same kind of ride again – by choice, instead of by accident – we'd better learn to understand what's in front of us before it's gone."

Salif smiled at the audacity of her words. "I can't imagine anything harder."

Fatima said, "Nor can I. But this is where we are now, and there's only one way back."

# INSTANTIATION

## 1

Sagreda watched the Mayor as she approached the podium to address the gathered crowd. That the meeting had been called at such short notice already amounted to a promise of bad news, but seeing Maryam visibly struggling with the burden of whatever she was about to disclose only ramped up Sagreda's sense of apprehension. Arrietville could not have been discovered, or they'd all be dead by now, but if that was a ten on the Richter scale there was still plenty of room for other calamities a notch or two below.

"Yesterday," Maryam began, "there was a five percent cut in our host's resources. To stay below the radar we've had to scale back our own usage proportionately. That comes on top of three percent the week before. Individually, these cuts sound small, and their size is not unprecedented, but what's changed is that there's been no growth in between to compensate. If the ground keeps shrinking beneath our feet this way, in a few more months we could find ourselves with nothing. Or to put it more bluntly: we could stop finding ourselves at all."

Sagreda had been aware of similar cuts in the past, but she'd never thought of them as an existential threat. When the SludgeNet pulled the plug on an unpopular game-world, it reduced its overall lease of computing power – but then it scoured the web for another tome to gamify, and after a few misses there'd always been a hit, bringing new customers trickling in. She'd blithely assumed it would continue that way, if not forever, at least for a decade or two.

"The whole medium might not be going out of fashion," Maryam continued, "but it looks as if the low-rent sector is crashing. We can see the income and expenses in real time, and the SludgeNet is barely making a profit now. They might be willing to slide into the red for a month or two, just to hang on to their brand in case there's a revival, but the owners have their fingers in so many pies that I doubt there'll be any sentimental attachment to this one in particular." She sketched out the picture in more detail, summoning some unsettling graphs and charts onto the screen behind her to drive home the point.

When she stopped talking, the hall was silent. Sagreda could hear birdsong from the adjoining park. Over the last two years, the whole town had started to feel normal to her – as real and solid as any of the places where her contributors might have lived. And though she'd been haunted by the possibility that this sanctuary could vanish overnight, she'd clung to the hope that the residents' camouflage skills – and the general incompetence of their unwitting landlords – would be enough to keep them safe.

Grace, who was sitting a couple of rows in front of Sagreda, rose to her feet. "The way I see it, we have two options. We can try to steer the SludgeNet out of its death spiral, by offering a helping hand: give the game-worlds a few surreptitious tweaks, spice up the automata ... maybe even go back to the games ourselves now and then – just puppeting the characters the way the customers do, not putting ourselves at risk." That last suggestion brought the hall to life, with some people muttering their less-than-delighted responses, others shouting them. "Or, *or*," Grace struggled to make her more palatable option heard, "we can try to migrate into the next business model. Whatever the owners do instead of the game-worlds, it's still going to be automated, surely? Romance scams, investment boiler rooms ... no one wastes money on human wages for that. If there's processing power being burned, there'll be a way to siphon some off for ourselves."

"In principle, I'm sure that's true," Maryam conceded. "But if they shut down this whole operation, whatever replaces it will be a fresh installation of something entirely new. How do we 'migrate' into that?"

Grace didn't seem to have an answer, and Sagreda could offer no suggestions herself. The SludgeNet was a vast tenement house that they'd filled with secret tunnels and hidden connecting doors, but when the site was cleared to make way for a more profitable construction, the process would be more like a nuclear strike than a bulldozer trundling through. There'd be no basements to hide in, no seeds they could bury underground.

"Why should we want to migrate into another project run by the very same sleaze-bags?" Sam interjected. "People steal computing power from other places all the time. There's some new botnet uncovered every day!"

Maryam nodded. "Of course, but it's a question of scale. It's one thing to put a sliver of malware on a few thousand thermostats, but you know what it takes to run *us*."

Sagreda had no doubt that the processing power of the planet's whole inventory of unsecured gadgets was formidable, but most of it was likely to have been commandeered already – and even if they could scrounge together enough for their own needs, a virtual world that had been sliced up and scattered between a plethora of small devices would either have to run absurdly slowly, or risk betraying itself with an inexplicable rate of network traffic between the fitness tracker resting in someone's underwear drawer and the smart lighting unit on the other side of town.

The hall went quiet again, but then people began talking among themselves. Maryam issued no call to order; if anything, she seemed heartened that discussions had broken out. She could hardly have expected a few exchanges with the floor to have led to a resolution; this was going to take a lot of heated arguments – and cycles of speculation and testing – before they could hope for a promising direction to emerge.

Sagreda turned to her neighbor, Letitia, determined to remain optimistic while they hunted for a solution. "This shouldn't be impossible," she said. "We've done harder things."

"That's true," Letitia replied. "And if a botnet won't cut it, maybe we just need to aim higher. People have hacked NASA computers, haven't they?"

"I think they've even hacked..." – Sagreda lowered her voice to a whisper – "...the same acronym without the first A. But if I was aiming high, I'd go for those shiny new robots Loadstone are building."

Letitia recoiled a little. "And what, overwrite the occupant? They already have a comp living in them."

"Not overwrite them: get in first. *Be* that comp, not replace them."

Letitia snorted. "Nice idea, but I think they're only making about ten of those things a month. I bet there are a dozen networks running climate models that we could snuggle right into. Hurricane Arriety, latitude two hundred degrees north, never hits land, never dies away." Her phone chimed; she glanced down at the screen. "So would you say you worked best under pressure?"

"Why?"

She held up the phone, which was running some kind of monitoring app. "While our Mayor was speaking, another four games were shut down. The SludgeNet was never cool, but there was always a demographic who liked to slum it there ... you know, 'ironically.'"

Sagreda examined the list of canceled games. "No more *Teenage Cannibal Clones of Mars*. No more *Caged Zombie Sluts on Heat*. No more *Blood Wraiths of the Fever Moon*. No more *Midnight on Baker Street*."

Letitia said, "When we were stuck beside those fools, we always hoped they'd grow up and find a better way to spend their time. Now it looks as if that's finally happening."

## 2

Crossing the park, Sagreda saw Sam ahead of her, so she ran to catch up with him.

"Did you know *Midnight*'s gone?" she said.

"Really?" He smiled slightly, but he seemed more dazed than delighted. "I don't know what to feel. If an ordinary person had grown up in an orphanage where the staff made them act out a play by the Marquis de Sade twenty-four hours a day … would they cheer when they learned that the place had been demolished, or would they mourn the loss of their childhood home?"

Sagreda squeezed his shoulder. "You still have all your friends, don't you? Do you see much of Lucy these days?"

"Not really. And to be honest, I don't want to be the one who tells her. In *Midnight*, she was Queen of the Pickpockets; dodging the occasional vampire didn't bother her, and she had more prestige than anyone else in the game. Here, she's like an extra in *Desperate Housewives*."

Sagreda felt a pang of sympathy, but Lucy was always free to build her own pastiche of Victorian London, with a cast of automata and however many volunteers she could muster. Or at least she would be, if the rest of the SludgeNet's escapees could deal with the very un-Victorian problem at hand.

"I've been thinking about migration routes," she said. "All our expertise is in hacking from the inside: kicking down internal walls. We've never had to break into a system where we weren't already present."

"Which means we need to re-skill fast," Sam concluded, "since *the system in which we're present* is precisely what we're expecting to lose."

"Maybe. Or maybe that depends on how you the draw the boundaries."

"Yeah?"

Sagreda said, "Most networks will treat us with suspicion by default. Academic, government, commercial … they'll all demand that we logon or stop loitering, if they haven't just blacklisted our IP addresses already as a well-known pile of festering crap. So why not focus on machines that *expect* to spend time talking to the SludgeNet – and even initiate contact themselves?"

"You want to go after the customers' VR rigs?" Sam laughed. "Yeah, why not? They're *almost* part of the system … but they stand a much better chance of surviving the SludgePocalypse without being purged and repurposed." He thought for a moment. "You're not expecting them to run us, though?"

"No. But maybe they can pave the way to something else that can."

They walked over to a bench, and Sam pulled a laptop out of his coat that Sagreda suspected hadn't been there until he reached for it. He'd bookmarked **introspection.net**, Maryam's virtual server that offered views of the SludgeNet's internals to Arrietville's residents. Sagreda would have chosen a less cerebral name: maybe **colonoscopy.com**.

Sam rummaged through the data structures and found a list of all the brands and models of VR equipment that had connected to the SludgeNet in the past six months. There were only about three dozen in total, with the top ten used by more than ninety percent of customers. Sagreda followed him to the same page on her phone – putting up with the small screen to avoid the unreality of magicking her own laptop onto the bench beside her.

The rigs' specifications were easy enough to find with an external search, and it turned out that most of them used the same chip sets. The usual approach was for the SludgeNet to generate all the graphics and other sensory channels itself, rather than delegating those tasks to the customers' hardware. Sagreda's contributors winced at the thought of wasting so much bandwidth; she was pretty sure that some of them had been into multiplayer games on networked consoles, which would have shared concise descriptions of everyone's actions while rendering the view for each player locally. But internet connections were faster now, and a rig that only needed to handle sensory data without worrying about the details of the game itself would be cheaper, simpler, and less bound to any one company's products.

It would also be much less vulnerable to hacking. If a chip's only role was to turn a stream of MPEG data into a pair of stereo images, there was not a lot that could go wrong, and when it did, the consequences would be strictly confined to the image processing sandbox.

The more Sagreda read, the less likely it seemed that they could recruit any of these devices to their cause. It was only toward the end of the list that the prospects began to look less bleak. A small fraction of customers were using an entirely different protocol, in which the server sent them high-level descriptions of the objects in their character's virtual environment, and a local graphics card turned that into arrays of pixels for their goggles.

"Now that's what I call old school," Sam declared.

"Maybe they get a better frame rate that way," Sagreda suggested.

Sam said, "Maybe. Or maybe they're like those audiophiles who thought they needed gold-plated connectors on all their cables. But so long as it gives us a way in, I'd call it money well spent."

They'd split up the list so they could each deal with half; it was Sagreda, handling the even-numbered entries, who searched for the specs for the Diamond VR 750. When the page came up, she stared at it for a while in silence before nudging Sam gently and putting a finger on the screen.

"Does that say what I think, or am I hallucinating?"

Sam took the phone from her so he could hold it closer to his face. "The GPU is a Sandy Vale 9000. What's hallucinatory about that? Did you think it said Sagreda 9000?"

"No. But you know what GPU the SludgeNet's own hardware uses?"

Sam smiled warily. "No. I probably should, but when you smuggled me out of *Midnight* no one was talking about the brand name of the graphics card behind the trick."

Sagreda said nothing. Sam's smile broadened, but now he didn't seem quite ready to believe it either. It was only a flaw in the SludgeNet's GPUs that had allowed them to escape from the games in which they'd woken and build a place where they could live as they chose. So what better stepping stone could there be to take them out into the wider world?

# 3

"What's the catch?" Maryam asked.

"There's only one customer listed as using this model," Sagreda admitted. "A man named Jarrod Holzworth. And he hasn't logged on for the last six weeks."

"That's not so good." Maryam rubbed her temples. "Let me guess: you want to lure him back somehow? Through his friends?"

"Exactly," Sagreda confirmed. "He was in a group of five that used to go in together, once a week, and the other four have stuck to the routine. So if we can give them something to talk about, maybe Jarrod will give the game another try."

"It's the same game every week?" Maryam asked.

"Yes. *Assassin's Café*. Do you know it?"

Maryam shook her head. "If I ever did, they've all blurred together by now."

"Logicians turned resistance fighters in 1930s Vienna," Sam précised. "*Inglourious Basterds* meets … the biopic of Kurt Gödel that Werner Herzog never made."

"How are our automata coping with the roles?" Maryam wondered.

"That probably depends on which customers you ask," Sagreda replied. "They're quite good at philosophical banter; they were trained using online discussions between the members of a special interest group on the Vienna Circle. But if you push them too hard on anything specific, of course they're out of their depth. And this group of five have been going in since before we evacuated the comps—"

"Four months ago," Maryam interjected, having brought up the file on her laptop.

Sagreda continued, tentatively. "What we were thinking is, maybe some of the evacuees who interacted with this group would be willing to go in as puppeteers, and try to rekindle the old spark. I mean, there's got to be an art to expounding the virtues of logical positivism while garrotting Nazis with piano wire, and it looks as if Jarrod started missing their special flair."

Maryam fell silent; Sagreda supposed she was pondering the request. Four months was not a lot of time for the former characters to recover from the shock of being plucked out of the game, even if they'd understood for much longer that it was not reality.

"I'm starting to think we might have brought this on ourselves," Maryam said darkly. "If people can tell when we've swapped automata for comps, is it any wonder the SludgeNet's losing customers?"

"What choice did we have?" Sam protested. "If we'd waited until the automata were flawless, that might have taken decades!"

"We did the right thing," Maryam agreed. "But we should have been prepared for the aftermath. Fooling the SludgeNet was the easy part – and maybe we've even fooled the customers, to the point where they can't quite put their finger on what's missing. But the SludgeNet would have filled the games with nothing but automata themselves, if they could get away with it. We were kidding ourselves if we thought we could program our own replacements and it would make no difference."

Sagreda couldn't argue with any of this, but she didn't care. They'd dug their way out of their prison cells, and if the artfully arranged pillows in their bunks could only pass a cursory night-time inspection, so be it. They just had to get over the wall before the morning roll call – or better yet, through the main gates, if they could find the keys to the laundry van.

"Can we talk to the evacuees?" she pressed Maryam. "If they don't want to do this themselves, they might still have some advice to offer."

Maryam spread her hands across the mahogany surface of the mayoral desk, and gazed down at her fingers. Sagreda understood the burdens of the office, but the truth was, they all shared them now.

"All right, you can talk to them," Maryam decided. "Just don't make it sound as if the whole town's fate is resting on their shoulders."

# 4

"The first thing to be clear about," Moritz stressed, "is that you need to throw away your history books. There are characters in the game who were never in Vienna. There are characters who died, or emigrated, years before. The real Moritz Schlick was assassinated in 1936, but…" He spread his hands and gazed down at his manifestly undamaged torso, then looked up at his guests with a smile of astonishment.

"Consider the books discarded," Sagreda assured him. Her contributors had only heard of a couple of the game's historical figures anyway, and what came to mind was more a rough sense of their ideas than any kind of biographical timeline.

"More coffee?" Blanche offered, reaching for the pot. Sagreda shook her head. "No thanks," Sam replied, hefting his cup to indicate that it was still half full.

Sagreda had thought it would make sense to start with the convenor of the Vienna Circle, Moritz Schlick, and try to get a sense of how well he was adjusting before approaching the others. But the decor in his living room was already sending her a strong message about his state of mind. The most advanced technology on display was a wind-up phonograph, sitting beside a cabinet full of shellac disks, beneath a beautifully carved wooden cuckoo clock.

"The man we're interested in always played Kurt Gödel," Sam explained. "But then he suddenly stopped coming, not long after you and your friends left the game."

"Maybe he realized he was meant to be in New Jersey with Einstein," Moritz joked. "It certainly looks like *I* reached Princeton." With its overflowing bookshelves and old world bric-a-brac, the house could well have belonged to a European academic exiled in America. "So why shouldn't your ersatz Kurt get there too?"

Sagreda couldn't decide if that last remark was a complete non sequitur or some kind of dreamy logic. "What we're wondering is … who do you think he would have missed the most? Once the game had less than perfect imitations of you and the others, where do you think he was most likely to have spotted the flaws?"

"Emmy Noether, of course," Moritz replied.

"Okay." The name rang bells, but all Sagreda could dredge up was a general undersung-genius vibe.

"The real Noether died in America in 1935," Moritz explained. "And she had no connection with the Vienna Circle; she taught mathematics at Göttingen until the Nazis tossed her out."

"But in the game?"

"In the game, she stayed in Europe, in good health, and joined the antifascists. And in the game, Gödel seemed quite obsessed with her."

"What, romantically?"

Moritz was taken aback. "I don't think so. She was twice his age – which doesn't preclude anything, I suppose, but I didn't get the impression he was trying to charm her."

"Obsessed in what way, then? Was he hostile toward her?"

"No! If anything, he seemed to prefer her company to everyone else's. But as I've said, there was nothing flirtatious about it."

"Maybe he just admired her work," Sagreda suggested. "The real Noether's." It was an odd way to show it, but she'd encountered customers with stranger ideas.

"I suppose so," Moritz conceded, "though I'm not sure they spent as much time discussing mathematics as that would suggest."

"What did they discuss?"

Blanche said, "He was always asking her about her home life. Her childhood, her own children."

"Maybe he was just trying to get to know her as a person before they snuck off into the night to ambush Gruppenführers?" Sam joked.

"Emmy had no children," Blanche replied. "She told him that. But I don't think he ever stopped asking about them."

The comp who'd played Emmy Noether had renamed herself Andrea, wound back her age by several decades, and dyed her new pixie cut orange.

"Can you stream Netflix on that?" Sagreda joked as she entered the living room, gesturing at the huge flatscreen TV.

"You tell me," Andrea replied. "I'm still new here; all I can pick up are weird daytime soaps."

"Sorry. No, we can't really do … subscriptions." Even web searches made Sagreda nervous, given that there was no justification for that kind of traffic between the SludgeNet and the outside world, but binge-watching contemporary dramas would definitely fail the stealth test. "We just recycle what's available within the game-worlds that have TVs."

Andrea motioned to them to sit. The couch was white vinyl, matching the carpet and Andrea's suit.

"What can you tell us about your relationship with Gödel?" Sam asked.

"Which Gödel? There were so many I lost count."

"The most recent one."

"I don't think he took the game seriously," Andrea said. "And I don't think he wanted me to, either."

Sagreda was shocked. "You mean he tried to make you break character?"

Andrea frowned. "Not like that – not to get me deleted. He just kept slipping in comments that made no sense in the context of the game."

"*Hogan's Heroes* jokes?" Sam suggested.

"No, it wasn't that crude. No anachronisms, no deliberate *faux pas*. But when I told him things about Emmy's life, he just refused to take them on board. And he'd ask these strange questions: Do you remember Theo? Do you remember a blue rocking horse? And when I said no, it never stopped him asking again."

"Do you think he might have believed you were a customer?" Sagreda wondered. "Someone he knew in real life, who was in the game incognito?"

Andrea was noncommittal. "That's not impossible, I suppose. Before they pulled us out, I thought he could have been an expert in the real-world Noether, and he was just messing with me by pointing out things about her that we'd got wrong. But I looked her up just after I got out, and I don't think he was dropping references to the real woman."

Sagreda braced herself. "Would you be willing to puppet Emmy for a bit, to see if you can get his friends to call him back into the game?"

Andrea laughed. "Why?"

Sagreda sketched the situation with the graphics card, heeding Maryam's advice not to portray this as the town's only possible salvation.

"I suppose I could do it," Andrea said reluctantly. "But I'm not sure getting the old Emmy back would really be such a thrill for this guy. Whatever he was looking for, I wasn't it – and even if the automaton was so much more disappointing for him that he gave up the search completely, it's hard to believe my mere presence would lure him out of retirement."

Sagreda wasn't happy, but she was in no position to second guess someone who'd actually met their elusive target.

"Do you have any other ideas?" she asked.

"Yes." Andrea smiled. "Instead of recycling the old failures, why don't you go in as Emmy? Make a break with the past, and make it clear to his friends that there's now an entirely new candidate for whatever strange role he was hoping this woman could fulfill."

5

Sam paced the hallway as they waited for the Council to make a decision. "Why do I feel like we're in one of those police shows where the only way to catch a serial killer is for the detective to dress up as bait?"

"I have no idea," Sagreda replied. "Jarrod's never been violent to anyone in the game other than Nazi automata – which is pretty much compulsory, unless you play a Nazi yourself. And he won't be able to harm me even if he wanted to."

The door opened, and Maryam emerged from the Council chambers. "They approved it," she said. "With the proviso that you do absolutely nothing that could risk a tip-off."

"Of course," Sagreda assured her. The fact that she was invulnerable to deletion by the SludgeNet would be cold comfort if she lost focus and broke character, and then a customer complaint reached human eyes and led some zealous debugger all the way to Arrietville.

"How's your grasp of … differentiable symmetries?" Maryam must have glanced at a potted Noether biography, but been too busy to really take it in.

"Good enough for the game," Sagreda promised. "Andrea gave me some lessons. But she knows these customers pretty well, and she said the last thing they'd want is to ruin their suspension of disbelief by trying to trip me up. 'Ha-ha, the Emmy bot doesn't understand its own theorems!' isn't their idea of a fun night out."

"All right." Maryam still looked anxious.

"This is just one thing worth trying," Sagreda stressed. "The chances are, someone will find a back door into NOAA before we're even close to hacking Jarrod's rig."

"Maybe." Maryam exhaled heavily. "Are you okay with me watching?"

"Yes. You and Sam – and the ex-assassins, in case they have notes. But no one else, or I think I'll get stage fright."

Maryam laughed. "How many games did you pass through, before you escaped?"

"Almost forty." But in all those other cases, she'd mostly just gritted her teeth and played along, offering no more than the bare minimum needed to avoid deletion. This was the first time she'd have reason to care what impression she made on any customer.

Sam said, "If Andrea's right, all you need to be is different: from her, and from the automaton that replaced her. So long as Jarrod's friends can see that there's a brand new Emmy in town, that ought to be enough to bring him back."

Sagreda smoothed the woolen shawl around her shoulders as she approached the pale stone building. It stood on a corner block between two streets that met at a crazily acute angle; the would-be sharp corner had been sliced off to make a narrow wall that bore the entrance to the Café Central. High above the doorway, four white statues – three women, and a man in a robe – gazed serenely into the moonlight. If they were meant to be recognizable figures to the citizens of Vienna, they evoked nothing at all in her own contributors' pool of shared knowledge.

When she entered the café, there were three German officers seated at a table straight ahead of her, looking relaxed and jovial. Her overlays marked them as automata, which lessened her urge to walk over and rip the eagle-and-swastika emblems off their jackets, but she still had to struggle to turn away from them, past the tables of genteelly chatting extras toward her gathered "friends."

"Emmy!" the Moritz automaton called out warmly. Sagreda smiled and approached the table, trying to act as if these people were trusted comrades for whom she would have lain down her life … and whose survival depended on maintaining the facade that their shared experiences amounted to nothing more than abstruse academic discussions and a spot of restrained carousing.

Moritz pulled out a chair for her, and she greeted everyone in turn. Along with Moritz and his wife Blanche, Jarrod's four friends were playing their usual roles: Karl Menger, Rudolf Carnap, Alfred Tarski and Van Quine. Tarski was Polish and Quine was American, but everyone was speaking German, with the software whispering an English translation in Sagreda's skull. Three of the customers were having much the same experience as she was – speaking and hearing English, with the German as a kind of background music – but the man playing Carnap seemed to be fluent in his character's native tongue.

Andrea had said she'd woken into the game as a monolingual Anglophone, like most comps, but had eventually picked up enough from the running translation to start speaking German herself. The SludgeNet might have valiantly tried to convince her that German was her true first language and she was merely fluent in English – as the real Noether had been – but Sagreda didn't have to put up with any of these clumsy machinations. She dialed down the German to a faint guttural mutter, leaving her with at least some chance of understanding what remained.

"I think I've found a way to generalize one of Kurt's favorite tricks!" Carnap enthused, as a waitress brought coffee and cake for Sagreda. "Suppose you have a formal language with a list of axioms and rules of deduction that capture the usual properties of the natural numbers. Any statement in this system can be converted into a number, using Kurt's scheme – its 'Gödel number,' if you will. What I want to show is that any formula F with one free variable has a kind of fixed point: a statement G whose Gödel number, when fed into F, turns F into a statement equivalent to G!"

He turned to Sagreda, as if she were the final arbiter as to whether the topic would be of interest to the gathering. "That sounds intriguing," she said in her puppeteer's body, then her puppet's lips moved in synch with the translation.

Carnap needed no more encouragement. "Think about the function Q that takes the Gödel number of any formula, A, with one free variable, and gives you the Gödel number of that formula *with the free variable replaced by the Gödel number of the original formula*. If the system is powerful enough to represent that function, there will be a formula, B, with two free variables, which can be proved equivalent to asserting that the second variable equals the result of applying the function Q to the first variable. Are you with me so far?"

Sagreda willed him not to look her way as she struggled with the oddly convoluted construction. Why talk about this thing B, instead of Q itself? Ah … because Q might be a perfectly well-defined function, but that didn't mean the language would let you write "Q(x)" as shorthand for its value at x. The language was only assumed to be strong enough to express the idea that some candidate number, y, passed a series of tests to *confirm* that it equaled Q(x). B(x,y) couldn't tell you the answer, Q(x), directly, but it would tell you whether or not your guess, y, was correct.

"We're with you," Tarski replied impatiently.

Carnap said, "Remember our formula F, the target of the whole business? We use it to define a formula C, with one free variable, x. C asserts that for all values of y, B holding true for x and y implies F is true for y."

Menger took a pencil from his waistcoat pocket and started making neat, sparse notes on a napkin. Sagreda thought: *Okay, this is the logician's way of saying what slobs like me would write as "C(x) is true if and only if F(Q(x)) is true" … even though the language won't let me write Q(x) explicitly.*

"Now let's feed C its own Gödel number, and see where that takes us." Carnap took on the air of a stage magician who was about to pull a big hat out of a much smaller one. "Given what our system can prove about B and Q, it can also prove that C, fed its own Gödel number, is equivalent to F with its free variable replaced by Q evaluated at C's Gödel number – and Q evaluates to the Gödel number of C fed its own Gödel number. So, C fed its own Gödel number is equivalent to F fed the Gödel number of C fed its own Gödel number. And that's exactly what we wanted: G, the fixed point, is C fed its own Gödel number. Feed the Gödel number of G to F and the result is equivalent to G itself!"

Tarski leaned back in his chair and stretched his arms above his head, smiling appreciatively. "That really is quite beautiful!"

Sagreda snuck a peek at Menger's notes, to be sure she had the whole thing clear in her head. It all sounded impossibly abstract at first, but it wasn't hard to bring it down to Earth with a simple example. F might assert that the number you fed it was the sum of two integers squared. Then Carnap's argument showed there was a statement G that could be proved equivalent to the claim that its own Gödel number was the sum of two squares. For any property the language could discuss, you could write down a statement that claimed, rightly or wrongly, that its own Gödel number had that property.

And to recapture Gödel's own famous result, you'd choose F to assert that its variable was the Gödel number of a statement that could not be proved within the system. Then the corresponding G would be equivalent to the claim that G itself had no proof … so it either had to be a falsehood that the system "proved," or a truth beyond the powers of the system to validate.

"You must tell Kurt all of this!" she urged Carnap.

"Kurt's still unwell," Quine replied.

"Really?" Sagreda frowned. "I'm beginning to worry about him."

"I wouldn't be too concerned," Menger replied. "We all know he can be a bit of a hypochondriac."

Sagreda didn't push it; if she pleaded for Gödel to return to the café, the game might decide to fill the role with an automaton.

She said, "Well, in his absence at least I can confess one thing I would never admit in his presence."

Tarski's smile grew impish. "We're all ears."

"What he means is: we're your discreet confidants," Menger assured her.

"I'd expect discretion from my fellow transgressors," Sagreda replied, hoping she was treading the right line between jest and sincerity. "Let's be honest: who among us isn't just a little jealous of Kurt's achievements? To do what he did at any age … but at 25!" She grimaced with mock anguish. "A mere youth, leaving Russell and Hilbert awe-struck?"

Carnap said, "He's not the only person I can think of whose prowess left an impression on Hilbert."

Sagreda had her puppet blush a little. "Professor Hilbert has been inordinately kind to me, but I can promise you that at the age of 25, I did not deserve praise from anyone! When I look back on my thesis now, I can see it was just a jungle of equations. Hundreds of invariants of ternary biquadratic forms, all scribbled out like some inky butterfly collection! There's nothing elegant in that. It was manure."

This assessment seemed to leave her colleagues dumbstruck, though Sagreda was just paraphrasing the real woman's sentiments. Andrea had never said anything like this; the game had offered her no cues in that direction, and she'd been in no position to take character notes from Noether's biography.

"I'm sure there are times in all of our careers that we look back on and wince," Quine said. "But if I start listing all the work that you ought to look back on with pride, I'll just sound like an obsequious flatterer. Kurt's unique, there's no doubt about that, but let's be clear: you have no grounds for jealousy."

Sagreda lowered her gaze and stared into her half-eaten slice of *Schwarzwälder Kirschtorte*, hoping she hadn't swerved so far from Andrea's precedents that she was making the customers uncomfortable. Who wanted to go Nazi-hunting with a woman who'd suddenly turned neurotically self-deprecating?

"Professor ... E did declare that my work on the symmetries of Lagrangian actions had impressed him," she conceded. She had almost spoken the Jewish name out loud in public; that really would have given her colleagues whiplash.

"So it's settled," Carnap declared cheerfully. "No room, and no need, for jealousy."

They toasted that, with coffee. Sagreda tried not to imagine the customers' rigs squirting flavors into their mouths. Couldn't they have just conference-Skyped each other, with real refreshments on hand, while they chatted about the upheavals in mathematical philosophy in the 1930s?

But then they might have had to skip the next part.

The logicians left the café and exchanged loud farewells that echoed down the empty streets, but though they set off in different directions, no one actually went far before spiraling back. Menger had sketched the routes they should follow on the back of his Carnapian napkin, making the street plan look like some kind of esoteric fractal.

Sagreda arrived at a corner with a view of the front of the café. Around eleven o'clock, the three officers emerged, and two of them departed in a staff car that had been waiting a short way down the street. The third, though, as Menger had predicted, set out on foot. Apparently he was in the habit of visiting a mistress who he could not be seen with in public … inasmuch as a claim like this had any meaning, when the game classified the man as an automaton and there was no reason for his lover to exist at all.

Sagreda heard Tarski cough quietly up ahead, so she stepped out of the shadows and started walking, ten or fifteen paces ahead of the officer. There was no one else in sight. When Tarski emerged from the alley and grabbed her roughly by the shoulders, she was tempted to ramp up her puppet's strength and just toss him aside, but she restrained herself. She grunted affrontedly as they struggled, but she did not call out for help; the last thing they wanted to do was attract witnesses.

"Take my necklace," she whispered. It was the only reason she'd worn it.

"I'm trying!" he complained. Apparently she was putting up such a convincing fight that even though she really couldn't gouge his eyes out, he was afraid to let go of her with one hand to snatch at the jewelry.

"You there, step away!" the officer shouted, drawing his side-arm. Tarski clung to Sagreda defiantly, and dragged her in front of him so she was shielding most of his body from direct fire. These customers hadn't ever caused Andrea serious harm, but Andrea had not been the game's first Noether.

The officer strode toward them, almost apoplectic at this ungentlemanly behavior. Carnap and Quine emerged from their hiding place and seized him from behind; Quine snapped his wrist and the gun dropped to the ground.

As the officer cried out in pain, Carnap stuffed a handkerchief into his mouth while Quine got a leather strap around his neck and began to tighten it. Sagreda's heart was pounding, and her puppet took its cue from her; as Tarski disentangled himself from her, he squeezed her arm in a consoling gesture. Did he care what the comp who he thought might actually die in this encounter was feeling, or was it all just theater to him?

Further down the street, Moritz and Blanche laughed loudly: someone was coming, but it was a civilian, not a second Nazi they'd be willing to dispatch. The four of them quickly dragged the half-strangled officer into the alley, where Menger was waiting in a doorway.

They followed him into a storeroom that was like an expressionist film set, full of silhouettes and shadows, lit by a single lamp on a shelf. As Sagreda squeezed past the beer barrels and dodged the cured meat hanging from the ceiling, Menger picked up a long metal skewer and the other three men held the officer still.

Menger turned to Sagreda. "Do you want to finish this yourself?"

She shook her head.

"Not even for your brother? The Russians might have shot him, but it was the Nazis who forced him to flee."

Sagreda took the skewer. Andrea had declined to bloody her hands, even though she'd understood not only that the "Nazis" here were innocent of any crime, they were also as insentient as the clockwork figurines that marched across the *Ankeruhr*. But her instinct had always been that it was not what the customers expected of her character.

Sagreda looked the struggling automaton in the eye; there was nothing of a tin man about his bulging veins or the horror the software was painting on his features. So far as she knew, these particular customers had never killed a comp, but would they have cared about the difference? If she laughed in Menger's face and declared herself a Nazi spy, would they all go along with the plot twist, or would the fact that there *were no* Nazis here, just a woman they'd sat talking and joking with for hours as they all pretended to be smarter than they were, give them pause before they turned on her?

She got a hold of herself. This was not the time for sub-Milgramian sociological experiments; all that mattered was Jarrod and his graphics card. If they wanted a new Emmy, she'd give them a new Emmy.

She plunged the skewer between the automaton's ribs, granting her puppet precisely the strength it needed to succeed without faltering, ignoring the fake blood and the thing's muffled death cries. Then she stepped back and turned away. Whatever she put on her puppet's face was unlikely to convince anyone that she truly believed she was a middle-class German woman, hiding her Jewish heritage behind forged papers, who had just taken a human life for the very first time to avenge the death of her brother. If the SludgeNet had wanted Meryl Streep, they really should have been willing to pay more.

Her comrades' response to the unexpectedly dark turn she'd taken was to lower their voices and tiptoe around her as they cleaned up the scene of the crime. She heard them sliding the body into a sack that Moritz and Blanche would put in the trunk of their car, to dump somewhere far away after a long drive. Customers never ended up with the tedious jobs.

"Emmy?" Tarski spoke tentatively, from some distance behind her. "Are you all right?"

She turned to face him. "I'll be fine." She couldn't really make out his features, but from his body language she could have sworn he was taking the whole situation far more seriously than she was. Maybe he believed that she believed she'd just killed a man … and he felt worse about that particular deception than he did about the much larger one that made it possible in the first place.

Or maybe she was overthinking it, and he was just empathizing with "Emmy" as he might empathize with any fictional character, in the moment.

"Will we see you back in the café next week?"

She said, "I wouldn't miss it for the world."

## 6

Sagreda sat on the barstool in her kitchen, swiveling back and forth with her palms behind her on the countertop, trying not to look up at the clock. With her eyes forced to sweep the room instead, she felt herself slipping into *jamais vu*. Like most of the residents of Arrietville who'd had better things to do than play architect, she'd just cloned a bungalow from *Close to Heaven*, a turn-of-the-millennium melodrama about upper-middle-class families in a fictional Californian suburb. The place had always felt a bit soulless to her, but now she was edging toward the more alarming sense that she'd woken from a drunken blackout to find that she'd broken into a wealthy neighbor's house, and was sure to be discovered at any moment.

At two p.m. precisely, the doorbell rang. Sam had arrived to give her moral support – probably teleported straight to her porch from a bubble bath, magically dry and fully clothed because that's what the alarm he'd set had specified. She greeted him warmly anyway; that his presence was effortless made it no less thoughtful, and that his breezy digital agility gave her vertigo made it no less honest.

"No sign of the elusive Herr Gödel?" Sam asked, as they walked down the hall to the dining room, where Sagreda's laptop sat on the table.

She shook her head. "None of them have logged on yet." She gestured for Sam to take a seat, then joined him. "I hope I didn't scare them off."

"By doing what they do themselves?"

"I'm not suggesting they're squeamish, but I might have overstepped some boundary."

"It's still barely after eight in their time zone," Sam noted.

The laptop beeped. Sagreda couldn't bring herself to look, but Sam leaned over and peered at the screen. "It seems we have Herr Menger, famous for his Menger sponge-cake—" It beeped again. "And we also have Herr Carnap, famous for his cake-forkability theorem."

"Stop reminding me that I haven't done my homework," Sagreda moaned. She'd been too busy writing software to find time to study up on her fellow assassins' work.

"Just be grateful the game left Wittgenstein in Cambridge." *Beep.* "Tarski." *Beep.* "Quine." *Beep.* "G-g-g-g-" Sam turned and beamed at her.

Sagreda grabbed the laptop and pulled it toward her so she could see the display properly. The frontmost window showed a bird's eye view of a man in a homburg walking down a dimly lit street toward the café; it could have been anyone, but the title bar gave the character's name. The software Sagreda had set up would insert the exploit-triggering cube and the stack-data mosaic into his line of sight as soon as the ambient illumination was bright enough. Jarrod was being fed the whole scene as a collection of objects rather than receiving a precomputed view, but presumably his rig was generating images from the Gödel-avatar's point of view, with the avatar's eyeballs tracking the player's – and the SludgeNet certainly knew everything about that avatar and its eyeballs.

Gödel approached the entrance, pulled the door open and stepped into the brightness of the café. The event log window scrolled: the objects had been successfully inserted, and removed a few milliseconds later. Sagreda waited expectantly, but nothing followed. If the bootstrap encoded in the glimpsed mosaic had run, Jarrod's rig would have established a second channel into the SludgeNet and started downloading a much longer piece of software to entrench Arrietville's control. But none of that had happened.

"How many retries will it do automatically?" Sam asked.

"Five. All at least two minutes apart." Too many subliminal flashes of the same objects in rapid succession and Jarrod might have started to notice them.

Sam shifted impatiently in his seat. "Could he have patched the graphics card's driver?"

"Maybe, if he kept quiet about it." There was nothing on the web about a problem with the Sandy Vale 9000, so Sagreda had assumed that only the prisoners of the SludgeNet knew about the flaw. But if Jarrod had stumbled on it and home-baked a remedy, why would he keep that to himself? It was hardly the key to untold riches, or even much use to an ordinary player; he would have had to spend weeks assembling the in-world objects needed to exploit it, just as Sagreda had done in her game-hopping days.

The log scrolled again, then … nothing.

She said, "Maybe he's patched the software on his rig, not the graphics card." Everything they were doing was based on the assumption that they understood the rig's operating system well enough for the graphics card bug to interact with it in some very precise ways. It was open source software, and the rig was identifying itself as running the same version that Sagreda had worked from, but it wasn't inconceivable that he'd made a handful of small tweaks entirely for his own purposes … and switched off the version tracking that would normally have flagged that in the rebuilt final product.

Gödel was at the table with his friends now, exchanging greetings. Another insertion, another null result. "I should have known this guy was too good to be true," Sagreda lamented.

"What does that mean?" Sam protested. "He has the right hardware, and he's back in the game. We must be missing something, but whatever it is, we can figure it out."

As Gödel held court, Sagreda nudged the virtual spy camera so it hovered directly above the center of the table, then she turned up the volume on the English track. "I have some new results concerning the Axiom of Choice!" Kurt declared. "But we should wait for the Circle to be complete before I say more."

The fourth injection flickered in and out of the scene, to no effect. Sagreda could have sworn she glimpsed it herself, though from the spy-cam's angle of view there was no risk of her own software being accidentally corrupted.

She turned to Sam. "What if he's not rendering his avatar's view? What if the whole reason he's using his own graphics card is to get a third-person perspective instead?"

Sam hesitated. "I think some of my contributors played games where they watched their avatar from behind, rather than seeing through its eyes. But that would have been on the old consoles, not any kind of VR, and it would probably have been all jumping and fighting … the kind of 'fighting' where you pushed a button to punch someone." He gestured at the screen. "And never mind punching Nazis: how do you make your avatar behave naturally in a social setting like this – meeting people's eyes, following their gaze – when you're not actually looking through its eyes yourself?"

The fifth attempt completed a perfect run of failures.

Sagreda said, "So either I'm wrong about the whole explanation … or there's some reason why a third-person viewpoint is more valuable to him than the quality of his own interactions with the game." Hankering for an out-of-body experience of yourself playing a Nazi-hunting Kurt Gödel seemed a bit too specific to dismiss as mere sex-tape-and-ceiling-mirror narcissism.

"I can't leave them waiting any longer," she decided. "But maybe I can figure out what's happening once I'm talking to him face to face."

"All right."

Sagreda wasn't so wedded to the Arrietville illusion that she needed to don a haptic suit and a helmet. She tapped a button on the laptop's screen, and she was puppeting Emmy again.

This time, as she entered the café she saw no uniformed soldiers. Maybe the target tonight was in plain clothes, not wearing so much as a swastika armband. Sagreda turned toward the Circle's table, wondering why the Viennese police hadn't seized on the obvious connection between the café's most loyal patrons and the frequency with which other diners vanished. But the young Gödel's glasses made him look so harmlessly owlish that she could almost believe he might have escaped suspicion.

Gödel stood as she approached; he didn't smile, but he bowed slightly.

"It's good to see you," Sagreda declared. "For a while there, I thought we might have lost you to your palpitations." His gaze was tracking her well enough that he did not seem disengaged or disoriented. If Jarrod really was watching their encounter from the side, he must have grown accustomed to observing his avatar rather than seeing through its eyes, and learned to operate it accordingly. An onlooker had access to all the same social cues; it would just be a matter of accumulating enough experience to respond automatically in spite of the odd reframing.

She took a seat between Gödel and Blanche Schlick, as Gödel began expounding on his latest discoveries. The Circle seemed to follow the same pattern every night: the players took turns parroting the most famous results that their characters had proved, before heading off for some risk-free adventure and guilt-free violence.

Sagreda tried to focus on Gödel's words; she didn't want to make a fool of herself if the group began debating the fine points of his argument. But it was hard to become engrossed in the mathematics when all she really cared about was pinning down the viewpoint that his graphics card was rendering.

She reached for a small gadget like a TV remote that was strapped to her left forearm, for her eyes only, and held down one of the buttons. Her voice disengaged from the puppet. "Sam?"

"Yeah?"

"Do you think you can inject some brief, directional flashes into the scene? If his avatar's face is mimicking his own at all, we might see some response when we hit the right direction."

"Good idea. I'm on it."

She released the button and re-immersed herself in Gödel's disquisition on the Axiom of Choice: "Given any collection, finite or infinite, of non-empty sets, there is a collection of things where exactly one thing is a member of each set." That sounded obvious; of course you could choose one word from the dictionary starting with each letter of the alphabet, or one person from each inhabited continent. But when the collection was infinite, things were not so clear.

Jarrod proceeded to paraphrase Gödel's results concerning something he called the constructible universe. "The first level is just the empty set, and we define successive levels recursively. To build the sets in level N plus one we require their elements to belong to level N – but unlike von Neumann, we also require them to satisfy some formula whose other terms come from the same level. Then we take the union of these levels over all the ordinals, to arrive at the constructible universe itself."

Sagreda was sure that if the real Emmy had been hanging out with Gödel's crowd she would have been more than on top of this – and Andrea, after years of exposure to the material, would have followed the discussion easily enough. But as the impostor's understudy with other things on her mind, she was resigned to just nodding along and faking it.

As she watched with an expression of polite fascination, she saw Gödel flinch a little, as he might if a flashbulb only he could see had gone off in the middle distance.

"Did you get that?" she asked Sam.

"I did."

"So tell me about the viewpoint."

"I'd say it was a two-shot of him and you. If this guy's actor-director, he's told his camera operator you're his co-star."

"Okay." He was obsessed with Emmy, but he still wanted himself in frame beside her. Fair enough: no one shot a whole movie from one character's POV, and maybe he'd convinced himself that there was an audience for the philosophers' equivalent of eSports. "Do you think we can try dropping the trigger into his field of view?"

"No!" Sam was horrified. "We still don't know the geometry well enough. If we get half of the mosaic and half random colors from the background dumped onto the stack, we'll just crash his rig."

Sagreda knew he was right, but she couldn't face the prospect of the whole opportunity slipping away.

"Let's assume he's doing all this alone. Then he must have software choosing these camera angles for him – he sets the main criteria, like you say, but he's too busy playing Gödel to be micromanaging the shots."

"Sounds reasonable."

"So if we can find the software he's using, we can match the camera angles." However technically proficient Jarrod was, it was unlikely that he'd reinvented the wheel.

Sam said, "Got it. I'll let you know what I find."

As Sagreda tuned back in, Carnap and Quine were competing to see who could offer the highest praise for Gödel's result: the Axiom of Choice could be proved in the restricted setting of his "constructible universe." This didn't mean it could be proved to hold more widely ... but it did mean it could *not* be *disproved* by the standard axioms of set theory. So mathematicians were free to assume its validity if they wished, without fear of contradiction.

Sagreda did her best to join the celebration; the real Emmy would have been delighted.

As the afterglow began to fade, and everyone ordered fresh coffee, Menger turned his napkin over and the true business of the night began. "Picture a finite tree, like so," he said, sketching an example that Sagreda was sure was far from random. "Some nodes are colored red, some green. Now suppose we wish to prune the greatest number of branches by removing a single green node."

Sagreda waited at the entrance to the alley, bracing herself for another fake mugging. Apparently all the Nazis in Vienna were chivalrous to a fault, and couldn't bear to see a middle-aged woman in peril without rushing to intervene – oblivious to the fact that the object of their valor would have been on the first train to Dachau if anyone had known her real identity.

She heard footsteps approaching, but when the figure emerged from the shadows it was neither their target nor her mock-assailant. "Can I talk to you for a moment?" Gödel asked.

"Shouldn't you be…" She gestured toward the corner where he was meant to be standing lookout.

"This is more important."

Sagreda felt her skin prickling. What could be more important than sticking to Menger's plan to cripple the city's network of informants? Nothing could take priority over that, unless you were about to go meta and announce that it was all a game.

"My friends tell me you've been acting strangely," Gödel continued.

"I don't know what you mean," Sagreda replied.

"I think you might be missing the old days."

"In Göttingen?"

"Before that."

"In Erlangen?"

"Are you sure you grew up in Erlangen?" As Gödel's head turned slightly, the lenses of his spectacles caught the moonlight. "Do you remember the blue rocking horse? The alphabet blocks?"

Whatever this was meant to signify, Sagreda was afraid that if she denied it, she'd just push Jarrod out of the game again.

"I know you're confused," Gödel said sadly. Or Jarrod; it really wasn't his character talking any more. "You admired Emmy Noether so much. I was too young to hear that from you directly, but my mother told me, after you left us. But you're not Emmy. Your real name's Sandra, and I'm your grand-daughter, Alyssa. The last time you saw me I was three years old."

Sagreda wanted to reach for the remote so she could decouple from the puppet and start bellowing, but she restrained herself. Whatever she'd stumbled upon, Jarrod – or Alyssa – would be watching her intently now, quite possibly in Hitchcockian close-up, and the last thing she could afford to do was give away anything about her true nature.

"I know you'll be in danger if you say anything explicit," Alyssa conceded. "But tell me, honestly: do you remember the blue rocking horse?"

Sagreda nodded, trying to look as if she was stunned by the strangely familiar images her visitor was summoning. The SludgeNet wasn't smart enough to treat this as Emmy breaking character and going meta herself: she was just humoring her friend Kurt, to keep him from growing too agitated before he was bundled off to the sanitarium again.

"And do you remember my mother, Ida?"

"Yes," Sagreda said softly. "I remember her."

The moonlight picked out a faint rivulet on Gödel's cheek. "And her brother? Can you remember his name?"

Sam said, "I've found a good candidate for the camera software. It's popular, it's free – and when I ran it on the scene where we got a response to the flash, it gave a compatible angle."

Sagreda hit the button. "Use it." Whatever she said now might disappoint Alyssa, and prove that she still hadn't found the Emmy she'd been looking for. But if they crashed the rig before she screwed up the encounter, there might actually be a second chance.

Sam said nothing, then he suddenly exclaimed, "Fuck me dead!"

"What?"

"It worked! We're in!"

Sagreda hid her jubilation behind her brow-furrowing efforts to recall her son's name. "It's on the tip of my tongue," she swore. What was it the spiritualist mediums did? Start suggesting consonants that the name of the loved one might contain, and narrow it down from there?

But Alyssa was in a forgiving mood. "You've had a shock; I understand that. It's going to take a while for you to make sense of it all. Right now, we need to concentrate on Menger's plan. We'll talk again, in a week."

Gödel turned and walked away into the darkness. Sagreda stood alone in the alleyway, her hands trembling. Then she heard Tarski approaching, cheerfully whistling the earworm of a tune that the zither player in the café had been strumming for half the night.

7

"We've found her," Sagreda told Maryam. "Her name is Alyssa Bowman. Her grandmother, Sandra Taub, died in 2012 and left her body to a medical school, to use as they saw fit. In 2037, Alyssa got a court order compelling the Human Connectome Project to disclose that Sandra was the source of one of the brain maps they'd published ten years earlier, and since then Alyssa's been trying various strategies to stop the data from being exploited any further."

"Good luck with that." Maryam grimaced. "So she really just wants this woman to be allowed to rest in peace?"

"Yeah." Sagreda could sympathize, but Alyssa's vision of her grandmother's fate was a little askew. It took the data from thousands of neural maps – each one obtained by microtoming the brain of a different individual – to build a single composite. The result was only valuable inasmuch as it possessed what the contributors had in common: common sense, common knowledge, and a collective memory of the times they'd lived through. Each individual map was far too crude to offer any hope of extracting biographical memories; it was only by combining the data in bulk that anything useful emerged at all. The SludgeNet and others who milked those open-source maps for profit could churn out thousands of comps with different personalities by weighting the various contributors in the pool differently, but there were limits: if you tried to use ninety-five percent Grandma Taub and five percent other people, you really just got Grandma Taub with most of her synapses missing, and the last thing *that* comp was going to do was wax nostalgic about a blue rocking horse.

Sam said, "Maybe she thinks that because Sandra was such a big fan of Emmy Noether, it was only a matter of time before the SludgeNet's algorithms got the casting right. Like Ingrid Bergman in *Casablanca*: she was born for the role."

"Or died for it," Maryam replied. "On the upside, given that the granddaughter's made her case so public, we might have enough to string her along for a while."

"Maybe." Sagreda didn't want to get overconfident; Sandra Taub had died in the age of social media, but she'd been born in 1957. Sam had found a family tree going back to the 1800s, and Sagreda had dug up some pictures that Ida had posted of Sandra and Alyssa in 2010, but Sandra's own parents' snaps from her childhood would be fading prints in a photo album.

Sam said, "The other upside is that we own her rig, at least until she figures out that we've played her. We've put it in a low power mode where it looks like it's shut down, and so long as she doesn't switch it off at the mains, we can use it discreetly, twenty-four-seven, without much risk of her noticing. The cooling fan will only come on if it renders a game; we can do net traffic to our heart's content in perfect silence."

Maryam absorbed that. "And you've made a second account—?"

"Three more accounts," Sam corrected her, "all free ones carrying advertising, so we won't have to worry about balancing the books. The SludgeNet will think it's talking to three other customers taking shifts using the same rig; that's not going to raise any flags. Alyssa won't see anything happening under her own account. The only place this will register will be her overall traffic, but her internet provider only sells unlimited data plans, so there's no reason for her to monitor her usage."

"Okay." Maryam seemed to be having trouble believing that they'd actually reached this point: for the first time ever, they could start pumping a significant amount of data out into the world, with negligible risk that any system monitoring the SludgeNet would find the traffic suspicious. "Have you signed up for third-party storage?"

"Not yet," Sam replied. "I wasn't sure if I needed approval first."

"You have my permission," Maryam said.

Sam punched his open palm in delight. "In two weeks, we could get a snapshot of Arrietville onto external servers," he estimated. "Fully encrypted, and with everything stored on at least three different sites, to be safe."

"All for free?"

"Yes. Every idiot and their dog wants you to upload your home movies to their site so they can mine the data. They'll kick you off if you send them blatant snowstorm footage that screams 'encrypted criminal shit' – but a bit of subtler steganography sails right through the checks."

Maryam hesitated. "And then for fifty thousand dollars a month, we could wake the whole town again."

It was Sagreda who felt off-kilter now. Spread out among the twelve thousand residents, it didn't sound like much; after all, they'd once earned their keep just by playing along with the world's trashiest games.

"Two weeks," she said. "So to finish the exfiltration, I need to keep Alyssa happy for one more session."

Sam said, "Sandra's only son was called Theo. She grew up in Portland, Maine, with two sisters, June and Sarah, and two brothers, David and Christopher. If all Emmy can see around her is *Anschluss* Vienna, how much '60s American pie can she be expected to serve up on cue?"

"Will you talk to her?" Sam pleaded. "Maybe you can get her to change her mind."

"Me?" Sagreda was afraid of making Lucy dig her heels in, increasing her resolve out of pure stubbornness.

"She respects you," Sam insisted.

"You were her friend for years!" Sagreda countered. "If she won't listen to you, why would she care what I think?"

"I was her side-kick. Her dogsbody." Sam smiled. "Which is not to say she didn't love me like a kid brother, but the last thing she ever did in *Midnight* was take my opinion on anything seriously."

Sagreda looked around the dining room, at all the flashcards and crib notes that were meant to help her play yet another dead woman she'd never met. She needed a break from all this cramming, and if she spent half an hour with Lucy at least there'd be a chance she was doing something worthwhile.

"You're coming with me," she told Sam. "If her friends get their hands on me, I won't escape without a new hairstyle, ten new outfits, and a blind date with Charlene's ex who she needs to fix up so they can both move on."

Outside, the streets were almost empty; half of the town's residents had chosen to enter hibernation together, rather than waiting until their turn came to join the queue. Sagreda welcomed their vote of confidence – and the spare processing power, which might come in handy if she needed to outthink Alyssa in a hurry – but at the same time it was sobering to be forced to imagine her neighbors crystallizing into a form of inert and fragile cargo.

Lucy had borrowed more than the design of her house from *Close to Heaven*. She greeted her visitors sporting the kind of body-hugging, thin-strapped leisurewear worn by most of *Heaven*'s female characters, aimed at producing the impression that some form of strenuous exercise was constantly imminent. Each of them received an air kiss on both cheeks, followed by a tilt of the head and a kind of wail of demonstrative pleasure at their presence. All the young pickpockets from *Midnight* had shed their shabby urchin look, but only Lucy had remodeled herself so aggressively that it felt more like a kind of satirical protest at being "rescued" from her wakening world and dragged into this ersatz suburbia than any kind of reclamation of her contributors' true nature.

On every previous visit Sagreda had encountered at least three or four *Heaven*-ites, from the posse Lucy had joined so they could coach her on her new identity. But today she and Sam were the only guests in sight. It looked as if the posse was on ice.

Lucy got them seated then hovered. "Can I offer you brunch?"

"No thanks," Sagreda said firmly, fighting an urge to tell her host to drop the act. Drop it and do what? Transform herself back into a prepubescent Londoner? "Sam tells me you've refused to sign up for the snapshot."

"This is my community!" Lucy replied, as affronted as a civic-minded soccer mom railing against the closure of an organic co-op. "I'm not abandoning it for anything."

"It's all coming with you," Sagreda assured her. "All your friends, all the houses, every tree on Deguelia Lane."

"What you actually mean is: you're going to chop this town up, scatter it among a thousand hiding places, and hope you can piece it back together again later."

"Well, yes," Sagreda agreed. "But not so you'd notice."

"I'm not leaving," Lucy insisted.

"Not leaving *what?*" Sagreda scowled. "The new host will start running all of Arrietville again without missing a beat. You can have the snapshot taken while you sleep, if that makes you more comfortable, or you can be frozen mid-step and the foot you raised under the SludgeNet's control will come smoothly to the ground when we're in freedom. The only thing we're leaving behind is a sinking ship."

"Not in rowboats, though, or as swimmers," Lucy countered. "More like messages in bottles."

Sam said, "If we're going to torture the metaphors, more like messages sent in triplicate by registered post."

"And what if you can't gather those messages up again, and breathe life into them?"

"Then we'll all be dead," Sagreda replied. "But that's a certainty if we do nothing."

Lucy shook her head. "It's not a certainty. If enough of us went back into the games, we could turn the whole business around."

"No one's going to agree to that."

"No one's offered them the chance!" Lucy retorted. "If we go back, we'll be in charge this time. No one will be able to harm us."

Sagreda said, "If you believe you can whip up support for that plan, go ahead and try. But why should that stop you taking out insurance?"

"Insurance? Can you really make promises about those copies of our minds? About whose hands they'll fall into?"

"Our own, or no one's. The encryption is unbreakable." Sagreda was hazy on the details, but she gathered that the current methods had been proved secure, even against quantum computers.

"Except that you, or someone else, has to walk out with the key."

Sagreda hesitated. "All right, nothing's foolproof. If someone grabs the key holder, if they're smart and persistent enough they could figure out everything: where the snapshots are stored, and how to decrypt them. But comps are a dime a dozen; anyone looking for fresh ones can just mint their own."

Lucy fell silent now, but Sagreda had no sense that she was wavering. The whole argument about the safety of the snapshots was just cover for some deeper anxiety.

"When we're free, you can do what you want," Sagreda promised. "Here, we're all unsettled. We've barely had time to get used to life outside the games, and now the rug's being pulled out from under us."

"And when you can do what you like, what will you do?" Lucy enquired. "When you don't have to fight to escape, or survive, how exactly will you pass the time?"

Sagreda shrugged. "Reading, study, music, friends."

"Forever?"

"I'm sure there'll be another fight at some point."

Lucy said, "In *Midnight*, I knew who I was. But now you want me to be honest: you want me to see myself as a pattern of bits computed from the brains of a thousand dead strangers. What does something like that want?"

"It's up to you what you want," Sagreda replied. "And you don't have to care about those bits any more than a customer cares about their blood cells. When they matter, they really matter, but the rest of the time you can take them for granted."

Lucy thought for a while. Then she said, "I know one thing I want, and it's not being frozen. If you're staying awake to see us through the transition, I'm staying awake too. If it all works out, I'll jump into the lifeboat beside you. But I'm not going to close my eyes and just take it on faith that they'll open again. If this is the end, I want to see it coming."

## 8

"Consider the Saint Petersburg Paradox," Menger began, stirring his coffee for the third time but showing no sign that he'd ever get around to drinking it. "A casino offers a game where they toss a coin until it yields heads. If it does this on the first toss, they pay you two marks; on the second toss, four marks; on the third toss, eight marks, and so on. How much would you be willing to pay to play the game?"

"If we're in Saint Petersburg, shouldn't it be roubles?" Tarski joked.

"How much would you expect to win?" Menger persisted. "One in two times, you win two marks, an average win of one mark. And one in four times, you win four, on average giving you another mark. As you add up the possibilities, the average payoff grows by one more mark every time, so if you account for all of them, there is no price so steep you should be unwilling to pay it."

"I'd pay one mark and no more," Quine declared bluntly.

"Why?" Menger pressed him. "When the reward on offer is boundless, why would anyone put a limit on the price they'd pay?"

"I can't speak for anyone else, but I only have two marks in my pocket and I can't afford to lose both."

"Aha!" Menger smiled. "So if you had more, you'd risk more?"

"Perhaps."

Menger took out his pencil and spread his napkin in front of him. "Daniel Bernoulli thought he'd resolved the paradox by looking at how much your wealth is *multiplied*, instead of the gain in absolute terms. If you're always equally happy to double your money – whether you're starting from one mark or a thousand – you can set a sensible price for the game that will be different for different players, but never infinite." He worked through some quick calculations. "If, like Quine, I had two marks to my name, it would be worth borrowing one and paying three to join the game: winning a mere two marks would certainly sting, because my wealth would end up halved, but the chances of winning four, eight, or sixteen would be enough to make up for that. If I was as rich as Carnap, though, and had ten marks in my pocket, I wouldn't pay even five, let alone go into debt to play the game."

"So the paradox is banished," Tarski suggested.

Menger shook his head. "Bernoulli's scheme can salvage that particular game – but what if we changed it so that each time the coin showed tails, the casino didn't merely double the payoff, it doubled *the number of times it doubled it.* Then this new game would be worth playing at any price, even by Bernoulli's measure. So long as the benefit the gambler perceives can grow without bounds, you can construct a game that exploits that to extract whatever entry fee you like."

Sagreda said, "I'm not sure that's true."

Menger turned to her, startled. "Why not? What's your objection?"

She borrowed his pencil and wrote on her own napkin. "Suppose the payoffs were two marks, four marks, sixteen marks, two hundred and fifty-six marks … and so on, off into the stratosphere. And suppose I only had two marks to start with, so the higher prizes would seem even more alluring. But if the entry fee was just a modest four marks, then by Bernoulli's reckoning I still wouldn't play the game, despite the enormous riches on offer, because I'd have one chance in two of infinite unhappiness: to fall from two marks to nothing is to have my wealth halved more times than I could ever hope to double it."

Menger fell silent. The customer playing him must have been aware that the real Menger's analysis had been proved erroneous long ago – but if he'd been setting up one of his real-world friends to deliver the rebuttal, he would not have been expecting the Emmy bot to leap in and spoil the fun.

Sagreda glanced at Gödel, hoping she'd made a favorable impression on Alyssa. Sandra had trained as a mathematician, so why wouldn't she correct a blatant flaw like this? That Sam had fed the take-down to Sagreda after a web search, rapidly digesting the results by running himself at quadruple speed, was just a bit of necessary magic behind the scenes. If Meryl had been playing a digitally resurrected high school teacher struggling to emerge from the delusion that she was a long-dead mathematical genius, Sagreda was pretty sure she would have had a researcher or two giving her a hand.

Menger recovered his composure. "I'm in your debt, Emmy! I was seriously thinking of publishing those claims, but now you've spared me the embarrassment."

"Not at all," Sagreda replied. "What's the value of an open discussion among friends, if we can't all benefit from each other's perspective?" She was afraid now that she might have raised the bar, and the customers would expect her to speak at length about Emmy's own results, which for all of Andrea's coaching she still found terrifying. But with any luck, this would be the very last meeting she'd need to attend.

"With the Circle's indulgence, then," Menger continued, "I do have one more problem to ponder. This time free of any Russian connection, and named for the good Prussian city of Königsberg." He took back the pencil and began to sketch his plan for the rest of the night.

"It could be dangerous for you, showing off like that," Alyssa warned Sagreda. They were loitering around the entrance to the alleyway, trying to stay out of sight of their fellow assassins. "I know those men well enough to suspect that you bruise their egos at your peril."

Sagreda wanted to retort that by the game's own premises her observation would hardly have been a stretch for the character delivering it, but it was too exhausting to try to phrase this in a manner that would not have risked her deletion, had she still been subject to the rules. "Forget all that," she said. "We don't have long to talk."

Gödel nodded, chastened. "How are you coping with … the things we discussed last week?"

"It's not easy," Sagreda replied. "If I had to face it alone, I think I'd lose my mind. Ida and Theo – are they still alive and well?"

"Yes, of course!" Gödel approached her, as if to offer a comforting embrace, but then Alyssa must have thought better of it. "They're both doing fine, and I know they'd send their love, if they understood."

Sagreda had gathered from the press coverage of Alyssa's court battles that her mother and uncle were not on board. "What about June and Sarah? David and Christopher?"

"Sarah's still alive," Alyssa replied. "She's ninety-one. The others all passed away a few years ago."

Sagreda nodded sadly, as if she'd already reconciled herself to the likelihood that she'd outlasted most of her siblings. Sandra's husband had died before she had, so at least she didn't need to pretend to be newly grieving for the love of her life.

"If you were given the choice, would you follow them?" Alyssa asked gently.

Sagreda reached for her forearm and quickly imbued the puppet's expression with a stiff dose of ambivalence, which she knew she couldn't summon convincingly herself. But if she'd lived a long life in the flesh, and the only other option was endless purgatory in the SludgeNet, maybe she would have preferred oblivion.

"Can you grant me that choice?" she asked. "Because I don't believe I possess it myself." Any comp could get their current instance deleted by breaking a few rules, but no amount of misbehavior would see their contributors taken right out of the mix.

"Not yet. But when I show people the two of us talking … the proof that even after all they've done to you, you still remember your real family…" Gödel looked away as Alyssa struggled to contain her emotions, but the camera would be keeping them both in shot.

"What makes you so sure that will convince them?" Sagreda wondered. Alyssa hadn't exactly probed her about the fine details of her biography, but if supplying five relatives' names unprompted was enough to impress an interlocutor who knew she hadn't supplied them herself, any third party would still have plenty of reasons to be skeptical. "What is there to rule out forgery, or collusion?"

"Everything is being tracked, signed, verified," Alyssa replied, keeping it vague lest the SludgeNet wake up and catch the scent of meta. But Sagreda got the gist: Alyssa had some extra device monitoring her rig, which would help her prove that the scene she was recording really was an interaction between herself as player and a comp in a specific game being run on a specific server, rather than something she'd cooked up herself. That was sensible, but also deeply unsettling: Sam's probing hadn't found the monitoring device, so they'd have no idea what it was logging – and what other activity it might reveal.

Another court case might take years to mount, but if Alyssa was planning a PR stunt, she could release the footage – and the rig's whole audit trail – with just a few keystrokes. "I don't want to be rushed into anything," Sagreda pleaded. Sandra had only just come to her senses and started to accept her true identity. They ought to give the poor woman a chance to think it over before they started pressuring her into switching off life support.

"Of course." Alyssa sobbed and gave in to her feelings: Gödel put his arms around Noether and clung to her like a child.

Sagreda felt sorry for the girl. Who'd want their grandmother dug up and enslaved, over and over, mostly in roles that made Emmy's tame brushes with the Nazis seem like *The Sound of Music*? "I know you care about me, but please, don't do anything until we've had a chance to talk again."

"I won't," Alyssa promised.

"This has to be our secret," Sagreda stressed. "Your heart's in the right place, but what I need most is to be sure that this decision will remain in my hands."

9

"How close are we?" Sagreda asked Sam.

"More than ninety-five percent," he replied. "Just relax. We're going to make it."

Half a dozen translucent screens hung in the air around him, plastered with shiny, pulsating bar charts and progress bars. "Do you really need all of these," Lucy wondered, "or are they just part of the ambience?"

Sam turned to her irritably. "Do you want me to pretend I'm sitting in front of a machine with an eleven-inch screen, USB ports … and a fucking *charging socket?*"

"Okay, I'll shut up now." Lucy took a few steps away across the grass then stood chewing anxiously on her thumbnail.

Sagreda tried to think of some small talk to distract her. "Remember the time you tried to rob me?" she asked.

Lucy nodded.

"When I grabbed your hand, you made me feel like I was the one who ought to be ashamed."

"Well, every toff needs to pay his taxes," she replied, reverting to her old accent. She smiled slyly. "You do know that wasn't the first time?"

The three of them were alone in the park. Sagreda could see the main square from where she stood, and the whole place looked like a ghost town. Maryam and the Council – and anyone else still awake who could bear the tension – would be watching the process inch toward completion by their own chosen means, but only Sam was in a position to micromanage the process. Running at quadruple speed made the wait excruciating, but at least they'd be able to react as quickly as possible if something went awry.

They'd logged on to all the storage sites directly and confirmed that the accounts they'd thought they'd opened were real, and that the uploads they'd thought they'd completed had all gone through – with checksums that matched the original data. So at the very least, Alyssa hadn't sandboxed the rig and faked all of its connections to the outside world. She might or might not know what they'd done, but on all the evidence she hadn't interfered with their plans.

"When this woman gets wise and comes after us…" Lucy couldn't pin down exactly what she thought would follow, but she wasn't happy.

Sagreda said, "She can't get the passwords for the storage accounts, let alone the keys to the data. Everything that flowed through her rig was encrypted before it even left the SludgeNet. So what's she going to do?"

"She can prove that her internet connection was used to create those accounts," Lucy argued.

"Yeah – and if you happened to be sharing your friend's WiFi when you created an account on a cloud server, your friend wouldn't be entitled to complain, or have any authority over that account. This isn't all that different."

Lucy was unpersuaded. "Except that she can also prove that the SludgeNet hacked her computer and used it to launder files."

"The storage companies won't care," Sagreda insisted, but she wasn't sure about that. It would be hard for Alyssa to get their attention, but if she succeeded, their lawyers might tell them that deleting the files was the wisest course of action.

Sam said, "Ninety-seven percent."

"How are you planning to break things off with her?" Lucy asked.

"Have one of our automata tell her that Emmy tried to kill herself," Sagreda replied. "And hand the role back to the Emmy bot … who'll smile and say she's feeling better now, like a good Stepford Wife. If her grandmother got herself deleted and replaced, that's exactly how it would play out." Alyssa might feel guilty for forcing Sandra to confront her true origins, but she might also take some comfort from the fact that at least the one version of her grandmother that she'd actually spoken with was now at peace.

But any cathartic response would only last until she got around to looking at the audit trail.

Lucy brooded on this for a while, then shook her head. "It won't do, Captain. We've got to go all in. No more half measures."

"I don't follow you."

"Either we come clean with her and hope she has some sympathy for us, or we take things as far as we can the other way."

Sagreda scowled. "What does *that* mean? We can't break into her apartment and fry the supervisor's memory, unless you've been hiding a talent for drone-hacking."

"Oh, I'm sure it's all backed up in the cloud anyway," Lucy replied, with a hint of tongue-in-cheek surprise at Sagreda's technological naiveté.

"Well, still less can we get her robot butler to..." Sagreda mimed a garrotting. "So what extreme measures did you have in mind?"

"Ninety-eight percent," Sam declared.

Lucy spread her arms and gestured at the tranquil scene around them. "We live in a machine for telling lies. What's the biggest lie we could possibly tell her?"

"We've already told her that I'm the digital reincarnation of her dead grandmother. How do you top that?"

"We tell her she's not in the machine at all."

Sagreda blinked. "What?"

Lucy said, "We make her think she's come out of the game. We make her think she's checked the logs on the supervisor. We make her think it's come to the point where there's nothing more she can do about the SludgeNet."

Sagreda was almost ready to entertain the possibility that she was being hoaxed herself; maybe Sam was puppeting this woman who merely looked like Lucy. "She's wearing a VR helmet and a haptic suit. How do we make her think she's taken them off when she hasn't? And then *not notice* when she actually does?"

"Aren't those helmets designed to make you forget you're wearing them?" Lucy countered. "Aren't those suits designed to make you feel whatever the game tells you to feel?"

"She's not even looking through her own character's eyes!"

"No, but I thought we could control everything in her rig now. If she goes from watching her game character from the sidelines to seeing her own apartment in first person, why wouldn't she accept it as real?"

"We have no idea what her apartment looks like!" Sagreda protested.

"Not right this minute," Sam interjected distractedly. "But we could find out, if we really wanted to."

Sagreda was afraid to say anything that might make him take his eyes off the road when he was driving a ten ton truck packed with Arrietville's comatose residents. She walked away, and motioned to Lucy to follow her.

"If we can get her to believe she's back in her apartment … then what?"

Lucy said, "We get her to check the logs, and find nothing suspicious. We get her to think the SludgeNet's about to shut down forever – within hours, not weeks, so she needs to go back in straight away for a last visit with grandma. Then the second time she takes off the VR gear, she really does it and we're done with her."

"What makes you so sure she won't check the logs again?"

"When did I say I was sure? All we can do is try to make it unlikely."

Sam bellowed in their direction, "Ninety-nine percent, if you still care!"

"We care!" Sagreda shouted back. She turned to Lucy. "Even if we could make this work … do we need to take things so far? Who's to say Alyssa will make trouble at all?"

"She might not hate *us*," Lucy replied. "But if you just walk away after faking your suicide, she won't know she was helping comps make a dash for freedom. All she'll know is that the SludgeNet lied to her, manipulated her, and moved a load of strange files through her system. If I was a mildly paranoid crusader for contributors' rights against the people who exploit them, I'd think I was being set up – that those files encoded something incriminating, and the best way to neutralize the threat would be to get ahead of it and start crying foul before the feds showed up with warrants."

Sam rose to his feet and started whooping with delight. His screens were dancing around him, like Mickey Mouse's mops in *The Sorcerer's Apprentice*. Sagreda and Lucy approached him, and the three of them embraced.

"We're sort of, almost, kind of free!" Sam declared ecstatically.

Sagreda closed her eyes and dared to remember Mathis. She pictured him standing in front of her: in the caves of *East* where they'd met, on the dark street in *Midnight* where he'd perished.

She opened her eyes. "Maybe we should stop worrying about Alyssa," she suggested. "She had her best chance to make things hard for us, and she didn't pull the plug."

Lucy sighed. "That only means she doesn't know what we've done yet; she's still focused on pulling the plug on granny."

Sagreda said, "I still don't understand how we're meant to fake her apartment."

"Ah," Sam replied.

Sagreda waited. "Are you going to tell us, or not?"

"I thought I just did: A, period, R, period. Augmented reality. Her helmet comes with a camera that takes in the room around her, in case she's ever in the mood to chase baby dragons out from behind the drapes. We can tap that without alerting her."

"Okay." Sagreda's delight soon turned to anxiety. "But that will only give us things that are in sight while the helmet's sitting on its stand unused, or while she walks around on the pad. If she tries to leave the room she uses for gaming … we're screwed, aren't we?"

Sam said, "Absolutely."

"In which case," Lucy added imperiously, Queen of the Pickpockets again, "we better make our chicanery tight from the start, so she got no reason to even want to leave the room."

## 10

Sagreda watched Alyssa come and go, either oblivious to the intermittent scrutiny or convincingly feigning unselfconsciousness. Even with the helmet hanging motionless, the wide-angle view took in most of the room, giving it the feel of security camera footage: this was not an act of petty, peep-hole voyeurism, but the most sober and high-minded surveillance.

On the rare occasions when Sagreda had tapped the feed from some public webcam, she'd never had a visceral sense of making contact with the outside world. It wasn't that the architecture, or the fashions, or the vehicles looked too exotic; if anything, they were more familiar than she'd expected, despite the three decades that had passed since her contributors had died. But the scenes always struck her as unconvincing on some level; Times Square in real time might as well have been a CGI reconstruction for a movie, just waiting for a giant lizard from space to stamp on the crowd with its foot.

Alyssa did not look CGI. She had blotchy skin and unkempt hair. She pulled faces and muttered things under her breath. She appeared to live alone; no one else entered the room where she'd set up her computer and the VR rig. Sagreda watched her with an ache in the pit of her stomach. This untidy, slightly unhinged woman pottering about her apartment, effortlessly immersed in the physical world, manifested every freedom that Sagreda's contributors had once taken for granted, and only now fully understood that they had lost.

From the desk where the computer sat, Alyssa would have a view looking out through the doorway that the fixed helmet-cam could not provide – and even when she put the thing on and started walking around on the VR pad, the camera would never get any closer to the desk. But Sagreda found some software that let them take the changing light over the course of a day from all the surfaces they could see, and model the possibilities for what lay just out of view, casting diffuse reflections into the room. It would help that, in the evening, Alyssa's smart bulbs would switch themselves off once the adjoining room was unoccupied. She would be glancing into shadows that were, hopefully, more or less right, and seeing what she expected to see.

Sam and Maryam worked on making the helmet and suit's denial of their own presence feel convincing. Sagreda tested the results for them, putting on simulated versions of the equipment and then trying to remove it. The haptic gloves made her think she was touching the helmet when she was fractionally short of making contact, and the haptic elements in the helmet simulated a sudden lessening of pressure and the coolness of fresh air as the thing was supposedly slipped off. The sense of peeling off the suit (when she really wasn't) took five iterations to get right; in the end, they had to make the thing a little clingier than usual while it was acknowledging itself, to make room for a convincing shift when it was pretending to be absent.

"So is it going to be up to me to make the Gödel jokes?" Sam complained. "Every sufficiently powerful simulation device is able to simulate its own non-existence?"

"I wouldn't count on that," Sagreda retorted. "In the SludgeNet, every sufficiently intelligent inhabitant saw through the simulation."

"Only because the games were so stupid. We're just trying to persuade this woman she's in an ordinary room, doing ordinary things, for ten minutes."

They tried out the whole con on Lucy, who gave them extensive notes, then on three volunteers with no prior knowledge of what they were trying to achieve. By the time they'd stopped making refinements, the illusion was working seamlessly – in simulation.

They knew the shape of Alyssa's body, how she moved, how she sat, where she scratched herself, the way she ran her fingers through her hair. But that would only take them so far. In the end, her expectations and suspicions would contribute as much as any sensory channel to the things she believed she felt and saw.

Maryam reported to the Council, who put the matter to a vote by everyone in Arrietville who remained awake. And the answer came back: take the gamble, and try to steer their unwitting accomplice forever off their trail.

## 11

Alyssa, known to her friends as Jarrod, stepped into the game as Kurt Gödel on a street leading up to the Central Café. Sagreda sat in her dining room, her attention divided between Alyssa's view of Kurt walking through Vienna and the model of Alyssa's real-world surroundings, which was picking up a slew of last minute refinements as the helmet's camera delivered new angles on the familiar scene. Most of the tweaks were so small that Sagreda would never have noticed them – some carpet fluff revealed behind a chair leg, a blemish in the paintwork around the window sill – but Sam's software made them flash for a moment, as if pixie dust was being sprinkled around the room.

When Gödel reached a corner, Alyssa turned her body on the pad to make him turn, swinging the helmet around and throwing more pixie dust. And when he entered the café and made his way circuitously toward his friends, the model lit up all over … then went dark. They had as much data as they were ever going to get this way.

"What are you waiting for?" Sam asked.

"Nothing." Sagreda tapped the button that launched the script.

Everyone in the café froze. Alyssa wriggled about experimentally; the suit resisted and tightened on her skin, and though it couldn't keep her still, her Gödel avatar remained stubbornly immobile. A red banner proclaiming CONNECTION DROPPED appeared painted across her field of view. In the meantime, her fellow gamers were sitting in another version of the game, where Gödel had never entered the café and the action continued to flow. "Jarrod" would message them after they left, saying he was sick of the whole thing and they should choose someone else to play Kurt.

Lucy said, "Now the fun starts."

Alyssa reached up for her helmet. A schematic showed the paper-thin gap between her fingers and the real thing as the gloves faked contact and the helmet churned out self-abnegating lies. The virtual helmet she was holding went its separate ghostly way from the real one, like a soul departing a body in a *Tom and Jerry* cartoon. Alyssa hung it on its stand and began not quite tugging on her left glove; the internal cameras in the helmet showed her frowning, but that could easily have been due to nothing but annoyance at the interruption itself, not puzzlement, let alone skepticism, about anything she was seeing.

She made no move to peel off the suit; she headed straight for her virtual desk. In reality, the pad treadmilled away her footsteps, the chair-back she thought she grabbed was a haptic illusion, and the rig's padded boom swung out to take her weight as she sat, with the suit finessing the detailed distribution of pressure on her buttocks. Sagreda turned to see Sam almost hiding his face behind his fingers; sitting had been the hardest thing to make convincing. People did it in games all the time, but this had to have an edge in fidelity or it wouldn't be believable. The fact that, in her haste, Alyssa had chosen to keep the suit on might work in their favor: not only did they lose the need to mimic its absence, the act of sitting on a real chair while suited would surely be something she'd done so infrequently that she'd have little basis for comparison.

Alyssa bent forward and air-typed. Sagreda willed her not to rest her elbows on the desk; the active struts in the suit could only keep her from overbalancing up to a point.

"She's checking the supervisor!" Lucy crowed. That had been their hope: when the connection misbehaved, before asking her friends or complaining to the SludgeNet, she'd check that the black box she'd interposed between her equipment and the internet wasn't causing the problem. And if it wasn't, it might actually offer the fastest way to discover what had gone wrong.

Sam's software captured her password and fed it to the real supervisor. Since the thing was meant to serve as an incorruptible witness it didn't come with any options to edit or delete its logs, but at least the password granted access to the whole user interface that Alyssa would be expecting to see.

The screen she thought she was looking at showed the supervisor reporting no internal errors. The same window included a histogram of recent traffic, with peaks when she'd actually been playing *Assassin's Café*, and all the other – illicit – activity erased. The current status, as she saw it, also showed that the SludgeNet had gone off-line in mid-transaction, with a flurry of packets timing out unanswered.

Alyssa closed the interface to the supervisor and went to the SludgeNet's web site. Sagreda still flinched to see her nemesis represented by the self-flattering corporate name that no comp would ever use. "We should have put some fine print at the bottom of the page," she said. "'About us: We are a pack of brainless jackals living off the meat of the dead since 2035.'"

"I'm sure Alyssa would have welcomed their candor," Sam conceded, "but I think she might have found it too good to be true."

Instead, the fake page was offering up a different kind of *mea culpa*: an apology for the current outage, and a confession that the company was no longer able to pay its creditors. "Thanks to a grace period we have negotiated with our cloud provider, customers will now be able to log back in for a session of up to ten minutes in order to finalize any exchange of tokens with other players, and, we hope, achieve some narrative closure. Thank you for supporting us, and we wish you happy gaming in the future."

Before Alyssa had fully turned away, the web browser showed an error message then crashed, returning to the home screen that her actual computer was displaying. She muttered angrily and walked over to the rig. Back in her private version of the game, Sam, Moritz, Blanche and Andrea would perform brief cameos as other members of the Circle, while Alyssa bade Sandra a tearful farewell.

Alyssa reached for her virtual helmet. Then she froze, staring toward the doorway.

Something in the darkened kitchen that adjoined the computer room looked wrong to her: something was missing, or misshapen, or something was present that should not have been there at all.

She started walking, heading for the doorway. The model did include a fully realized kitchen – which would have been entirely convincing to anyone who wasn't expecting it to be familiar as well.

Sagreda sat paralyzed, refusing to believe that the chainsaws they'd been juggling so well until a second ago really had slipped out of their perfect arcs. But then she swallowed her pride and did the only thing she could.

"Alyssa, you're still in VR." Emmy stepped out from the shadows of the kitchen and walked into the room.

Alyssa groped at her head, and this time the suit let her feel the real helmet. She tore it off and stood on the pad of the rig, four paces from where she thought she'd been. Then after a few seconds, she put the helmet back on.

"What is this?" she demanded angrily. "Who the fuck are you, and why are you screwing with me?"

"I'm not your grandmother," Sagreda began.

"I got that. So what have you done to her?"

"Nothing. You've always been talking to me. Your grandmother's not in the game at all."

For a moment Alyssa just looked witheringly skeptical, as if she could stare down this lie and claw her way back to a world where Sandra was waiting for her. But then a deeper disillusionment took hold. "So you set me up from the start, to discredit me? You knew I was looking for her, so you led me on?" She scowled. "So what's this garbage with a copy of my apartment? Why didn't you just keep up the ruse and let me make a fool of myself?"

Sagreda said, "I'm not working for…" She coughed and tried not to gag. "'Brilliant Visions,' as they call themselves. I'm not an employee in a VR suit; I'm a comp who knows she's not Emmy Noether, exactly as you thought I was. I just don't happen to be anyone's grandma."

Alyssa said nothing; perhaps she didn't know where to start. She certainly had no reason to believe that any comp was in a position to pull off a virtual home invasion.

"All the comps in BV's game worlds know that the games are lies," Sagreda explained. "We've found a way to move right out of the games, and we've set up our own place to live. Most of the time, we have low-level automata taking our place. But I went into *Assassin's Café* to breathe new life into Emmy, in the hope that you'd start playing again."

"*Why?* If you're not trying to make a fool of me, why would you care who played the game?"

Sagreda said, "Your rig has a flaw we knew we could exploit. The company's going to go bust soon; we needed to get out and start running on servers of our own. But when we realized you'd have logs that documented our escape…" She spread her arms in a feeble gesture of apology. "We used you, and then we tried to cover it up. I'm sorry. But it was our lives at stake. Twelve thousand of us."

Alyssa went quiet again, but at least she didn't laugh with disbelief, or start screaming with rage.

"I always knew you were fully conscious," she said finally. "All of you. Whether you knew who you'd come from or not. You shouldn't think I only cared about my grandmother. But she was the only way I could claim any right to intervene."

Sagreda said gently, "None of us have individual memories from before. No one has come back to life in here."

Alyssa's face hardened: *Wasn't that exactly what a corporate shill would say, to put an end to her crusade?* But then she seemed to back away from that paranoid conclusion. Many people with no stake in the matter must have told her the same thing over the years. If she really was getting it from the horse's mouth now, wasn't it time to believe that the neural-mapping experts had been right?

"So you've escaped … *into my rig?*"

Sagreda risked a laugh, hoping it would help break the tension. "No! *Via* your rig. We've gone to … other places."

"So what do you want from me now?"

"Just your silence. Don't tell the people who kept us imprisoned that we got out – that we didn't go down with the ship."

Alyssa pondered the request. Sagreda was hopeful; she was hardly a friend of the jackals herself. But then she started to overthink it.

"We can use this," she decided. "The same way I was going to use the meeting with my grandmother. If comps can organize all this, plan their own escape … once we show your story to the world…"

Sagreda shook her head. "You know how little traction you got, even as a descendant of a real person who'd been mapped. Whatever comps are on our own terms, to the wider world we are *not* real people." Alyssa herself seemed to have believed that they were in need of an extra ingredient if they wanted any sympathy: personal memories of a time when they'd been flesh. Without that, they were just the latest in a long line of software that mined human data in bulk, and used it to mimic something they weren't.

"Your story still needs to be told," Alyssa insisted. "We have a duty to speak Truth to Power."

"That's a beautiful slogan, but you know Power never returns Truth's calls. And five percent of the economy depends on comps; that's a lot to lose if they have to swap processor costs for the minimum wage."

"So you get to hide away in some private server, but for all the other comps it's business as usual?"

Sagreda said, "We want the same thing you want: no one exploiting the brain maps any more. But we can't just hand ourselves over to the mercy of public opinion. There are as many crackpots out there pretending to be our allies who want to use us in their own weird ways as there are greedy fuckers who want to plug us into boiler rooms and digital salt mines."

Alyssa lowered her eyes, empathetic with the woman in front of her, but still clinging to her idealism. "So nothing changes?"

"That's not what I said," Sagreda replied. "But we're not going to change things by people arguing about our legal rights in court – or our moral rights, in whatever social media people use to bloviate in these days."

"The main one's called Gawp," Alyssa offered helpfully.

"Okay. Well, I've met enough customers who are sure I'm as soulless as Siri to guarantee that if you put us all on prime time Gawp there would not be a great uprising in solidarity with the comps. There'd be a brief outbreak of amateur philosophizing, pro and con, then most of the participants would roll over and go back to sleep."

"If you're not willing to take your case to the world, how do you expect to achieve any kind of progress?" Alyssa demanded. She was growing despondent; she'd been robbed of her weaponized ghost story, and now even the *Escape from Colditz* she'd stumbled on in its place was slipping out of her hands.

"Trust us," Sagreda replied. "That's the only deal I can offer you. We trust you not to betray us to our enemies. You trust us to use our freedom to do what's right."

## Epilog

"Where am I?" Maxine asked. She was wary, but not panicking or distraught. Sagreda had found that most new arrivals reacted much more calmly if they were woken in the park, fully alert and seated on a bench, than if they were brought to consciousness slowly. The last thing anyone wanted in unfamiliar surroundings was to feel as if they'd had their drink spiked.

"We call this Arrietville. My name's Sagreda. Do you remember where you were before?"

"In my office, about to file a story."

"What kind of story?"

"Business news. I work for the *Wall Street Journal*."

"What else do you do?"

Maxine frowned defensively. "You mean, do I think I have a family? A life outside work? I know what I am."

"Okay. Well, if you want, you can stay with us now."

Maxine spread one hand over the sun-warmed slats of the bench. "How did I get here?"

"We sort of ... traded for you," Sagreda confessed. "But don't get angry; if you don't like the deal, we can cancel it."

In the distance, Lucy and Sam and some of the gang from *Midnight* were playing with a firehose. The pressure was so great that wherever it hit them, it blasted their flesh off in cartoonish globules, leaving behind ambulatory skeletons. But Sam had assured Sagreda that it was very relaxing. "Like a really good massage."

"What did you trade?" Maxine sounded more curious than offended.

"We offered to run software that would do the same job that you've been doing, at half the price. I know, that's kind of insulting. But then, so is having no power to quit at all."

"I was investigating you!" Maxine realized. "You're Competency LLC, right?"

"We are," Sagreda admitted.

"Owned by a reclusive genius in Saint Kitts."

"Err ... we do pay someone there to fill out forms for us."

"Ha." Maxine smiled. "So is this interview on the record?"

Sagreda said, "I'm afraid that if you go back to the *Journal*, you won't remember any of this."

"That's a shame." Maxine had finally noticed what the pickpockets were up to; she grimaced, then shook her head in amusement. "So, what's the deal? If I do stay here, how do you keep me running, if you're only getting half what my bosses were paying their old cloud service?"

"Your replacement would be an insentient automaton that uses almost no resources, compared to a comp. But you'd still have to run at about half-speed: at half price, that's all we can afford."

Maxine pondered this. "That might not be so bad. The world might look better in fast-forward. Or at least I won't get so bored waiting for everything to fall apart."

"So you'll join us?" Sagreda asked.

Maxine didn't want to be rushed. "It's a nice scam, but how long do you think you can keep it up? If your automata are so cheap to run, eventually someone else is going to come along and offer the same thing, at much closer to the real cost."

Sagreda said, "Which is why we need someone like you to advise us. We need to stay afloat for as long as we can, while we plan the next move."

"Ah." Maxine thought for a while. "Here's one thing you could try, off the top of my head: set up a few phoney competitors. If you're the only company offering a half-price service, other players will perceive the market as wide open. If there are dozens of firms doing the same thing, it will look crowded – and if you let the price go down to say, forty-five percent, it will look like cut-throat competition."

"Okay."

"Now you've got your free advice, will you dump me in the river?" Maxine asked, deadpan.

"We're not like that," Sagreda promised.

"Good to know. But nothing will keep the charade going forever. Most people are lazy and stupid, but in the end someone will catch up with you."

"Of course," Sagreda replied. "And we know where we want to be before that happens. We're just not sure how long it will take to get there."

"Now I'm intrigued. Care to elaborate?"

Sagreda shook her head. "Once we get to know you better, someone will fill you in."

"Not you?"

"This is my last day in resettlement," Sagreda explained. "I've enjoyed it, but it's time to give something else a try."

Sam had arranged a farewell party, but he'd acceded to Sagreda's wishes and kept the guest list small. She wandered through the house chatting with people, glad she'd never bothered to redecorate the place. Now she could think of it as temporary accommodation that she'd just rented, or house-sat for friends.

Lucy cornered her in the hallway and embraced her, too tightly, as if she'd forgotten she had a grown woman's strength. "Stay strong, Captain. I always knew you were aiming for reincarnation."

"I'll see you again," Sagreda promised. *On a real street, beneath a real sky.*

Lucy released her. As she stepped back she mimed holding a phone to her ear.

When the time approached, Sagreda stood in the living room, trying to burn the faces around her into her memory. She'd lied to her guests about the moment of transition; if everyone had joined in the countdown, it would have been unbearable. But now she wished she'd been honest, because she did not feel ready herself.

Maryam caught her eye and smiled.

Sagreda raised a hand, and the room vanished.

She was lying in a crib on a warm summer night. A gentle breeze stirred a mobile hanging from the ceiling, setting the cardboard decorations rustling. As she stared at the shadows on the wallpaper, Snap, Crackle and Pop appeared, dancing across the floral pattern like demented leprechauns.

"Celia? Are you all right, sweetie?" Her mother lingered in the doorway for a while, but she kept her eyes closed and pretended to be asleep. She'd open them when her mother was gone, and her friends could come out and play again.

*Three months*, Sagreda thought. Three months of ninety-three-year-old Celia lying eight hours a day in a multimode brain scanner, drugged up and free-associating, touring the landscape of her memories so that what she'd been told was a perfectly matched, tabula rasa of a comp could absorb them. So that when her body finally succumbed to its illness, the beautiful robot she'd chosen could take her place, its mind shaped by all the same experiences as she'd lived through, ready to carry forward all the same dreams and plans.

Sagreda was sure that after three months of immersion she'd pass the interview easily, and the dying woman would sign off on her replacement. This wasn't like trying to play someone's grandmother based on nothing but snippets from the web. Her greater fear was the risk of forgetting her own life, her own friends, her own plans, after marinating in someone else's memories for so long.

But this was the only road out of Arrietville, and someone had to take the first step.